the Devil Wears Black

OTHER TITLES BY L.J. SHEN

Stand-Alones

Tyed
Sparrow
Blood to Dust
Dirty Headlines
Midnight Blue
The Kiss Thief
The End Zone
In the Unlikely Event

Sinners of Saint (Contemporary Romance)

Defy
Vicious
Ruckus
Scandalous
Bane

All Saints High (New Adult)

Pretty Reckless
Broken Knight
Angry God

Boston Belles (Contemporary Romance)

The Hunter
The Villain
The Monster (TBR)
The Rake (TBR)

the Devil Wears Black

L.J. SHEN

This is a work of fiction. Names, characters, organizations, places, events, and incidents are either products of the author's imagination or are used fictitiously.

Published by Montlake, Seattle

www.apub.com

ISBN-13: 9781542025553
ISBN-10: 1542025559

Cover design by Hang Le

Printed in the United States of America

For Lin and Lilian. You ladies are my favorite book club ladies.

Two things the devil and the color black have in common?
They are always dark and never out of fashion.

—Chase Black, COO of Black & Co.

PLAYLIST

- Trevor Daniel—“Falling”
- Healy—“Reckless”
- Kasabian—“Fire”
- The Waterboys—“Fisherman’s Blues”
- MAX feat. Quinn XCII—“Love Me Less”
- The Cars—“Drive”
- The Rolling Stones—“Sympathy for the Devil”

CHAPTER ONE

Maddie

October 10, 1998

Dear Maddie,

You are currently five, and very fond of the color yellow. In fact, yesterday you asked me if you could marry it. I hope you still wear it all the time.

(I also hope you found someone a bit more suitable for marriage.)

Fun fact of the day: When the Spanish explorers reached the Americas, they thought sunflowers were made of gold.

The human brain is so imaginative!

Stay creative, always.

Love,

Mom. x

◆ ◆ ◆

It was official. I was having a stroke.

All evidence pointed in that direction, and at this point I felt confident I'd watched enough *Grey's Anatomy* to self-diagnose:

Confusion? Check.

General numbness? Check.

Sudden headache? Trouble seeing? Difficulty walking? Check, check, check.

The good news was I was seeing a doctor. *Literally.* I was walking back to my apartment with one when the symptoms occurred. At least I had the luxury of immediate medical attention if I needed it.

I shoved my fists into my yellow sequined jacket with the purple dots (a personal favorite), squared my shoulders, and squinted at the large figure sitting atop the stairway of my brownstone rental, willing it to disappear from my vision.

He stayed put, the bluish glow of his phone illuminating the planes of his face. Midsummer air danced around him, crackling like fireworks. Every whiskey-colored light on the street caught his profile, like he was standing onstage, demanding everyone's attention. White-hot panic washed over me. I only knew one person who made the universe dance around him like aloha girls.

Reluctantly, I ruled out having a stroke.

No. He wouldn't dream of showing up here. Not after how I left things.

". . . So my little patient leans down to me and says, 'Can I tell you a secret?' and I'm like, 'Uh-huh,' thinking he is going to spill the beans about his parents getting a divorce. But he just says, 'I finally figured out my mom's job.' I ask him what it is, and he says—wait for it, Maddie." Ethan, my date, held a hand up, crouching with his other hand resting on his knee, clearly overestimating the comic potential of his story. "'She slipped a new iPad under my pillow the day I lost my first tooth. My mommy is the tooth fairy. I'm the luckiest boy alive!'"

Ethan threw his head back and laughed, oblivious to my internal meltdown. He was handsome, with his hair, eyes, and loafers almost the exact same shade of walnut brown, his lean runner's body, and his Scooby-Doo tie. True, he wasn't Dr. McDreamy. More like Dr. McReality. And yes, he had shared *twelve* stories about his young patients over the course of the Ethiopian meal we'd enjoyed, nearly toppling over each time he'd recited their whiplash-smart observations. But Ethan Goodman was *exactly* the kind of guy I needed in my life.

The man on my stairway was the very person who'd taught me this painful lesson.

"From the mouths of babes." I played with my dangling sunflower earring. "I miss my innocence. If I could keep one thing from my childhood, that'd be it."

The figure on my stairway stood up, turning in our direction. His eyes slid up from his phone, catching mine effortlessly. My heart deflated like a balloon, soaring in erratic circles before dropping into a heap of saggy rubber in the pit of my stomach.

It was *him*, all right.

All six-two chiseled angles and ruthless sex appeal of him. Wrapped in a crisp black dress shirt rolled to the elbows, exposing forearms as thick as my thighs, corded with veins and muscles. Layla, my childhood friend turned next-door neighbor, called him a real-life Gaston. "Easy on the eyes but begging to get thrown from a roof."

He was frowning as if he himself couldn't figure out what he was doing here.

With the tousled black hair.

Slanted blue-gray eyes of a manga character.

With that Greek-god bone structure that made you consider committing war crimes for a chance at running your teeth across his jaw like an animal.

But I knew he wasn't Mr. McDreamy *or* Mr. McReality.

Chase Black was the devil. My personal devil. Always clad in black, a cruel comment ready on the tip of his tongue, his intentions as tainted as his smirk. And me? I'd been dubbed Martyr Maddie for a reason. I couldn't be mean if my life depended on it. Which, luckily, it did not.

"Really? If I could keep one thing from my childhood, it'd be my first baby tooth that fell out. My dog swallowed it. Oh well," Ethan peeped enthusiastically. My head snapped back to my date. "Of course, accidents with dogs *always* happen. Like that time another patient of mine—God, wait till you hear this story—came into my pediatric clinic because of a suspicious rash—"

"Ethan?" I stilled midstep, unable to focus on another sweet story. Not that the stories weren't riveting, but calamity was literally at my doorstep, ready to explode all over my life.

"Yeah, Maddie?"

"I'm so sorry, but I think I'm a little nauseous." Not technically a lie. "Think we can call it an early night?"

"Oh no. Do you think it was the *tere siga*?" Ethan frowned, giving me a puppy look that broke my heart.

Thank God he was too busy talking my ear off about his patients to notice the gigantic man standing in my doorway.

"No way. I've been feeling off for a few hours. I think it's finally hitting me." I glanced at Chase behind Ethan's back, swallowing hard.

"Are you sure you'll be okay?"

"Positive." I smoothed his Scooby-Doo tie over his chest with a smile.

"I like positivity. It makes the world a better place." Ethan's eyes lit up. He bent down to kiss my forehead. He had dimples. Dimples were great. Ethan, also, was great. So why was I eager to bid him farewell just so I could murder my unexpected guest on the stairway to my apartment for the entire street to witness?

Oh, that was right—because Chase Black had ruined my life and left me to piece it back together, each shard of our broken relationship cutting me deep.

More on that in a second.

I just had to say goodbye to my perfect, almost-saved-me-from-a-stroke Dr. McReality.

As I walked the rest of the way to my building, my heart flapping against my sternum like a fish out of water, I fantasized about the various ways I was going to greet Chase. In all of them, I appeared blasé, five inches taller, and wearing femme fatale Louboutins as opposed to my green Babette shoes.

Funny, I don't remember leaving the trash outside. Allow me to escort you back to the recycling bin, Mr. Black.

Oh, you want to apologize? Can you be specific as to why? The cheating part, the humiliating part where I had to take an STD test afterward, or simply for wasting my time?

Are you lost, sweetie? Would you like me to escort you to the brothel you are obviously looking for?

Suffice it to say, Chase Black did not bring out the Martyr Maddie in me.

I stopped three steps away from him. My nerves were as tattered as my peach-patterned dress, and I hated the flutter of excitement skimming through my chest. It reminded me how stupid I'd been for him. How convenient. How submissive.

"Madison." Chase tilted his chin up, looking down his nose as he examined me. It sounded like an order more than a greeting. The patronizing pinch of his eyebrows also didn't look too inviting.

"What are you doing here?" I hissed.

"Let me come up?" He tucked his phone into his front pocket. Straight to the point. Not *can I* but *let me*. No *How have you been?* Or *Sorry about that time I crushed your heart to dust* or even *How is Daisy, the Aussiedoodle I gifted you for Christmas, even though you told me you were allergic to dogs no less than* three times, *and your friends now dub her Assholedoodle for her tendency to piss in people's shoes?*

I clutched the lapels of my thin summer jacket, furious at myself for the way my fingers shook. "I'd rather not. If this is about you screwing your way through New York, you've got the wrong address. You can checkmark my name."

Summer heat bled from the concrete, curling over my feet like smoke. The darkness of the night did nothing to dim how hot it was. Manhattan was sticky, bloated with sweat and hormones. The street buzzing with couples and shark packs of tourists, rowdy coworkers, and college kids up to no good. I didn't want a public scene, but I wanted him in my apartment even less. Know the expression *If anyone can have it, I don't want it*? That applied to his body. After we'd broken up, it had taken me weeks to rid my bedsheets of that singular Chase Black smell. He'd followed me everywhere, like a dark cloud with a bellyful of rain. I could still feel the fat swell of tears behind my eyelids when I thought about him.

"Look, I know you're upset," he started, his tone guarded, like he was entering a negotiation with an undomesticated honey badger.

I cut him off shakily, surprised by my own assertiveness. "Upset? I'm upset about my laundry machine breaking down. About my puppy chewing her way through the crocheted blue poncho I bought last winter, and about waiting for the next season of *The Masked Singer*."

He opened his mouth, no doubt to protest, but I held my hand up, waving it for emphasis. "What you did to me didn't upset me, Chase. It *devastated* me. I don't mind admitting it now, because I'm so over you I forgot how it even felt to be *under* you." I barely took a breath before spewing more volcanic arson his way. "No, you're not coming up. Whatever you have to say to me"—I pointed at the ground beneath me—"this is your stage."

He ran a hand through his hair, so black and soft looking it made my chest tighten, eyeing me like I was a ticking bomb he had to diffuse. I couldn't tell whether he was annoyed, remorseful, or exasperated. He seemed like a mixture of all three. I'd never known what he felt, even when he was deep inside me. I'd lie there, looking into his eyes, and see my own reflection staring back at me.

I crossed my arms, wondering what had prompted his visit. I hadn't heard from him since we'd broken up six months ago. But I had heard from Sven, my boss, about the women Chase had brought back to his penthouse in the aftermath of our breakup. My boss lived in the same glitzy Park Avenue building as Chase. Apparently, the latter hadn't been crying himself to sleep.

"Please." The word twisted in his mouth uncomfortably, like it was made of gravel. Chase Black was not accustomed to asking for things nicely. "It is a rather personal issue. I'd appreciate not having your entire street as an audience."

I fished for my keys in my little clutch, stomping my way up the stairs. He was still on the first step, his eyes burning a hole through my back. The one time he looked at me with anything but frost, and I was completely immune to it. I pushed the building entrance door open, ignoring his plea. Funny, I'd always thought it'd feel divine to dismiss him the way he'd dismissed me. But right now, my feelings swirled among hurt, anger, and confusion. Triumph was nowhere in sight, and glee was miles away. I was almost past the threshold when his next words gave me pause.

"Too scared to give me ten minutes of your time?" he challenged, the smirk in his voice like a stab in my back. I froze. *Now* I recognized him. Cold, calculated. Playfully ruthless. "If you're so over me and not at all tempted to be *under* me once we get upstairs, you can go back to your blissful, Chase-free existence after I say my piece, no?"

Scared? He thought I was *scared*? If I were any more immune to his charms at this point, I'd actively throw up at his sight.

I swiveled, jutting my hip out, a polite smile on my lips. "Cocky much?"

"Just enough to get your attention," he deadpanned, looking awfully like a man who didn't want to be here.

What is he doing here, anyway?

"Five minutes will do, and you better behave." I pointed at him with my clutch.

"Cross my heart and hope to die." He put a hand on his chest mockingly.

"At least our hopes are aligned."

That drew a chuckle out of him. I fled up to my apartment on the second floor, not bothering to glance behind me and see if he followed. I tried to sort through the reasons he was here. Maybe he'd just gotten out of rehab for treating his destructive sex addiction. We'd only dated for six months, but during that time, it had been pretty obvious Chase wouldn't rest until I had carpet burns all over my back and walked wonky the next day. Not that I'd had any complaints at the time—sex was a part of our relationship that had worked well—but he was an insatiable tomcat.

Yes, I decided. This was probably a part of his twelve-step recovery process. Make amends with those he'd hurt. He was going to apologize and leave, and we'd both have our closure. A cleansing experience, really. It would make starting things with Ethan even more perfect.

"I can practically hear you overthinking," Chase grumbled, ascending the stairs behind me. Funny, he didn't sound apologetic at all. Just his usual jerk-face self.

"I can practically feel your eyes on my ass," I ping-ponged flatly.

"You can feel other parts of me on it if you're so inclined."

Don't stab him with a steak knife, Maddie. He is not worth the prison time.

"Who's the guy?" He yawned provocatively. There was always a devilish edge to his words. He delivered everything in a deadpan manner, a touch of irony to remind you he was better than you.

"Gee. Wow." I shook my head, huffing. He had some nerve asking me about Ethan.

"G-Wow? Is he a rapper? If so, he needs a makeover. Tell him about the Black & Co. Club. We're running a fifteen percent promotional discount on personal-stylist services."

I flipped him the bird without turning around, ignoring his dark chuckle.

We stopped by my door. Layla lived opposite me, in the other apartment that had been converted into a studio when our landlord had cut his property bang in the middle. Layla had been the first to move to New York after we'd graduated. When she'd told me the studio apartment in front of hers was going to be available because the couple had moved to Singapore, and the landlord preferred a tidy resident who paid on time, I'd jumped on the opportunity. Layla was a preschool teacher by day and a babysitter by evenings to supplement her income. I found it difficult to remember seeing her not holding a toddler in her arms or doing cutouts of letters and numbers for class the next day. Layla plastered a word of the day to her door each morning. It was a great way for her to talk to me even when we weren't talking to each other throughout the day. Over the years, I'd grown attached to Layla's daily words. They were companions, little signs of a sort. Predictions on how my day was going to be. I'd forgotten to look at it today in my haste to get to work.

I glanced absentmindedly as I shoved my key into its hole.

Danger: exposure or liability to injury, pain, harm, or loss.

A sinking feeling washed over me. It settled at the base of my spine, applying persistent pressure. "You aren't here to apologize, are you?" I breathed, my eyes still on my door.

"Apologize?" His arm came from behind me to rest above my head. His warm breath skated over the back of my neck, making the little hairs on it stand on end. *The Chase effect.* "Whatever the hell for?"

I pushed the door open, letting Chase into my apartment. My domain. My *life*.

Painfully aware of the fact that the last time he'd barged into my kingdom, he'd also burned it down.

CHAPTER TWO

MADDIE

July 2, 1999

Dear Maddie,

Today, we pressed Mrs. Hunnam's wilted daisies into your old books together. You said you wanted to give them a proper burial because you felt bad for them. Your empathy made my throat clog up. That's why I turned around and walked out of the room. Not because of the pollen. Of course not. God, I'm a florist!

Fun fact: Daisies symbolize purity, fresh starts.

I hope you are still compassionate, kindhearted, and that you remember every day is a new beginning.

Love,

Forever,

Mom. x

◆ ◆ ◆

I kicked my shoes against the wall. Daisy rushed from her bed on the windowsill by the flowers, wiggling her tail as she began licking between my toes in greeting. Truth be told, it wasn't her most ladylike habit, but it was among the least destructive ones.

"To what do I owe the displeasure, Mr. Black?" I peeled my yellow jacket off.

"We have an issue." Chase gave Daisy a pat before sauntering deeper into my studio. It seemed unfair, almost twisted, that I had wasted so many tears and sleepless nights coming to terms with the fact he would never stand casually in my kitchen again, only to . . . well, have him standing in my kitchen again, looking casual AF. Like nothing had changed. But that wasn't true. *I'd* changed.

Chase opened the fridge, plucking out a can of Diet Coke—*my* Diet Coke—and cracked it open before leaning against the counter and taking a sip.

I stared him down, wondering if *he* was the one suffering from a sudden stroke. He looked around my crumpled, tiny space, no doubt taking inventory of the changes I'd made since he'd last been here. New wallpaper from Anthropologie, fresh bedsheets, and (least noticeable, but nonetheless existent) the new dent in my heart, the shape of his iron fist. He flicked the lights on—I had one set for the entire apartment—and whistled low.

Under the unforgiving LED lights, I noticed that he looked disheveled and unshaven. His eyes were bloodshot, his shirt a little wrinkled. His $200 haircut was in desperate need of a trim. Very unlike the handsome, immaculate rake he prided himself on being. Like the world had finally decided to press its crushing weight on his glorious shoulders.

"My family seems to have taken a liking to you," he admitted coolly, like the prospect was about as unlikely as a straight unicorn.

I marched toward him, snatching the Diet Coke from his grasp. I took a sip on principle and put it on the counter between us. "And?"

"My mother can't stop talking about the banana bread you promised to bake for her, my sister's lifelong dream is to become your BFF since you knit her that hat, and my father swears you are every man's dream woman."

"I happen to think very highly of your family too," I said. It was the truth. The Blacks were nothing like the spawn they'd mistakenly spewed into the world. They were sweet and compassionate and welcoming. Always smiling and, above all, frequently offering me a glass of wine.

"But not me," he supplied with a hedonistic smirk that suggested he took pleasure in being disliked. Like he'd achieved his goal. Unlocked a level in a video game.

"Not you." I gave him a curt nod. "Which is why flattery will get you nowhere."

"Not trying to get anywhere with you," he assured me, his chest expanding under his shirt. A phantom of his scent—woodsy, aftershave, and male—drifted into my nostrils, making me quiver. "Not in the way that you think."

"Get on with it, Chase." I sighed, looking down and wiggling my toes. I wanted him out of here so I could dive under the duvet and binge-watch *Supernatural.* The only thing that could save tonight was a healthy dose of Jensen Ackles combined with unholy amounts of chocolate and impulsive internet shopping. Also, wine. I would kill for a bottle. With the victim preferably being the man in front of me.

"There's a problem," he said.

There always was with him. I stared at him blankly so he would continue. Then he did the weirdest thing. He . . . sort . . . of . . . *flinched*? The Chase Black.

"I may have forgotten to mention we broke up," he said cautiously, averting his gaze to Daisy, who was currently humping the couch's leg with an enthusiastic dog smile.

"You *what*?" My head snapped up, my teeth clashing together. "It's been six months." And three days. And twenty-one hours. *Not* that I was counting. "What were you *thinking*?"

He rubbed his knuckles against his stubble, eyes still trained on my hussy pup. "Frankly, I thought you'd realize you overreacted and come back."

If I were a cartoon character, my jaw would drop to the floor, and my tongue would roll out like a red carpet, bumping into the door, through which I would later hurl Chase, leaving a hole the shape of his body.

I pressed my fingers to my eye sockets, drawing a ragged breath. "You're joking. Tell me you're joking."

"My sense of humor is better than that."

"Well, I hope your sense of direction is just as good, so you can go back to your family and tell them we're definitely done." I stomped to the door, throwing it open and motioning for him to leave with a head jerk.

"There's more." Chase remained propped against my counter, his hands tucked into his pockets nonchalantly. He had a few signature positions that were inked into the backs of my eyelids and saved for rainy Magic Wand days.

Chase casually leaning a hip against an inanimate object.

Chase holding the top of the doorframe, his biceps and triceps bulging out of his short-sleeved T-shirt.

Chase with one hand tucked into his front pocket, his sex eyes undressing me slowly.

Essentially, I had an entire catalog of my ex inspiring self-induced orgasms with his looks alone. Which, admittedly, was a level of pathetic that needed a new name.

"I was going to tell them we were done a couple weeks ago, but my father beat me to it in the bad news department."

"Oh shoot. Has the superyacht broken down?" I put a hand over my chest, feigning concern. Ronan Black, the owner of Black & Co., Manhattan's busiest department store, led a charmed life full of vacations, private jets, and grandiose family gatherings. Still, speaking ill of the people who'd welcomed me into their house left a sour taste in my mouth.

"He has stage-four cancer. Prostate. It spread to his bones. Kidneys. Blood. He wasn't screened. My mother had been begging him for years, but he didn't want the discomfort, I guess. Needless to say, it is incurable. He's got three months to live." He paused. "Generously speaking."

He delivered the news flatly, keeping his face blank. His eyes were still on Daisy, who neglected the couch, spreading her legs at his feet, begging for a belly rub. He leaned down and scratched her stomach absentmindedly, waiting for me to absorb the news. His words soaked into me like poison, spreading slowly and lethally. They hit me somewhere deep, in that tight ball of angst I kept lodged in my belly. My mom ball. I knew Chase and his father were close. I also knew Chase was a proud man and would never break down, especially in front of someone who hated him. My knees buckled, the air slamming against the back of my throat, refusing to make its way into my lungs.

I resisted the urge to erase the space between us and hold him. He'd translate my warmth into pity, and I didn't pity him. I was crushed for him, having experienced losing my mother to breast cancer when I was sixteen after her on-again, off-again battle with the disease. I knew all too well that it was always too soon to say goodbye to a parent. And that watching someone you loved lose the battle against their own body was as painful as ripping open your own flesh.

"I'm so sorry, Chase." The words finally stumbled out of my mouth, clunky and weightless. I remembered how much Dad had hated being told that. *So what if they're sorry? It's not going to make Iris feel better.* I thought about Mom's letters. I typically started every morning with one of her letters and a strong cup of coffee, but this morning I had read two of them. I'd had a gut feeling today was going to be a challenging one. I hadn't been wrong.

I hope you are still compassionate and kindhearted.

I wondered what she'd think of my nickname. Martyr Maddie. Always down for saving the day.

Chase's hooded eyes dragged from Daisy to meet mine. They were frighteningly empty. "Thank you."

"If there's anything I can do . . ."

"There is." He straightened up swiftly, patting himself clean of Daisy's hair.

I tilted my head in question.

"In the days after my father broke the news to us, my family was a mess. Katie didn't show up for work. My mother didn't leave her bed, and Dad ran back and forth, trying to comfort everyone instead of taking care of himself. It was, for lack of better words, a fucking shit show. And the show's still going."

I knew Lori Black had battled with depression before, not through Chase but through an in-depth interview she'd given *Vogue* a few years back. She'd spoken candidly about her dark periods while promoting the nonprofit organization where she volunteered. Katie, Chase's sister, was a marketing executive at Black & Co. and a shopaholic. That was less endearing and quirky than it sounded. Katie suffered from bad anxiety attacks. Her episodes included going on intense, out-of-control shopping sprees to bury whatever it was that made her nervous. Knee-jerk spending made her breathe slightly better, but she always hated herself afterward. It was like binge eating emotionally, only with designer clothes. That was how she'd gotten diagnosed, in fact. Six years ago, she'd gone into a spending frenzy after her boyfriend had broken up with her. She'd spent $250,000 in a little less than forty-eight hours, maxed out three credit cards, and been found by Chase buried under a literal mountain of shoeboxes and clothes in her walk-in closet, crying into a bottle of champagne.

Chase must've read my mind, because he pressed home, his eyes holding mine intensely. "Considering my mother's track record, it wouldn't be far fetched to assume she's on a straight path to Depressionville. When I went to check on Katie, her door was blocked with Amazon packages. I needed a sacrificial lamb."

"Chase." My voice croaked. I had a feeling I was the poor animal about to get tossed into the smoker. His face was blank, his tone measured.

"I had to think on my feet. So I made an announcement of my own."

He grabbed the can between us, taking another sip, his eyes on me. Quiet. My heart spun like a hamster on a wheel. The tips of my fingers tingled. Panic clogged my throat.

"I told them we were engaged."

I didn't answer.

Not at first, anyway.

I picked up the can of Diet Coke and threw it against the wall, watching it splash into an avant-garde painting of brown fizz. Who did something like that? Told his family he was engaged to his ex-girlfriend, whom he'd cheated on? And now he was here, not even half-apologetic and still a full-blown jerk, delivering the news offhandedly.

"You son of a . . ."

"It gets worse." He raised a palm, his eyes cutting to my window seat, which was crowded with potted flowers in various colors and Daisy's bed. "As it turned out, the engagement announcement was just what the doctor ordered. Family is a divine principle for the Blacks. It gave Mom something to be excited about and took away Dad's thoughts from the big C. And so it appears that you and I are having an engagement party in the Hamptons this weekend."

"An engagement party?" I echoed, blinking. I felt seasick. Like the ground beneath me swayed in the same rhythm as my pulse. Chase nodded curtly.

"Naturally, we both must be in attendance."

"The only thing natural," I said slowly, my head a jumbled mess, "is the fact that you're still delusional. The answer to your unspoken request is no."

"No?" he repeated. Another word he wasn't used to.

"No," I confirmed. "I will not accompany you to our fake engagement party."

"Why?" he asked. He looked genuinely baffled. I realized Chase, despite his thirty-two years of existence, had very little experience with rejection. He was handsome, smart, so filthy rich he couldn't spend all his money even if he dedicated his entire life to the cause, and of enviable Manhattan pedigree. On paper, he was too good to be true. In reality, he was so bad it hurt to breathe next to him.

"Because I'm not going to celebrate our fauxmance and deceive dozens of people. And because doing you favors is very low on my to-do list, somewhere under plucking my eyelashes individually with a pair of tweezers and picking a fight with a drunken Santa on the subway." I was still holding the door open, but I was shaking. I couldn't stop thinking about Ronan Black. About how it must've hit Katie and Lori. About Mom's letter telling me to stay compassionate. Surely she hadn't meant this.

"I'll fire you," he said simply, not missing a beat.

"I'll sue you," I retorted with the same nonchalance, feeling much more hysterical about his threat than I let on. I loved my job. Plus, he knew damn well I lived paycheck to paycheck and wouldn't survive even the briefest unemployment.

No wonder his last name was Black. His heart certainly was.

"Is money tight, Miss Goldbloom?" He arched an eyebrow, his voice deadly.

"You know the answer." I bared my teeth. A Manhattan apartment, no matter how small, cost a fortune.

"Perfect. Do me this solid, and I'll reimburse you for your time and effort." He turned from bad cop to good cop in a second.

"Blood money," I said.

He shrugged, looking bored with my antics. "Blood? No. A few scratches, probably."

"Are you offering to pay me for companionship?" I ignored the pulse flicking in my eyelid. "Because there's a word for that. Prostitution."

"I'm not paying you to sleep with me."

"You don't have to. I foolishly did that for free."

"Didn't hear any complaints at the time. Look, Mad—"

"Chase." I mimicked his warning tone, hating that he used his nickname for me—not Maddie, not Mads, just Mad—and that it still made the pit of my belly swarm with butterflies.

"We both know you'll do it," he explained, with the thinly veiled exasperation of an adult explaining to a toddler why they should take their medicine. "Spare us this little tango. It's late, I have a board meeting tomorrow, and I'm sure you're dying to tell your friends all about your little date with Scooby-Dull."

"We do?" I parroted, my eyes dangerously close to setting him on fire purely through the power of revulsion. I didn't even touch his last dig. That was just Chase being Chase, beating his own Guinness World Record at being an asshole.

"Yes. Because you're Martyr Maddie, and it's the right thing to do. You're selfless, considerate, and compassionate." He listed those traits matter-of-factly, like they didn't chart positively in his book. His eyes drifted from my face to the wall behind me, on which I'd pinned dozens of squares of delicate fabrics. Chiffon and silk and organza. Materials in white and crème from all over the world, along with penciled sketches of wedding gowns. I shook my head, knowing what he was thinking.

"Reel it in, Cowboy Crabs-anova. I'd never marry you."

"That's good news all around."

"Is it? Because I think you just asked me to be your fiancée."

"*Fake* fiancée. It is not your hand in marriage I am asking for."

"What *are* you asking for?"

"The courtesy of not breaking my father's heart."

"Chase . . ."

"Because not coming? Mad, it will *shatter* him." He dragged a shaky hand through his tresses.

"This'll snowball." I shook my head. My fingers were dancing, they quivered so badly.

"Not under my watch." He held my gaze, not a muscle twitching on his face. "I don't want you back, Madison," he said, and for some reason, the words cut me open and bled me dry. I'd always suspected Chase had never truly wanted me, even when we were together. I was like a stress ball. Something he played with absentmindedly while his thoughts drifted elsewhere. I remembered feeling acutely unseen whenever he looked at me. The way he huffed when he took in my quirky dresses. The side-eyes he awarded me with, which made me feel just a tad less attractive than a circus monkey. "I don't want my father leaving this world when it's in chaos. Mom. Katie. Me. It's too much. You can relate, can you not?"

Mom.

Hospital bed.

Scattered letters.

My hollow, aching heart that never quite recovered from losing her.

I felt my resolve chipping, one crack at a time, until finally, the layer of ice I'd coated myself with when I'd let Chase into my apartment fell with a soundless clank, like a warrior ridding themselves of their armor. He remembered our conversation all those months ago, when I'd told him my mother had died in the same month my father had filed for bankruptcy for their business, Iris's Golden Blooms, and I'd failed a semester. She'd left the world worried and anxious for her loved ones.

The fact she hadn't gone peacefully still gnawed at me every single night.

It didn't matter that I'd ended up graduating from high school with honors and even gotten a partial scholarship for college, or that Dad had gotten back on his feet and our flower shop had thrived afterward. It always felt like Iris Goldbloom was stuck in the limbo of that hellish period in our lives, forever waiting to see if we'd pull through.

As much as I loathed Chase Black for what he'd done to me, I wasn't going to force another calamity on his family in the form of a canceled engagement party. But I wasn't going to play by his rules either.

"Where did your family think I was for the past six months? Wasn't it weird to them that I haven't been around?"

Chase shrugged, unfazed. "I'm running a company that's richer than some countries. I told them we were seeing each other on evenings."

"And they bought it?"

He flashed me a sinister grin. Of course they had. Chase had the uncanny ability to sell anxiety to a new bride.

I grumbled. "Fine. What happens when we finally break up?"

"Leave it to me."

"Are you sure you've thought this through?" It sounded like a horrible plan. Straight-to-cable rom-com material. But I knew Chase to be a serious guy. He nodded.

"My mother and sister would be disappointed but not crushed. Dad wants me happy. Moreover—I want *him* to be happy. At any cost."

I couldn't argue with that logic, and frankly, it was the one thing Chase had over me. My sympathy to his situation.

"I'll go this weekend, but that's where it ends." I lifted my index finger in warning. "One weekend, Chase. Then you can tell them I'm busy. And whatever happens, this engagement mumbo jumbo will be kept top secret. I don't want it to come biting me in the ass at work. Speaking of work—after we cancel our so-called engagement, I get to keep my job."

"Scout's honor." But he only raised one finger. Specifically, the middle one.

"You've never been in the Scouts." I narrowed my eyes at him.

"And you haven't been bitten in the ass. It's a figure of speech. No, wait." A slow-spreading grin tugged across his face. "Yes, you have."

Pointing at the door, I felt my neck and face burning with a blush as I recalled the time that I had in fact been bitten in the ass. "Out."

Chase shoved his hand into his back pocket. Dread curled around my throat like a tight scarf as he pulled out a small Black & Co. Jewelry velvet box and threw it into my hands. "I'll pick you up Friday at six. Hiking attire mandatory. Sensible clothes optional but fucking appreciated nonetheless."

"I hate you," I said quietly, the words scorching their way up my throat as my fingers shook around the plush box with the gold lettering. I did. I really, truly did. But I was doing it for Ronan, Lori, and Katie, not him. That made my decision more bearable somehow.

He smiled at me pityingly. "You're a good kid, Mad."

Kid. Forever condescending. Screw him.

Chase stalked to the door, stopping a few inches from me. He frowned at the discarded soda can at my feet.

"You may want to clean that up." He motioned to the sprayed Coke on my wall. He lifted his arm and rubbed his thumb over my forehead, exactly on the spot Ethan had kissed, erasing his touch from my body. "Scruff is not a good look, especially on Chase Black's fiancée."

CHAPTER THREE

MADDIE

August 10, 2002

Dear Maddie,

Fun fact: The flower lily of the valley has a biblical meaning. It sprang from Eve's eyes when she was exiled from the Garden of Eden. It is considered to be one of the most gorgeous and elusive flowers in nature, a true favorite among royal brides!

It is also deadly poisonous.

Not all beautiful things are good for you. I'm sorry you and Ryan broke up. For what it's worth, he was never the one. You deserve the world. Never settle for less.

Love (and a little relieved),

Mom. x

I'd been planning my wedding day ever since I was five.

My dad loved to tell the story of how the day before first grade, I'd been seen running after Jacob Kelly along our cul-de-sac, clutching a bunch of backyard flowers, roots and mud intact, yelling at him to come back and wed me. I got my way in the end, after much bribing. Jacob looked appalled, with both himself and me, as my friends, Layla and Tara, dutifully performed the ceremony. He refused to kiss his bride—which was more than fine by me—and chose to spend our honeymoon hurling pine cones at squirrels running across my backyard fence and complaining there was no more of my mom's famous cherry pie.

I didn't stop at marrying Jacob Kelly. By the time I was eleven, I'd been wed to Taylor Kirschner, Milo Lopez, Aston Giudice, Josh Payne, and Luis Hough. All of them still lived in the same town I'd grown up in in Pennsylvania and still sent me Christmas cards taunting me for being blissfully single.

It wasn't about the romance. My interest in boys was saved for morbid curiosity as to what made them dirty, rude, and prone to fart jokes. It was the wedding part I absolutely loved. The butterflies in your stomach, the festiveness, the guests, the cake, the flowers. And above all—*the dress*.

Fake-marrying boys gave me a reason to wear the white puffy dress my cousin Coraline had gifted me when she got married. I was her flower girl. I squeezed into that thing for five consecutive years, until it was clear the dress couldn't fit a preteen, even one as comically short as me.

I had been obsessed with wedding dresses ever since. Rabid, more like. I'd begged my parents to take me to weddings. Even went as far as sneaking into strangers' ceremonies at the local church just so I could admire the dresses. To make my obsession worse, my mother was a florist and would oftentimes allow me to tag along when she delivered wedding flowers to plush, beautiful venues.

Becoming a wedding dress designer seemed like a calling, not a career choice. You were your most beautiful, flawless self on your wedding day. In fact, it was the only day in your life where anything you chose to wear, no matter how costly, extravagant, or lavish, was fair game. People often asked me if it felt stifling to limit myself to designing one type of outfit. Honestly, I didn't know why any designer would choose to make regular, normal clothes. Designing wedding dresses was the professional equivalent of eating dessert every day for breakfast, lunch, and dinner. It was like getting my Christmas presents all at once.

Maybe that was why I'd always been the last to leave work. To turn off the lights and kiss my latest sketch goodbye. Not this Friday, though.

This time, I actually had plans.

"I'm off. Happy weekend, everyone!" I slipped into my hot-pink pumps, turning off the light illuminating my drafting table at Croquis.

My corner of the studio was my little haven. Designed to cater to my needs. My drafting table had silver stationery trays, which I filled with pencils, funny-shaped erasers, Sharpies, brushes, and charcoal. I made it a point to put a vase with fresh flowers by my desk every week. It was like having Mom around, making sure she watched over me.

I gave the flowers in my vase—a medley of lavender and white blooms—a little pat, watering them ahead of the weekend. "Be good." I wiggled my finger at them. "Miss Magda will take care of you while I'm gone. Don't give me that look," I warned. "I'll be back Monday."

Whoever said flowers didn't have faces obviously hadn't seen them wilt. Usually, I'd take my flowers home with me and put them on my windowsill to people watch and get some sunrays next to Daisy, but this weekend, I was going to the Hamptons to accompany Satan, and Daisy had a sleepover at Layla's.

"Talking to your plants again. Cool. Totally sane." I heard a mutter from across the studio. It was Nina, my colleague. Nina was my age yet an intern. She was supermodel perfect. Willowy as a swan, with an upturned nose and the skin complexion of a Bratz doll. The only negative thing I had to say about her was she severely disliked me for no apparent reason other than my ability to breathe. Literally, she'd dubbed me "Oxygen Hogger."

"Move along now." She waved her hand, eyes still glued to her screen. "If your plants pee, I will change their diaper. Just as long as you get out of my sight."

Taking the higher road, I turned away, making my way to the elevators. I bumped right into Sven. He planted a hand on his waist, leaning forward and tapping my nose. My boss slash sort-of friend was in his early forties and wore black head to toe. His hair was so shockingly blond it flirted with white, his eyes so light you could almost see through them. He always wore a touch of gloss and dangled his hips when he walked, à la Sam Smith. As department head at Croquis, a wedding-gown company that was in partnership with Black & Co. to sell their lines exclusively at their stores, he called the shots and attended meetings with the executive board. Sven had taken me under his wing when I'd been fresh out of art school and given me an internship that had swelled into a full-time position. Four years later, I couldn't imagine working for anyone else.

"Where to?" He cocked his head.

I looped my courier bag over my shoulder, making my way to the elevators. "Home. Where else?"

"Lorde help me, thank God you design better than you lie." He meant the singer, *not* his Almighty. Sven did the sign of the cross, following my footsteps, his Swedish accent raising the intonation on final syllables. His foreign accent made a subtle cameo only when he was excited or drunk. "You never leave on time. What's going on?"

My eyes flared. Had Chase opened his mouth? Sven knew Chase, and they ended up at the same meetings frequently. I wouldn't put it past him. I wouldn't put *anything* past him, bar starting a third world war. Chase would be freaked out by the commitment. A war could last months—even years. He didn't have the stamina to see it through.

I stopped by the elevator bank, punching the button and popping two pieces of gum into my mouth. "Nothing's going on. Why would you ask that?"

Sven cocked his head sideways, like if he stared me down long enough, the secret would spill itself out of my mouth. "Are you okay?"

I let out a high-pitched laugh. Sven and I were close but still professional. I'd like to think that if he weren't my boss, we'd actually probably be best friends. But we both understood that for now there were boundaries and certain things we could and couldn't talk about. "Never been better."

Someone get me out of here.

The elevator dinged. Sven slid in front of it, blocking my way inside. "Is this about . . . *him*?"

My jaw nearly dropped to the floor.

"'Him' can burn in hell a thousand times, and I wouldn't spit on him to put the fire out," I hissed. "I can't believe you brought him up."

If I had a penny for every time Sven had caught me crying about Chase in the kitchenette, my station, the restroom, or anywhere else in the office, I wouldn't have to work here. Or at all, for that matter. I didn't even know why. In the six months we'd dated, I'd only met Chase's family a handful of times, and not even his brousin (brother-cousin) and his wife, whom they were close with. He hadn't met my family—only Layla and obviously Sven. Things hadn't been serious by any stretch of the imagination.

"Harsh words. What did the poor guy do? You've only been dating for three weeks." He tapped his lips, scrunching his eyebrows. "What's his name again? Henry? Eric? I remember something all-American and wholesome."

Ethan. Of course he meant Ethan. My heart slowed, almost to a complete stop. Crisis averted. The doors to the elevator closed, and I frowned at Sven, pushing the button to call it once again. It was already on its way back down. *Darn it.*

"Patience is a virtue," I pointed out.

"Or a definite sign he is playing for the other team." Sven adjusted the collar of my blue patterned blouse. "Firsthand experience, sister.

I had a girlfriend throughout high school, Vera. Her virtue remained intact until she left for college in the States, where it was probably shredded by a pack of frat boys to make up for lost time."

"Poor Vera." I licked my thumb and rubbed a coffee stain off the corner of his lips.

"Poor *me*." Sven swatted my hand away. "I was so busy trying to be the man I thought my parents wanted I completely missed out on my ho years. Don't let that happen to you, Maddie. You go and be that ho we all want to be."

"You're projecting." I winced.

"And *you* are missing out," he countered, poking me in the breastbone. "It's been months since you broke up with Chase. It's time to move on. *Really* move on."

"I did. I mean, I have. I *am*." I pressed the button to the elevator three times in succession. Click click click.

"Oh, look, an incoming text message from Layla." Sven held his phone up to my face. Oh, I forgot to mention that since Sven and I couldn't be best friends, my best friend had actually become his best friend. It really messed with my work/personal-life balance, and I'd be lying if I said it didn't bother me at times. Like now. "Let me read that for you: 'Tell your employee to take this weekend to enjoy herself. Force her to have fun. Make mistakes. Sleep with the man of her dreams.'"

"I'm not . . . ," I started, but he shook his head, turning around, waving his hand as he sauntered back into the studio and bent over Nina's shoulder, glancing at what she was working on. The doors to the elevator opened. I walked in, shaking my head.

"Over my dead body."

Half an hour before Chase was supposed to pick me up, I knocked on Layla's door. She opened, pushing a stray lock of emerald-green hair behind her ear, holding a kicking, screaming four-year-old in meltdown mode. Layla was a curvy, the-only-dimples-I-have-are-on-my-ass-and-that's-the-way-I-like-it girl, with the most enviable wardrobe, consisting of boho-chic dresses, floaty skirts, and over-the-shoulder knit sweaters. She didn't seem to mind his advances at tearing her eardrum. The pocket money must be worth it.

"If it isn't Martyr Maddie," she chirped lovingly, giving me a one-arm squeeze. I hadn't changed from my work clothes. A blue blouse with printed cherries, paired with a gray pencil skirt and pink pumps. "Shouldn't you be with your ex-boyfriend right about now?"

"Just came by to drop off my keys."

Okay. That was a blatant lie. Layla had a spare in case of an emergency. I just needed to talk to her before I left. "Thanks for watching over Daisy. I usually walk her three times a day, for twenty minutes minimum. She likes Abingdon Square Park. Specifically chasing after a squirrel named Frank and catcalling other dogs. Just make sure she doesn't run into the street. There's a measuring cup in her food bag—one scoop in the morning, one in the evening. Her vitamins are by the utensils drawer, yellow pack. Don't worry about changing her water too much. She drinks from the toilet bowl anyway. Oh, and don't leave anything on the counter. She will find a way to open and eat it."

"Sounds like me after a night out." Layla grinned. "Frank, huh? Are things serious between them?"

"Unfortunately for him." I winced. I recognized Frank by the bald spot between his eyes. Daisy loved that squirrel, so of course, I fed him every time we went to the park.

"She also might pee in your shoes in protest when she realizes I am gone," I added.

"Jesus, she is worse than a kid. That see-you-next-Thursday ex-boyfriend of yours really made sure you'd never forget him with this parting gift."

I shrugged. "Better than C-H-L-A-M-Y-D-I-A."

"I know how to spell." The kid poked his tongue out, making both of us look at him incredulously.

"Thanks, I owe you one," I said.

"Don't mention it."

The kid in her hand was now tugging at her hair, yelling his mother's name.

"Ground control to Martyr Maddie, are you there? I asked you if Sven read you my text," Layla said, ignoring the ball of commotion in her arms. I hated that nickname. I also hated that I kept earning it by never turning people down when they asked for favors. Exhibit A: attending my own fake engagement party in the Hamptons this weekend.

"Yup." I plastered a cheerful smile on. "Sorry, I drifted. He did. You're insane."

"And *you* look like you're on death row."

"I feel like it too."

"I'm sorry, honey. I know how devastating it is when a gorgeous, well-bred gazillionaire whisks you off for a weekend in the Hamptons after slipping a four-hundred-fifty-K engagement ring on your finger. But you *will* survive it."

Let the record show I hadn't been the one doing the investigation on how much the ring cost. That was Layla, over a bottle of wine (okay, spiked Capri Sun) the minute Chase left my apartment building. I'd summoned her to an urgent meeting, during which she browsed Black & Co. Jewelry's website and concluded the engagement ring was a limited edition and was no longer for sale.

"You know what it means." She wiggled her brows then, pouring a shot of vodka into a cup and squeezing the Capri Sun into it. I'd shut her down immediately.

"Yes. That he wants to make sure his family thinks the engagement is legit. That's all."

Now, I was still trying to douse her optimism with a good portion of reality.

"Really, I prefer to look at it as being kidnapped by a cheating, lying, arrogant piece of sh—" I eyed the kid, who went completely silent, bug eyed, waiting for me to complete the sentence. I cleared my throat. "Sheep."

"She said a potty word." He pointed at me with a chubby finger.

"No, I didn't. I said 'sheep,'" I protested. I was arguing with a four-year-old. Ethan would have had a heart attack on impact had he found out.

"Oh." The kid poked his lower lip out, mulling it over. "I love sheep."

"Apparently, we don't love this one, Timothy." Layla patted his head. She closed the door half an inch. "Can you promise me one thing?"

"Do I have to?" I sulked. I knew she'd want me to be positive and optimistic.

"Try to make the most out of it. Instead of thinking about *who* you are going to spend the time with, think about *how* you're going to spend your time. The one-hundred-fifty-million-dollar property you will be staying in on Billionaires' Row, eating clambake delicacies, sipping wine that costs more than your rent. Bring your sketchbook. Take a breather from city life. Make this trip your bitch."

"Potty word!" Timothy perked again.

"I said 'beach.' Surely you like building sandcastles."

"Uh, *duh*, I do."

I loved my best friend, but she was a role model to children like I was a can of soup. She didn't even want to have any (children, not soup. Layla *loved* soup). Nevertheless, Layla had a point. I was going to attend my fake engagement party with the man of my nightmares, but I was going to do it in style. Chase and I had spent Christmas at his Hamptons estate before we'd broken up. It was the kind of place you only got to see on HGTV or celebrity Instagram stories. Problem was, Layla was a notorious commitment-phobe. Spending time with the man who'd broken her heart would never pose a problem, because her heart would never get broken.

"You know what? You're right. I'll do just that. High five, Timothy." I offered the kid my open palm with a smile. He stared at me vacantly, unmoving.

"Mommy says not to let strangers touch me. I could get kidnapped."

Not if the kidnapper knows what your lungs are capable of.

"Well, then it's settled. You're going to have fun, not overanalyze every moment, and allow yourself the luxury of an oopsie hate flock without getting attached."

"Hey! You said—" Timothy started.

"Flock. I said 'flock.' Thanks for coming to my TED Talk." Layla slammed the door in my face before I had the chance to moan about my upcoming weekend.

That was when I noticed Layla's word of the day.

Birthday: the anniversary of the day on which a person was born, typically treated as an occasion for celebration and the giving of gifts.

It was his birthday when Chase had cheated on me.

And just like that, my mood turned sour again.

Chase was five minutes late. Deliberately, no doubt. Punctuality had always been his forte. But if riling me up were an Olympic sport, he'd have an array of gold medals, a book deal, and a steroids scandal by now.

He double-parked in front of my building, blocking traffic with the nonchalance of a psychopath who truly didn't care what people thought of him. He got out, rounded the car, and wordlessly pried my suitcase from my fingers before throwing it into his trunk. People honked and shook their fists out their windows behind us, yelling their opinion about his poor driving skills while wishing him acute injuries in various creative ways, their heads poking out of their cars. He slipped back into his vehicle and buckled up, in no hurry. I was still glued to the sizzling curb, trying to come to terms with the idea of spending time with him. He rolled the passenger window down, giving me that barely patient smile he awarded his employees that made you feel so stupid you needed to wear a helmet indoors.

"Stage fright, *love*?" He said the word *love* like it was profanity.

I had to remind myself his mind games didn't matter. Ronan Black mattered. His sister and his mother mattered. Their hearts. My conscience.

"Sure," I bit out sarcastically. "Wouldn't want my fake in-laws to think their fake future daughter-in-law is not as charming as they initially thought."

"Ever heard about the term *fake it till you make it*?"

"I'm sure the women in your life are familiar with it," I quipped.

He smirked wryly. "Our relationship might've been fake, but the orgasms were anything but."

The cars behind him honked loudly, not pausing for a breather. The sound began to echo in my head. I wanted Chase to know I was not going to be some yes-woman who'd cater to every whim and idea he had, even if I'd agreed to help him.

"Get in, Mad. Unless you want me to get in a fight with half the street."

"Tempting," I bit out. I mean, it *was*.

He smirked, completely oblivious to the chaos teeming behind him as more and more cars began to honk. It wasn't like me to keep people waiting, but making my point trumped being polite. He needed to know I was serious.

"If you get nervous, just picture everybody naked."

"All right, then," I said, my eyes traveling as south as they could down his body at this angle. "Are you cold, Mr. Black?"

He laughed, enjoying our exchange. "I don't remember you being so feisty."

"I don't remember you being this intolerable," I shot back. I realized it was true. When we'd dated, he'd seemed way more polite and closed off, and I was . . . well, less *myself*.

I hopped into his car, opting to stare out the window throughout the drive, watching Manhattan's high-rises sliding by in slow motion. Like flicking through a magazine quickly, the scenery changed frequently, glossy through the filter of the squeaky-clean window. All the hysteria I'd somehow managed to shove under piles of to-do lists and work throughout the week simmered back up as we left the city. How was I supposed to mask the sheer loathing I had for this man? I couldn't kiss him or hold his hand. Jesus, I'd just realized I was supposed to share a room with him. No way, José.

It had been hard enough to explain the situation to Ethan a couple of days after agreeing to this fiasco, when I'd met him after Chase dropped in for a visit. I relayed the entire situation to him, including Chase's cheating, his dying father, and my own experience of losing a parent. Then I told him about the nickname Sven and Layla had slapped on me. *Martyr Maddie.*

"Are you sure you're okay with this?" I asked Ethan for the millionth time over *xiao long bao* and Chinese beers. I was treading carefully. I understood how crazy it all sounded. Ethan and I had never discussed exclusivity. We dated casually but hadn't slept together, let alone put a label on what we were. We had shared a few sloppy kisses, nothing more. I wanted him to put his foot down and tell me he wasn't comfortable with the idea. It'd have been the perfect excuse. But Ethan, who saw the good in everything—serial killers included, I suspected—simply nodded, grabbing another dumpling with a chopstick and tossing it into his mouth.

"Sure? I am more than sure. I'm honored to be dating someone like you. The only thing this weekend in the Hamptons is going to prove is that you"—he pointed at me with his chopsticks—"are an amazing person. Chase Black was a fool to cheat on you, and you're still helping him out. You're fantastic."

I watched him, waiting for the other shoe to drop.

"Besides, we aren't really exclusive, are we?" He rubbed the back of his neck, blushing. "We haven't even . . . you know."

I did know.

"So"—he shrugged—"it's not like I'm in any position . . . what I mean to say is that I'm good with it. Really."

For some reason, his reaction had unsettled me. I wanted him to be at least a little unnerved by the prospect of my spending the weekend with my ex-boyfriend. Which was completely irrational, since I wasn't possessive toward Ethan at all, and because he was right—he and I weren't really exclusive.

Back in reality, Chase read my thoughts.

"Does he have a name?" He snapped me out of my reverie, his eyes still glued to the traffic jam we were approaching. It seemed like the entire world was headed to the Hamptons. A bottleneck of trucks, Priuses, and convertibles waiting in a never-ending line of vehicles.

"Don't start," I warned.

He tutted. "Touchy. I'd be, too, if my partner was dumb enough to send me off to a weekend in the Hamptons with someone who'd previously fucked me to three consecutive orgasms in less than twenty minutes."

"Can you be any cockier?" I whipped my head around to scowl at him.

"Yes, but then I'd have to wear a condom."

There had been some relief to breaking up with Chase. Six months into our relationship, I was still flustered and constantly berating myself for saying the wrong thing in his presence. My voice was always high pitched when he was around, and I filtered my words, my *thoughts,* to try to be the woman I thought *the* Chase Black would date. He felt so far out of my league that I concentrated on not making errors more than I did on getting to know him and having fun. I'd always felt less. Less attractive, less stylish, less smart. Hating him now was so much easier than trying to worm my way into his bitter heart, like I had when we were dating.

"So. His name." Chase returned to the subject at hand.

"How is that your business?" I began to scratch at my nail polish to keep my hands from strangling him.

"It is my business who my fiancée is fucking," he said matter-of-factly. I paused midscratch, pulling at the delicate flesh around one nail and tugging at the dead skin until it ripped.

"*Fake* fiancée," I corrected.

"And a *real* pain in the ass."

"Gosh, Chase, how are you single? You're just about the most charming man I've ever met."

"I *choose* to be single," he fired back, smiling patronizingly. "Just like you choose to date anyone under the sun, just as long as you're not alone."

Ouch. Awkward silence filled the car. The banter was fine, but when we started speaking truths, that was when it got too much. Not that I did date anyone under the sun, but I was pretty sure Chase actually believed what he'd said. I decided to play along. It wasn't like I had anything to hide. I was proud of Ethan.

"Ethan. Ethan Goodman."

"Goodman," Chase repeated, whistling low.

"Nice job, Chase. I didn't know you had that word in your vocabulary. How did it taste?"

"Like two point three kids, a suffocating mortgage on a Westchester house you hate, and a midlife crisis consisting of mild alcohol abuse at forty." His eyes were still hard on the road. "What does Ethan Goodman do for a living?"

"Doctor." I kept it vague, feeling my cheeks heat.

"Hmm. I'm going to rule out plastic surgeon on the grounds that it is too sexy—actually, any kind of surgeon; he doesn't seem the steady-hand type—and go with dentist." He paused, frowning at the row of vehicles ahead of him. "No. That would actually be profitable. I changed my mind. Ethan Goodman is a pediatrician." He swiveled his head, flashing me a smirk so sinister I physically felt it licking at my skin.

"You say that like it's a bad thing." I narrowed my eyes. "He saves lives."

"Private practice." He ignored me, hitting the nail on the head once again. "So technically, he fills out growth charts with handwriting nobody can understand and examines butt rashes. Let me guess—he did a tour somewhere to give back to the community. Gain perspective. South America? Asia? No . . ." He paused, grinning so widely I was tempted to punch him square in the face. "Africa. He is committed to the cliché."

"Yeah, the cliché of saving lives and helping others." Seriously, my face felt so hot I was one blush away from exploding. "He's a good man."

"Clearly. It's in his fucking name. And you're here because Ethan the good man has some commitment issues of his own."

"Excuse me?"

"Why else would he be okay with this arrangement? He wants to see how you and I play out."

"*We* are not a thing. Ethan and I met at SeriousSinglesOnly.com," I couldn't help but blurt out, and I immediately regretted the decision. It wasn't something I wanted to advertise, but Chase needed to know he was wrong about at least one thing. I mean, obviously, his very existence was wrong on multiple levels, but I was talking specifically about Ethan.

"You could have met him at WillMarryAnyoneForABlowJob.com, and I would still think the same. He is no more committed to you than you are to me, and you two are forcing this shit upon each other despite you having zero chemistry just because you don't want to be alone. Called it now. Thank me later."

"You're one to talk," I muttered, returning to the task of scratching off my nail polish. It was a nasty habit I was trying to kick, but the need to taint his precious Tesla with dry flakes of Moroccan Nights pink was overwhelming.

"I can do more than talking," he mumbled.

"As much as you shutting up is tempting, no thanks."

I swiveled my head back to my window, to the safety of watching other people in their cars, trying to lower my heartbeat to a normal rate. I thought we were done talking. I hoped so, anyway. And then . . .

"Hope you're okay with fifty years of lights-off missionary, eating rolled oats for breakfast every day, and naming your pets after trashy reality-TV celebrities your kids idolize." He kept baiting me. I wanted to crawl out of my skin and jump out the window, but I didn't trust Chase not to do unholy things with the body I'd shed and leave behind.

I put my hand to my heart, feigning shock. "The horror of living a good, quiet life with an honest man, pets, and kids will haunt me forever. I beg you, stop."

He sent me a sidelong glance. "You wear sarcasm well."

I waited for the strike to come. Chase didn't disappoint.

"Unfortunately, it is the only thing you wear that doesn't look ridiculous."

"Can you just shut up? It's bad enough you forced me into coming here. Don't offer me unsolicited commentary about my style or analyze my current relationship. I just want someone nice and normal."

It was hard to admit, even to myself, that now I was even more nervous about sex with Ethan. If he wasn't going to rip my clothes off and take me against a spiked wall in a BDSM dungeon, I was going to be disappointed, solely based on the fact Chase had been right about pretty much everything else about him.

No, I chided myself. *Ethan doesn't have doubts about dating me.* We'd been hanging out for three whole weeks and still hadn't slept together. He was obviously in it for the long run.

I could see Chase shaking his head in my periphery, chuckling to himself. "You don't want what normal people want, Mad."

"You don't know what I want."

More silence. My soul was banging its head against the futuristic-looking dashboard. Why did I have a soft spot for people I didn't know? Why had I thought this was a good idea? But I never really could refuse small acts of kindness. That was why I didn't narc on Nina from work for bullying me. I knew intern jobs in fashion were hard to come by, so I sucked it up while Nina verbally abused me daily. I kept a chocolate bar in my purse in case *others* fainted on the subway and needed sugar to spike their blood pressure. It was an Iris Goldbloom trait I'd inherited.

"Friendly reminder—you have to pretend that you like me," Chase snapped after a while, tap-tap-tapping his steering wheel with his perfect long fingers. I closed my eyes and breathed through my nose.

"I know."

"Convincingly."

"I could be convincing."

"Debatable. There may be touching involved. Light patting in non-strategic areas and so forth." His eyes were still on the road.

"Are you out of your mind?" I hissed.

"Presently, yes, hence why you're here. As a result, we're going to have to play the loving couple."

"We will. Now can you please, *please* be quiet? I'm doing you a favor. A huge one. Don't make me regret it," I finally barked, feeling dangerously close to falling apart. My face was hot, my eyes watery, and it felt like someone had punched my nose from the inside.

To my surprise, he zipped it.

We zoomed past Long Island, the Tesla's quiet buzz the only background noise accompanying the drive. I closed my eyes, feeling my throat bob with a swallow.

I longed for a truce. For Chase to take a step back and let me gather my ragged self-esteem and frayed thoughts. For a sign what I was doing was the right thing and not destructive to both my heart and his family.

Most of all, I longed to run away. Somewhere far, where he couldn't grab my heart with his poisonous claws again and devour it.

See, I had a secret I didn't share with anyone. Not even Layla.

Sometimes, at night, I could feel Chase's claws sliding across my heart, sharp as blades. I still wasn't over him. Not truly. I didn't even think it was love—there was nothing about Chase's personality I particularly enjoyed.

I was obsessed.

Consumed.

Completely enamored.

Problem was, Missionary Ethan, I knew, would be kinder on my heart than Reverse Cowgirl Chase.

CHAPTER FOUR

Chase

First thing I'd noticed about Madison Goldbloom when I'd hit on her in Croquis's elevator? Her beautiful hazel eyes.

Okay. Fine. It was her tits. Sue me.

To anyone else, they were probably average, pleasant-looking tits. They were even modestly tucked inside a perfectly sensible, albeit visually offensive white turtleneck with a tacky lipstick pattern all over it. But they were so perky—so goddamn erect and round—I couldn't help but note they were the perfect size for my palms.

In order to test that theory, I had to wine and dine her first. Since nature all but conned me to pursue her, I took Madison to one of Manhattan's finest restaurants that same evening and spared no expense—nor compliment—for the sake of my palm-to-tit ratio research.

(Which turned out to be a success. Science, baby. Never failed.)

Madison was smaller than the average human being, which was preferable, seeing as I hated people, so the less there was of them, the better. Alas, this specific person was a honey trap. Because what she lacked in size, she made up for with enthusiasm. She was perky and charitable and got breathless when she spoke about things she was passionate about. She cooed at babies and patted dogs on the street and made eye contact with strangers on the subway. She was in-your-face alive in ways I wasn't accustomed to or comfortable with, and that didn't sit well with me.

As for her clothes . . . part of me wanted to take them off her because they were horrendous, and it had nothing to do with the sex part.

It was never supposed to be more than a fling. The thought of it exceeding the shelf life of a week hadn't even crossed my mind. My relationships typically coordinated their expiration dates with my milk cartons. In my thirty-one years of existence prior to meeting her, I'd only had one girlfriend, and it had ended in a farce that reminded me that humans, as a concept, were faulty and unpredictable and, although unavoidable, should be kept at arm's length.

Then came Madison Goldbloom, and *poof!* Girlfriend number two materialized. If we were being technical here, she didn't earn the title. She *stole* it.

Mad and I went out the evening I'd met her (the no-fraternization rule didn't apply since we technically didn't work in the same company). She had very big, very brown-green-whatever eyes rimmed by brown and gold speckles, a pixie haircut that gave her a dramatic, will-slowly-steal-your-heart-if-you're-not-careful Daisy Buchanan look, and lips so full and pillowy I got a semi every time they moved.

Which was every time she spoke.

Which was *a whole fucking lot.*

After I slept with Mad on the first date, we texted back and forth. She told me she didn't normally sleep with first dates and that she would like to take it slow. Which, of course, made me want to sleep with her again almost immediately. I did just that. The third time we texted, she threw her rules out the window and began to play according to mine. Before I knew it, we got into a comfortable arrangement of eating dinner together, followed by having sex. This arrangement occurred frequently during the week. In hindsight, *too* frequently. It was the tits, and the fact that underneath her (I cannot stress this enough) truly horrid clothes, she wore sexy chemises and matching lingerie.

Perhaps I was not entirely without fault when it came to setting the tone for our extended fling. At some point, I made a strategic error. It made logistical sense Madison would have access to my apartment. Having her at my disposal was convenient, and buzzing her up constantly grated on my nerves. No emotions were involved while making the decision to give Mad a spare key. My housekeeper and PA had one, too, and I was not in danger of proposing to either of them. In fact, I changed PAs as often as I did underwear.

And just for clarification, I was a highly hygienic person.

As for occasionally taking Madison to the movies—I genuinely wanted to watch whatever we went to see. Sue me for being a Guillermo del Toro and Tarantino fan. It wasn't like we cuddled in the theater or even shared popcorn (she poured a bag of M&M'S into her bucket of popcorn on our first outing to the movies. That should have been my first clue the woman was raised in the wilderness).

It took me five months to find out I was in a relationship. Mad was the person to point it out to me. She did it in a sly, adorable way. Not unlike a Care Bear with a butcher's knife. Said her father was in town the week after the next and asked if I wanted to meet him.

"Why would I want to meet him?" I asked conversationally. Why, in-fucking-deed. Her answer made my whiskey go down the wrong pipe. The same Scottish single malt I'd been sipping at a friend's party I'd taken her to, *not* because we were dating but because it was less hassle than making the journey to her place when I was done.

"Well, because you're my boyfriend." She batted her eyelashes, cradling her cosmo cocktail like she was a tourist trying to live her best Carrie Bradshaw life.

(Note to self: She *was* a tourist. She'd grown up in Pennsylvania. I should have checked if I could deport her back there, although at this stage, it had been way past fourteen business days.)

It was in that come-meet-my-dad moment that I realized I hadn't screwed anyone else since I'd met Madison, and I didn't have any desire to do so in the near future (voodoo vagina). And that we spoke regularly on the phone (even when we didn't, technically, have much to say to each other). And that we had sex all the time (I was attached to a dick; enough said). And that I naturally assumed my weekend plans included her (again—I was attached to a dick).

That, coupled with the fact I brought her over to see my parents at Christmas, was how things started getting serious and not at all fling-like.

More specifically—how they crashed and burned, setting my entire life philosophy on dumpster fire. I was now officially taken and with a girlfriend, two things I'd promised myself would never happen again. So I did what I had to do to remove Madison Goldbloom from my life. Got rid of her Band-Aid-style, once and for all.

I thought we were over.

Done for good.

I *wanted* to be done with the little, mouthy, sex-on-atrocious-Babette-shoes woman who thought wearing petticoats at twenty-six was adorable, as opposed to deranged.

Then my father had thrown a burning curveball straight into my hands, and here I was, tossing it from side to side, actively spending time with Madison. Doing the very thing I'd vowed not to do.

"You're here!" Mom pounced on my windshield like a frenzied kangaroo as I parked the Tesla by the Hamptons estate. Madison jolted awake from her slumber beside me. She patted her chin to see if she was drooling—she was—and sat up, rearranging her pearl headband.

Rather than offering her a few seconds to get ready, I did what any other world-class dick would do and shoved my door open and rounded the car to hug my mother.

"How was traffic?" Mom's french-manicured nails dug into my shoulders. She peppered kisses across my face, thinly concealing her eager peeks into the car. She was quivering with barely restrained excitement.

"Bearable."

"I hope Madison didn't mind the traffic."

"She loves traffic jams. They're her favorite hobby."

Right after trapping innocent men into relationships.

Anyway, since when was Madison above trivial inconveniences such as traffic? That was what happened when you never brought anyone home. The first so-called partner I had, and my parents treated her like the Second Coming of Jesus.

I opened Madison's door, helping her out of the car but really thrusting her right into reality's arms. She shimmied her pencil skirt down, trying to make a graceful exit.

Mom tackled Madison like a professional linebacker, plastering her to the car. To her credit, Mad played the part of a happy fiancée semiconvincingly. Meaning she was awkward but not above her usual gracelessness. After they squealed at each other, Mom examined her engagement ring from all angles, oohing and aahing like it was the first time she'd seen a diamond in her life. It was a nice piece from the Black & Co. exclusive line. I'd asked for the most stupidly expensive, generic thing they had. Something that said *the fiancé is rich* but also *and knows nothing about his bride-to-be*. Something perfect for the two of us.

"I hope you don't mind, but it'll be a smaller event. We haven't had much time to prepare since Ronan . . ." My mother trailed off, apologizing to Madison.

Madison shook her head almost hysterically. "No, no. I totally get it. The fact that you're doing anything at all considering the circumstances is . . . ah . . ." She looked around herself. "Amazing, really."

"Don't worry. You'll still be the belle of the ball." I patted Madison's shoulder, looking down at her with the warmth of a butter knife. I might or might not have watched several Hallmark movies in order to mimic a loving fiancé. As I'd been jogging on the treadmill. Real talk, the cardio was the only reason I hadn't fallen asleep during the BS overload.

"You're too kind." Madison put her hand over mine on her shoulder, squeezing it in the hopes of breaking a few bones.

I bit back a smirk. "Never too kind for you."

"Oh, stop it." She smiled tightly. *"Really,"* she stressed.

Mom looked between us, basking in whatever she thought she was witnessing and clapping her hands together. "Look at you two!"

Although Madison did not do anything overtly bad to fuck things up, she was far from Oscar-worthy in the loving-fiancée department. She tucked her head down whenever she was asked a question that needed to be answered with a lie. Her cheeks were so beetroot red I thought her head was about to explode. And she regarded me with polite, fake enthusiasm, like I was bad macaroni art made by a particularly distracted child.

"Katie is dying to see you, and I don't think you've met Julian, Chase's older brother, and his wife, Amber, yet. They weren't with us last Christmas. They celebrated with Amber's family in Wisconsin," Mom blabbed, snatching Madison's hand and leading her into the house after ten painful minutes. "Clementine, their daughter, is *such* a peach."

"Sounds fruity," Mad squeaked, getting whisked away by Mom without sparing me another glance.

Sounds fruity. She'd actually said that. I'd been inside this woman at some point. What in the holy fuck had I been thinking?

Two uniformed employees materialized from the entrance, rushing to carry Madison's suitcase. I directed them to the room we were going to share—yes, *share*—glancing at the golf cart by the Tesla. I entertained the idea of heading straight to the golf course to interrupt Julian and Dad, then thought better of it. I wasn't some hysterical preteen begging to be included. Besides, I had to go upstairs and work the Madison angle. Prep her before she met the rest of the Black clan.

My father had the uncanny ability to see past bullshit and dissect situations and dynamics successfully. I wouldn't put it past him to call me out on this engagement if he noticed my bride was contemplating murdering me with a steak knife. Yes, I decided. The crap with Julian could wait. It wasn't like we were going to go for each other's throat near Dad, anyway.

Reluctantly, I headed to our room on the left wing of the estate. The side reserved for immediate family. Julian and his family resided in the right wing. The official reason was because they needed more space. If it were three years ago, I'd have bought it. Not now, though. Now, Julian felt like an outsider through and through.

I found Madison caught in a mindless conversation with Katie and Mom in our room. Amber was probably taking a bubble bath somewhere in the mansion, trying the latest skin-care fad. Koala blood or turtle shit or whatever it was she smeared on her face to appear younger. The women in my family were still holding Madison's hand hostage in turns, cooing at the engagement ring like it was a newborn. Clearing my throat, I stepped inside and wrapped an arm around her shoulders.

The gesture didn't feel familiar or pleasant. I'd never done it before, even when we were seeing each other. Madison had slim, narrow shoulders, something I'd never truly noticed before. It didn't feel right, the weight of my entire arm on this woman. Other men obviously didn't have partners Mad's size, or they'd bury them completely. How I'd been able to be on top of this girl several times a week was a mystery to me. She looked so fragile standing next to me in that moment. I decided not to put the full weight of my arm on her shoulders, which resulted in my arm sort of hanging in the air an inch from her body. It was inconvenient, but she was tiny.

So tiny she couldn't possibly count as an entire person.

I technically only had *half* an ex-girlfriend.

Just admit you had a fucking girlfriend, you full-size piece of shit.

"I was just asking Maddie how come we haven't seen her for so long." Katie turned to face me, fiddling with the pearls on her neck. She was tall for a woman, with long dark hair and an impeccably malnourished figure she liked to wrap in elegant dresses. She was the type of person to blend in with the furniture and take up as little space as possible. The opposite of small, olive-skinned, chatterbox Madison.

"You mean grilling her," I corrected. I didn't want my fake fiancée to be under unnecessary scrutiny. Her lying game was probably as weak as her fashion sense. Katie recoiled visibly, insulted by my dig, and I immediately felt like a douchebag. For all my resentment of romantic relationships, I was usually a decent human to my family.

"Thank you, Chase. I can take care of myself." Madison smiled tightly.

And you might need to with the asexual fool you're dating.

"You're right, sweetheart. I know firsthand how good you are at taking care of yourself." I elevated a suggestive eyebrow, referring to the arsenal of sex toys I'd once found in her kitchen drawer while looking for a spoon for my coffee. ("I'm space efficient, okay?" she'd yelled. "This is a studio apartment!") Madison, as predicted, turned crimson in a second.

"Self-care is important." She looked up at the ceiling, presumably trying not to combust.

"Preach, sister." Katie sighed, our innuendos flying over her head. "I'm thinking of going back to therapy now that we found out about Dad."

Mad's eyes dropped back to Katie, her face crumpling from horrified to sad. "Oh, honey." She touched my sister's arm. "You should do whatever it takes to put yourself in the best state of mind. I think it's a great idea."

"Did you go to therapy? During . . . ? After . . . ?" Katie asked hopefully. My sister was a little older than Madison and yet ten times more naive. I chalked it up to a sheltered upbringing, combined with the luxury of never knowing true hardship.

"Well, I couldn't really afford it." Madison scrunched her nose, making Katie's eyes bulge out with horror. Yeah. She forgot shrinks were a perk not everyone could afford. "But I had my dad. And anyway, lots of family, so . . ." She shrugged.

There was an awkward pause in which Katie probably felt like dying, I felt like killing someone, and Madison . . . who the heck knew what she felt at that moment?

"Well"—Mom clapped with a cheerful smile, snapping us out of our reverie—"let's leave you lovebirds alone to settle in. We're having a late snack at ten. Nothing formal, just a bit of food and a chat. We'd love to have you, if you are not too tired."

Mom gave Madison one last hand squeeze before dragging my sister out of the room and closing the door behind us.

I removed my arm from Mad's shoulders at the same time she swiveled toward me, stomping on my foot with all her might. It took a second to register her foot was on mine. She weighed practically nothing. Most of it was fabric and accessories she'd probably found in a Claire's discount basket.

"We're *not* staying in the same room." She wiggled her finger in my face. I began to loosen my tie, sauntering into the walk-in closet, in which a full-blown wardrobe was waiting for me, appropriate for all seasons. I knew she'd follow.

"Fact-check that statement, Madison, because it looks like we are."

"This place has like three hundred rooms." She was at my heels, waving her arm around.

"Twelve," I corrected, opening the watch drawer. *Rolex or Cartier?* The least heavy one was the right answer, in case there was more shoulder hugging. I knew I'd have to at least pretend to like her in front of my old man, and touching her was, unfortunately, a part of the charade. If he'd be half as happy as Mom and Katie were to see her, my place in heaven was secure.

God, I hope they serve booze there.

"Still enough for me to sleep elsewhere." Madison jutted a hip against the shelves in my periphery. Narrow waist. Wide hips. Not disproportionately so, like that reality-TV family of human clones. She was deliciously feminine. Everything about her delicate and small and round. I wondered if that Dr. Goody Two-Shoes appreciated that about her.

"Why would two lovebirds like us sleep in separate bedrooms?" I closed the drawer, beginning to undress. I trusted Mad could turn around if she felt offended by my partial nudity. Not that it was something she hadn't seen before. *Up close.*

"Lots of reasons," she said breathlessly, snapping her fingers together. "Celibacy. Let's pretend I'm saving myself for marriage."

"Sweetheart, you sang your carols in the pantry, Jacuzzi, three of the bedrooms, *and* the pool when we stayed here last Christmas. Your virtue couldn't find its way back to your body with a map, a compass, and a GPS."

"They heard us?" Her eyes widened, and she blushed again. Admittedly, she was a cute blusher. She had apple cheeks and a soft jawline. Too bad she also had the ability to trick me into commitment when I wasn't paying attention.

"Yes, my family heard us. People in Maine did too."

"Jesus Christ."

"Now, now, we celebrated JC's birthday, but it was me who did all the dirty work."

"I don't recall you complaining."

"A bit hard, since my mouth was strategically placed between your legs."

She swatted my bare chest before turning around and pacing back and forth. She linked her fingers behind her neck as I continued to strip down to my briefs, flexing every muscle in my body. I was not above vanity (in truth, I was not above most things).

"I'm not sharing a bed with you." She shook her head. Stopped. Pointed at the floor. "You're welcome to the carpet."

Resisting the urge to ask her if she meant another round with the one between her legs, I bowed my head. "Not sure you are aware, Mad, but it is possible for two people to sleep in the same bed without having sex. Cases of that have been recorded throughout history."

"Not where you are concerned." She gave me the stink eye, ignoring my state of undress. Fair point. I wasn't used to her calling the shots or refusing me in general. Back when we were dating, Madison went with the flow and danced to my tune.

She definitely wasn't doing that now, and I didn't know what to make of it.

I was going to launch into another counterargument when she began to unzip her suitcase and fling her clothes out of it. They landed on the floor in a heap of patterned fabrics. Perfect to start a bonfire.

"You're not going to convince me otherwise, Chase, so I suggest you just make yourself comfortable on the floor with a pillow and a blanket. I will not hesitate to go back home if you don't respect my boundaries."

"With what car, exactly?"

"Uber, if need be. Don't test me, Chase. I am not your prisoner."

"Nor was I yours," I muttered.

"Excuse me?" She snapped her head up.

"Funny, I didn't know you were into that."

"Into what?"

"Respecting boundaries."

"When did I not respect your boundaries?" Her eyes were so wide I could see my entire reflection in them.

When you made me your boyfriend without my consent.

I realized, even as I said that internally, how carnally pussy it sounded. I could have walked out of my relationship with Madison at any given moment. I'd chosen to stay. I chose her superior baking skills and the excellent fucks and the comfort of deleting hookup apps over my principles.

I also chose to screw it all up.

I made a rough calculation. If I cheated on her, she'd go away, then come back eventually (they all did), and we'd fall into a more casual, no-strings-attached arrangement. I wasn't a total pig. I'd move her into a nicer place, get her nice things. I just didn't want to settle down. The mere term bothered me. *Settle.* You settled for an ugly car to make sure it was secure enough for your family. You settled for a boring date so you could fuck her at the end of the night. You did *not* settle when it came to your entire goddamn existence.

Thing was, Mad never came back. She blew up, broke up with me, and left for good. She *did* end up sending me a birthday present, though, in the form of a bag of Daisy's hair balls and her latest vet bill (which, let it be known, I was enough of a good sport to pay). I still remembered the note she'd added to the invoice.

Chase,

I got Daisy spayed. I think we can both agree nothing that comes from you should ever reproduce. Feel free to pay this at your earliest convenience.

—Madison

Back in reality—in our shared room—I felt my jaw tightening. I answered Madison through clenched teeth. "Fine. If you are so worried about grinding your ass against my crotch at night, I'll sleep on the carpet."

"Thank you." Her lips puckered. She was fighting a smile, I realized. Why would she smile? I noticed my ears felt hot. I resisted the urge to touch them. I wasn't blushing. This was a fact. I never blushed.

"Stop looking at me." I tapered my eyes, throwing a bath towel over my shoulder.

"Stop pointing at me." She went back to tossing her horrendous dresses out of her suitcase, biting down a smile. Point at her? Was she crazy?

I looked down.

Oh.

Oh.

I turned around, rearranging myself through my Armani briefs, thinking, *Fuck, fuck, fuck.*

"Yeah, I know." She sighed behind my back. "That's usually what you think about when your body reacts this way."

I'd said that aloud? What in the ever-loving hell was wrong with me?

"Go make yourself presentable," I muttered, stomping my way to the shower before I did more female things. Like blushing again, or maybe fucking swooning in her arms. "And for the love of God, try not to wear anything patterned."

She wore a patterned outfit, head to toe.

Her black heels had little white cross prints, her dress was flowery, and she had a checkered headband. She'd done that thing I fucking loved with her hair. Her bangs were iron straight, but the rest of her short hair was messily wavy and falling over her face and neck like a waterfall.

Her style reminded me of her apartment. A crowded, color-clashing mess that looked like a piñata full of secondhand furniture and bad decisions had exploded inside. I wouldn't call her a hoarder per se, but her apartment didn't look pretty. It was possible Madison Goldbloom was the most sentimental person on planet Earth. She collected everything, including—but not limited to—flowerpots, fabrics, sketches, postcards, wedding invitations, hair elastics, touristy knickknacks, a poodle-shaped mannequin made solely from wine bottle caps, and even a Prince-shaped Chia Pet.

Clutter. Clutter. Clutter.

I had no idea what I found appealing about this girl, other than her talent to offend any pair of working eyes in a two-hundred-mile radius. She designed wedding dresses for an exclusive bridal company that didn't suck. I knew that for a fact—their designs sold like hotcakes; that was why we were in partnership with them. Sven said she was his most valuable employee. I did not question that at the time we were dating.

I should have.

Mad descended the stairway while the rest of us were seated in the dining room. The staff sprang into action, serving the food as soon as she slipped into the seat next to me, smiling at everyone and waving hello. "Sorry, I didn't realize you guys were waiting."

Madison had the ability to be a shy wallflower to the world and a little nymph in the bedroom. I used my foot to pull her chair closer to me so our arms and legs were touching. It dragged along the marble floor noisily, making everyone in the room chuckle.

"He already misses you. That's so sweet." Katie put her hand to her chest, her voice hoarse with emotion. Madison let out a hysterical, nervous laugh. I gritted my teeth silently.

Don't screw it up, Goldbloom.

"Caja-China-roasted Mecox farm pig, bacon cake, buttermilk coleslaw, scallion on a bed of pretzel rods," one of the hostesses explained to Madison, pointing at the different dishes on the table. As far as ten o'clock snack went, this was a full-blown feast. My parents couldn't help themselves. It irked me that I'd have to break it to my mother and Katie that Madison and I weren't together. Although I wouldn't have to deal with it until after Dad . . . *after Dad.*

I couldn't get past that sentence.

My father was dying, and there was nothing within my power to help him. I'd grown so accustomed to throwing money at my problems; the idea I was defenseless against something so profound, that would alter my life in such a radical way, made me irrationally angry.

Madison smiled and nodded dutifully where appropriate. She leaned forward at the long table, addressing my father, who sat at the head, looking smaller than he had before we'd found out. "Thank you so much for inviting me, Mr. Black."

"Well, I didn't really know how much time I'd have to get to know you." He awarded her one of his rare real smiles. Her throat worked. "Chase and you must've really taken to one another. Marriage is an important decision after less than a year together, and with your busy work schedules, that didn't allow us to get to know you."

I was beginning to feel marginally sorry for Madison. My family had a way of cross-examining her, and everybody seemed to be playing the bad cop.

"May I just say how sorry I am that you're . . . well, that you . . . ," Mad started.

"Are dying?" He finished the sentence for her, his tone dry. "Yes, sweetheart, I am not too happy about that either."

She blushed, looking down at her lap. "I'm sorry. Words fail me at times like these."

"Not your fault." He took a sip of his whiskey, his movements slow and measured. He was an older version of me, with a headful of white hair, a tall frame, and arctic eyes. "I doubt anyone is good at talking to a dying person about their state. At least I know Chase has someone to lean on. He is not as tough as he always seems, you know." He arched an eyebrow.

"He is also right fucking here"—I pointed at my own head, knowing he'd find my annoyance amusing—"and a part of this conversation."

"Trust me, I know Chase has a fragile side." Madison patted my shoulder, still smiling at my father. An obvious dig at me. One–zero to the away team.

"Fragile is a bit of a stretch." I smiled good-naturedly.

"Delicate, then?" She whipped her head around, blinking at me with a bright grin.

Two–zero.

"*Touchy* is the word you are looking for." Julian clucked his tongue, his Cheshire cat grin on full display, at the same time that Mom snort-laughed. "Nice to meet you. I'm Julian."

He extended his hand over the table. Mad shook it. A sudden urge to flip the table upside down struck me.

"Touchy." Mad tasted the word on her tongue, smiling at my cousin. "I like that. He is like a porcupine on Shark Week."

That made Katie, Mom, Dad, Julian, *and* Amber burst into laughter. It was such a normal family moment that I wasn't even overtly annoyed with Madison for making fun of me or with Julian for existing. It was the first we'd had since we'd found out about Dad and the first time I'd seen Julian looking pleased in years.

Everyone began to dig into their food. Other than Amber, but skipping meals in favor of alcohol was just another Tuesday for her. Mad shrank into her seat, downing her glass of champagne like it was water. At first, I didn't pay much attention to what she was doing. I hadn't eaten since breakfast. But when ten minutes had passed and her plate was still empty, I felt my teeth gritting in annoyance.

"What's wrong?" I hissed sideways at her.

The food was fine. More than fine. A Michelin-star culinary phenomenon had cooked it, not some asshole sous-chef who'd made his way from Brooklyn to make a fast weekend buck.

"Nothing," she said, just as her stomach began to growl. It wasn't a feminine rumble either. It sounded like her intestines were trying to pick a fight with the rest of her body.

I leaned toward her, brushing my lips along the shell of her ear so it appeared that we were sharing an intimate conversation, one that didn't include the subject of her stomach making Freddy Krueger sounds. "You're a terrible liar, and I'm an impatient bastard. Spill it, Madison."

"I have no idea what any of the things the waitress said mean," she whispered under her breath, her blush making another guest appearance. "Some of these things are unrecognizable to me. I'm sorry, Chase, but bacon cake sounds like something that should be outlawed in all fifty states."

I pressed my lips together, resisting a chuckle. Taking her plate, I started filling it with food, knowing it earned me brownie points in the fake-fiancé department. Mom quietly glowed as I slid the plate back to Madison, smiling at her with what I hoped looked like warmth (inspiration: Jesse Metcalfe in *A Country Wedding*).

"You'll like these . . ." *Don't say* sweetheart. *Don't be that cliché.* "Baby."

Baby? Could I sound like any more of a douchebag?

"How are you so sure . . ." She hesitated, too, aware of how all eyes were on her. *"Darling?"*

Amber nearly spat out her wine, laughing.

"I know your taste."

"Doubtful."

"Trust me," I gritted out through my fake smile.

"Never," she whispered.

Still, she took her fork and stabbed at a sautéed brussels sprout coated with bread crumbs, herbs, and cream. Her eyes rolled inside their sockets after the third chew. The sound that followed, coming from the back of her throat, made my dick jerk in appreciation.

"Now I see the light." She sighed. I wanted to show her other things. To drag her into my dark side for a little while, then spit her back out to her sunshine existence.

"So. Madison," Amber purred from across the table, running her long, pointy fingernail along her champagne glass in a comically wicked manner. I braced myself. Amber was, without doubt, the most dangerous person at the table. "How did our Chase propose?"

Our Chase. Like I was a fucking vase. She wished.

Amber had witchlike acrylic pointy nails, enough hair extensions to make three wigs, fake eyelashes, and cleavage that left nothing to the imagination. Smugness hung around her like a cloud of perfume. She was my age—thirty-two—and her hobbies were limited to plastic surgery, finding the new workout/diet craze celebrities were fawning over, and having public arguments with her husband. Julian put his arm around his wife's shoulder, wiggling his brows, as if to say it was showtime.

Brace yourself for an Oscar-worthy performance, coz.

"How did he propose?" Mad repeated, her smile more frozen than Amber's forehead. All eyes were on her. I supposed Madison wanted something a bit more romantic than the story of how we'd met. One morning, we'd walked into the same elevator, the one Black & Co. and Croquis shared, and instead of continuing my way up to the last floor in our high-rise building—a.k.a. management floor—I'd slipped into Croquis's studio with her, leaned against her drawing table, and asked her what it'd take to get into her pants, though in not so many words. Madison chugged her second flute of champagne before putting it down and lifting her eyes to meet Amber's.

"The proposal was actually really romantic," she said breathlessly.

Is she drunk? I needed her sober. She was swimming with the sharks, bleeding in the fucking water. No, she was just being New Maddie again, meaning she was about to rip me a new one.

"It was?" Julian's eyes hooded skeptically. I didn't like his eyes on her. Let me rephrase—I didn't like him these days, period. But I especially didn't like the way he looked at Madison. There was something sinister about the obsidian quality his eyes took on. I wasn't the possessive type, but punching a hole through his face seemed inevitable if he continued staring at Madison like this. Like he wasn't entirely sure if he wanted to have sex with her, mock her for how socially unpolished she was, or both.

"Yes." Mad munched on the side of her lip, stealing glances at me. *God dammit.* "We were at the Brooklyn Heights promenade, enjoying the romantic view—"

"Chase went to Brooklyn?" Amber cut into her words, raising a microbladed eyebrow. Rookie mistake. Everybody knew anything south of the East Village and north of Washington Heights was dead to me in the city. Hell, I considered Inwood fucking abroad.

Madison made a *mm-hmmm* sound, taking another sip of champagne. She looked like a trapped animal, cornered and frightened. But helping her out would look suspicious. I felt like a turtle mother watching her wonky-ass hatchling wobbling offshore to the ocean, knowing it had a 5 percent chance to survive.

Then, lo and behold, a Christmas-in-July miracle happened. Madison cleared her throat, straightened her back, and found her voice.

"I was leaning on the banisters, taking in the sights. Before I knew what was happening, he was on one knee before me, a sweaty, blabbering mess. I thought he was going through a mental breakdown. He was *so* nervous. But then he said the sweetest thing. Remember what you told me, honey?" She turned to me, blinking angelically. I gave her a curt smile. She wanted something along the lines of *You're the love of my life, my moon and my stars* or *I can't live without you and frankly don't see the point in trying to* or even [insert any other Hallmark cliché I'd listened to during my research, which had triggered my gag reflex].

"Of course." I took her hand, brought her knuckles to my lips, and brushed them along her flesh. Goose bumps rose on her arms, and I grinned into the back of her hand, knowing we still shared enough sexual tension to make the mansion explode. "I told you you had a mustard mustache, then wiped your pretty face clean."

Mad's smile dropped. Amber let out a metallic chuckle. My parents and Katie smiled. Julian narrowed his eyes, his gaze ping-ponging between us.

"Carry on." He rested his chin on his knuckles. Julian was a decade older than yours truly. A Saturn-looking man. Tall, surrounded by rings of fat, with a shiny, bald head that made you want to rub it and see if a genie would come out of his ear.

Mad looked between us, picking up on the murderous vibes. "He helped me clean my, uh, mustard stain, then told me he originally wanted to wait a bit longer—a year is nothing in the grand scheme of things—but his love for me was just too much. That I was his entire world. I think the word he used was *obsessed*. He began to gush. It was kind of embarrassing, actually." She pressed her foot over mine under the table, daring me to defy her story. "Like, really going at it. To the point he started crying—"

"Chase? Crying?" Amber wrinkled her nose, visibly appalled now. It was sixty-nine steps too far, and I was eager to drag Madison back to our room and spank her for every lie she'd spat out at dinner.

"I wouldn't go as far as weeping, but . . ." Madison turned to me, doing that auntie arm pat again, giving me a three-nil-for-the-away-team look. I couldn't contradict her version of our proposal story. Not publicly, anyway, when we were supposed to sell ourselves as a loving couple. I was, however, going to retaliate for this little stunt.

"It was emotional," I concluded, taking a small sip of my whiskey. "Although, truth be told, the mist in my eyes was mostly due to your brown-and-green-checked dress with the blue dots, sweetheart. It was a lot to take in."

"But a pleasure to take off, I assume." Julian was baiting me, a cold smile playing on his lips.

My father dropped his utensils on his plate, clearing his throat deliberately. Julian looked up and waved away the discomfort at the table. Sometimes riling me up trumped acting like an actual human being in company. It was a recent development and one I didn't appreciate at all. "That was highly inappropriate of me. I apologize, Madison. Brotherly banter gone too far."

Brotherly, my ass. I wouldn't trust him with a plastic spoon.

"Please, call me Maddie." She bowed her head.

"Maddie," my father repeated, sitting back. I made a mental note to remind Julian I was not above hurling him out of an open window if he were to sexually harass my fake fiancée.

"I must admit we were having our doubts since we haven't seen you since Christmas. We thought Chase might've gotten cold feet," Dad piped, pinning me with a glare.

"Nothing cold about this man." Madison smiled big at Dad, pinching my cheek. Christ, I was glad this was going to be over in a couple of days. The woman was bound to drive me to alcoholism. "The hottest man I've met."

She blurted the sentence out before she realized what she was saying. I turned my head and stared at her with a smug smile. Her cheeks turned pink. Her neck and ears were quick to follow.

"Thank you for marrying this savage of a man." Dad smiled.

"You owe me one," she joked. Everyone laughed. *Again.*

We fell into pleasant conversation as more courses were served. Thirty minutes later, Katie's back straightened, and she frowned.

"Where is Clementine?" She stabbed a berry swimming in her club soda with a toothpick and tossed it into her mouth. I hoped the lack of alcohol in her glass was a telltale sign that she was back on her meds. That was an encouraging development. Katie's anxiety brought everything else in her life out of focus, and even though she was great at what she did, marketing, I knew she wanted to meet a nice guy and settle down. She couldn't do that as long as she was mentally frail.

"Asleep upstairs." Amber flipped her platinum-blonde hair, cutting her gaze to mine pointedly. "She didn't even get to see her favorite uncle."

"She will tomorrow," I said, clipped.

"Thanks for clearing some time in your schedule to see her. I know how busy you are." More sarcasm.

I raised my glass, pretending to make a toast. "Anything for my niece."

And nothing for her parents.

"Maddie, I don't suppose you'll be in the mood to play Monopoly with us afterward? You must be exhausted." Mom turned to my fake fiancée, batting her eyelashes. She was laying it on thick. "It's a tradition the Black women keep every time we're in the Hamptons."

Mad perked up. "Really? I don't remember us doing it during Christmas."

That's because Mom just made this tradition up, I refrained from saying. My family went gaga over this woman, and I wasn't entirely sure why.

"We wanted to give you and Chase some, er, alone time as a new couple."

It alarmed me that Mom was more invested in Madison than I was in the stock market. Maybe she simply liked the idea of me not dying an old, solitary grinch. Madison was the only woman I'd brought home since She Who Shall Not Be Named.

"I would love to," Mad exclaimed sunnily. I didn't doubt her enthusiasm. Knew she'd rather take a bath in a deep fryer than spend a minute with me.

Katie and Mom exchanged the Look. The one they shared whenever they watched *Pride and Prejudice* and Colin Firth was stuttering something charming onscreen.

I stabbed at my steak like it had tried to stab me first, watching it bleed juicily onto my plate, feeling an impending calamity hanging over my head.

Mad was digging her obnoxiously patterned, colorful roots into the Black family, and my parents and sister were falling hard and fast.

Unlike me. I was the only Black who was immune to her charms. To her smiles. To her heart.

I promised myself that.

CHAPTER FIVE

Maddie

March 1, 2001

Dear Maddie,

Today was not a good day. I know you were upset when we told you we couldn't afford to pay for your school trip to the Statue of Liberty. Your father and I are struggling financially; that's not a secret, but I wish it was. I wish we could keep this fact away from you, to afford all the things you want to do.

There is so much I want to give you, but I can't. My treatments are getting pricier, and ever since your father had to hire an assistant to run the shop while I'm in treatment or recovering, we've been treating things we took for granted like luxuries.

What broke my heart today wasn't even that you were sad about the trip—but that you tried to hide it from us. Your eyes and nose were red after you came back from your room, but you smiled like nothing happened.

Fun fact of the day: Jasmine is called queen of the night in India, because of its strong scent after sunset. I left some in your room. My version of an apology. Remember to tend to them. You can learn a lot about a person's sense of responsibility and devotion by the way they keep their flowers.

Thank you for tending to us, even when we can't tend to you in all areas in life.

Love,

Mom. x

"To be honest, I thought you didn't like us very much." Katie dragged her thimble over the Monopoly board, her brows furrowed in concentration. The drawing room was bathed in golden light. The rich carpets over exposed wood, Pinterest-worthy fireplace, and handmade crème-and-blue throws made me feel like I was cocooned inside one of those Jen Aniston movies where everything looked perfect all the time.

In the last couple of hours, Katie had purchased all four railroads on the board and was in the process of acquiring over three houses on the orange-colored group. Last I paid attention, she'd been driving Lori and me to the ground, leaving us with measly small sheds in the bad parts of town and the clothes on our backs. Luckily, Lori and I were sharing a bottle of wine and pieces of gossip about the royal family, which, it turned out, we both shared an unhealthy obsession with. We'd spent the last hour dissecting Kate Middleton's wedding dress before moving to the grave topic of Meghan's wedding tiara.

"Are you kidding me?" I pressed my wineglass to my blistering cheek, enjoying its cool sensation. I was probably slurring. The four glasses of champagne and one glass of wine on a relatively empty stomach weren't a good idea, but I had to dull all the Chaseness around me. He was a lot to deal with. "I love you guys. Ronan is, like, a legendary fashion icon, Lori is the mom I wish I still had, and you . . . Katie, you're . . ." I paused, blinking at the Monopoly board. I hated the idea they thought I wasn't around because of *them.* Hated that Chase had kept the truth from them and villainized me in the process. "You're seriously someone I would be good friends with. The first time we met, at

Christmas, my dress tore up across my ass. You didn't even blink before ushering me to your room and giving me something to wear." A Prada something, to be exact. It had taken everything in me to send it back with a thank-you note. "You're amazing, Katie. Like, really amazing." I leaned forward, putting my hand on her arm. I couldn't tell through the fog of intoxication if we were having a tender moment or an awkward one.

Her eyes clung to mine. "Really? Because I thought maybe it was me."

"Why would it be you?" My eyes widened.

"I don't know," Katie said, so sweetly shy she looked like a kid, even though she was older than I was. Her voice was like broken glass.

"No, you're perfect." I hiccuped. "I love you."

Had I just declared my love to a relative stranger? That was my cue to retire before Martyr Maddie became Creepy Maddie and passed out over the Monopoly board.

"I think I better head to bed. Who won?" I squinted at the board. It was blurry, the little pieces swimming around it like they were chasing one another. I hiccuped again. "Me?"

"Actually, you owe me two thousand dollars and a house on Tennessee Avenue." Katie laughed, starting to remove the Scottie dog, top hat, and thimble from the board. I yawned, my eyes flickering shut as I took spontaneous one-second naps between blinks. Somewhere in the back of my head, I realized I was being a mess, not at all the brilliant, responsible fiancée Chase wanted me to be. Screw him. I owed him nothing. As long as his family was having fun.

"I hope you like fixer-uppers and accept coupons, Katie, because I'm broke as all hell," I snorted out.

"That's all right. It's just a game." Katie folded the board and tucked it back into the box as she hummed to herself. She was so agreeable and docile. The opposite of her older brother. Almost like he'd hogged every drop of ferociousness in their DNA pool before he was born.

"Yeah, well, I'm flat-out broke in real life too." I snickered.

Time to go to bed, Miss Hot Mess Express.

I stood up on wobbly feet. My knees felt like jelly, and there was a strange pressure behind my eyes. Knowing I'd be coming face-to-face with Chase made me break out in hives. I'd tried to postpone our reunion as much as I could, hoping—*praying*, really—he'd fall asleep before I got back to the room.

"Not for long." Lori laughed.

I laughed too. Then paused. Then frowned. "Wait, how do you mean?"

"Well"—Lori offered me a one-shoulder shrug, picking nonexistent lint from her dress pants as Katie put the Monopoly box away—"you're going to marry Chase, honey. And Chase is . . . well endowed."

Katie choked on her soda, while I used every ounce of my self-control in order to not break into giggles. "Oh, Lori, you have no idea," I said.

Now Katie cackled. It was a sight. The willowy, dark-haired beauty with her hair pinned back carefully let it all out and laughed. I grinned. I wondered when the last time she'd actually had fun was. Then resisted the urge to invite her for a night out with Layla and me. Martyr Maddie needed to be switched off this weekend to make sure things wouldn't get overly complicated.

Lori wasn't wrong, though. Chase was a billionaire. His level of rich was golden toilet seats and private jets containing sex swings. It was burn-the-money-just-to-see-if-it'd-make-you-feel-anything rich. The scary, jaded type of wealth that seemed wholly untouchable from where I was standing.

It hit me then that I'd never considered Chase's money as a factor when we were really dating. His wealth was in the backdrop of our relationship, like a massive piece of furniture I learned to overlook, even though it was a part of the view. When he asked me what I wanted for Christmas, I told him I needed a new heating pad. It was twenty-five bucks on Amazon, available on Prime, with a gift-wrap option included for an additional fee. Chase laughed and got me a pair of $10K earrings instead. He couldn't fathom why I wasn't enthralled by the lavish gift. The truth of the matter was I was broke post-Christmas and had really been counting on that heating pad.

I didn't want something expensive and useless. I wanted something not so expensive and use*ful*.

Lori's comment made me sober up momentarily. I nodded, getting back into delighted-fiancée mode. "Oh yeah. Sure. But I'm going to be very responsible with his money. I mean, *our* money. Money in general." *Shut up, shut up, shut up.* "I don't spend a lot."

"Well, we all know I have the opposite problem." Katie looked down at her feet.

Desperately eager to change the subject, I clapped my hands, standing in the middle of the room. "Where is Amber, by the way? I really wanted to get to know her."

And by *really* I meant *not really*, but it seemed like something I should say.

Katie and Lori exchanged looks. I was drunk but not stupid and could tell they were doing this eye-communication thing Dad and Mom used to do when she was still alive to decide something I wasn't supposed to know.

"She was tired," Katie said at the same time Lori mumbled, "I think she came down with something."

Huh.

So Amber disliked me. For no apparent reason, as far as I could tell.

"That's unfortunate," I said.

"Very," Lori muttered in a tone that conveyed it really wasn't. Then I remembered Lori and Amber hadn't really communicated very much during dinner. Then again, Amber had been either busy with her phone or glaring at Chase and me simultaneously, waiting for one of us to spontaneously combust.

I kissed Lori's and Katie's cheeks goodbye and turned toward the door. I promised myself not to read into Amber's reaction to me. I'd done nothing wrong.

Other than deceiving the entire Black family, a little voice inside me said. But Amber wasn't privy to that, was she? Then I remembered she hadn't seemed sold on my Brooklyn story. Neither had her husband, Julian. It worried me that I may have blown it. If Ronan knew Chase and I were lying, he'd be devastated, and I wouldn't be able to live with myself.

I ascended the stairs barefoot. The velvet carpet pressed between my toes lusciously. Everything was crème and navy and powder blue. Nautically rustic, with big pieces of furniture and white-painted wood. It felt almost unreal to be a part of this place. Like I'd cheated my way in. Which, in a way, I had.

I reached the second floor, holding the banisters for dear life, still buzzing with alcohol. I zigzagged past the hallway doors. One of them was ajar. It was a double door.

A low, gravelly growl seeped through the crack. "Over my dead body."

I froze, recognizing Chase's diabolical voice. He sounded ready to murder whoever was with him in that room, and I didn't want to be there when it happened.

Move along, something inside me whispered. *Nothing to see here. Not your business, not your war.*

I checked the time on my phone. One a.m. What the hell was he doing up, and who was he arguing with? Curiosity got the better of me. I leaned against the wall, holding my breath, careful not to get caught.

"If that's what it takes," Julian drawled sardonically. I recognized his voice too. He had traces of a Scottish accent, littered in his words sparsely. Ronan Black's family was originally from Edinburgh. Julian, Ronan's late sister's son, had been flown from Scotland when he was only six to live with the family after his parents died in a fatal car crash on Christmas Day. The Black couple, Lori and Ronan, once said in an interview Julian was the best Christmas gift they'd ever received. I'd read about it on the Black family Wikipedia page when I was Chase obsessed during the first month of our relationship. Julian and Chase grew up as brothers and, according to Wikipedia, were close. Whoever had written this page had been high, because during my six months with Chase, he'd rarely mentioned his cousin to me and never made an introduction. Now that Julian was here, he and Chase acted like sworn enemies.

"Don't mistake my devotion to my father for weakness. My focus is on his health and well-being. If something happens to him . . ." Chase left the sentence unfinished.

I stuck my nose in the gap between the doors and peeked through it. They were standing in a darkened library. It was a gorgeous room, with floor-to-ceiling white shelves containing thousands of books seemingly arranged by the color of their spines. Chase was leaning behind a heavy oak desk, his knuckles pressing the exposed wood. Julian was standing in front of him, tall but not as tall as Chase, my fake fiancé's shadow cast over him like a dark castle.

Julian threw his arms in the air, exasperated. "Something *will* happen. He is dying, and you're not a good fit to replace him. Thirty-two and barely out of your corporate diapers. You'll spook the shareholders and drive the investors away."

"I'm the COO," Chase boomed. It was the first time I'd heard him raise his voice to anyone. He was always deadly quiet and in complete control.

"You're a fucking thief, is what you are," Julian bit back. "You proved it three years ago, and I still haven't forgotten."

Three years ago? What had happened three years ago? Of course, I couldn't very well walk in there and ask. One of the more unfortunate side effects of eavesdropping.

"He chose me as next in line. He chose you as CIO. Deal with it," Chase barked, his eyes hooding.

"He chose *wrong*," Julian deadpanned.

"You have some nerve talking to me about this bullshit on my engagement-party weekend." Chase leaned back, opening a drawer and removing a cigar from it. Rather than lighting it, he broke it in two and fingered the material inside.

He was trying not to snap, I realized.

"About that." Julian took a seat on a chair behind him, crossing his legs. "As soon as I met little Miss Louisa Clark, I realized something was amiss."

"Louisa Clark?" Chase frowned.

"*Me before You*. I watched it with Amber. She cried a lot."

"I would, too, if I had to fuck you on the reg," Chase muttered. "Is there a point to your little story?"

"Your fiancée. She is a Louisa Clark. You don't truly expect us to believe you are marrying this . . . this . . ."

"This?" Chase stopped squashing the tobacco between his fingers and cocked an eyebrow, daring him to finish the sentence. I swallowed. My heart was thrashing helplessly against my rib cage. I didn't want to hear whatever came next but couldn't unglue myself from my spot either.

"Come on." Julian snorted. "Before we were enemies, we were brothers. I know you. This eccentric, artsy-fartsy, quirky-but-full-of-depth chick isn't your type. You like them severely malnourished and personality-free. Your type wears designer clothes and doesn't get sloppy drunk during family gatherings. I see through you, Chase. You want to show Ronan you're good for it. That you're ready to settle down, have kids, the whole enchilada. And with a normal, average girl, no less. Is that who you are now, brother? Grounded? Reliable? An all-around stand-up guy?" Julian threw his head back and laughed. He stood up, shaking his head. "I don't buy your sudden engagement, and I don't buy this relationship. You're just vying for the CEO seat to get back at me by acting all high and mighty. You can play house with a girl who's a six all you want, but I don't for one second believe you'll marry below ten."

A six. I felt nauseous, so much so the need to throw up almost overwhelmed me. I wanted to slap Julian across the face. How dare he put a number on me? And how dare Chase just stand there and listen to this? I *was* his fake fiancée. In fact, screw that. I was his ex-girlfriend. A human being. He couldn't let Julian speak this way.

"You think I want to become CEO to get back at you?" Chase smirked, amused.

"Why else? You didn't even care for the job when you graduated."

"Oh, fuck you, Julian."

"Not if I fuck you first."

"Well." Chase let loose a smile so frigid it made my insides twist painfully. "As it happens, the vacancy for CEO is not available just yet, so you'll have to sit pretty and watch as my so-called fake engagement unfolds."

Unfolds?

Unfolds into *what*?

I'd told Chase this was a one-off. I wasn't going to start playing the dutiful fiancée part like this was some sort of Kate Hudson rom-com. He knew full well whisking me off to the Hamptons was already pushing past my boundaries. Setting them on fire, more like.

He also knows you're Martyr Maddie and will stop at nothing to please others, no matter who they are or how you feel about them.

It took me a few seconds to realize Chase was stalking to the door. I jerked back, before darting to our room, tripping over my own feet. Once inside the room, I knocked a vase down in my haste to close the door. Not wanting to get caught, I left the shattered glass on the floor, dashing into the bathroom. I locked the door behind me and plastered my back to it, panting.

A few seconds later, I heard the door open, then the sound of crunched glass as Chase stepped over the broken vase. There were jasmines inside. Their scent soaked the air now, filling it with thick sweetness that seeped under the crack of the bathroom door. I felt bad for the flowers, squashed under Chase's shoe. My heart had once suffered a similar experience.

"Madison!" he roared into the silence. His voice pierced the air.

I winced. I didn't much care what he thought, but I hated that it was common knowledge I was sloppy drunk tonight and that Julian had thrown it in his face.

"I know you're in there." His words got closer, darker. My dinner clogged my throat, begging to purge itself. Knowing the door was firmly locked, I hurried to the toilet, threw the seat up, and lurched into the bowl. My whole body convulsed as my stomach pumped up the little I'd eaten tonight.

"Should've hired a sorority girl for the job," he muttered under his breath behind the door, giving the handle a firm shake. "Fun drunk beats sad drunk every day of the fucking week."

Fun drunk is not an option when a jerk like you is in the vicinity.

I continued throwing up. Tears ran down my clammy cheeks, snaking into my mouth, their saltiness exploding on my tongue. I never got drunk. I must have been more anxious than I'd realized.

We were supposed to be wide awake and ready to go on a family hike tomorrow at ten a.m. I very much doubted I would be in any shape to get out of bed, if I even made it to it and not straight to the ER tonight.

"Madison!"

"Leave me alone." I scrambled up to brush my teeth. I got as far as the sink and tumbled back down. The pressure in my head made it impossible to open my eyes. Julian's words spun inside it, circling like clothes in a washing machine. *A six.* I was so painfully average and so royally out of my depth here.

I was on my second attempt to hoist myself over the sink and try to brush my teeth when Chase kicked the door down. Unhinged, it flew to the floor, landing with a thump. Luckily, the Jack-and-Jill bathroom was more spacious than my studio, and the door landed a few feet away from me. I looked up and blinked at him, my mouth slack.

Asshole kicked the door down.

"You . . . you stupid . . ." I squinted, trying to find adequate words. And failing. He strode over to me, picked me up from the floor, and righted me against the sink. He turned on the tap and began to wash my face for me, running his big palm over my nose and mouth. He held me by the waist to keep me from falling.

"Finish that thought, Mad. I've a feeling it's going to be amusing," he said tonelessly, plucking my toothbrush from the silver container by the sink and applying a generous amount of toothpaste onto it.

"Conceited . . . arrogant . . . egotistical . . ."

"Nah-ah. You don't get to use synonyms. That's cheating."

"Bastard!" I roared.

"Now we're getting somewhere." He stuck the toothbrush in my mouth, applying gentle pressure as he brushed my teeth for me. He was a thorough brusher. *Of course he was.* "What else have you got?"

"Stupid . . ."

"You already said 'stupid.'"

"Okay, dumb . . ."

"How about we continue this tomorrow?" He cut through my stream of insults. "I promise to be convincingly insulted and cry into my pillow the minute you're done." He finished brushing my teeth, rinsed the toothbrush, and filled a glass of water for me to gargle.

I was too disoriented to pretend to care he was taking care of me. In all of the six months we'd been dating, I'd been careful not to expose him to any part of my less glamorous side. I'd brushed my teeth before he'd woken up to avoid morning breath, gone number two while the shower was on so he wouldn't hear (which had also cornered me into taking frequent showers at his place), and categorically pretended my period hadn't existed, sparing him any mention of Mother Nature's visits to my body. Now, here I was, letting him clean traces of my puke straight from my mouth with his ring on my finger. Oh, irony really did have a sick sense of humor.

I gargled the water he helped me sip before spitting into the sink and side-eyeing him. "You're not the boss of me."

"Thank fuck for that, you'd be a nightmare to tame." He didn't spare me a look, picking up my pink bag of toiletries and plucking two sheets from my makeup-removal wipes. He began to scrub my eyes, probably worried my $5 waterproof mascara would stain his $5,000 linens.

"And you'd be a tyrant to work for," I slurred. He chuckled, tossing the dirty wipes into the trash can, picking me up honeymoon-style, and carrying me back to the bedroom. I was still trying to come up with creative insults, refusing to cave to temptation and wrap my arms around his neck. The aftertaste of puke still lingered on my breath, but I was oddly unbothered when I spoke directly to his face.

"You're not even that attractive," I muttered confrontationally as he put me down on the bed. He removed my shoes, then reached for the hidden zipper in the back of my pencil skirt and rolled it down. He was stripping me bare. It felt too good to get rid of my work clothes to care. Anyway, it wasn't anything he hadn't seen before. And we weren't exactly seducing one another. I was half-dead, and he'd basically admitted my mediocrity to Julian by not defending me.

Oh, also—I hated his guts.

"And you're cold and sarcastic and lack basic empathy." I continued listing his shortcomings. "Just because you're helping me now doesn't mean I forgot who you are. The devil incarnate. You're far from Prince Charming. For one thing, you're rude. And not the saving-princesses kind. You'd probably send someone over to save them for you. Also, you'd look ridiculous on a horse."

I was half-sorry I wasn't still puking. Vomit was favorable to what left my mouth as I tried to insult Chase. That was some second-grade stuff right there.

"Permission to remove your bra," he said thickly.

"Granted," I huffed.

He unclasped my bra with one hand, then produced a Yale sweatshirt from his nightstand drawer. He pulled it over my head, then stopped, staring at my breasts for a few good seconds.

"Take a picture. It'll last longer."

He tugged the sweatshirt down in one go, his throat bobbing with a swallow. The fabric was warm, soft, well worn. It smelled of Chase.

"And what kind of name is Chase Black, anyway?" I let out an unattractive snort. "It sounds made up."

"Sorry to break it to you, but it's as real as your hangover is about to be tomorrow morning. I suggest you chug this." He unscrewed an Evian bottle that sat on the nightstand and handed it over to me. He rolled his black dress shirtsleeves up his elbows, exposing forearms so veiny and muscular I was surprised I hadn't humped them months ago, when I'd still had the chance. "I'll go get you some Advil."

"Wait!" I called out to him when he was at the door. He stopped but didn't turn around to face me. His back was so deliciously ripped inside his dress shirt that I was half-mad at myself for never exchanging nudes with him when we were a thing.

"Pick up the jasmines and put them in a vase full of fresh water. They don't deserve to die," I croaked. "Please."

He made a grumbling sound, shaking his head like I was a lost cause.

The last thing I remembered was gulping the two Advil Chase put in my mouth and passing out.

I woke up with a pounding headache the next day. The clock on the nightstand signaled eleven. It was official—the weekend had started off with me being a spectacular failure, as far as my duties as a charming fiancée went. First, I'd gotten accidentally drunk; then I'd missed the Blacks' family hike. The room was empty, save for a tray with bacon, eggs, fresh bread toasted with butter, and a steaming cup of coffee. There was a new vase full of slightly distressed jasmines on the dresser by the door. A neatly folded blanket and a fluffed-up pillow were sitting on top of one another tidily on the floor.

And a note on the nightstand.

M,

Went hiking. Jasmines are alive. Assuming you are, too, soak up the alcohol with the breakfast I left for you.

PS:

I'd look fantastic on a horse. #Fact.

—C

I spent the rest of the weekend working hard on redeeming myself in the eyes of the Blacks.

At lunch, I was glued to Katie's and Lori's sides, making pleasant conversation and helping Lori stitch back a part of her favorite vintage dress that had gotten torn. I then rolled up my sleeves and made scones for everyone, bantering with the family baker (because what kind of family didn't have a baker on their payroll?) and laughing with Katie, who didn't participate in the baking but was content to sit on the counter and tell me about the half marathon she was training for.

"It's the only thing that makes me feel accomplished. My dad gave me a job and threw enough money at my education, but running? No one does it for me. It's all me."

When the family went wine tasting, I opted to stay behind, seeing as I'd drunk my own body weight the previous night and was afraid even the scent of alcohol would upset my stomach. I sketched and watched the sunset at Foster Memorial Beach, the ocean crashing ashore tickling my toes with its foam. The air was salty and clean. My heart twisted painfully. Mom would have loved this beach.

My phone pinged with a message.

Layla: Welllllllll? 🔪

Maddie: Wellllllll? 😮

Layla: What's going on? Also, I think Sven is onto you. He knows the Blacks are in the Hamptons this weekend. Coincidentally, he dropped by your apartment earlier and I had to tell him you're out. Anyway, should I be worried for Ethan's marshmallow heart?

Maddie: Nope. Chase is gross as ever.

Layla: Totally gross. In a want-to-have-his-sociopathic-babies way, right?

Maddie: First of all: I cannot believe they let you work with children. Second: I told you. He is a cheating cheater who cheats and we are not warming up to him (we = me and my body).

Layla: This sounds a lot like you trying to convince yourself.

Layla: Also, I just want to point out, I was voted teacher of the month last July. So HA.

Maddie: You mean during summer break, when kids are not at school?

Layla: Bye, party pooper. Tell the cobwebs on your va-jay-jay I said hi.

I must've gotten carried away with my sketching, because when I got back to the Black mansion, the door in our en suite bathroom was back on its hinges, unlike yours truly. Chase was already showered, dressed, and looking like the billion bucks he was worth, ready for dinner. I'd managed to successfully avoid him throughout the entire day by spending time with his family. I refused to thank him for taking care of me last night on the grounds that he cheated on me and was still a jerk, and I decided to continue ignoring his good deed. Chase asked if he could count on me not to spontaneously puke at the table. I flipped him the finger and headed to the still-steaming shower. He went downstairs to spend time with his father and niece while I threw three bath bombs into the hot tub, lay in it until my skin became prune-like and I'd shrunk to the size of a ten-year-old, and chose my outfit for the night (A-line black dress with cat ears on the shoulders paired with an orange cardigan and blue heels).

I did not drink a drop of alcohol through dinner and politely ignored Amber's death stares. The stainless beauty of her, paired with the fact her husband thought I was subpar, rattled something I hadn't known existed in me. Luckily, her daughter, Clementine, who looked to be around nine years old, turned out to be an unexpected delight. I hit it off with the little ginger thing immediately. We talked about which princess dresses were the best (Cinderella and Belle, hands down), then about our favorite superheroines. (That was where we agreed to disagree. Clementine exclaimed Wonder Woman was her first choice, while I thought the clear, obvious answer was Hermione Granger. Which led to another subargument about whether Hermione was a superheroine or not.)

(She *definitely* was.)

Clementine was fantastic. Open and bright and full of humor. It helped that she looked nothing like her grim father and gorgeous mother. A completely fresh entity, with different coloring, a constellation of freckles on her nose, and uneven teeth.

I got into bed early, avoiding all communication with my fake fiancé, and was delighted when I woke up in the morning and not only felt brand new but found Chase sleeping on the floor again. I took a moment to watch the frown between his eyebrows as he slept, the thick slash of his dark eyebrows pinched together. A pang of something warm and unwarranted unfurled in my chest.

Devilishly handsome.

I turned my back to him and slept through the morning, but not before writing him a note and leaving it exactly where he'd left his, on the nightstand.

C,

Thank you for brushing my teeth Friday night.

Next time don't use all the hot water.

PS:

You'd look ridiculous on a horse.

—M

CHAPTER SIX

Chase

I crumpled Madison's last note while she was in the shower before slam-dunking it into the trash can. I scribbled another one before she came out.

M,

Can't help but notice you failed to comment about the jasmines. No wonder we broke up. You've always been unappreciative (Xmas diamond earrings come to mind).

PS:

Re: me on a horse. Do I smell a bet?

—C

I had trouble wrapping my head around the fact my convenient, timid ex-girlfriend had turned into a feisty, take-no-bullshit warrior.

There was a knock on the door.

"Come in." I put the pen down. I expected Dad. We hadn't had time to talk one-on-one during the weekend, and I wondered if he'd picked up on the tension between Jul and me. We hadn't had many weekend-long family gatherings with Julian in the past three years. Not since Dad had announced I'd be chief operating officer of Black & Co., the second-in-command to his CEO and chairman position. He'd given

Julian the CIO position—chief information officer—and the message was clear: I was to inherit the CEO seat when it was time for Dad to retire.

Julian had been resentful since then. He thought, considering he was the elder "son," that he would be the natural successor. Only he didn't feel so much like a son anymore and opted out of most family gatherings these days. In fact, I was surprised he'd come to the Hamptons. But of course he had—he'd wanted to see Madison, find out what kind of woman I'd decided to marry.

I looked up at the open door. It wasn't Dad. It was Amber.

Fucking Amber.

She wore a pair of leather pants tighter than a condom and a blouse she'd conveniently forgotten to button around her generous, surgically enhanced rack. Her dyed-blonde hair was freshly blown out, and her face was immaculately made up, including her painted-on eyebrows, which gave her a Bert-from-*Sesame-Street* edge. I jutted my chin out in hello but didn't stop shoving Mad's clothes into her suitcase. My fake fiancée's unaccountability infuriated me. She had nonexistent organizational skills. I couldn't trust her to be ready in time, and I wanted to be out of here before we hit traffic. Another prime reason we were a terrible fit.

And here was another one, in case I was tempted to dip into Madison's jar ever again—she was a *dreadful* drunk. On a scale of one to Charlie Sheen, she was a solid Mel Gibson. Embarrassing to be associated with. Still, I applauded myself for being pleasant and supportive of her when she'd been about to pass out. Of course, I'd had to be. She was my fake fiancée, and tossing her to another room, letting her fend for herself, seemed cold, even by my arctic standards.

"Are you alone?" Amber pouted, crossing her arms over her chest to push her tits out. She was all class.

"Madison's in the shower," I supplied without looking up.

She took that as an invitation to waltz in and park her ass on the edge of the bed, on which the suitcase was open. I continued cramming burnable fabrics into the open jaw of the luggage, wondering who the fuck made the weird clothes Madison was purchasing with gusto. I tried to look at the labels, but there weren't any. Very promising stuff.

"Clementine wanted to say goodbye." Amber leaned toward me, pushing her chest even tighter. I really didn't want it to burst. It would delay my trip back to New York by at least a few hours.

"I'll come see her before we leave," I tried to clip out, but I couldn't help it. My voice came out softer than intended where Booger Face was concerned.

"We need to talk about her." She put her hand on my arm. If she thought it'd stop me from moving, she was dead wrong.

"Booger Face or Madison?"

"I wish you wouldn't call her that," Amber huffed.

"Same," I deadpanned.

I resented Julian and Amber for calling their daughter a name with zero nickname potential. Clemmy sounded like it was short for chlamydia, and Tinny made her sound like a mini can. I therefore referred to her as Booger Face, even though long were the days since she had sported actual boogers. When Clementine was born, Amber had asked me what I thought about the name. I'd said I didn't like it. I was certain that was why she'd chosen it.

"Fine. Tough crowd. Let's start with your fiancée. Is it real?" Amber glowered.

I zipped Mad's overflowing suitcase wordlessly. What the heck kind of question was that?

"She's a bit of an oddball." Amber's palm slid from my arm, her fingernail running circles on her thigh absentmindedly.

"She suits me."

But she didn't, and we both knew that. I hadn't considered the fact that Madison wasn't my obvious choice back when I had dated her, simply because I hadn't thought there was anything to consider. She was supposed to be a fling. Nothing more. Now that Julian and Amber had pointed it out, I had to admit they weren't wrong. I liked my women the same way I liked my interior design: impractical, obscenely expensive to maintain, with zero personality and frequent updates.

"About Clementine . . ." Amber stopped circling her fingernail over her thigh, digging it into the fabric. She was nervous.

"No," I snapped, looking up. She reared her head back like I'd slapped her. "We've discussed it, and my demands were clear. Either you accept them or you zip it."

"Are these my only options?"

"This is your only *ultimatum*." My gaze flicked to the closed door of the bathroom. The stream of water stopped, and the glass door squeaked open. For a reason I didn't care to explore, I didn't want Madison listening to this clusterfuck of a conversation.

"You think I'd lie?" Amber's emerald eyes flared. She had the audacity to put her hand to her neck and fake a dainty gasp.

"I think you'd do anything bar selling Booger Face to the circus to get what you want," I confirmed nonchalantly.

She stood up, fists balled at her sides, no doubt about to spew something out. Another lie, probably. The bathroom door whined. We both glanced at it, Amber's mouth still agape.

"Out," I growled.

"But—"

"Now."

Amber stepped toward me. Her face so close to mine I could catch the individual freckles under her three pounds of foundation. Her tits brushed my chest. They were hard and big, unnaturally enhanced. Nothing like the soft, small ones Mad had.

Don't think about her tits Friday night when you put your sweatshirt over her body.

Oops. Too late for that.

"This isn't over, Chase. It'll never be over."

My father once told me, "If you truly want to know someone, make them mad. The way they react is a telltale sign of who they are." Amber was working extra hard on riling me up. Little did she know, my number of fucks to give was constantly on the decline and reserved for immediate family and true friends only.

"It was over before it started," I hissed into her face, smirking tauntingly. "Before I even laid a finger on you, *Amb*."

She galloped to the bedroom door and slammed it in my face, making a scene. She wanted Madison to know, to ask what had happened, to plant the seed of insecurity in her. My fake fiancée opened the bathroom door a second later in a bathrobe, rubbing a towel into her short locks. Odd timing. I eyed her suspiciously.

"Was that the door?" She tilted her head sideways, letting the towel fall to the floor. She strode to the bed, flicked open her suitcase, and—check this—began to *unpack* everything I'd packed for her as she sifted through her clothes. She lifted one frock at a time, examined it, then threw it over her shoulder, in search of something else to wear.

"What the hell are you doing?" The question came out in wonder more than anger. Her eccentric behavior always took me by surprise.

"Choosing an outfit," she chirped. "What else would I be doing wrapped in a bathrobe, fresh out of the shower?"

Sucking me off.

"So?" she asked again. "Who was it? I heard you talking to someone."

"Amber," I grunted, my eyes tracing the outline of her body under the bathrobe hungrily. I hated that I wanted to pound her like a piece of schnitzel. (Madison, not Amber. I wouldn't touch Amber if it brought world peace.)

"I'm guessing you two are close," she said as she continued to look through her clothes. Her tone was neutral, matter of fact.

"You're guessing wrong," I bit out.

"But you have so much in common."

"We both breathe. That's the only thing we have in common."

"You're both also insufferably bitter."

There was a beat of silence, in which I quickly reminded myself explaining to Madison how *unlike* Amber and I were wouldn't matter.

"You're welcome, by the way," I groaned.

"For having my things sifted through by you without permission?" She turned to look at me, still all sugar and smiles. "That was extremely generous of you."

"You know, I don't remember you being so argumentative when you had a regular supply of vitamin D." I tapered my eyes, hoping my semi wouldn't blossom into a full-blown erection as we butted heads again. That part was true. Madison had done a complete one-eighty on me since I'd landed at her doorstep asking her to accompany me to the Hamptons. This new version of her was also the *real* person she was, and it pissed me off I'd never gotten to truly know her.

It pissed me off that she was actually funny.

And sarcastic.

And a handful, in a bizarrely attractive way.

But most of all, it pissed me off that she'd *lied* to me about who she was.

"I wanted to make an impression on you back then. That ship has sailed."

"More like sank in the middle of the fucking ocean."

"Well." She shrugged, clutching a red-and-purple dress to her chest, choosing her outfit for the day. "You were the one to direct it into a six-ton iceberg in the middle of the ocean. Don't you ever forget that, Chase."

I smiled tightly and went downstairs to break something valuable in the kitchen. Breaking her, I realized, was not on the menu anymore. She was different. Stronger.

A few more hours, and I wouldn't have to see her again.

We were in the foyer, the staff ushering our suitcases to my Tesla, when Julian made his first chess move. I'd been anticipating it all weekend, trying to figure out his game, why he was here. Not that I was complaining: Julian and Amber were train wrecks, but I was always game for spending more time with Booger Face.

I called bullshit about Julian's six remark. Madison was a solid twelve, on her worst days. She wasn't just wholesomely beautiful but also sexy in a way women who weren't worried about being sexy were. What nagged him about her was that she was indifferent to the numbers in his bank account and his Armani suits. She was what he called a postfeminist. A girl with a we-can-do-it mentality who made her own path in the world. He, in contrast, had a let-the-butler-do-it mentality. Of course they were like oil and water. But if he thought I was going to flip my shit when he called her a six, he was in for a surprise. Letting him rattle me was not an option.

When I was a kid and Julian had come back from boarding school or college, we'd always played chess. Neither of us were big fans of the game, but we had this underlying competition between us. We competed over everything. From our sports accomplishments—we were both rowers for our high school and college teams—to who could stuff himself with more turkey at Thanksgiving. Despite that, Julian and I were close. Close enough that we talked on the phone regularly when he was away and hung out more than two brothers with a decade between them should when he was home. We'd play chess in the weirdest way.

We'd leave the board in the drawing room and move our pieces throughout the day. It had the shine of an extra challenge, because we always had to remember what the board had looked like before we'd left it. No king, queen, bishop, or pawn went astray. We both watched our game with hawklike eyes.

It was a lesson in resilience, planning ahead, and patience. To this day, whenever Julian and I were at my parents' house together, we'd play.

Most of the time, I'd win.

Eighty-nine percent, to be exact (and yes, I was counting).

Still, Julian always gave a good fight.

But now we weren't close anymore, and I suspected neither he nor I was going to abide by the unwritten rules of our new game.

"Maddie, Chase, wait." Julian clapped twice behind us like we were his servants. Madison stopped first, and I had to follow through with her foolish decision.

My parents and Katie gathered around us. Dad was holding Clementine. He adored her more than anything else in the world. At nine, Clementine was almost a preteen, and yet he still held her like she was a toddler.

That was the thing about my father, though. He had the eerie capability to be the best dad and grandfather in the world—the best husband, at least from where I was standing—and still be a mean *son of a bitch* when it came down to business. We had weekly hangouts consisting of drinking beer and watching football and talking smack about our competitors. Then he'd take Mom on a date night and read to her when they came back home. He'd take Booger Face to the zoo in the morning and buy-to-destroy a competitor in the evening. He really was the entire package. For a while, I'd thought I'd follow in his footsteps.

Perfect businessman.

Perfect husband.

Perfect everything.

But then something had happened to change everything I'd believed about my family. About women.

I realized I was going to bizarre, unlikely lengths to pacify my father. I wasn't an idiot. People didn't fake engagements outside of Ryan Reynolds's movies. To understand my sacrifice, you had to remember—those dents you saw in families, the wear and tear of being holed up together during summer vacations and Christmas holidays and winter breaks? The tension, the underlying bitterness, the rile-you-up buttons your loved ones pressed when they wanted to make you snap? The Blacks didn't have them. My immediate family, for the most part, remained a shiny, untouchable thing without any real indentations. No nasty arguments. No hostile baggage between siblings. No infidelities, money problems, dark pasts. I'd come to realize that almost every family in the world suffered through a lot of their relatives' unbearable traits. Not so with mine. I didn't tolerate my family. I *worshipped* them.

Well, three out of the four, anyway.

Mad turned around, looking at Julian with a patient, saintly smile. She didn't trust him, but she didn't want to come off as rude either. "Yes, Julian?"

"I was thinking." He stepped toward us, swirling the thick liquid of his whiskey in his tumbler.

"An unpromising start," I deadpanned. People snickered uncomfortably around us. I wasn't joking, but whatever.

"We haven't really had time to get to know you at all. On Friday, you were . . . *indisposed*." He said the word like she had puked buckets on the dinner table, as opposed to tipsily slurring her words when she'd retired to the drawing room with my mother and sister. "And on Saturday, you didn't join us on the hike or wine tasting. You're a difficult woman to pin down, huh?" He smirked.

She opened her mouth to answer, but he soldiered through with his speech, not giving a damn about what she had to say.

"It was impossible to get ahold of you, get to *know* you, and you are going to be a part of the Black clan. You'll practically be my sister-in-law."

"Not practically." I wrapped an arm around Madison. "We're not brothers, a fact you seem to forget only when convenient."

"Chase!" my mother chided at the same time my father frowned, looking between us. Julian took a step back, tutting.

"No need to be scandalized on my behalf, folks. That's just Chase being an unruly baby brother. At any rate, Amber and I would love to invite you guys over—along with Ronan, Lori, and Katie, of course—for a festive engagement meal. Say—Friday? Unless, of course, Maddie is busy again for the next six months."

Motherfucker.

Queen's gambit. He'd begun our mental chess game with the classiest chess opening, by pretending to offer a pawn. In this case, Madison. She'd been disposable to me a second ago, but now, when Julian was trying to prove his point, she became the queen. The most important piece in my game.

I smiled, clapping his shoulder good-naturedly with my free hand. "What a lovely offer. We accept." I felt Mad's shoulders stiffening under my arm. Her eyes darted to my face in surprise. I ignored her, still looking at Julian. "What can we bring?"

"Maddie's banana bread," Katie suggested. My sister hadn't had cake for at least five years straight, so I wasn't sure what business she had choosing dessert. "She told us she makes a mean banana bread yesterday."

"Shocker." Amber rolled her eyes.

Mad's eyes ping-ponged between everyone. She said nothing, probably channeling the majority of her energy to muster the self-control not to maim me.

As soon as we buckled up in my car, she opened her mouth. She looked like a little woodpecker. Prettily annoying and ready to give me a headache. I was certain I liked Real Maddie even less than I liked Girlfriend Maddie, who had continuously tried to please me. Unfortunately, I had to make do with Real Maddie, because my family fawned over her, and because Julian's newest mission in life was to uncover our fake relationship.

"I'm not going."

"Yeah, you are."

I prided myself on being a skillful negotiator. I also knew that, logically, starting the negotiation from an aggressive, dogmatic stance would get me nowhere. However, where Madison Goldbloom was concerned, I simply couldn't help myself. She called to the four-year-old asshole kid in me. And he came running, ready to pick a fight.

She crossed her arms over her chest. "I told you it was a one-off. *No.*"

"I will pay your rent. Twelve months up front." My fingers curled over the steering wheel firmly.

"Are you deaf?"

Are you? *I'm offering you free fucking rent to do something most women would sacrifice a kidney for.*

I had the sense to keep this as a thought and not spit it in her face.

"Do you want a bigger apartment?" I asked, willing to bend over backward to make this happen. It wasn't even about Dad anymore. Not fully, anyway. My father looked sufficiently convinced Madison and I were an item. I'd kill Julian if he uncovered the truth. And I meant that literally. "There's a vacant one in my building. Three bedrooms, two baths, sick view. Doesn't your little friend from Croquis live there? Steve?"

"Sven," she groaned. "And he's my boss."

I knew who Sven was. We did business together. I just wanted to work the "friends" angle and remind her why she wanted to live next to someone she was friendly with.

"You could be neighbors. The place is ready for Daisy to compromise every piece of furniture inside it."

And I, apparently, was ready to never get her deposit back and shell out close to 750K in total for the pleasure of taking her on another date.

"Daisy is content humping dollar store plant pots to satisfy her needs," Madison replied sunnily, opening her little pocket mirror and applying lip gloss. I liked that she didn't paint her face to a point where she looked like someone else. She normally put on lipstick and mascara and called it a day.

"Money? Prestige? Black & Co. shares?"

I was officially the worst negotiator in the history of the concept. If my Yale professors heard me, they would take my degree, roll it into a cone, and smack me in the ass with it. I drove slowly to prolong our negotiation. I was not above kidnapping her if that didn't work.

She shook her head, still staring out the window. She confused and infuriated me. The dazzling simplicity of her—of not doing something just because it didn't feel right—was both refreshing and frustrating. In my experience, everyone had a price, and they were quick to name it. Not this chick, apparently.

"What would it take?" I grumbled, trying another tactic. The ball was in her court. I *hated* her court. I wanted to buy it, pour gasoline on it, and then burn it down. For the first time in my life, someone else had the upper hand. An unlikely someone else. And all because my idiotic brother-cousin (what was he to me, anyway?) had a hard-on for seeing me fail. Everyone else in the family ate up our romance and asked for a second serving. Katie had even prodded me about who was planning Mad's bachelorette party. She wanted to take her future fake sister-in-law to Saint Barts, for fuck's sake.

The worst part was that Julian was barking up the wrong tree. I didn't give a crap about the CEO throne. I mean, I did, but I also knew my place as Dad's successor was secured. For the first time in my life, I'd done something for an entirely unselfish reason. Whoever said giving was better than receiving was high, because I was definitely not having a merry time doing the charity work.

Still, if Dad found out I'd lied about Madison, he'd be heartbroken, and that was a chance I wasn't taking.

"Anything?" Madison tapped her lips thoughtfully. "You'd do *anything*?"

Well, lookee here. I'd finally found something she enjoyed other than getting eaten while sprawled on my granite kitchen island—busting my balls.

I offered her a curt nod.

"And remember, whatever it is you give me, I will only go to *one* dinner with you," she warned.

"Crushed," I drawled sarcastically—again, zero self-control. "Get on with it, Mad."

She bit her lower lip in concentration, giving it some genuine thought. I imagined she was going to try to inflict as much damage as possible. This was a person who preferred a heating pad to a Tiffany & Co. pair of earrings. A highly unpredictable specimen of a woman. She'd castrate me if she could.

Finally, Madison snapped her fingers in the air. "I know! I've been wanting to sleep in for a while now. But ever since you gifted me Daisy—bless her heart—I need to walk her at six in the morning. Any later than that, and she starts scratching the door, crying, and pissing in my shoes. If I go to that dinner thing, you have to walk her every morning for a week. Weekend included."

"I live on Park Avenue. You live in Greenwich," I retorted, twisting my head in her direction so she could appreciate how aghast I felt toward her idea.

"And?" She snapped her pocket mirror shut and shoved it back into her purse. We held each other's gaze on a red light for a moment. I felt my jaw tightening so hard my teeth ground one another into dust. A honking sound from behind us snapped me out of our stare-off.

"And nothing," I muttered, willing the throbbing vein in my forehead not to pop all over the leather seats. "It's a deal."

She laughed with delight, her throaty, sexy voice filling my car and giving me an uncomfortable semi. "Jesus, I can't believe I dated you."

I can't believe you chose this bullshit over a brand-new Park Avenue apartment.

"I don't know what we were thinking," I agreed solemnly.

We weren't dating. You were dating me without my knowledge. If I hadn't woken up in time, we'd probably be married and pregnant by now.

Now I was thinking about pregnant sex with Madison, and the semi became a full hard-on.

"It was just the sex, wasn't it? And movies. And eating. No real talking was involved," she murmured, resting her head back against her seat, her hazel eyes dim.

That sounded about right. We'd talked very little in the months we'd seen each other. Madison had seemed intimidated by me, something I hadn't bothered rectifying, as it had made our eating-fucking-sleeping arrangement supremely comfortable for me.

"If it makes you feel any better, my no-mingling policy extends to all humans, not just girlfriends," I offered.

"That does not make me feel any better. I walked around thinking you thought I was stupid," she accused.

"Not stupid." I shook my head. "Not overtly brilliant, either, but definitely competent."

Didn't they say the truth would set you free? Why did I feel so fucking chained into this uncomfortable moment, then?

"Wow. You are like Mr. Darcy's evil twin, but sans the charm."

"So basically an asshole?" I groaned.

"Pretty much."

I double-parked in front of her entrance. Pediatric Guy was slumped on the stairway. His kneecaps, ears, and Adam's apple looked like they should be attached to a person at least twice his size. He was lanky in a half-formed-teenager way, his chest caving inward. He had glasses and an intelligent nose I highly suspected women like Madison found attractive. His cheek was propped against his knuckles as he read a wrinkled paperback like some kind of Neanderthal. An actual book with pages and everything. I bet he physically went to the supermarket for his shopping and got his own takeout instead of ordering Uber Eats. This was the kind of heathen she was associating herself with these days.

I bet he wrote her love letters and didn't even mention her rack or ass. *Prick.*

She glanced at him, then at me, then at him again. What was his name? I remembered it was as generic as the rest of him. Brian? Justin? He looked like a Conrad. Something that was synonymous with *douchebag.*

"Ethan's here," she announced.

Ethan. I'd been close.

"I need to tell him about that stupid dinner. You still have my email, right? Send me the details." She hopped outside without sparing me a look. I unloaded her suitcases like I was a goddamn bellboy. To save the remainder of my pride, I dumped them by her building without even glancing at her or her dudebro, not offering to help her take them upstairs. Let Dr. Douche do it himself.

I rounded my car and got back inside, watching her ass in that ridiculous A-line dress as she approached Ethan, flung her arms over his shoulders, and kissed his cheek. *Cheek.* Something not terrible happened in my chest when I realized that probably meant they hadn't slept together. *Yet.*

I breathed through my nose, sending a little prayer to the universe that Ethan wouldn't fuck my fake fiancée tonight, and looked down to retrieve my phone from my pocket.

There was a note stuck to the passenger seat. The same sticky white one with my family name engraved at the top from the Hamptons. She'd put it there when I wasn't looking. Sneaky.

C,

You saved those jasmines because they are living things, not because I asked you to.

Also: We broke up because you're a cheating cheater who cheats.

Also 2: What's up with Julian?

PS:

Re: you smelling something unfamiliar. It might be a good time for your bimonthly STD check.

—M

CHAPTER SEVEN

MADDIE

June 3, 1999

Dear Maddie,

Fun fact of the day: The poppy has astonishingly flourished on battlefields, smashed by boots, tanks, and the first industrial war the world had ever seen. It is a token of remembrance in Britain.

Poppies are strong, stubborn, and impossible to break. Be a poppy. Always.

Love,

Mom. x

◆ ◆ ◆

Objectively speaking, as far as mornings went, today's was a particularly glorious one. The type Cat Stevens wrote songs about. I woke up at eight thirty without the help of my alarm. Layla had let Chase in at dawn, while I'd been fast asleep and she'd been bidding one of her many flings goodbye. I managed to bring my best friend up to speed about my little arrangement with Chase via text messages. Chase took Daisy on a lengthy walk. I was still dead to the world when he brought her back. I woke to him pushing the door open, cursing under his breath, complaining about Daisy not wining and dining his leg before humping it, pouring food into her dish, and scolding her for drinking vigorously from the toilet bowl. ("You're really not winning any seduction points right now, Daze.") I smiled as I stretched lazily in my bed, thinking about the inconvenience the journey to my neighborhood had caused him. When I opened my fridge to take some orange juice out, I found a note plastered to the door.

M,

Not everything alive is worth saving. My cousin-brother, Julian, is a prime example of that (don't ask me what he is to me, it changes from day to day).

Also: Let's pretend I cheated. You weren't exactly honest either. You gave me a watered-down personality, leading me to believe you were sane. WHICH YOU ARE NOT.

Also 2: Yes, the capitals were necessary.

Also 3: Addressed the Julian issue above.

PS (technically Also 4—too much counting for you?): attached is a picture of me on a horse, age six, adorable as all fuck.

PPS:

Noticed Nathan didn't sleep at your place. I take it he's still a virgin? ☹

—C

Something fell from the sticky note. A picture. I picked it up and flipped it over. It was the kid version of Chase smiling to the camera—two front teeth nowhere to be found—sitting on a pony. He had carefully trimmed tar-black bangs and a smile so jarring that the vividness of it jumped out of the picture. Begrudgingly, and only to myself, I could admit that he was right. He did look good on a horse. Not like the Old Spice dude but sufficiently adorable.

And what did he mean—*Let's pretend I cheated*? He *had* cheated. I'd seen him with my own eyes. Kind of. Well, there was little room for interpretation. Anyway, I wasn't opening that can of worms. I was with Ethan now. Sweet, wonderful, reliable Ethan.

The sensation of something cold and liquid on my toes broke me out of my musing, and I looked down to realize I'd been pouring orange juice into an overflowing glass for a full minute. I jumped back. Recovering, I dabbed at the pulpy stain at my feet with one hand as the other reached to write Chase a note back.

C,

Flowers symbolize life. I would never trust someone who doesn't take care of their flowers.

Also, I will allow the statement that you were cute on a horse. Once upon a (very long) time.

PS:

Please do not touch my things again (pens, sticky notes, SUITCASE, etc.).

PPS:

It's Ethan, not Nathan. And actually, we had wild sex all night. He had to leave for an emergency.

—M

So I lied. It wasn't that much of a big deal. Only in Manhattan was it expected that anyone twenty-two and above should have sex after three dates. In that sense, I missed Pennsylvania.

I was going to do Chase this solid, give him his ring back, and say goodbye.

This time for good.

No more negotiations.

No more bargains.

No more heartache.

I met Ethan at a new Italian restaurant the same evening. He was twenty minutes late. For all Chase's faults (and there were many; I could write a *War and Peace*–length book about all of them), he valued people's time and never left me hanging. He wasn't late, and on the rare times he was, he always texted with a reasonable explanation.

Chase also isn't saving children for a living, I scolded myself inwardly. *Cut a guy some slack.*

I spent the time waiting reading an article about a woman who had made a dress for her upcoming wedding out of toilet paper and recycled material because she didn't have the money to buy or rent anything fancy. I found her Facebook page, wrote her a message, and asked her for her address and dress size. I had a few dresses lying around my apartment from when I'd been a design student I could get rid of, and my Martyr Maddie instincts kicked in. I also shot Layla a quick message thanking her for letting Chase in this morning and forwarded her a picture of the Italian restaurant I was in, with the caption *Maybe the perfect moment will be tonight?* along with a winking emoji. It wasn't necessarily a possibility I was excited about, but I tried to hype myself up for it. Layla's response came after seconds.

Layla: Nothing more romantic than garlic bread and a man who is twenty minutes late.

Maddie: Be happy for me.

Layla: I'm being honest with you. That's so much more important in a good friend.

Maddie: He could be the one.

Layla: Keeping my fingers crossed for you. But honey, don't date him just because you're afraid of the Chases of the world.

It bothered me that Chase and Layla were singing the same tune, but I shoved this worry to the bottom drawer of my brain.

Ethan arrived disheveled and a little sweaty, his hair sticking up everywhere. He wore casual clothes—a pair of jeans and a faded tee—not his usual doctor clothes. He kissed me on the cheek, his breath smelling uncharacteristically sweet, and took a seat in front of me, patting himself like he'd forgotten something.

"Well? How was it?" He cut straight to the Chase. *Literally.* He'd come to say hi to me the previous night, but that was just to lend me a book I'd pretended I wanted to read about managing infectious diseases in preschools. It occurred to me that I was making the same mistake I had with Chase back when we were dating. I was pretending to be someone who wasn't completely me to try to appear more appealing to the person I was dating. It wasn't so much that I was a completely different person, but I rounded the edges a little.

What Chase had told me after we'd gotten back from the Hamptons had struck a chord with me this morning, when I'd realized I had no intention or will to read a medical book just to make Ethan happy. Chase felt fooled, and as much as I wasn't #TeamChase, I could still see where he was coming from. I decided to be completely honest with Ethan to avoid that. To show my absolute true self.

"What, the Hamptons?" I picked up my water and chugged it down to buy time. "It was understandably weird. I got trashed at the family dinner. Chase slept on the floor. We fought every waking moment his family wasn't watching. Overall, we looked more on the brink of a bitter divorce than a blissful engagement."

Ethan grabbed a breadstick from a basket and nibbled at it as he cooed, "Poor baby."

"And then his cousin-brother—I'm not sure what they are to each other; biologically they are cousins, but they were raised as brothers—invited us . . . no, more like *challenged* us to go to dinner at his place to celebrate our engagement. He and Chase have this weird rivalry going on. So I kind of had to agree to that."

I blinked at Ethan from across the table, eagerly awaiting his reaction. He put his breadstick down, frowned, and then looked back at me with his good-natured smile intact.

"Sure. I mean, we're still casual, right?"

"Right." I nodded. "Of course. Casual. Is that what you see us as?"

"For now. Yeah."

I was beginning to hate the word with a passion. Then something occurred to me.

"You didn't come from work, did you?"

Ethan shook his head, helping himself to another breadstick. Now it was his turn to stall. My eyes didn't waver from his face until he was forced to add words to his lackluster explanation. "Nope. I was at a . . . friend's house." He looked uncertain, rubbing the back of his neck.

"You take showers at your friends'?" I raised an eyebrow.

"A special friend?" he offered, tucking his chin down and blushing.

My brain short-circuited for a second. He was sleeping with someone else?

"I see." Frankly, I didn't see anything. I was blindsided and annoyed but surprisingly unemotional about the discovery.

"It's nothing serious. I just want to be up front and honest with you since your last boyfriend wasn't. This thing with Natalie stops as soon as you and I are more established. But I figured since we're not intimate yet, and you are doing this fake-engagement thing . . ." Ethan trailed off, the tips of his ears so red they practically glowed.

I decided to take it in stride. Ethan wasn't Chase. He'd never let me think we were exclusive, then gone and slept with someone else. He hadn't given me a key to his apartment or invited me to parties or gifted me a living thing. It was still early days. We'd only kissed a couple of times. Anyway, what business did I have getting riled up about it? I'd spent the weekend wearing my ex-boyfriend's engagement ring and Yale sweatshirt. True, we hadn't done anything together, but it was hardly behavior worthy of a girlfriend-of-the-year award.

Also, again: the fact Ethan had slept with someone else this evening simply didn't bother me enough to give him grief about it, no matter how much I felt like I should.

A waitress came to take our order. Once she disappeared, I sat back, watching him with a weird mixture of awe and confusion.

"Where do you want to live when you grow up?" I blurted out. It was such a weird thing to ask, three weeks into seeing a guy. But I worried Chase might have been right about Ethan being everything I thought I wanted but not what I actually *did* want. I didn't want to hurt Ethan's feelings or drag both of us into something that was doomed from the beginning.

"I *am* grown up." Ethan looked perplexed, helping himself to some more breadsticks.

"You know what I mean. When you have a family."

"Oh," he said, looking around us distractedly like I'd just asked him if he was willing to change my adult diaper.

Say Brooklyn. Say Hempstead. Hell, say Long Island for all I care.

"Westchester, I suppose. Great school districts, clean, safe . . ."

Boring. Then again, so what? Lots of young professionals who lived in New York ended up in Westchester once they started reproducing. Monica and Chandler from *Friends* had.

Yes, but you're a Rachel, not a Monica, I heard Layla saying in my head.

And it's also a sitcom, not real life. Now it was Chase's voice that teased me.

"Can I ask you another question?" I peeled off the sticker holding the napkin together. Ethan took a sip of his wine, nodding. He didn't understand this game much. Neither did I. I was just trying to figure out whether Chase had really read Ethan so well or not.

"Anything, milady."

"What did you have for breakfast?"

"Eggs on toast," he said without missing a beat. I sighed in relief, as if this were all the evidence I needed that Chase had it wrong. It wasn't oats. Ethan probably hated oats.

"My turn," Ethan said. "Best way to start the day?"

Coffee, doughnuts, and talking to Dad on the phone. Mostly listening to the small-town gossip he had to offer. I was about to answer, *Jogging, a granola bar, and listening to podcasts about climate change,* before remembering I'd promised myself to be honest this time. So I gave him my real answer. Ethan scrunched his nose.

"What?" I winced, bracing myself for his disappointment.

"Nothing. Just . . . I don't do gossip. I also don't drink caffeine. It gives me terrible tremors."

"Right," I said. At this point, between Diet Coke, coffee, and energy drinks, caffeine had surely embedded itself into my blood type. Not that it mattered. Ethan and I didn't have to be compatible in *every* single way.

"Favorite TV channel?" I smiled sunnily. "On a count of three."

"Three . . ."

"Two . . ."

"One . . ."

"HBO," I piped up at the same time he said, "National Geographic." We laughed, shaking our heads.

"Favorite smell?"

His eyes lit up, just when his pasta and my pizza arrived. His was loaded with vegetables, seafood, and exotic mushrooms. Mine consisted of pepperoni, bacon, and extra cheese. We counted to three again. I said puppies. He said vanilla.

I repeat—*vanilla*. Just like the sex Chase had promised we'd have.

Ethan and I continued this tango for the rest of the evening, amused by how morbidly different we were. It was actually a kick-ass icebreaker. If it weren't for the fact I knew he'd slept with someone else mere hours ago, not to mention that I was going on a second date with my ex-boyfriend come Friday, I'd actually say the evening brought us closer.

Ethan walked me back home and had the good sense not to kiss me on the mouth when we parted ways. He kissed my cheek again, smiling shyly as he cast his gaze downward.

"I'd invite you to come up, but—" I started at the same time he opened his mouth.

"That thing with Natalie—"

We both stopped.

"You go." I felt my cheeks heating.

"She just broke up with someone, it was long term, and she and I have this thing when we're both single. I'm really interested in you. I'm not the sleeping-around type of guy. Honestly, I wanted to show myself that I was okay with you going out with your ex." He rubbed at his temple. "And for the most part, I am."

"I understand," I said quietly. Although a part of me didn't. I wished Ethan would have just told me the truth before we'd both compromised the beginning of our relationship. But there was no going back from what it was right now. A messy shot in the dark made by a blind, intoxicated cupid.

"Maybe it's best if we don't have sex until everything with Chase is over. It obviously makes you feel weird. Like I'm not fully committed to this," I suggested.

Ethan nodded. "That's fair. And I promise to end things with Natalie after your last date with him. You're seeing him Friday, right?"

"For the second and last time," I confirmed.

I pushed the door open to my building and closed it, plastering my back against it with a heavy sigh. My phone pinged in my purse. I plucked it out, thinking it might be Ethan, wanting to soften the blow of our goodbye by saying something sweet or playful.

Unknown: Don't forget the banana bread on Friday. It's Chase, btw.

Maddie: How do you know I deleted your number?

Unknown: When the nights get cold, the memory of your ex burns hotter. You seem like the type to self-preserve.

Maddie: You seem like a conceited idiot.

Unknown: That may be true, but you just admitted to deleting my number.

Maddie: Can I ask you something?

Unknown: Seven inches.

Maddie: Har. Har.

Maddie: Where do you want to live when you're "settled down"?

Unknown: I will never "settle down."

Maddie: Humor me, jerk.

Unknown: Fine. I'll stay in Manhattan. You?

I pushed the door to my apartment open. Daisy jumped on my legs excitedly, nuzzling her wet tennis ball into my hand. I glanced at the overhead clock above my fridge. Almost eleven. Chase was going to be here to take her out in seven hours. The thought of him in my apartment made my head swim. I added him to my contacts, purely for logistical purposes. I'd delete him again on Saturday morning, post our fake-engagement dinner.

Maddie: I don't know. Maybe Brooklyn. What did you have for breakfast?

Chase: I think her name was Tiffany.

Maddie: Dear God, you're stabbable to a fault.

Chase: Relax. A protein pack.

Chase: Do NOT make a jizz joke.

Maddie: Favorite channel?

Chase: Is that a real question? Is there a right answer other than HBO?

Maddie: Best way to start the day?

Chase: You sitting on my face.

Maddie: Thank you.

Chase: For the riveting visual?

Maddie: For reminding me why we broke up.

Chase: Any-fucking-time.

Maddie: 🖕

I shouldn't have gone to bed with a smile on my face, yet I did.

Chase Black was the devil. A sinister, cold creature that somehow managed to scorch his way into my veins. But whatever he was . . . being next to him made me feel alive.

◆ ◆ ◆

On Tuesday, I woke up to zero sticky notes from Chase. Considering I'd specifically asked him not to touch my things, I should have felt a lot more cheerful than I did when I glanced at the shelf of my fridge, offended by its stark emptiness.

Not that it mattered. No Post-it Notes from Chase meant I didn't have to clean up all his mess when I got back to my apartment. It gave me a good chance to bake something and bring it to Ethan's office. (This was not retaliation against Chase for not leaving me any notes. No sirree. Just me trying to be nice to Ethan.)

Wednesday, however, was a game changer. Two days away from the festive engagement dinner, I found a slew of black sticky notes stuck to my fridge. Not the same color as my turquoise ones with the leopard print that I kept on my counter to make supermarket lists. Bastard had brought his own notes. That was why he hadn't written anything on Tuesday. He'd probably asked his assistant to provide him with the stationery he required to continue our written beef. There was no way his Royal Highness had descended down from Olympus himself and visited Office Depot. The pen he'd used was gold. He had a lot to say, so he'd spread it over a few notes, sticking them one below the other in succession.

M,

What are you wearing Friday night? We need to coordinate, although I doubt I own anything purple and green with patterned smiling pigs. Or sequined, feathery hats with pom-poms and bow ties.

Or anything else completely grotesque, for that matter.

PS:

Daisy seems to be obsessed with the same squirrel. I am afraid they will create a subspecies. Squog. Squirrel dogs.

PPS:

Bull. Shit. What was Pediatric Boy's emergency? Testosterone transplant?

—C

Frantic, I scrambled to the trash can to retrieve the last notes we'd written to each other to see what he was referring to in the second PS. The trash can was full to the brim. I looked down at it, aghast, before flipping it over, squeezing my eyes shut while breathing through my mouth.

Garbage rained down on the floor. I sifted through it as Daisy sniffed around banana peels and string cheese wrappers, tail wagging, until I found our last notes. I smoothed them on the floor, reading them over. Chase had taunted me that Ethan was still a virgin. I'd told him we'd had crazy sex the night he'd dropped me off from the Hamptons. Obviously, he wasn't buying it.

I scowled at Daisy, who was licking the inside of a chicken-salad can, making slurping sounds.

"No one can know about this, Daisy. No one."

She replied with half a bark. I picked up my pen and wrote, pressing it against the paper so hard the words dented the rest of the pages.

C,

Haven't thought about my attire for the evening. But now that you're asking, why, yes, I will go for the sequined purple dress with the green jacket (velvet) paired with brown heels. No smiling pigs, but I think I have something with Michael Scott on it.

PS:

Ethan is more of a man than you'd never be. He is honest and loyal and NICE.

PPS:

Yes, the squirrel's name is Frank. Let them be. They're dysfunctional but good together.

PPPS:

I'm suspiciously low on orange juice. Please do not help yourself to anything while fulfilling your side of the Daisy bargain.

—M

On Thursday, there was radio silence. I did *not* analyze the lack of notes while riding the train on my way to work. I didn't care. Truly, I didn't. But if I *had* given it some thought (which, again, I hadn't), the natural assumption would be that Chase had forgotten to bring his black notes or golden pen or both.

Which meant that continuing this conversation wasn't something he thought about regularly.

Which, again, was completely okay with me.

The day slogged by painfully slowly. I texted with Ethan back and forth. We weren't able to see each other for the rest of the week because he was training for a half marathon—the same charity marathon Katie had told me in the Hamptons she was going to do—and had to wake up super early. Sven said I was surprisingly useless that day. I wanted to believe it was because I wasn't going to be seeing Ethan, but realistically speaking, it was Chase that made my mind drift away from work. When Sven was out of sight, Nina helpfully added I was turning into one of my plants. "A burst of color and inefficiency." She click-click-clicked her mouth, her eyes glued to her Apple monitor. I had to take the sketch I was currently working on home to finish since it was due the next day.

Then, on Friday, another note waited for me on the fridge:

M,

Daisy doesn't like her food. I brought her something new. The guy at the store said it's the dog equivalent of caviar. Left it on the counter.

She also tried to hump Frank this morning. Are you projecting on the poor dog?

PS:

I cannot believe we pay you to design clothes. You do know not every fashion statement needs to be screamed?

PPS:

Re: orange juice. I admit I did help myself to some, but only because I was thirsty and you only drink tap around here. Very poor hospitality to point it out. How unbecoming for a southern girl.

I picked up my phone and texted him a response. Normally, I was firmly against any communication with him, but my body was simmering with unrestrained rage. How dare he?

Maddie: I'm from Pennsylvania, NOT the South, Satan McDevil.

Chase: Pennsylvania = South. South of New York. Know your geography, Goldbloom. Knowledge is power.

Maddie: WHY ARE YOU SO INFURIATING???

Chase: All caps. This pent-up sexual frustration is going to kill you one day.

Maddie: Good! Being dead would beat spending time with you today.

Chase: If you're trying to get my feelings hurt, it's working.

Maddie: Really?

Chase: No.

Maddie: You know, when I saw you on my stairway, I thought you were going to apologize as a part of your postrecovery steps for your sex addiction treatment.

Chase: If I were a sex addict, I'd hardly treat it.

Maddie: Remind me why I'm helping you again?

Chase: Because you are a good person.

Maddie: And why are you accepting?

Chase: Because I'm not.

Chase: Don't forget the banana bread.

Chase: Have you slept with him yet?

Chase: That's a no. Thought so. See you in the evening.

I resisted the urge to hurl my phone against the wall. I had a feeling if I adopted the habit of smashing things every time Chase pissed me off, nothing in my apartment would stay intact, walls included. Instead, I stomped to the counter, grabbed Daisy's new bag of food, and poured a cup into her bowl. She wolfed it down so fast she nearly took my hand in the process.

I told myself it'd all be over in less than twenty-four hours.

I told myself I didn't care.

Most of all, I thought Chase might be a little right. Maybe I did need sex to calm me down. It *had* been six months, after all. I texted Ethan.

Maddie: Let's meet at my place on Saturday after your marathon. Unless you think you'll be too exhausted?

Ethan: *half marathon.

Seriously? That was what he took from my message? My phone glowed to life with a second message a few seconds later.

Ethan: And I will adequately perform, even post–half marathon. It's a date. x

CHAPTER EIGHT

CHASE

"So lay it on me. How's my old man doing?" I sidestepped a kid on a scooter as I walked with Grant to Madison's apartment. Grant Gerwig had been my best friend ever since I was four. Currently, he was a Colin Firth–looking, prestigious oncologist with a private clinic in the Upper East Side. He was one of those assholes you read about who accidentally found the cure to an incurable disease at a bar eating stale peanuts while waiting for their Tinder date. The kind of smart that made you wonder if there was a secret meaning to life that he wasn't telling you about. We jogged every morning together and made it a point to have a weekend drink, no matter our schedules, if we were both in town. When we'd found out about Dad, I'd physically dragged Ronan Black to Grant's clinic for a second opinion, despite him muttering that he clearly remembered having to help Grant "take care of business" when my best friend had had an accident while watching a horror flick with me when we were five. "I just don't like the idea of getting my medical verdicts from people I knew before they were fully potty trained."

Anyway, both young Grant and the old doctor Dad had gone to initially were on the same page. The cancer was too advanced, too incurable. Still, I felt slightly less helpless having Dad treated by my best friend.

"You know I'm not at liberty to discuss it." Grant stuffed a fist into his khaki pants, using his free hand to redirect a kid on a scooter so he didn't collide with a tree. The kid's mother thanked him as she raced down the street after her son.

Mad's bohemian, colorful street suffered from the greatest problem of our nation, New York's number one enemy: the stop-and-take-a-picture-in-the-middle-of-the-fucking-road tourist. There were people everywhere. Taking selfies with a vintage candy shop in the background, waiting in line to a gay bar, browsing secondhand books on stands outside an independent bookshop. The slimness of life didn't touch this street. It was vivid and alive and bursting with color.

It made me resentful that the sunken-cheeked kid with the nylon backpack and the **Anti Social Social Club** hoodie, the middle-aged dog walker with the sundress, and even the goddamn four dogs she was trying to shepherd were going to outlive my father. The man who'd created Black & Co. Who provided thousands of jobs and was responsible for a third of the textile business in New York. Who'd contributed to the US economy and attended my rowing tournaments religiously and helped Jul turn his summer town house in Nantucket into an eco-friendly monster that basically lived off the grid with his bare hands and sat through Katie's high school theater shows and *God fucking dammit,* life was unfair.

"Chase?" Grant peered into my eyes. He was heading for a date. We'd figured we'd grab a quick beer beforehand. "Did you listen to what I said? Patient-doctor confidentiality and so forth."

I grunted, kicking a soggy garbage bag sitting at the curb. I was already annoyed with the prospect of sharing Dad with Julian, Amber, and Madison tonight. I'd visited him every day for the past week, even though we worked together in the same office. He seemed to be getting progressively worse, and some of the other employees were starting to talk.

"He's in a lot of pain." The words came out like *I* was in a lot of pain too.

"Tell him to give me a call. There's a lot we can do about it."

"He's a stubborn bastard," I countered.

"Doesn't run in the family, obviously." Grant smiled wryly.

We both stopped in front of the same brownstone. He raised an eyebrow. So did I.

"Well, I guess I will see you tomorrow for golf?" he asked.

"That's the plan." I took the steps up. So did Grant. We stopped again. Stared at each other.

"Yes?" I asked impatiently. "Is there anything you want to tell me?"

Had Madison decided to date every doctor in New York?

The entrance door swung open, and Layla, Madison's even-crazier friend with the funky green hair, burst out like a stripper from a cake.

"Grant! You're here!" She flung her arms over his neck. It was a highly unorthodox way to greet a man you weren't planning to get into bed with in the next few hours, unless . . .

Unless he started dating her weeks ago and didn't want to tell me because I was being a miserable piece of shit trying to come to terms with Dad's situation.

"Layla," I said curtly.

"Prince of Darkness," she answered in the exact same manner. "I'm praying for my best friend's sake that you'll be nice this evening."

"Even God can't interfere with my nefarious behavior, but thanks for the royal title. I see you're dating *my* best friend," I drawled.

"Sleeping with him," she amended. "Yes."

Grant flashed me an apologetic smile. "You weren't exactly in the right headspace to talk about this, and as Layla said, she laid down the rules pretty strictly. This is casual and should not affect your or Maddie's lives."

Not in the mood to touch this BS with a ten-foot pole, I rolled my eyes, ambling through the door. When Madison and I had broken up,

Grant was another person who'd pinned the downfall on me. While I'd forbidden him to keep in touch with her, I didn't put it past Madison to have played matchmaker to him and Layla. Another trait I absolutely *despised* about Martyr Maddie—she was always in everyone's business and forever tried to hook people up with dates, furniture they needed, and social activities.

I especially hated that she'd paired these two together, because Grant actually wanted the whole white-picket-fence-and-sane-wife dream, and the first time I'd met Layla, she'd launched into a forty-minute speech about why monogamy was unnatural. Daisy and Frank would make a more sensible pairing than those two.

I knocked on Madison's door, hearing Daisy barking excitedly. Mad opened, and I became weak in the knees and hard everywhere else, because *what the fuck?*

Madison wore a little black dress, snug in all the right places—completely pattern-free—paired with black velvet heels and a turquoise neckpiece. Something between a necklace and a studded collar. Her short brown hair was extra messy in a just-got-fucked purposeful way, her lips were scarlet, and her olive eyes were winged with a dramatic black femme fatale liner. My cock stood for a round of applause, throwing imaginary roses at her feet. The rest of me wondered what had inspired me to do anything else with her back when we were dating other than sleep with her until there was nothing left *of* her.

"You look great." I narrowed my eyes into slits, the compliment coming out as an accusation.

She grabbed her purse and keys, frowning at me. "Didn't you say you wanted to coordinate clothes? I remembered you are very fond of black. Black glossy door, black furniture, black satin sheets . . ." She began to count all the black things in my apartment.

"You forgot the black blinders. Would you like to pay my bedroom another visit?" I offered her a wolfish smirk.

"Hard pass."

That's not the only thing that's hard right now, sweetheart.

I had a violent urge to touch her. Push a stray lock of her hair behind her ear, kiss her cheek in greeting, or perch her on my lap, spread her ass cheeks, and eat her from behind. Before I had the chance to do that (I was going for brushing lint off her sleeve, although orally devouring her was my personal preference), someone tapped me on the shoulder from behind.

The day had been entirely full of unpleasant surprises, but Pediatric Dudebro in his dress shirt, stupid tie, and running *tights* was the cherry on the shit cake. He grinned at Madison, giving her two thumbs up for the outfit.

"Maddie! I came to get a good-luck kiss before the half marathon." He was running in place on her threshold beside me, both of us outside her door. I didn't care how nice this man was. He was oozing douchebagness in radioactive quantities.

"Hi." He turned to beam at me, offering me his hand. I shook it, making sure I pressed hard enough to almost crush his bones. The only reason I didn't go for full destruction was because his patients were minors and I had enough reasons to suspect I was the first name on karma's shit list. If he were a plastic surgeon, catering to bored housewives and vain men, his hand would be marshmallow right about now.

"Chase Black."

"Ethan Goodman."

"Ethan is . . ." Mad trailed off, allowing herself a moment to think about what he was to her. We both looked at her expectantly. A slow smile spread across my face. They hadn't had *that* conversation yet. They weren't anywhere near as serious as she wanted me to think they were. Mad cleared her throat. "We're seeing each other."

Ethan nodded in confirmation, pleased with her bullshit explanation. If I were introduced as anything other than boyfri . . .

Finish that thought, idiot. My brain pointed a gun at my temple from the inside. *I fucking dare you.*

"Nice tie. Is that from Brioni's newest collection?" I jutted my chin in its direction, dead-ass serious. He wore a *PAW Patrol* tie. Specifically, with Chase on it, wearing his firefighter helmet. I only knew the dog's name because Booger Face used to call me Doggy Chase for a while, and I'd been worried and disturbed about her knowing my favorite sexual position.

Also, why weren't we talking about the fact he wore tights?

"Brioni?" he echoed, still running in place. "Is that a designer brand?"

"Close. An Italian dish," I deadpanned.

I felt like an asshole. No doubt I looked like one too. And for the first time in a *very* long time, it felt like crossing an invisible line. I'd always been sarcastic and brash, but never completely off-the-rails rude. In Ethan's case, I couldn't stop myself. I imagined him pressing his tights-clad crotch (seriously, were we just going to ignore the tights?) against Madison's soft curves and kissing her, and frankly, that made me want to drink myself to death, smash the bottle of whiskey on a brick, and stab him with it.

"Chase!" Madison stomped her high heel, which, for the record, I wasn't opposed to removing with my teeth later tonight. My cock was stirring uncomfortably in my briefs every time I caught a waft of her perfume. Pumpkin pie, coconut, and Daisy's smell. She smelled like home. A home I categorically wasn't invited to, but a home nonetheless. Ethan jutted his chin out at me, a glint of wildness in his eyes. It was a carnal spark that told me he knew Madison was a catch, and he wasn't backing down.

All yours, Pedi Boy.

"I admit I'm not very knowledgeable when it comes to clothing. I'm hoping Maddie here helps me out." He flashed her a smile and a wink. I ran my eyes along his body, assessing him.

"Sucks for you. The pot and the kettle going shopping. No retinas will be safe."

I was now insulting both of them. Very bad form, considering she was about to help me. But they seemed wrong together, and she was so oblivious to it I couldn't stop myself.

Mad rolled her eyes. "See what I mean about you not ever having to worry about him? He's insufferable. I'll see you tomorrow, Ethan." She leaned forward, touching his chest as she kissed his cheek. Her lips lingered on his skin a moment too long, and my hands curled into fists, itching to grab her waist and physically remove her from him. "Good luck with the marathon."

"Half marathon," he corrected, hugging her tight.

Don't look at his tights. If he has an erection, you might have to kill him, and your lawyer is in the Maldives on vacation.

When Mad and I stepped out of her building, my pulse returned to its regular rhythm.

"Do you smell that?" She sniffed the air theatrically.

"Smell what?"

"The urine from the pissing contest you just launched at my doorstep."

I laughed. The 2.0 version of her was considerably more fun to hang out with, despite the constant headache she gave me. I said the thing I thought would rile her up the most, because seeing her cheeks turn pink was one of my favorite pastimes.

"I didn't know golden showers are your jam. I am happy to accommodate this."

"Chase!" she shrieked.

"What? It'd save water. I'm just being an environmentalist." Somehow I thought Greta Thunberg still wouldn't approve.

"That's it—now I know it. The devil wears Black."

She meant both my favorite color and my last name.

"Better the devil you know than the angel you don't."

"I can't *wait* to get to know the angel better," she retorted.

"I bet the angel doesn't know how to do that thing with his tongue you like so much."

"The angel makes me happy," she snapped, reddening under her understated makeup. Mad was always good at that. Looking put together without resembling a Kiss band member.

"Bull. Fucking. Shit. He makes you comfortable."

"What's wrong with comfortable?"

"Comfortable would never set you on fire."

"Maybe I don't want to burn."

"We all want to burn, Mad. It is dangerous, ergo, we want it."

We proceeded to the subway. I decided grilling her about Grant and Layla would garner more hostility. As it was, if hate translated into electricity, Madison would detonate my ass. We took the train to the Upper West Side. Driving in Manhattan on Friday night was the equivalent of rubbing your dick across a grater: Technically possible, but why would you want to try?

When we exited the train, Mad stopped dead in her tracks, a look of horror marring her face. I turned back to her. "What is it now?"

"I forgot the banana bread." She slapped a hand over her mouth. "Oh shoot. How did you not remind me? I was so flustered when you and Ethan were doing a dance-off on my threshold I totally forgot to bring it."

Like anyone gave a shit. Katie and Mom just wanted her to feel like they were looking forward to something other than her royal presence. Her ability to tolerate me mystified them. They weren't *actually* looking forward to the banana bread. In fact, they weren't looking forward to consuming anything that wasn't wine or bad reality TV shows.

"It wasn't a dance-off," I pointed out.

"It was," she insisted. "And you lost. Metaphorically speaking, you dance like everyone's drunk uncle."

"I do not dance like ev—" I closed my eyes, massaging my temples. I was not going to reduce myself to the intellect of a woman who could distinguish everyone in the Kardashian clan by name. *Willingly.* "They'll manage without the banana bread."

"But it's *dessert.*"

"Hate to break it to you, but no one was counting on your banana bread. Julian and Amber probably had three catering companies and Gordon Ramsay himself working the kitchen since last night."

"Well, I promised!"

Is it even legal to fantasize about doing things to her? I pondered at this point. *She is mentally fifteen.*

"They probably forgot."

"I texted with Katie and Lori all week. They definitely haven't."

They were texting all week? Was that why Mom had gotten out of bed and Katie had actually showed up to work? A twinge of something ridiculous and unwarranted squeezed my chest. I ignored it, keeping my expression carefully blank.

"There's a bakery around the corner." I inhaled through my nostrils. "Do you want to buy a replacement, or is Martyr Maddie above tricking people?"

"A bit late to pretend I'm above that." She waved her hand between us. Right. I'd made her tell a much bigger lie.

I realized Madison was the whole package. I should be acknowledged somehow for my stupidity. I'd thrown away a supreme fuck just because I was afraid she . . . what, exactly? Would trick me into marrying her somehow? That was never going to happen.

Tell that to the engagement ring she is wearing right now, which you gave her.

I suddenly remembered exactly why I'd stayed with Madison for longer than a week, even though I hadn't had one serious conversation with her the entire time:

1. The sex was out of this world.
2. The baking was sinful.
3. She treated my family like, well . . . family.

In return, I'd cheated on her—that was what she thought, anyway—and never had met her father while he'd visited the city. Chances were, getting in her pants wasn't in the future for me. It was best to get this over with as soon as possible.

I bought two loaves of banana bread from Levain Bakery while Mad dashed into a supermarket to get a baking tray. We met at an intersection just in front of Julian's building. She took the banana bread from my hand, still wrapped in a brown paper bag, held the bag by the tip, and began to batter the bread against a building violently. I stared at her, as did the rest of the street.

"May I ask what in the goddamn world are you doing?" My voice came out more cordial than I thought was necessary. She was assaulting a baked good, after all. Very publicly, if I might add.

"No homemade banana bread looks as perfect as the ones from bakeries. I'm just making it look authentic," came her swift reply, as she poured the distressed loaves into the tray she'd bought and covered them in plastic wrap. She was panting, her tits rising and falling in her tight dress.

I looked away, *not* thinking about how perfect her breasts felt in my palms.

"You should put more of that effort into trying to look like you can tolerate me," I noted sourly.

"That's above my pay grade."

"I don't pay you."

"Exactly."

We crossed the street, glaring at each other. Another one of our unspoken staring contests.

"You know," I started, "I could—"

"Nope. Please don't try to bribe me with apartments and cars and golden helicopters. God, you're predictable. I'm so glad I met Ethan."

A man who wore tights and a *PAW Patrol* tie was besting me. Now was a good time to off myself.

In the elevator, I ducked my head toward her. I didn't know why. She just looked . . . Mad-like. Sexy in a cute, retro-chic kind of way. The kind teenagers liked masturbating to. Or, you know, thirty-two-year-old tycoons too.

"Did you just sniff me?" She turned around, eyes wide.

"No." *Yes.* Dammit.

"You're like a feral animal."

"Better than a *PAW Patrol*–collared Chihuahua."

She rolled her eyes like I was a one-trick pony, took my hand, and put it over her bare collarbone. I resisted the need to gulp. Her skin was hot, silky, and perfect; there was nothing sexual about what she did when she rubbed her delicate neck with my big palm, but I was pretty sure a pearl of precome graced the crown of my cock by the time she was done.

"There." She pushed my hand away. "That'll give you a good portion of my smell until tomorrow morning, and you'll smell like me when we get in there. Happy?"

"With you? Never," I spat out.

She smiled.

I frowned.

The elevator slid open, and we both stepped out.

It was going to be a long fucking night.

Julian lived in an Upper West Side five-bedroom penthouse overlooking the city that held an uncanny resemblance to a brothel, including red-upholstered furniture, dripping chandeliers, and an extensive wet bar. The minute we entered the premises, I ushered Dad to Clementine's room for some privacy. His cheeks were sunken. Life leaked out of him in slow motion. I wasn't sure what I was expecting, exactly. I knew there wasn't a treatment for his level billion of cancer. Grant said putting him through chemo—if his blood tests would even allow for him to go through chemo—was a waste of time and effort and would only make him feel even sicker. At this point, it was about keeping him comfortable.

Only he wasn't looking anywhere near comfortable to me.

"Chase." Dad frowned. "Why are we in here?" He looked around Booger Face's room. It was the only space in the apartment that didn't look like you might catch an STD if you sat on a piece of furniture. All pink-hued walls and ceilings and white fixtures.

"Because you're not taking care of yourself," I spat out. "You need to take your meds."

"I don't like to feel sedated," he countered. "I want to be present."

"I don't want you to suffer," I argued.

"It's not your decision to make."

After a ten-minute argument, in which I badgered him to call Grant and failed to convince him, I dragged myself to the open kitchen area, joining the rest of the family. I left Dad in Clementine's room, too angry to look him in the face. When I got to the kitchen (more chandeliers, crème-and-gold countertops, flower-patterned fucking everything, and no trace of actual food), I stopped dead in my tracks.

Booger Face was sitting on the counter, dangling her purple sneakers in the air, laughing in delight. Mad was twisting Clementine's unruly orange hair into a french braid, blabbering about warrior princesses. Amber was side-eyeing them behind her flute of champagne, not even pretending to listen to my mother's litany of every store in town that had run out of the sandals she was after. Julian, who stood next to his wife, gave me a death stare, his white-knuckled hold on his champagne nearly smashing the glass to dust. A stab of petty glee prickled my chest.

Madison was giving them no reason to suspect we were less than two lovebirds. *Good.* So good, in fact, I had to remind myself why having a girlfriend, even if it was sexy, capable Madison, wasn't a good idea:

1. Girlfriends wanted to get married at some point. Most of them, anyway.
2. I didn't want to get married at *any* point.
3. If I were to date Madison—which, again, would never happen—I would be suspicious and resentful. I'd make her miserable beyond belief. Losing her for the second time would be embarrassing to the point I'd have no choice but to punch my own face.
4. Punching myself in the face, deliberately, was very low on my to-do list.

I sauntered into the kitchen, dropping a kiss on Clementine's crown of crazy orange hair. I wrapped my arm around Madison. "What's good?"

"Everything!" Mom turned to me, her voice shrill. "Everything is great. The banana bread looks delicious. Thank you, Maddie."

"Looks awfully similar to the one they sell at Levain down the road," Amber muttered into her drink. Her short red minidress was perfect for a pelvic examination or amateur college porn.

"Been hitting the bakery often, Am?" I deliberately swept my eyes along her toned, fit frame just for shits and giggles.

She turned the color of her dress, narrowing her eyes at me. "Actually, I lost three pounds. I'm doing this new hot sculpt yoga class five times a week."

"Your accomplishments know no bounds."

"What about you, Maddie—do you exercise?" She turned to my fake fiancée, smiling at her sweetly.

Madison, pretending to be oblivious to her host's passive-aggressiveness, snapped Booger Face's braid in a thin pink elastic. "Not unless you count walking from the living room to the kitchen to fetch some ice cream while *The Walking Dead* is on commercial break. I really should switch to AMC Premiere, but I need the physical activity. And there are *so* many commercial breaks."

I stifled a grin, delighted by Mad's response to a paling, thoroughly annoyed Amber.

"Wow. I can't imagine my life without working out." Amber played with her diamond necklace.

"It's a terrible existence," Maddie agreed easily, "but someone's gotta do it."

I wanted to kiss her.

I wanted to kiss her bad.

The fact I technically could, because she was my so-called fiancée, didn't help matters. I knew Martyr Maddie wouldn't slap me in the face if I tried to kiss her publicly, but I couldn't muster enough assholeness to go from rude and surly to straight-up bastard.

The meal was buffet-style. All the dishes were still in their prepacked catering containers, spread across the massive U-shaped kitchen island. As with everything Julian and his wife did, it was beautifully impersonalized.

There were honey-glazed crab cakes and artichoke bottoms stuffed with crabmeat, miso-marinated Hawaiian butterfish and cucumber bites. This time, Mad took a chance on most of the dishes. It was Clementine who sat in horror in front of her plate, her big green eyes staring at the heap of dead sea creatures.

"But Mom . . . ," she kept saying. "Mommy. Mommy. Mom. Mommy."

"Jesus Christ, Julian, just give her some Cheerios," Amber finally snapped, when it was obvious she couldn't continue telling Katie her story of how she'd been mistaken for Kate Hudson at Saks Fifth Avenue.

"But I don't want Cheerios." Clementine pouted, her brows diving down. "I'm tired of eating them all the time. I want Grandma's pancakes."

"Grandma doesn't have that special grandma mix." Mom dropped her utensils on her plate, her eyes softening. Clementine spent a good amount of time at my parents' house, and Mom braved the kitchen to treat her granddaughter to the one thing she made by herself and didn't ask the cook to fix—instant mix pancakes.

It was my understanding that Amber and Julian's relationship was an endless string of arguments, with Julian getting kicked out of the house frequently and Amber crying herself to sleep on a weekly basis. My parents tried to shield Booger Face from this reality as much as they could.

Madison watched the exchange with thinly masked alert. I could see the wheels in her brain turning. She didn't want to overstep, but she didn't like Amber's treatment of Booger Face. I didn't think anyone did. That kid lived off cereal, Pop-Tarts, and air.

"What mix do you usually use?" Madison turned to my mother, placing a hand on her wrist. "For the pancakes?"

"Quick Wheat."

"Okay, so flour, sugar, eggs, water, milk, and salt. Hershey's Kisses if you have them too. Where's your pantry?" She turned to Amber, her eyes daring her host to refuse. Yet again, I found myself hard. Was there anything Madison did that didn't give me a raging erection? I tried to think. I hadn't been hard when she'd assaulted the banana bread publicly. Although, if I was being honest, she'd still looked fuckable. Tie-able, too, though.

Amber smiled politely. "She can eat what everyone else is eating. In our household, everyone is having the same dish or no food at all. It's a parent thing. You wouldn't understand."

Right under the belt. I looked over at Madison, who kept her smile fresh and sweet.

I agreed with Amber's sentiment, but this was a pile of bullshit in Clementine's case. Booger Face never had what everyone else was having. Amber simply wanted to punish Clementine for warming up to Madison. Only Clementine wasn't privy to that.

"Isn't she sensitive to shellfish?" Dad frowned at Julian. Julian turned his gaze helplessly to his wife. *Jesus Christ.* Katie dragged Clementine's plate away from her. "Mildly allergic. It gives her a rash."

"The doctor said she will develop immunity if she eats shellfish regularly." Amber blushed under her makeup. I almost pitied her. She wasn't a neglectful mother, but she had the maternal instincts of a bag of Cheetos. Booger Face had private tutors, and Amber took her to ballet lessons and taught her how to swim, ride a bike, and do cartwheels. She even took her to French lessons. Julian's involvement in his kid's life, however, was minimal and limited to patting her head like she was a Labrador every evening when he came back home. I had a theory that Amber had lost her soul the day she'd chosen Julian Black for a husband. Of course, being the president of the I Loathe Julian hate club for the past three years, I was a little biased. At any rate, I had a feeling I could recruit Mad as our newest member, judging by her interaction with the couple.

"Shouldn't she start with small quantities?" Katie turned to Amber.

"I'm hun-grayyyyyy," Clementine whined, throwing her head back.

"Really, it'll be no trouble at all. It will take me ten minutes," Madison began to explain in the cacophony of voices that spoke over one another.

"Just let her have pancakes!" my father boomed all of a sudden, slamming his fist on the table. The room fell quiet. Madison sprang into action, scurrying to the kitchen.

I turned my attention back to my food.

"Aren't you going to accompany your fiancée?" Julian sat back, starting a new shitstorm.

I shrugged. "She can find her way around your kitchen."

"Can you find your way to the twenty-first century, though? That's quite chauvinistic."

I fought an eye roll. "Since when is it chauvinistic to insinuate that my girlfriend can make her own food? Doesn't it make her independent? Anyway, when was the last time you fixed yourself a plate of something that wasn't bought at Whole Foods?"

"Girlfriend?" Julian arched an eyebrow that said *busted.* "Thought she was your fiancée."

"Chase. Julian. *Stop,*" my mother bit out. "You're upsetting your father."

He started it, I wanted to protest. For obvious reasons, I didn't.

I could see Madison making herself comfortable in Julian and Amber's kitchen. Heard the sound of the sizzling butter as it hit the pan. The scent of warm sugar wafted through the air, and I didn't think there was one asshole at the table who wanted to eat crab stuffed into organic vegetables instead of what my fake fiancée was making.

"I really like Maddie." Booger Face sucked on her organic boxed juice, sighing.

"That's nice, sweetheart." Amber looked away from her plate, blinking rapidly.

"I really, *really* like her," Clementine continued, not winning any tact points this evening. "It is nice of her to make me pancakes. I hope I see her in the clinic again soon."

Amber snapped her head up like a guard dog who'd just heard a twig crunching under a boot. "In the *clinic*?"

"Yeah. When I went to get my shots. I wanted to say hello, but you were talking on the phone and said there was no time, remember?" Clementine glanced at her in confusion, and something very dark and very cold uncurled inside my chest. I bet Amber hadn't been paying attention to what Clementine said at the time. "I saw her when I went to the doctor to get my shots. Maddie hugged my doctor. She hugged him hard. For a long time. Like couples in movies do. It was so disgusting." Booger Face shivered, shaking her head with disgust.

The room was so quiet I could hear my own heartbeat. All eyes slowly slid in my direction. I had nothing to say. Nothing other than *WHY WAS MADISON HUGGING THE ASSHOLE WITH THE TIE AND TIGHTS LONG AND HARD LIKE COUPLES IN MOVIES DO?*

Hugging led to other things, and all those things assaulted my brain in a collage of Mad and Dr. Tights going at it like bunnies in front of a pediatric clinic. Him grabbing the back of her neck roughly, thrusting his tongue into her mouth. I took a sip of my water, concentrating on not tossing the table and everything on it through the floor-to-ceiling window. I wanted to do something radical and violent and shocking but knew it wasn't going to help my case.

I didn't trust myself to speak. To *think*.

"Is that so, sweetheart?" Julian poured more water into my glass, his voice like a snake's hiss. "What's your pediatrician's name again?"

"Dr. Goodman," Clementine purred, stupidly delighted to be acknowledged by her father. "He has the best ties, Dad. Of cartoons and Disney characters. And he lets me pinch him when he gives me shots. I like him, even though he hugged Maddie so hard there was no space between their bodies. Then he kissed her cheek. *Yuck.*"

I was going to commit murder. I was sure of it.

Amber's eyes were clinging to my face, but it was Katie who asked brokenly, "Chase? I mean . . . is this true?"

I had two options. Making Booger Face look like a liar—which she wasn't—or chalking this up to her wild nine-year-old imagination. There was also a third option, of admitting it to be true and coming clean. But that meant letting Julian win. Three years ago, I'd have bowed out of this gracefully.

Today, though, it was war.

"Maybe you saw someone who looks like her, Booger." I ran my hand through Clementine's braid.

She stared at me, serious as a heart attack, scowling. "No, I didn't. She wore the same green dress with the little avocados she did in the Hamptons. I told Mommy I want a dress like that, and she said she would rather set herself on fire than have me wear it."

Fuck my life in the ass. I'd chosen the most recognizable woman in New York to play my doting fake fiancée. Everyone was watching our exchange intently. My father, especially, looked pale and extra frail. He knotted his fingers together, tapping his index fingers to his lips contemplatively.

I gave Julian a meaningful stare.

He waved his fingers at me dismissively. He didn't fucking care.

Mad chose that exact moment to make her grand return with a big smile, oven mitts, and a plate stacked with a mountain of steaming pancakes. She slid the plate in Clementine's direction, drenching the pancakes in enough maple syrup to drown a hamster. "There you go, sweets."

"Maddie." Julian almost sprawled in his seat, he was so smug. "Clementine just shared something very interesting with us. She said she saw you hugging her pediatrician, Dr. Goodman, this week, and that he kissed your cheek. Is this true?" He elevated an eyebrow, feigning surprise.

"Chase says she must've seen wrong." Amber jumped on the shit wagon, recovering quickly from her failure to feed her own child. "But I know my daughter, and she is extremely observant."

Madison's eyes darted to me. I held her gaze. I wasn't sure what I was asking her, but I knew if she was going to refuse it, there was a good chance I'd set the world on fire.

Tick.

Tock.

Tick.

Tock.

Since when were clocks so goddamn loud? I waited for her to say something. *Anything.* How the tables had turned. Six months ago, Madison Goldbloom would bend over backward to make me happy (quite literally—we'd tried that position twice). Now, I was at her mercy.

Her lips parted, and the room sucked in a collective breath.

"Oh, Dr. Goodman!" she exclaimed with her big Maddie smile, but I could see right through it. The self-disgust laced with panic swimming in her big brown eyes. "Clemmy, you definitely saw me! Dr. Goodman and I are old friends. He is practicing for a half marathon. I just dropped by with some baked goods because I was in the area visiting a friend."

Of course. A friend. A *friend.* Why hadn't I thought of that?

Because the only women you talk to who are not blood related to you end up in your bed. You wouldn't recognize friendship with the fairer sex if it kneed you in the nuts.

Clementine seemed to be appeased by that, smiling her partly toothless grin at Madison like she'd hung the stars and moon for her.

Julian, however, wasn't impressed by this bullshit. He looked between Mad and me, arching an eyebrow. He was about to say something I 100 percent didn't want to hear, his mouth falling open, when a loud bang snapped everyone out of the drama. My gaze darted to the head of the table.

Dad.

CHAPTER NINE

Chase

I hooked Dad's right arm, propping him on my shoulder. Julian took his left side. We zigzagged across the living room unevenly, the height difference between Jul and me making Dad sway unconsciously between us like a rag flapping on a clothesline.

"Let's take him to my bedroom," Julian groaned, his knees buckling under my father's weight. We dragged him through the hallway, Mom and Katie on our heels. I heard Amber cracking open a bottle of liquor and Madison asking Clementine enthusiastically to show her her book collection.

The hallway was never ending, stretching for miles, and I pushed away the thoughts of Dad dying in my arms tonight. The pictures on the walls blurred. When we got to Julian and Amber's bedroom, we rested Dad on top of the bed. I dialed Grant's number. Fuck his date with Layla. I paced back and forth as Katie tried to pour a little water between Dad's dry, colorless lips. He regained consciousness, but that meant jack shit after his head had collided with his plate and he'd passed out on the table mere minutes ago.

As if remembering herself, Mom rushed back to the living room to fetch the medicine bag she'd brought for Dad (because carrying a medicine bag everywhere was now a thing). It was a big black device that had all kinds of oxygen masks and an array of orange pill bottles.

"Pick up, pick up, pick up," I muttered, my phone plastered to my ear, pacing back and forth in a room I never wanted to be in. Grant picked up on the second ring. I rehashed the events in a clipped tone.

"Put Ronan on the phone, please," Grant said, annoyingly composed. My four-year-old self wanted to throw sand in his eyes. *What are you so calm about? My dad is dying.*

Mom handed me the medicine bag. I unzipped it. Katie propped Dad's back against the headboard, a thin veil of sweat coating her forehead. I hurried to help her, pinning my phone between my ear and shoulder.

"Just tell me what to do."

"Chase, I can't."

"I'm your best friend," I hissed through clenched teeth, recognizing how childish it sounded.

"You could be the pope for all I care. You need to put your dad on the phone. He is the only person I can discuss his meds with, unless I get his verbal permission."

We both knew Dad wouldn't grant me permission to discuss his health while he was still in a position to make his own decision. He was stubbornly proud. Reluctantly, I handed Dad my phone. His fingers curled around the device shakily. He began to sift through the medicine bag in his lap as he *hmm-hmm*ed to the phone. Ranitidine, slow-release morphine, diclofenac, methylprednisolone. Hospice medicine, designed to make him comfortable, not better.

Katie galloped to the en suite bathroom, and I heard her retch as she threw up. It was too much for her. The realness of losing him.

Dad popped a few pills, drank more water, and answered various questions Grant had asked him. I didn't think it was standard procedure for a doctor off duty to sit around and listen to his patient's slow breaths for twenty minutes, but he did. Dad put Grant on speaker, and Katie got back to the room.

"Hey, Mr. Black, remember when Chase and I watched *The Shining* while we had a sleepover and I pissed my pants and you helped me clean it up? Bet you never thought things would turn out this way, huh?" Grant laughed. Dad did too.

I silently thanked the universe for gifting me a doctor best friend and not a douchey Wall Street broker of the variety I'd gone to school with.

"How could I forget?" He chuckled. "You've come a long way."

"Well, it has been a few years." I heard Grant grin.

Dad hung up and handed me the phone back, his stern father voice giving me whiplash. "Grant's going to drop by at my house in a little to make sure my head is okay. He's a good friend. Make sure you don't lose him or Madison. They please me."

"Really?" I cocked an eyebrow. "You just passed out, and that's what you want to talk about? My friend and girlfriend?"

"Fiancée," Julian corrected with a bleached smile.

Right. I needed to ink this onto my wrist in order not to forget. Julian was a skilled chess player. But he was also a predictable player, and his favorite method was to capture the pawns before going in for the kill.

In this case, Madison was the pawn, but I'd be damned if I'd see her knocked over by Julian as an afterthought.

"And yes, surrounding yourself with good people is the key to happiness. I found out about it the hard way. Now, I don't know what Clemmy was talking about out there"—Dad pointed at the door—"but you cannot lose this woman. She is too good to let go."

"What makes you say that?" I ran a hand over my jaw. I wasn't disagreeing with him. But I found it hard to believe we appreciated the same things in Mad. Frankly speaking, her great ass, fuckable mouth, smart-ass observations, and eccentric tendencies.

"She is smart, sassy, loving, and easy on the eyes."

Okay, maybe we *did* see the exact same things. They just sounded a lot less filthy coming from him.

"She respects your family. She works hard for what she wants. She always has a smile on her face, even though I'm sure she didn't always have it easy," he elaborated.

"Dad." Julian sat on the edge of the bed, taking Dad's pale hand in his. Sometimes I forgot Julian wasn't my brother. He *felt* like my brother. Until Dad had announced I was his successor, anyway. From that point onward, Julian had been quick to point out he was only a "mere" cousin. In fact, he called him Uncle Ronan 90 percent of the time these days, even though he knew it ripped my father to shreds. Julian patted Dad's hand awkwardly, like it was made out of slime. He couldn't fake his way to a genuine feeling if he had a *How to Be Human for Dummies* manual right in front of him.

"I think maybe it's time for you to take care of yourself. Spend more time at home with Lori." Of course, Mom was *Lori* now. All the sleepless nights she'd spent hugging him tight when he'd had nightmares after his parents had passed away. All the birthday parties she'd thrown for him. All the tears she'd cried when he was hurting. "Maybe it's time to . . . retire," Julian finished, his forehead crumpling in fake concern.

"Retire?" My father tasted the word on his tongue for the first time. He hadn't missed a day of work in fifty-five years. I doubted it ever crossed his mind. Working made him happy. He didn't know himself outside the context of work. "You want me to retire?"

"Nobody wants you to retire," I hissed, pinning Julian with a death glare. "You must've misheard. That's what happens when people talk with a mouth full of shit."

"Chase!" Mom gasped.

"He is struggling." Julian straightened his back, jutting his chin out. "What if there's a power outage in the building and he is in the elevator?

What if he falls? What if he needs his meds and there's no one to give them to him? So many things can go wrong."

True. I can accidentally push you out the window, for instance.

"Julian, shut up," I snapped.

"The shareholders are going to ask questions soon. It's a two-point-three-billion-dollar company, and it is being run by someone who is not well. I'm sorry—I'm just saying what no one else is brave enough to." Julian held his hands up in surrender. "It is ethically wrong to hide this kind of medical condition from the board. What if—"

"Shut up, Jul!" Katie barked, bursting into tears. It was not unlike my sister to cry. It *was* unlike my sister to be confrontational. Then again, Dad had gotten sick, and all of a sudden this family had turned into *Lord of the Flies*. And Julian, the classic middle management guy—good at nothing other than possessing a staggering amount of confidence—was the man who'd decided to replace him, no matter the fact the role had been promised to *me*. Katie stabbed me with a look. "I'll take Mom and Dad home."

"I'll take them." I picked up Dad's medicine bag, hoisting it over my shoulder.

"No, they can stay here. I . . ." Julian put his hand on Dad's arm. We both shut him up with a glare.

"I'll handle this," I assured my baby sister.

"C'mon, Chase. You came here by train. I have my car, and I wanted to crash at theirs, anyway. It's close to the half-marathon starting point."

I nodded, torn between joining them and getting Madison home. But I knew Dad didn't want an entire production—it would only make him feel more vulnerable if we all escorted him back home—and besides, I wanted to wrap things up with Mad. It was probably the last time we were going to see each other.

She is too good to let go, my dad had said.

Too bad I couldn't keep her.

I spent the ride back to Madison's apartment counting the reasons why she shouldn't be with Ethan Goodman in my head. I stopped at thirty when I realized that there were at least a hundred more in the pipeline and that I was too proud to say jack shit about it to her, anyway.

Madison alternated between glancing at me with concern and munching on her lower lip.

It was disgustingly hot and packed in the subway. Every single motherfucker inside was either sweating, holding a greasy takeout bag, or both. A baby whined. A teenage couple made out on the seat in front of us, partly masked by the backs of two men in suits who were standing and reading on their phones. I wanted to get out, take Madison with me, hail a cab—an Uber Copter if I could—and go back to my Park Avenue apartment, where I'd put Elliott Smith on blast and bury myself in my ex-girlfriend.

Which, there was no point denying at this stage, was what she was to me.

When we finally got out of the train and I walked her to her apartment, I realized it was probably the last time I was going to visit her street. Goodbye hung in the air, fat and looming and un-fucking-fair. But what could I do? She wanted marriage. She was obsessed with weddings—designed wedding dresses for a living, had flowers everywhere—and I thought marriage was the stupidest idea mankind had entertained. Never had I seen such a popular idea being utilized over and over again despite garnering such poor results. Fifty percent divorce rate average, anyone?

Nah, marriage was not for me. And yet . . .

The morning walks with horny Daisy.

Our arrangement.

Our banter.

Our Post-it Notes.

I'd grown to not completely hate all of that. Which was more than I could say about my interactions with most people.

"Are you okay?" Mad finally winced when we were at the stairway to her apartment building. The entire journey had been silent. Of course I was fucking okay. Everything was fine. The only thing that bothered me (*remotely*) was the idea of Ethan hopping up these stairs tomorrow after his half marathon. How he was going to fuck her. Bury himself in her sweet, warm body, which always smelled of freshly baked goods and flowers, and *fuck*. I started imagining her doing all the things she'd done with me. The vein in my forehead was ready to pop.

Mad surprised me by taking my hand, squeezing it in both her small palms.

"I want to tell you that it gets better, but it really doesn't. The only good thing about this situation is that experiencing the death of someone close heightens your senses."

"Heightens my senses?" I asked sardonically, feeling my nostrils flare. I'd once eaten an ortolan while covering my head with a napkin to heighten my senses. My senses were higher than the Empire State Building. They didn't need a pick-me-up.

Madison brushed her thumb along my palm, making a shiver roll down my spine. "Death is no longer an obscure idea. It is real and it is waiting, so you grab life by the balls. When you go through the horror of seeing someone you love die and still manage to wake up the next day to tie your shoelaces, to shove a tasteless breakfast down your throat, to *breathe*, you realize survival trumps tragedy. *Always.* It's a primal instinct."

I watched our entwined fingers curiously, realizing we hadn't held hands while we were together. Madison had tried. Once, a couple of weeks into our hookup. I swiftly untangled myself the first chance I got. She hadn't tried since.

Her fingers were slim and tan. Mine long and white and comically large against hers. Yin and yang.

"How did you concentrate on anything other than your mother dying?" I asked gruffly.

She smiled up at me, her eyes shining with fat tears. "I didn't. I faked it till I made it."

I bowed my head down, plastering my forehead to hers, breathing her in. I closed my eyes. We both knew there was not an ounce of romance in that moment. It was a pure this-planet-is-crazy-and-the-human-condition-is-trash moment. It was an end-of-the-world moment, and there wasn't anywhere else I'd rather be.

Our hairs touched, and I felt goose bumps on both our arms wherever we touched. I didn't want to let her go but knew with every fiber of my body that I should.

For her.

For me.

I couldn't pinpoint when, exactly, it turned into a hug, but before I knew what was happening, she was leaning into me, and I was leaning into her, and we were swaying in place like two drunks in a sea of summer lights.

She looked up, and her smile was so sad I wanted to wipe it off her face with a kiss.

"You're brave," she whispered. "I know you are."

She knew I was? I didn't know why, but that made me angry.

"I just wanted to . . . ," I started, the words dying inside my throat.

Fuck you one last time? Know if you really are having sex with that idiot? Burn down a pediatric practice?

In the end, I didn't say anything. Just wondered, why couldn't she be like me? Like Layla? Why couldn't she want fun and casual and un-fucking-complicated?

"Goodbye, Chase." She squeezed my hand one last time. She forgot to give me back the engagement ring. I didn't ask her for it, because (a) I didn't care about the damn ring, and (b) I knew she'd have to contact me again in order to return it. For all her faults, Madison was the furthest thing from a gold digger I'd ever met.

I leaned down and kissed her temple, letting my lips hover there. She took a step back and went inside.

I watched her disappearing behind her building door.

She kept glancing back.

I kept thinking she'd make a U-turn, like in the stupid movies she'd always tried to convince me to watch. Run back out, jump into my arms. We'd kiss. It would rain (even though it was summer). I'd hoist her up in the air, and she'd wrap her legs around my waist, and we'd go upstairs and make love, fade-to-black-style.

But after a few seconds of staring at me through the glass window of her entrance door, she shook her head and took the second flight of stairs.

I turned around and stumbled back home by foot, pressing my hand against my face, trying to breathe her in from the time she'd rubbed my fingers against her collarbone in the elevator.

Her scent was gone.

CHAPTER TEN

MADDIE

September 1, 2002

Dear Maddie,

Fun fact: The dandelion flower opens up in the morning to greet the sun and closes in the evening to go to bed. It is the only flower to "grow old." When you were younger, I took you to the park every day. Do you remember, Maddie? We used to look at dandelions and try to determine which ones would turn white and frail first. When they finally did, we'd pick them and blow them. They'd dance in the wind like snowflakes, and you'd chase them and laugh.

I told you it was okay to pick up dandelions and blow on them, because we spread their seeds. Each dandelion that died was responsible for the birth of a dozen like it!

There is a twisted, jagged beauty to the ending of life. It is a bittersweet reminder that it happened.

Seize the moment.

Every moment.

Until we meet again.

Love,

Mom. x

◆ ◆ ◆

Three Chase-free days had passed.

Three days without Post-it Notes.

Three days where Chase got in, took Daisy, got out, and was out of my hair, just like I'd begged him to be since he'd walked back into my life.

Three days in which Ethan and I were too busy—me with finishing a few sketches that were due by the end of the week, him with his post (half!) marathon rituals. Our official consummation date was postponed, since Ethan needed to sit in a bath full of ice and write a five-thousand-word post in his blog about the medical merits of ice baths (which he sent to me; I skimmed). I tried convincing myself that it was a good thing we didn't try to have sex the day his muscles were aching and I was still mulling over every single minute from that dinner night with Chase. I was especially bothered by Hug-Gate. I tried to assure myself that nobody thought anything of two adults hugging outside a pediatric clinic. It sounded completely platonic, but the fact that Chase had looked like he was about to maim someone with a butter knife at the table, paired with Julian's insanely sharp instincts, meant that I was still worried we were uncovered. If that could cause Ronan to faint, God only knew what could happen if he found out the truth.

Ethan and I made plans to hang out on Tuesday. Ethan suggested he bring Chinese food and I bring the "right mood." I tried to muster every ounce of excitement for our evening plans while I was at work.

I found a romantic-songs playlist on iTunes, shoved my AirPods on, and bobbed my head to some Peter Gabriel and Snow Patrol. I planned on putting on soft music on my old record player, maybe scattering some flowers around the house.

I was working on my drawing board, outlining a simple dress for our Mother of the Bride fall collection (I hated working on this collection; it was a painful reminder I *didn't* have a mother), when I felt a tap on my shoulder.

I turned around, fully prepared to see a DoorDash delivery guy holding a paper bag with my lunch. Or maybe Nina scowling at me and telling me to keep the music down on my AirPods. But I nearly fell off my stool when I saw Katie Black standing in front of me, waving at me with an apologetic smile.

"Hi!" I said too loudly, wobbling up to my feet. *Flustered* didn't begin to cover what I was feeling. Technically, I could see why she'd be here. She thought we were soon to be sisters-in-law. In practice, I knew my colleagues were going to ask a lot of questions if they saw us together. Namely, Nina, who was already peeking over her shoulder, trying to figure out what Katie freaking Black was doing talking to me.

I'd managed to keep my six-month relationship with Chase a complete secret while we were dating. Knew people would have a field day if they knew I was sleeping with the billionaire from the top floor. The one who owned the department store that kept *our* business alive. The irony of getting caught dating a man I hadn't really dated six months after we'd broken up wasn't lost on me.

"Hi. Hello. Hola." Katie waved again, her blush deepening. "Hope I'm not interrupting anything. I thought . . . well, I normally take my lunch at the office, but one of my meetings got canceled, and I thought it'd be a good idea if you and I maybe spent some time together. You know, just so . . ." She trailed off, looking at the ceiling and chuckling to herself, mortified.

"Yes!" I said too brightly, eager to get her out of the studio, fast. I patted my chair for my jacket before remembering it was a thousand degrees outside and I hadn't brought one with me this morning. I dragged her to the elevators. Physically pushed her in their direction. "What a great idea. I'm starving. Where do you want to eat?"

"La Table?" She stared at me with a mixture of surprise and worry, hoisting her Balmain bag over her shoulder. La Table was a $300-per-plate, fixed-price French restaurant under our building. It was reservations only (unless your last name was Black or Murdoch), which meant that I was in no risk of bumping into any of my colleagues. It also meant I was going to shell out enough money to pay a whole week's rent because of Chase's stupid lie, but as with Daisy's vet, I was fully prepared to send him the bill for this.

The elevator slid open, and Sven appeared. He looked at me in question.

"Hi. No questions, please. Bye." I all but shoved Katie inside while he stepped outside. Katie opened her mouth to ask me what was going on, but I beat her to it.

"So how was the marathon?" I asked cheerfully.

"Half marathon," she corrected (she and Ethan would get along; I inwardly smiled). "And it was really good, actually. I had fun, and we raised a lot of money for charity. I'm sure Chase told you he donated three hundred thousand dollars to sponsor me."

I almost choked on my saliva. He'd done that? I had no idea. I always thought Chase would be the kind of guy to support the cause of burning down rain forests and wearing fur. He seemed so infuriatingly soulless. Even when we'd been together, there was a shell of something dark, made out of steel and misanthropy, I couldn't quite get past. I nodded dutifully, still playing my role as a fiancée.

"Sure. Yes. Totally."

One affirmative is enough, Maddie.

We got out of the elevator. I asked her how Ronan was doing (not good), then complimented her on completing the half marathon. She told me she was planning on running a full marathon next year. Then asked why I wasn't wearing my engagement ring.

"I'd really prefer not to make a big deal out of it." I felt myself blushing. I mean, that, and the fact I wasn't actually engaged to her brother. Take your pick. Panic alarms rang through my body. It felt so completely, unbelievably shitty to lie.

"Why? He's not technically your boss. You know that, right?"

"I do, I do." I wasn't worried Chase would fire or demote me. I was worried he'd detonate my heart into miniscule pieces. "I still think it might rub people the wrong way, you know? Just because it's a sister company and I don't report to Chase doesn't mean that it smells kosher."

"Hmm," Katie replied. It was a good time to change the subject before my head exploded from overblushing.

"I really like your dress," I chirped. It was a brown knee-length number. Stern but really elegant.

Katie let out a surprised laugh. "I dress horribly. I want to blend in with everything."

"Why?" I wondered. Obviously, I had the exact opposite problem.

"Because I don't like to be seen. It's a part of my anxiety problem. I don't have the same confidence Julian and Chase seem to have been born with. I always think to myself, the first thing people see when they meet me is that I come from money and my dad gave me a kick-ass job because he had to."

"He wouldn't keep you if you sucked. I know that much about Ronan." I shook my head as we strolled out of the building. "And confidence is like a house. You build it brick by brick. Each brick may seem insignificant, but when you take a step back after a while, you realize you've made a lot of progress." Mom told me that. "Dressing confidently is the first step."

"We should go shopping together sometime. You can help me out," Katie suggested, biting down on her lip as we entered the restaurant. I was about to answer when the maître d' greeted us, seating us at a prime table by the window. Mistaking my silence for rejection, Katie cast her eyes down at her menu, her shaky fingers fluttering over her neck.

"I would love that, Katie," I said. "Although I'm not sure your brother is going to approve. He always taunts me about my clothes."

"That's just his version of pulling at your pigtails." She laughed, taking a sip of her water. "You must know how much he adores you. He thinks you're gorgeous."

He does? It was not far fetched to think Chase found me attractive—he had dated me for a while—but he rarely ever commented about my looks, unless it was to point out how awful my fashion sense was.

"Sometimes I think he'd like me to look more put together," I mused about my fake relationship with my fake fiancé to my fake almost sister-in-law. I had no idea what made me say that. It wasn't like it mattered.

Katie snorted, looking up from her menu. "I don't think so at all."

"You don't? Someone like Amber seems more fitting."

I was not so subconsciously baiting Katie for more information, but I knew it wasn't constructive. The waiter came to take our order. I let Katie order for both of us, mainly because I couldn't pronounce most of the things on the menu but also because I was too nervous to take a good look at it in the first place. Once the waiter was gone, Katie snapped the napkin open and spread it in her lap. "Well, we all know how *that* went."

"How what went?" I pressed.

Stop, Maddie, stop.

"Chase and Amber."

There was a Chase and Amber? And we all know how it went? Really?

Feeling my pulse punching the side of my neck unpleasantly, I nodded, confirming I knew all about Chase and Amber. Panic climbed up my throat.

"Yeah, they don't get along," I finally squeaked. A flashback from the Hamptons ran through my head. Of Amber visiting our room while I'd been in the shower. Hushed voices, followed by an intense silence. They shared a secret. I was sure of it.

"That's an understatement." Katie snorted, then chugged San Pellegrino. "Sometimes I'm surprised Mom and Dad accepted her into the family after what she did to him. Then again, they didn't really have much choice, did they?"

"No," I agreed, feeling my body coming alive with too many emotions to identify exactly what it was I felt in that moment. Anxiety? Excitement? Anger? "I agree. That . . . that wasn't nice of Amber."

What the hell did she do to him?

"Anyway, I'm so happy he found you. I'm going to be honest: I didn't think he'd ever bounce back from this. Not after things went down. He never had a serious girlfriend after Amber and before you."

Chase and Amber were dating? But how could that be? She's with his brother.

"That's me." I clinked my overpriced sparkling water glass to hers with a smile. "Full of surprises."

And lies. And guilt. And probably irritable bowel syndrome, thanks to all the built-up aggression and remorse my body contains.

I was about to try to dig deeper into #chamber (the Chase-and-Amber shipping name I'd made up on the fly), when Katie sprang up to her feet, waving her hand excitedly. I whipped my head backward to see who she was looking at.

Chase.

Making his way to us.

With a cocky, I-dare-you-to-say-anything smile plastered on his face.

He looked so ruthlessly stunning I allowed myself two seconds to appreciate the Chris Hemsworth-ness of him in one of his signature black suits—tall and broad and bigger than life—before I returned to my usual program of being furious with him.

What the hell was he doing here?

"I'm so glad you could make it! Gosh, look at her face. She *is* surprised." Katie laughed, mistaking my shock for delight. "We just ordered. Are you hungry?"

"No, I had lunch with a shareholder," Chase said casually, leaning down to where I sat, grabbing my neck (grabbing my neck!), and planting a firm, hard kiss (!@#^%$!) on my mouth. His lips were on mine. Warm and hard and full of conviction. It was a kiss that said, *This is happening,* not *Thank you for all you did. Have a good life.* It was a continuation of something we'd started when I'd found him sitting on my stairway. It was destruction wrapped in a toe-curling moment I wanted to erase from my memory.

It. Was. Perfection.

He leaned back, smirking devilishly at me as he took the seat next to mine, straightening his dress shirt and adjusting his cigar pants as rich men who knew how to dress did. I glared at him, still feeling that close-lipped kiss everywhere. My mouth. My cheeks. My chest. That place under my belly button he knew how to make throb.

"How did the meeting go?" Katie chirped. Chase launched into a rant about something Julian had failed to do and he'd had to clean up on his behalf. I took the opportunity to pluck my phone from my bag and write him a quick message. Yes, I'd been supposed to delete his number right after I'd come back home from dinner on Friday, but I guess I'd forgotten. It wasn't like Chase was the center of my universe or anything.

Maddie: Did. You. Just. Kiss. Me?!?!

I knew my message would be left unanswered, so I placed my phone in my lap and tucked into my starter, an extra cheesy onion soup. Chase took a breath from his business meeting story, and it was Katie's turn to tell him about how someone from the marketing department had screwed up so badly they'd had to can the entire fall catalog and start from scratch. Chase's eyes drifted down, a small grin tugging at his lips as his fingers began to fly across the screen of his phone.

Katie finished her story. Chase countered it with a story about how Julian and Ronan had once gotten food poisoning in the middle of an event and thrown up directly into an investor's lap. There was still no message back from him. I looked down to my phone every few minutes, confused.

"Do you have any embarrassing stories, Maddie?" Katie asked.

My head snapped up. I felt like I'd been called out on not being present in the moment. I cleared my throat, trying to recover. "Sure do." I side-eyed her brother. My blood was boiling with rage, but Katie didn't know that. She perched her chin on her hand, ignoring the main course they'd just served us—ratatouille—waiting for my delightfully funny input.

"You want an embarrassing story? Okay. So I was dating this guy back in the day . . . he was a real tool," I added, letting out a metallic laugh. Katie followed along, sending Chase an oh-my-God-so-juicy wink. "I have to say, we weren't exactly a match made in heaven from the get-go, but I wanted to see where it was going. Plus, I was under the impression we were serious. He gave me a key to his apartment, like, three months in."

"Maybe it made logistical sense to him," Chase said nonchalantly, taking a sip of his drink. He glanced at Katie uncertainly, like he and she were privy to something I wasn't.

I shot him a polite smile. "Sorry, honey, is this your story or mine?"

His jaw worked. His eyes clouded with warning.

Don't screw it up for me, they said. But I was past doing what was good for him—or for me. I was unhinged with vengeance. With bitterness that simmered in my body and rose up, spilling from my mouth after months of tears.

I turned back to Katie. "So I am dating this guy, and he gives me keys to his apartment. It's his birthday. I'm thinking, I'm going to surprise him in the most romantic, sexy way . . ."

Katie laughed. "Snap, Chase, you may want to cover your ears for this next part."

"Don't worry. He knows this story well." I speared him with a look, ready for my punchline. "I knew he went drinking with his friends. I waited for him in his bed, wearing nothing but the pair of Louboutin heels he bought for me earlier that month, a red thong, and a lacy black bra—you know, to match the heels—sprawled on his bed next to a white chocolate cake I made for him—"

"That made a mess all over his bed." Chase cut into my speech, then quickly backpedaled when Katie turned her head to look at him. "I'm guessing. Who puts a cake on a fucking bed?"

"To make a long story short," I bit out, drawing Katie's attention back to me again, "it turned out he didn't need my company after all, because he stumbled into the bedroom with a woman who wasn't me. Oh, and had a lipstick stain on his dress shirt. How cliché, right?" I smiled bitterly, reaching for Chase's whiskey—he was the only one who'd ordered a stiff drink—gulping it down in one go, and slamming it on the table. "How's that for embarrassing?"

By the look on Katie's face, horror mixed with pity and something else I struggled to read, I could tell that was not the kind of story she'd had in mind. Katie put her hand on mine, trying to catch her breath. I realized, albeit a little too late, that my eyes were glistening. I was holding back tears. But it made no sense at all. I was completely over Chase. I was.

"I'm so sorry this happened to you, Maddie. There is just no excuse."

"None," I agreed cuttingly, gulping my breaths, one fat inhale after the other. "None whatsoever."

"This is . . . heartbreaking," Katie said quietly. "So my guess is you didn't stick around beyond that."

I snorted. "You're guessing correctly. You know what they say—once a cheater, always a cheater."

"That's the stupidest shit I've ever heard," Chase interjected, signaling the waiter to refill his drink with a wave of his hand. "That's like saying that anyone who is involved in accidental manslaughter is a serial killer."

"Cheating is not accidental," I pointed out. "It's plain selfish."

"There are two sides to every story," Chase bit back, color staining his chiseled cheekbones. "Maybe if you bothered talking to the guy—"

"He seemed preoccupied with someone else at the time." I ripped off a piece of bread and shoved it into my mouth. He *still* hadn't answered my text message about the kiss. Katie looked between us, her jawline rigid, her posture surprisingly tight. I saw it in her face. The second she decided to let the subject drop and pretend like we hadn't stepped into a huge mine of feelings and secrets.

"So . . ." She cleared her throat, looking around us. "Seeing as you've now moved on with Chase . . . when are you thinking of getting married? Is there a date?"

"No date. Nope," I drawled, still holding Chase's bluest-shade-of-blue gaze. "We're thinking of taking a long time. You know, for planning and stuff."

"Like, a year?" Katie asked.

"More like a decade," I bit out.

I knew I was letting our charade slip and wished I could restrain myself. I genuinely wanted to make friends with Katie. Take her shopping and spend time with her, independently from how my fake engagement with Chase was going to pan out. I was just taken off guard by how Chase had shown up here, screwing this up for me, and then kissed me without permission, which had totally bent me out of shape.

I massaged my temples and closed my eyes, letting out a growl. "I think I'm coming down with something. How about I make it up to you later this week, Katie?"

"Sure." She looked between us.

When I opened my eyes, I saw Chase was taking care of the bill. I tried to pay my part, slide my credit card his way, but he just put his hand on mine and smiled at me.

"Never, sweetheart."

"Such a gentleman."

"You have no idea."

"That"—I sat back, fighting the urge to throttle him—"is true."

That's what happens when you muster some sympathy for the devil, I thought bitterly. *He drags you to hell, and you get burned.*

◆ ◆ ◆

Mothers of brides all over America were going to buy fuzzy-looking dresses with angry, sharp lines that fall. My designs were not up to par with my usual clean, romantic style.

I was so furious after the meal with Chase and Katie that I ripped three papers while trying to sketch. I was sitting in front of a blurry shape of the female body—no stitch of clothing on it yet—when my phone pinged with a message.

Chase: I bet you're still thinking about that kiss.

Maddie: I chugged bleach as soon as I got back to the office. It helped, a little.

Maddie: What the hell did you think you were doing?

Chase: Playing the loving fiancé.

Maddie: We're done playing. We had an agreement, and I did my part.

Maddie: You ambushed me. You knew I'd be there. Why did you do it?

Chase: I decided our engagement story needed more reinforcement, since you went and hugged Tights Guy publicly.

Chase: Extra long.

Chase: Like couples in the movies.

Maddie: I said he was a friend!

Chase: It still happened.

Chase: (it did happen, didn't it?)

Maddie: Yeah. I stress-baked extra cookies last week and decided to bring him some.

Chase: What kind of person makes out with her boyfriend at a pediatric clinic?

Maddie: IT. WAS. JUST. A. HUG!

I felt like Ross yelling at Rachel, "WE WERE ON A BREAK."

Maddie: Wait, why am I defending myself to you?

Chase: Because I'm your fiancé.

Maddie: FAKE FIANCÉ.

Chase: Tell that to the real engagement photo shoot my mother had scheduled for us next week. I'll email you the details in a bit.

"Gawwwd," Nina drawled behind me at the top of her voice. "You even type messages loudly. Do you realize you whisper everything you write? You're so basic."

I dropped my pencil, before storming to the elevators. I slipped into a closing one, kicking my leg inside to pry the doors open, then hit the button leading to the top floor—Black & Co.'s management. I'd never set foot in there before, and the prospect of storming in raising hell was less than appealing. But I couldn't take it anymore. It was obvious Chase was breaking all the rules in our agreement. I tapped my foot throughout the entire ride, imagining all the ways I was going to kill Chase when I finally got to him. *Knife. Gun. Arson.* The possibilities were endless, really.

The elevator dinged open. I purged myself out of it, advancing straight to the biggest fishbowl office on instinct.

"Miss!"

"Excuse me!"

"Do you have a pass?"

Stuttering receptionists and flustered secretaries were on my heels, stumbling behind me on their sensible wedges. A sleepy herd of suited men watched from the sidelines of the office, holding stacks of papers and files. I slapped the glass door to Chase's office open with my palm.

"You!"

Bastard didn't even look up from the documents he was reading. Just turned a page very slowly, making a show of frowning at whatever he was reading. I took it as an invitation to walk right in. Two receptionists popped up behind my shoulders.

"I'm so sorry, Mr. Black; she just burst in—"

"—didn't even see her name tag! Security's on the way."

"It's fine." He cut them off in a way that implied it wasn't fine. "Leave."

The two of them shared a confused look, then bowed their heads in unison and scurried out of his office. Chase finally looked up from his documents. He looked shockingly composed for someone who'd just gotten called out in the middle of his office.

"Miss Goldbloom, how may I be of help?"

I slammed the glass door behind me, refusing to take in the thrilling richness of his work environment. The chrome desk, huge Apple screen, floor-to-ceiling window overlooking Manhattan, and gray-and-white furniture.

"I—" I started, but he stopped me, lifting his palm up, then opened a drawer in his desk and retrieved a remote control he used to close the black shades in his office automatically. I blinked. Now we were alone *and* completely hidden from the world. His colleagues could see nothing, and I could only guess what they were thinking.

Office sex. Lord, I hated him and his games.

"You were saying?" He sat back, amusement flashing in his eyes. That was a good question. What *was* I saying? I shook my head.

"You're taking advantage of the goodness of my heart. I told you we were done after that dinner. You have no business kissing me or agreeing to photo shoots with me."

"I'll walk Daisy every day."

"Until when?" I scoffed.

"Until my dad dies," he replied flatly.

I tried not to let the weight of his sentence sink into me but felt my shoulders slumping nonetheless. "Chase," I said softly. "We both want him to live as much as he can. It's not fair on both of us."

"The hell with what we want—he has a couple months, at best," he growled, looking away from me. "Less, probably."

"This is not sustainable." My voice was so quiet it sounded more like a breath.

"We don't need to be sustainable. We're not fucking plastic bags."

"I would rather wrap one around my head than play house with you," I muttered, immediately regretting my words. He was hurting. His entire being bled this fact. The way he talked about his dad, had looked at him from across the table over dinner.

Chase rose from his seat, smirking darkly at me. "You're a terrible liar."

"I'm not lying."

"When you told Katie our breakup story, you had tears in your eyes. You're not over me." He leaned forward across his desk, only a breath away from putting his lips on mine. "However, contrary to your predictions, you will be *under* me."

I felt my lower lip wobbling and crossed my arms over my chest. I wanted to get out of here. I wasn't even entirely sure what had made me come to his office in the first place. Chase rounded his desk, every inch of him the cool businessman I loved to hate.

"Madison." My name was a command.

I jutted my chin out defiantly as he leaned against his desk, ankles crossed, hands shoved inside his pockets. "I would like to restart our fake relationship," he said.

"Too bad it's not a Windows PC."

"If it were, I'd reformat it completely and backdate it to seven months ago," he surprised me by saying. A waft of his scent made its way into my system. Pine and wood and male and richness that couldn't be bought. He was the sun. Beautiful and blinding and capable of burning you alive. And I was a mere star in his constellation. Small and insignificant, utterly indistinguishable to the naked eye.

"You screwed up long before I caught you with her."

But even as I said it, I knew it wasn't the truth. Not entirely, anyway.

I'd been a watered-down version of myself to appease him, forever a martyr.

And he was an egomaniacal, self-centered playboy who'd regarded me carelessly and never bothered to get to know me. But the thing was . . . the old Maddie had let him treat her this way. The person I was now, however, wasn't having it. Not at all.

My eyes dipped from his gaze to his mouth, determined not to show him what was behind my pupils. I wondered why he couldn't show me a fraction of the sympathy I showed him and leave me alone. The very existence of him was tearing me apart.

"Madison," he croaked.

"Chase."

His fingers fanned across the side of my neck, his gaze holding mine, penetrating the thin wall of determination I'd put between us. I wanted to die. Die because Chase touching my neck felt more sexually maddening than being fully kissed and groped by Ethan.

"He doesn't have long, and Julian will uncover our charade in less than a week if we stop seeing each other now."

"What are you suggesting?"

"That we'll start seeing each other for the time being."

"No." My stomach felt hollow, my voice bouncing inside it.

"Why?"

"Because I hate you."

"Your body told me a different story when I leaned in to kiss you earlier." He advanced toward me predatorily, his movements sleek and smooth. His hand clawed into the tender flesh of my neck, and my belly clenched deliciously, approving of his touch. He was right. He was everything dark and sinful. Impossible not to yield to.

"My body is a liar." The words felt heavy on my tongue.

"Your mouth is, and hell if I don't want to fuck the truth out of it."

I looked away, watching him in my periphery leaning nearer and nearer. I took three steps back. He ate the distance between us with one stride. I walked backward. He followed me. Finally, my back hit the black blinds. Chase boxed me with his arms above my head, a menacing sneer on his lips.

No more barriers. Just us and that thick, almost tangible tension lingering in the air like sweet smoke.

"If you pretend to hate me . . ." His voice was silk and velvet, his hot breath fanning the side of my neck. "At least do it like you mean it."

His knee poked between my thighs as his mouth descended in slow motion onto mine. His body molded into my frame. I stood there, eyes open, watching in gut-swirling horror as his mouth met mine. Yet I pulled him closer, my nails sinking into his shoulder blades. His lips were warm and soft. Softer than I remembered. They felt different. Like his soul was touching mine through this brief brush of our lips. It surprised and scared me, how charged it felt to be in his arms, to drink from the well of his scent and warmth and feel.

He tasted like a touch of whiskey and mint gum, exploring, probing, awaiting permission to plunge in with his tongue. I sighed into our kiss, feeling my muscles relaxing without my consent. I was a pool of desire when Chase put his hands on my cheeks, framing me with his strong fingers.

"This is a bad idea," I heard myself whispering, but I still didn't let go of him.

He groaned, the tip of his tongue touching mine. A current ran through both of us, and we shivered into each other.

"I wish you were someone else." His lips spoke into mine. "Soulless, like me."

The door flew open before I swallowed his words with a hungry kiss.

"Ronan is waiting on that growth report from quarter three . . ." Julian stopped on the threshold, a folder in his hands, his eyes on us. Chase's mouth left mine swiftly, and my gaze dropped to the floor. I was horrified, but I wasn't sure why. As far as Julian was concerned, we were an engaged couple fooling around in Chase's office. If anything, getting caught was beneficial, so why did I feel like a fraud?

Julian curled his fingers over the doorknob, cocking his head sideways. His smile wasn't that of someone who'd caught two lovebirds having a clandestine moment. He looked like he was dissecting a mouse with a scalpel. "Please, don't stop on my account."

Chase tucked me under his arm. It was the first time I felt protected by him, and I didn't know what to make of it.

"Unfortunately, this is not a peep show, hence the drawn blinds. And the fucking *door*. Were you born on a bus? Knock, God dammit."

Julian propped his shoulder against the doorframe, grinning fully now. "Are you blushing, brother? Is there anything I should know?"

"Yes. If I ever get a chance to piss in your drink, rest assured, I will do it. No second thoughts."

"You seem very . . . *prickly*." Julian rubbed at his chin, looking between us. "Dare I say, even uncomfortable together."

"We felt very comfortable yesterday, when we broke your bed together, weren't we, baby?" Chase dropped an impersonal kiss on my head. I nodded stiffly, more concerned with sticking it to Julian than berating Chase at the moment.

"Don't worry. I'll send a replacement this afternoon." Chase chucked my chin lovingly. He was disgustingly good at playing the dutiful fiancé.

"Make it white. I'm redecorating." I played along.

"Bull, meet shit. I wasn't born yesterday." Julian's beady eyes danced in their sockets. "You're lying. You're not together, but Chase is now working his way back into your good graces, and the naive little girl that you are—you are falling for it."

I swallowed down my pride—and anger—keeping my smile intact. A part of me had pondered the same thing. Whether Chase had suddenly begun to kiss me and take interest in me just because he needed to keep me close. I knew very well that he wanted us to be fake-real-dating. With all the perks of a couple, but without the commitment and feelings.

"I really don't appreciate what you are insinuating," I heard myself say in my bubbly, customer-oriented, can't-we-all-just-get-along voice. "Chase and I have been together for almost a year. I understand in light of what Clementine said, you are a little suspicious, but you are being unnecessarily crude right now."

"Oh, Maddie," Julian sighed melodramatically in the same tone he'd say, *Oh, you little idiot.* "We both know you two weren't together the entire time."

"We do?" I perked up, going for sarcasm. Chase's body quivered with an unrestrained chuckle next to me.

"Unless he cheated on you with at least three women. Chase here is not very good at keeping his private business . . . well, private. And I do like to pay him surprise visits, just to check on my baby bro." He winked at Chase.

I felt physically sick, even though Julian's information came as no surprise to me. I knew Chase had hooked up with women after we'd broken up. Sven had flat-out told me so. And yet feeling his arm draped on me and knowing it to be true made me want to curl into a ball of misery and self-loathing.

"All is forgiven and forgotten," I said breezily, swallowing down the bile in my throat. I hated Chase so much in that moment I wanted to stab him with a sketching pencil. I felt like Eliza Hamilton. Smiling to the world to save face while her brilliantly devastating husband owned up to his affairs.

"Is that so?" Julian arched a cynical brow.

"People make mistakes all the time," I gritted out.

"Yes. Your husband-to-be seems to be living proof of that. And now he is faithful, I'm guessing?"

"More than your wife ever will be." Chase shrugged.

"Watch it." Julian lifted a warning finger.

"Seen enough." Chase sucked his teeth, a taunting grin playing on his face. "And cut the brotherly bullshit. Our relationship died the day Dad announced me as the future CEO. Just remember, Julian, in war, there are winners and losers. Historically speaking, the winners don't take mercy on those who tried to dethrone them."

My eyes ping-ponged between the two men. I was trapped in the unfurling of a family calamity. Finally, I stepped between them, a referee of sorts.

"Okay, that's enough. Chase, give him the quarterly . . . growth . . . whatever." I gestured impatiently with my hand to the folder on his desk. Chase took the paper he'd been reading earlier and held it out to Julian. "Julian, please give us some privacy, and do knock next time. Thank you."

I physically closed the door behind Julian to speed up the process. Being around them together was exhausting. I turned to Chase. "About what we discussed. To continue this until . . ."

Your father dies. I couldn't complete the sentence. We both looked away. I thought about Mom. Specifically, about one of her letters, where she said there was beauty in everything. Even in losing someone. I'd been so mad when I'd read it that I'd taken a lighter to it and started burning it before chickening out. To this day, it was the only letter in less than pristine condition. It was blackened around the edges, marshmallow-like. "I'm sorry, Chase, but I can't do this. I would if I could, but I don't want to get hurt. And this"—I motioned between us—"it's already killing me, and it's not even real."

I shook my head, escaping his office before he had the chance to convince me otherwise. To lure me into his devil's den, which was full of dark, gorgeous things I wanted to explore.

I tripped back to the elevators, my feet moving on their own accord. I glanced at Chase's office, ignoring the blur of faces staring at me curiously from all corners of the room. The blinds were still drawn.

When I got back to the studio, an email from Nina awaited me. It was sent to my Gmail, as opposed to my company email, where it could be seen by HR in one of their random checks.

> Maddie,
>
> You've received flowers from some loser who thanked you for sending her a wedding dress after an article about her making herself a wedding dress out of toilet paper (WTF?).
>
> They're by your drawing board, right next to a picture of her in your dress. The dress looks hideous. So does the bride. Please stop hoarding flowers in the office. Some of us actually suffer from allergies.
>
> —Nina

I was tempted to write something back to her. Something vicious and offensive. Then decided I didn't want Sven to know there was trouble between me and the pretty intern. Instead, I collected my things, watered my flowers, grabbed the Polaroid of the bride I'd sent the dress to, and then slunk back home to lick my wounds.

CHAPTER ELEVEN

MADDIE

There were two delivery guys waiting at my building door. They were holding a huge cardboard box, yelling directions at each other, rolled cigarettes sticking from the side of their mouths. I squinted, rushing toward them. "Can I help you?"

"We sure hope so, ma'am," the sweatier one of the two grumbled.

"Bed frame delivery for Goldbloom?" The second guy, a pimply kid of nineteen, blew a dreadlock out of his face, dropping the rollie on the ground in the process. I felt my eyes widening.

No, he didn't.

"Yes, that's me. A *bed frame*?"

They nodded. "Don't look so surprised. You paid extra for rush delivery."

I fought a giddy smile. "Is it white?"

The teenager bristled. "Whiter than my knuckles, ma'am. Can we come in?"

I let them through. I resisted the urge to text Chase, even if just to say thank you, not trusting myself not to cave to his advances. Truth was, I couldn't afford to help him anymore. I was beginning to not hate him, and that was a luxury I couldn't afford, because Chase was still Chase.

The man who'd cheated on me.

The man who'd brought countless women to his bed after we'd broken up.

The devil in the dapper suit, who wore his smile like a weapon.

After the delivery guys left—promptly tipped and sent away with cans of Diet Coke—Ethan arrived. He showed up earlier than we'd arranged, carrying Mexican food. ("Can you believe China Palace closed early? Nothing is going as planned today!") We sat down at my coffee table, which also served as my dining table, seeing as my apartment was the size of a shoebox. Daisy was pestering us for scraps, shoving her nose into the food containers and whimpering. I focused on eating the broken chips only (for solidarity purposes), my mind still reeling from those two kisses with Chase. I knew what I had to do and dreaded the poor timing, especially on the day Ethan and I were supposed to sleep with each other. I put my taco down, turning to Ethan on the couch. We were watching the local news, after the record player had broken down on us, completely ruining the already tarnished mood. Ethan was eating with gusto, engrossed in a news piece about a new footpath gate in Brooklyn that was too noisy for the residents living around it.

"So I have to tell you something." I cleared my throat. He looked up, pieces of cheese and shredded lettuce peeking from his mouth. God, I really didn't want to do this.

"I saw Chase today. Not voluntarily. His sister invited me for lunch, and he showed up. One thing led to another, and we kissed. I'm really sorry, Ethan. I've been feeling shitty about it all day."

I was referring to the second kiss. The one with my full consent. The one that had felt like our souls were dancing together, that could have led to more than just a kiss.

Ethan put his taco down, reluctantly turning his attention from an elderly woman on TV complaining about the loud gate under her apartment building to me. "You kissed him in front of his sister?" he asked, confused.

What?

"Yes. I mean, no. I mean, yes, on the lips, a peck, I suppose. He initiated it. Then I went to his office to confront him about it, and we kissed again." Pause. "A real kiss."

"Let me get this straight." He frowned. "You went to yell at him about kissing you, then let him kiss you again?"

Admittedly, I wasn't explaining it really well. Not that there was a way to explain the insanity that was Chase and me together.

"I know it's weird. I can't even explain how it happened. One moment I was yelling my lungs out at him, and the next . . ."

He was shutting me up with a bone-melting kiss.

"What does he want from you?" Ethan scowled, dropping his taco on his paper plate. He wasn't so happy about my fake engagement anymore. Maybe because parts of it were beginning to feel real. "He can't seem to let you go, but he sure as hell did a fine job scaring you off when he had you."

I'm sorry, how is Natalie doing? I was tempted to ask. He wasn't really in a position to give me crap.

"He wants us to continue pretending until his dad passes away." I blinked at the shabby flowery rug under my coffee table. It was full of crumbles from the crunchy tacos. Daisy was nowhere in sight to clean them up, so my guess was she was trying to piss into Ethan's shoes, as she did with every person who entered her fort and wasn't me. I'd had the good sense to place his shoes inside a plastic bag on the stand by the door.

"And put your life on hold?" Ethan scowled. "How very considerate of him."

"I said no."

"Of course you said no!" Ethan threw his hands in the air, then paused. "Wait, why did you say no?"

Why had I, really? Who knew? Because I was scared. Because it had seemed like the right thing to do. Shout-out to the people who understood the ins and outs of their decisions. I wasn't one of them. I mainly went out on a limb and tried to follow my logic and whatever I thought Dr. Phil would say about my situation.

"Because of you."

I mean, it was half the truth. Well . . . maybe a quarter. The main reason was I knew Chase was more than capable of breaking my heart again.

Ethan scratched his smooth jaw. "I don't like him."

"Me either." *Another* lie.

"Then I don't see the problem." He picked up his taco again. "The fake engagement is over; you are officially back on the market. So what if you kissed? I . . ." He stopped himself at the last minute. "I did things, too, while we were each seeing other people. That's why we've decided to wait until now before we take things to the next level." He arched his brows meaningfully. "Welcome to the next level, Maddie."

"I'm not ready for the next level yet." I tore the already shredded lettuce between my fingers meticulously, not meeting his eyes.

"We don't have to today."

I shook my head, closing my eyes.

"Or tomorrow, even," he began to bargain.

"I don't know if it's a good idea, period. That kiss happened for a reason. Maybe I'm not completely over Chase. I thought I was when I signed up for SeriousSinglesOnly. I truly did. But now I'm not so sure."

"You just said you refused him because of me," Ethan pointed out.

"Yes, because I want someone like you," I agreed. "I just don't know if I'm ready to move on."

Our silence was punctuated by the robotic voice of the news anchor on TV, who moved to another item, about a nineteen-year-old criminal who carved his name onto his girlfriend's face. His name was Constantine Lewis. I bet if Chase were watching it right now, he'd say he hoped to hell he'd at least had the good manners to carve *Stan* for short.

I was predicting what Chase would say or think. How he'd react. I thought about him every waking moment. What he was doing, thinking, eating. Who he was seeing. I was *definitely* not over him.

"I'm really sorry, Ethan. I'm horrified that I put you through this. For what it's worth, you're absolutely perfect."

"You're giving me the it's-not-you-it's-me cliché." He clutched the left side of his shirt, but his voice lacked venom. "Ouch."

"It pains me more than it does you." I smiled tiredly.

"But you want to get over him. It's half the journey."

I said nothing, because it was the truth.

"Can I at least have a say in this? I'm the wronged party here, supposedly."

I chuckled. "That's fair."

"I'd like to think about it. About whether I want to forgive you for doing the unforgivable and kissing your billionaire, hotshot, not-ugly ex-boyfriend."

I full-blown cackled now. "Are you reserving the right to dump me?"

"Nicely," Ethan corrected. "And yes. I'm not sure I'm ready to give up on this, whatever it is. I appreciate your fair warning I might get hurt, but I might still want to give it a shot. Deal?" He offered me his hand. I took it, shaking it with a stupid smile. It was the nicest thing that had happened to me today.

"Deal."

We fell into comfortable silence, eating the rest of our meal, until we heard a thin sound of liquid coming from the door, followed by a puppy growl.

"Daisy!" I jumped from the couch, but it was too late. My chocolate-colored Aussiedoodle was already standing by the door, tattered plastic bag in her mouth, peeing straight into Ethan's shoes.

◆ ◆ ◆

I spent the next three days screening Chase's calls. Even though Ethan reserved the right to change his mind about us, I hadn't heard from him since our Mexican-food night. I was mildly relieved by this turn of events. It was one less thing to worry about. I did send Ethan an apologetic, lengthy text message before Layla told me to stop being more saintly than the pope. "The man dicked someone else the day he wined and dined you. You were obviously not *that* committed to one another."

Three days post the nuclear kisses and sort-of breakup from my nonboyfriend, Ethan, and I was beginning to breathe again. Shallow, tentative breaths of someone who knew it wasn't over yet.

Ronan was still sick.

Chase was a man who always got what he wanted.

As for me? I was slowly learning to stand up for myself.

I threw myself into work and finished three sketches for the Mother of the Bride collection. I made one of the sketches in honor of Mom, drawing the model with the same orange turban she'd worn when she'd been going through chemo. She had the same smiling hazel eyes as Mom and the same full lips and freckles. The dress was floral and big and lacy. Something Mom would've worn for my wedding. When Sven saw the final designs, I could see the confusion in his face. It wasn't common practice to put details into the face of a model in a sketch. Then the penny dropped, and he reached to squeeze my shoulder, exhaling. "She'd have loved it."

"You think?" I asked quietly.

"I *know*."

I prayed my next assignment wasn't going to be mother related. I missed my mom more than ever, wishing she were here to help me sort the Chase/Ethan mess. So when Sven approached me after I finished the Mother of the Bride collection, I was already holding my breath.

"Maddie, I need your attention." Sven snapped his fingers, swaggering his way to my corner of the studio. I fluffed my white and pink lilies, eyeing him curiously. He stopped a few feet from me, thrusting a stack of papers into my hands. "Your assignment."

I swiveled on my stool fully, crossing my legs and holding my pencil between my teeth like it was a cigarette. I opened the file he'd handed to me. It was a thin one, and when I flipped through it, I noticed it was because it didn't have all the things they usually gave us in a packet: mock-ups of the general fashion line, bullet points of what needed to be done, etc.

"It's been a long time coming, but you've worked the hardest for years, and I think you deserve this chance," Sven said as I read the words on the assignment packet again and again.

The Wedding Dress to End All Wedding Dresses: Croquis's Flagship Wedding Gown

My fingers trembled around the document, and my heartbeat pulsated in my neck.

"We are launching our fall collection at the New York Fashion Week in a couple months. Traditionally, the opening item is the Dream Wedding Dress. As you know, it is the most prestigious spot in the runway show. Usually reserved for our heavy-hitting designers. It's the dress all the Vera Wang, Valentino, and Oscar de la Renta folks are going to be looking at. The one the front-row celebrities will be ordering for their weddings. The cherry on the cake. *You're* going to design it."

I knew all of this. This was a huge deal. The person who'd designed it last year had moved up and now worked for Carolina Herrera. Rather than answering him with words, I chose the moment to ungracefully fall apart. Literally, I fell down on my ass from my chair, I was so stunned. I tried to keep my happy tears at bay, but it was hard, because I'd never thought I'd be able to secure something so prestigious so early into my career.

"Get a handle on gravity, Maddie," Sven muttered, offering me his hand, hoisting me back up to my feet. "When Layla told me you were going to fall on your ass, I didn't know she was being literal."

"Layla knows I got the assignment?" I gasped, covering my mouth with both hands. But of course she did. God, these two really annoyed me. "Sven, you won't regret it, I promise."

"Stop it. I chose you to be my star designer this year. More specifically, your designs didn't bore me to death. I want you to go really wild and off the wall with this one. You've shown that you can take instructions well, but now I want to see the mad hatter in you. The artist."

"You got it." I did my best not to jump up and down, laughing through my unstoppable happy tears, which I was no longer able to hold back. I usually reserved my tears for good news and Disney movies.

"When is it due?" I asked.

"A couple months, so you better get your butt in gear." He made a whiplash sound. "Oh, and before you ask—it doesn't come with a bonus," he pointed out dryly.

"Starving artist for the win." I fist-pumped the air. "How is Francisco doing, by the way?"

"Still wanting a child."

"And you?"

"Still wanting to run away with my Equinox trainer."

"Liar," I said softly, rubbing his forearm. I didn't press for more info, though. If Sven wanted to tell me more about his adoption case, he would.

I was busy browsing through my assignment packet, memorizing all the details, when I heard a bored voice behind me. "Maddie Goldbloom?"

"Right here," I singsonged, still on a high. I turned around, coming face-to-face with a young delivery guy in yellow overalls and a purple hoodie underneath. He was holding a bouquet of lilies.

"Delivery for you." He thrust a digital screen at me to sign. I did, stabbing the screen with the gray plastic pen.

"Ugh. Those things never work. My signature ends up being nothing more than a jagged gray line," I muttered, scribbling harder.

"Don't worry, dude. It's just for legal purposes. Nobody is planning to sell it on eBay." The delivery guy flipped his hair sideways. I took my white lilies, placed them next to my own flowers, and fished for the note. I knew Nina was going to have a field day about the addition of more flowers to my corner of the office.

I finally found the small note and opened it with shaky fingers. I didn't let myself hope. Which was a good thing.

Maddie,

After long and careful consideration, I decided whatever it is you are willing to give me—I'm willing to take it.

I'm in.

—Ethan

I took a picture of the note and sent it to Layla. Her name flashed on my screen after no longer than five seconds.

"Oh. My—"

"Don't you have class?" I cut into her speech.

"I do. Teaching preschoolers independency and self-management is highly important, I'll have you know." She snickered. I heard her voice echo as she settled in the empty hallway. "I'll be honest—I didn't think Ethan had a chance after Chase barged back into the picture, but this is a game changer. He is basically agreeing to be the sidepiece. *Juicy.*"

"No, he isn't," I protested.

"You know what you need to do?"

"No, but I have a feeling you're about to tell me."

"You have to screw both and see which one's better."

I already had a feeling I knew who took the cake (and orgasms). I stared at the note tucked inside the flowers, feeling nothing but dread and disappointment.

"That won't be fair to one of them." I munched on my lower lip.

"Hmm, no. It would just cement the fact Chase surpasses Ethan and that you have to put on your big-girl panties and just cut Ethan loose. I'm the first to admit Chase is not boyfriend material—the guy is the male version of me. But Ethan . . ." Layla tsked. "Nah-ah."

"Is that all?" I groaned.

"No. I also want to report Grant is excellent in the sack and congratulate you on your assignment. Love you."

"Yeah, me too." I hung up.

I texted Ethan a quick thank-you message, asking him if he wanted to grab coffee. It was the least I could do after his sweet gesture. His reply was immediate.

Ethan: I would very much like that.

I smoothed a blank page over my drawing board, blinking at it with a smile when I thought about my Dream Wedding Dress assignment. There was nothing that excited me more than a blank page. The possibilities were endless. It could be amazing or mediocre or bad or a masterpiece. The fate of the dress that was about to grace the page was yet to be written. It was my job to write its story.

"What am I going to do with you?" I whispered, tapping my charcoal pencil on my lips, grinning at the page.

"I'm thinking a good meal, followed by first base in the cab, followed by eating you out in the elevator up to my penthouse—sorry, I won't be able to resist—followed by a fuck-fest that would make Jenna Jameson blush."

I gasped, turning around to see where the voice came from. I recognized the deadpan, wry tone on impact. My knees buckled, but this time I didn't fall off my chair.

"You cannot sa—"

"Not your boss," he pointed out before I finished my sentence.

"Just because I don't work for you doesn't mean you're not sexually harassing me."

"Am I sexually harassing you?" He slanted his head sideways, cocking an eyebrow.

No.

My face must've conveyed my answer, because he let out a deep, rumbling chuckle.

"What are you doing here?" I scowled at Chase. He matched his black suit with a burgundy tie, hand tucked in his pocket, his Rolex poking out. He was the closest thing to corporate porn I'd ever seen in my life.

"Seeking you out," he said unapologetically, glancing at the three vases full of flowers by my desk. "One vase you keep because of your mom," he said, making my heart jolt in surprise. He remembered? "Who sent you the other two?"

"Someone I sent a wedding dress to."

"And?"

"Ethan."

"His are the lilies, right?" He approached the flowers, tugging at a petal. I flinched. "Nice choice. Is he mourning the premature end of your relationship?"

"The relationship with Ethan is not dead."

He threw his head back, laughing carelessly. "Put him out of his misery, Mad. It's game over for Dr. Seuss. A bunch of flowers aren't going to change that."

"A bunch of flowers change everything"—I slapped his hand away, protecting the flowers—"to a florist's daughter."

He cocked his head, looking at me funny now. I didn't like his look. It was the look of a man with a plan, and I didn't think Chase's plans and mine were aligned.

"Is that so?" A glint of mischief flickered in his eyes.

I looked away as if hit by his beauty. I hated the giddiness that seeped its way into my gut every time his eyes were on me.

"Come with me." He opened his palm. I didn't take it.

"I don't think so."

"It's not a request."

"It's also not the seventeenth century. You can't order me around."

"That's true, but I can make a scene that would make you wish you've never met me."

"I already wish that," I quipped, lying.

"You're wasting everyone's time. Ethan's, particularly. Martyr Maddie wants to have babies with Ethan. But the real you wants to take the plunge, drown with me. Come on."

It was pointless to argue with him. Moreover, I couldn't concentrate on creating the Dream Wedding Dress—DWD for short—when the mystery of what Chase wanted to show me hung above my head. It was disconcerting to think he had a sixth sense of when Ethan was making a move and had chosen the exact same day and hour to show up. I followed Chase to the elevator, dodging the curious looks of people around me. Sven had his back to us. He was tucked inside his glass office, talking on the phone animatedly with a fabric provider who had screwed up one of his orders. But Nina was there, poised elegantly in her seat, watching us while filing her nails. There were at least a dozen colleagues—designers, seamstresses, and interns—who eyed us curiously as we made our way out of the studio. Luckily, other than Nina, I considered most of them friends and knew they liked me enough not to think the worst of me. Still.

"People are going to talk," I complained under my breath.

"As long as you are the subject and not the one doing the talking, I cannot see how this is an issue."

We entered the elevator. "I'm not like you. I'm not untouchable."

"Madison Goldbloom, I wish you were touchable to me," he said earnestly as the elevator doors slid shut on us in slow motion. "I wish that very, very much."

CHAPTER TWELVE

Chase

I took her to the biggest flower shop in New York City. A Midtown florist by the Empire State Building.

Mad dragged her feet and scowled the entire time like a pouty teenager, throwing looks over her shoulder to make sure we weren't seen together. Most women I knew would pay good money to be seen with me. Not this one. Having her around felt liberating. Like taking a vacation from the chaos in my head. True, I was never going to offer her marriage, but I could still offer her a hell of a good time. This time, I was serious about making her mine.

Temporarily mine.

Hell, she could even reclaim her girlfriend title.

Bonus points: I'd get to keep Julian off my fucking case.

The plan was bulletproof.

We passed the florist's display window. Bouquets of colorful flowers and a sign that said **Love Is a Big Deal** stared back at us. No wonder she was so obsessed with marriage and love—her parents had crammed it down her throat since the day she was born. I pushed the door open, waiting for her to walk in. Once inside, Madison turned to me, crossing her arms over her chest. She wore a yellow chick-patterned dress with a darling collar and a black velvet necktie and a youthful blush. Which, unfortunately, made me look like her perverted older uncle.

"What now? You're going to buy me all the roses in the shop and proclaim your undying love for me?" She rolled her eyes.

"Not quite. I'm buying Ethan flowers."

"You're buying Ethan flowers?" Madison echoed, letting her mouth drop into a perfect O shape.

"Yes. And myself."

"*And* yourself."

"Are you just going to repeat everything I say?" I inquired politely.

"Yes, until you make some sort of sense to me."

"Very well." I took her hand in mine—the second time we'd held hands in a week—dragging her deeper into the store. The scent of pollen was so thickly sweet I almost gagged. I didn't know how Mad could like it. But of course she could. It smelled like her childhood and nostalgia and her *mother*. I didn't know how I hadn't thought of it before. Kudos to Ethan for figuring it out before me. Flowers. Simply fucking genius.

"I understand you have some reservations regarding our relationship and would like to tweak the fine print of our arrangement. Remember I told you I want to keep doing this until my father passes away?" I asked, ignoring how bitter the words felt in my mouth.

Dad was feeling like shit, but he continued coming to work every day. Julian was running around dropping hints about the state of Dad's health to shareholders and investors, anonymously tipping the media about a major change coming on the board. Grant had caught him in the act, after Julian had checked into a hotel room twenty minutes before a Wall Street reporter was directed into the same room. My best friend had been at the restaurant in the lobby of the hotel, having lunch with his mother.

My cousin was definitely going for what we called in chess "the double attack."

"By 'doing this,' you mean 'doing me,' right?" Madison frowned, her eyes roaming the place like it was a candy shop. She couldn't help herself. She touched an orange-purple flower, fingering its velvety petal between her fingers and shivering with pleasure. That was all it took to make my cock jerk in my pants.

"Yes," I said. "But I decided to give you the whole fiancée package at the discount price of just having your company."

"What does the fiancée package include?" She yawned. Not a good start.

"Dating, movie nights, restaurants, fucking, meeting your dad." I let that last one sink in, watching her face, but she remained stoic, focused on the flowers in front of her as she leaned down to sniff the sunflowers.

"I'm serious about this," I added.

"You cheated on me," she pointed out for the millionth time.

Not this old tune again. It was time she knew the truth. I touched her arm, making her gaze dart up to mine. "I didn't cheat on you."

She groaned, pretending not to care. "I saw you."

"No, what you saw was me coming into my apartment with someone else. You didn't see me touch her. You didn't see me kiss her. I never did."

"There were lipstick marks on your dress shirt." She turned around to me fully now. She wasn't whispering either. A thirtysomething couple who was very clearly looking at flowers for their wedding eyed us curiously.

Keep watching, assholes.

"It wasn't my shirt."

"Of course it wasn't." Mad threw her head back and laughed. A bitter laugh I never wanted to hear from her mouth again. It sounded foreign. Completely un-Madison-like. The woman next to the man beside us elbowed her beau, cocking her head in our direction. Un-fucking-believable. I gave the husband-to-be a what-the-fuck glare.

He shrugged helplessly. "Sorry, bro. Sounds like you kind of brought this on yourself." He chuckled.

I turned my attention back to Madison. "The shirt wasn't mine. It was Grant's. He hooked up with someone. No, let me amend—he was in the middle of hooking up with someone and got called in for work. Understandably, he couldn't show up wearing a shirt that suggested he was vacationing in Ho Island."

"So you volunteered your shirt." More sarcasm.

"Correct," I gritted out. "Remember that shirt? It was white. I don't wear white. I only wear—"

"Black," she finished for me, her eyes flaring. She had a light bulb moment. I'd worn black that day. Hell, I wore black any day. There was a beat of silence. The couple beside us looked invested in our exchange, and I'd have given them a piece of my mind if I weren't completely focused on explaining to Madison what she'd really seen that night.

"It doesn't matter, anyway. So what if it was Grant's shirt? The woman you brought home was real. I saw her. I guess she just followed you? No"—she held her hand up, smiling, but there was nothing happy about that smile—"she was just running away from an ax murderer, and you gave her shelter, right?"

The woman beside us giggled. Her fiancé tucked his chin down, hiding a grin. I was going to kill someone. Likely myself for coming up with that stupid plan in the first place.

"I brought her home because I knew you'd be there," I said dryly.

"You couldn't have." Mad shook her head. "I told no one other than . . ."

"Katie," I finished for her. "Katie told me. I mentioned I might spend my birthday weekend in Florida with Grant. She told me I wouldn't want to do that, then revealed your plan."

By the look on Madison's face, I knew the penny had dropped. Caught in an emotional tornado at the restaurant the other day, Mad had forgotten she'd told Katie about the birthday surprise prior to waiting in my apartment. So at the restaurant, she recited her story about the cheating bastard she caught, but she wasn't privy to the fact Katie had told me about Madison waiting for me in lingerie in my bed.

And she forgot she herself had informed Katie she'd be waiting for me in my bedroom.

Katie wasn't stupid. She'd done the math but hadn't said anything. At least one person in my family already knew what Julian was dying to uncover—I'd fucked up.

"And you brought her home so I'd catch you." Mad's nostrils flared.

"Yeah."

"Why?"

"Because I wanted you to see."

"Why?"

"Because things were getting too real too fast, and I don't do real, Madison. I think we both know I don't do fast either." I glared at the couple next to us pointedly. The guy blushed. *Really?* Now I didn't even care his girl was judging me. She was sentenced to a life with a prematurely ejaculating husband.

"My life will not be disturbed by senseless, messy emotions." I was mansplaining now. I needed to shut up.

"Okay, RoboCop," the woman beside us mumbled.

"You could've talked to me," Mad said.

"From experience, women don't get the message. They say they'll take it slow, but that just means biding their time. And no offense, but you are the most wedding-obsessed woman I've ever met. You design wedding dresses for a living, and between your apartment and office, you have enough flowers to put Holland out of business."

"You could've broken up with me." Mad's voice cracked midsentence. She wasn't wrong, and I hated when she wasn't wrong. I'd taken the coward's way out.

"I figured you'd get the message, get mad, then reappear in the form of a fuck buddy."

"Wow. For a smart person, you're really dumb." She sighed. In her defense, her face was full of awe rather than disdain.

"I concur." The woman beside us lifted her arm. "Super dumb move."

"Thanks for the input. I was anxious to know what a complete fucking stranger makes of my character." I threw her a polite smile before turning my gaze back to Madison and gathering her palms in mine. "I can't promise you forever, but I can promise you right now, and it's more than I've ever offered a woman before."

"Well, I appreciate your twisted, bizarre, backward-logic truth," Madison said, plucking her hands from mine and smoothing her dress over her thighs. "But even if you haven't cheated on me, the fact is you still hurt me. The answer is no."

"I figured you'd say this. Hence why I came here to buy Ethan and me flowers." I motioned around the flower shop like she didn't know where we were. It was not my brightest move, but the success of my plan was in jeopardy. "You know your flowers, right? I'm going to get an identical plant for both Ethan and me. The one that's most difficult to keep alive indoors—your pick. If Ethan really is Mr. Perfect and I'm such a shitbag, surely he can show his commitment by keeping the plant alive."

She blinked at me. "Not following your logic."

"The jasmines." I worked hard on not baring my teeth like an animal. "You said you care when flowers die, right? Gave me a whole goddamn speech about it, if I recall correctly. You're obsessed with flowers and keeping them alive." I took a breath, realizing that she associated the flowers at her desk with her mother, and her mother was dead, and flowers really meant a whole fucking lot to her. "You're rabid about the subject."

"You're really selling this grand gesture to me." Madison scrunched her forehead. "But can you turn the asshole in you down a notch while explaining this so I can see past the fog of wanting to punch you in the face? Thank you."

I suppressed a smile. Real Maddie really was much better than the light, fat-free, gluten-free version who'd entered my life some months ago. Yeah, she was a do-gooder, but she was no pushover, I'd learned.

"You said you care about plants. That how people take care of them is a testament of their character. Well, I think Ethan doesn't care. Not enough. Not about you, at least. Not as much as me."

There was silence. When I looked up from her face, I noticed that the entire store was watching us, not just that thirtysomething couple. We'd had a very vocal argument, consisting of my (not so) cheating past and a declaration of intent, and now people knew there was another man in the game. I was one plastic surgery and nude scandal away from being a guest on *The Real Housewives of Whereverthefuck*.

"Azaleas," she whispered, looking deep in thought. Her legs carried her to the far end of the store. I followed her, spellbound. The couple choosing wedding flowers followed *me*. I turned around to stop them, holding a hand up.

"That's it for you, Mr. and Mrs. Peepson."

"But I want to know how it ends," the woman whined.

"Spoiler alert: I get the girl. Move along now."

I caught up with Madison standing in front of a bunch of blooming pink, red, and purple azaleas. Her eyes shone.

"They like cool, humid spaces and are considered to be almost impossible to make bloom. They'll be a headache to keep alive in New York in August. The task is nearly undoable. Only one in eleven azalea plants survives. I remember my dad *hated* keeping azaleas in their shop. He listed all the reasons why his customers needed to choose another flower when men bought them for their wives." Pause. "But my mom . . ." She trailed off. "They were her favorite. So every Friday, no matter what, rain or shine, he brought her azaleas."

"I'll keep my azaleas alive," I clipped.

She tore her gaze from the flowers, frowning at me. "How do I know you won't task your housekeeper with keeping them? Or hire a gardener?"

"Because I'm not an immoral bastard," I said simply. She gave me a disbelieving look. I supposed she had a point.

"I won't be an immoral bastard about this," I amended, and I let her pick two plants of her choosing. We walked to the cashier. Mad asked for a Sharpie, told me to turn around, and marked both plants in a way that would make her recognize them in case I got a replacement. I would ask her where the trust was, but considering everything we'd gone through together, I guessed the answer to that question was the bottom of a fucking trash can. There was no trust between us whatsoever.

I paid for the flowers, then told the cashier to put whatever the nosy couple ordered for their wedding on my tab. Madison stared at me like I'd lost my mind. I shrugged. "I'll see your Martyr Maddie and raise you Charity Chase with a side of Blissful Black."

She laughed. I wasn't ready for that laugh. It came out throaty and genuine, her eyes crinkling at the corners. My dick wasn't the first responder this time around. It was another organ. One that had sat dormant for years. One that had no business waking up.

"Afraid I'm going to beat your little boyfriend at his own flower game?" I raised an eyebrow, all nonchalant and shit.

"He is not my boyfr—" she started, then clapped her mouth shut. I flashed her a smile full of triumph.

It was on.

CHAPTER THIRTEEN

Maddie

November 15, 2004

Dear Maddie,

I wanted to thank you for being the best daughter in the world. Yesterday, I felt sick all day and didn't go to work. You went to help your father in the shop even though you had an important test the next day, and when you came back, you brought a bouquet of azaleas with you. My favorite (you remembered. You always do).

You told me you ate the petals secretly. They tasted like sweet nectar, you said. We pressed them into books in my bed, watching Steel Magnolias *and drinking sweetened tea. The flower made me feel loved. I hope one day they'll make you feel the same too.*

Love,
To the moon and back,
Mom. x

◆ ◆ ◆

I gave the azaleas to Ethan when we met for coffee. (**Tea,** he amended in a text message. **Coffee is highly unhealthy. I'll send you an article.**)

Instead of relaying my bet with Chase, which I thought was rude and presumptuous, I simply explained that the flowers meant a lot to me and gave them to him as a gift. Azaleas were Mom's favorite flowers, I explained, and they required special attention and a lot of care, but in return, their bloom was breathtakingly beautiful.

"They're a lot of work, but they're worth it."

"Reminds me of someone." He took a sip of his green tea, his smile stretching across his face like a wound. He looked different. Tired. I couldn't help but suspect I had a lot to do with it.

Since Ethan didn't know about the bet, which was a clear disadvantage, I balanced it out by printing out specific instructions of how to take care of the azaleas. Ethan shoved the plant and instructions under our table, before ordering a gluten-free pastry and launching into a speech about how he'd been invited to talk at a conference about children who suffered from anxiety. I immediately thought about Katie. How she'd be interested in listening to this lecture.

Then I thought about the moronic mistake I'd made the other day, when I'd forgotten she was privy to my waiting for Chase on his birthday and had basically blown up our cover to the sky.

As for Ethan, it was nice to hang out with him, but it lacked that feeling I had with Chase. Where every interaction felt divine, before the aftermath, in which I'd obsess about every single thing we'd said to each other.

The weekend rolled in, forcing me to unglue myself from the DWD project. I made plans with Layla, Sven, and Francisco. The latter two hosted their annual roof party on their neighbors' rooftop, serving low-calorie, low-carb mojitos and putting George Michael on blast. Sven was religious about throwing the bash once a year, explaining that he needed to channel his inner Kris Jenner without maxing his credit card. He sold the tickets at a hundred bucks a pop. A ticket would secure you a plastic sun bed, watered-down cocktails, Costco sandwich wraps, and Sven's glorious company for a few hours. All the money went to a charity of Sven's choice. This year, it was the Animal Protection Society.

The rooftop was jam-packed with Francisco's and Sven's colleagues and friends. "Born This Way" by Lady Gaga made the ground shake. Layla and I secured a couple of sun beds on the far end of the roof, away from a school of high-pitched interns from Francisco's office. I couldn't help but notice the penthouse level of Sven and Chase's building was parallel to the roof where the party took place. Which meant that Chase's living room was right in front of my face. As with all high-rises, the windows had tinted film, which meant he could look outside, but no one could see into his apartment. Not that I planned on looking into his place. Or that I tried to when no one was looking.

I closed my eyes, letting my skin soak in the sunrays. My sun bed was wonky, and I was probably going to come back home with red streaks all over me, but there was nowhere else I'd have rather been in that moment than here with my friends.

"Speaking of men, how's Grant?" I asked my best friend. Shortly after Chase and I had broken up, Layla had announced that she was interested in sleeping with Grant and asked if it would be okay by me. Of course it was. Grant seemed like a trustworthy man. But that was before Chase had told me he'd exchanged the lipstick-stained shirt with him. Although if I were being honest with myself, between Grant and Layla, the person who needed to guard their heart wasn't my best friend. She was notoriously against any sort of long-term romantic relationships.

"Super lickable, as per usual. He went to a bachelors' party in Miami."

"And you aren't worried he'll be sampling more than Cuban food and fruity cocktails there?" I asked.

Layla shook her head. "I sure hope he does. I told him we are only a fling. I even cemented the fact by going out with a total Tinder fuckboy so he realizes we're not exclusive. Alas, Grant is the marrying type."

"And you're not the marrying type because . . . ?" Francisco came over to us, dumping burgers onto a tray and then putting it on a set table. He sat on the edge of my sun bed.

"I don't want to have children." Layla shrugged. "And although the two don't have to go together, let's admit it—one insinuates the other. I just don't believe in marriage."

"Ethan is like that," I mused. "The marrying type, I mean."

"Yeah"—Layla cocked her head sideways—"but Grant is, you know, interesting."

"Ethan is interesting," I protested. "That's unfair. You haven't even met him."

"Is that why you still haven't let him put the tip in, Maddie?" Layla looked unconvinced.

Francisco leaned forward and tapped Layla's shoulder. "Show me Grant."

"Okay, but don't get attached. Because again—he's a total family man, and we're bound to break up once he realizes I'm serious about not settling down," Layla warned, twisting her torso to fish her phone from her bag. She took it out, holding my flower-cased phone too. "Here, you have a message from the commitment-phobe."

I caught my phone in midair, surprised that my body was in sync with my brain. My heart bounced around erratically like a frat boy looking for easy prey at a party. Chase had sent me a picture of the vivid-looking azaleas on his coffee table. I recognized his living room in the background. The minimal, impersonal space that always reminded me of a sad, plush hotel room where rock stars went to die.

Maddie: Color me impressed. The Nobel Prize people are on the way.

Chase: Is this code for "put some pants on"?

Maddie: Why would you NOT be wearing pants midday?

Chase: I'll have you know some of my favorite things are done pantsless. What are you doing?

Maddie: Sunbathing on the roof right across from your building.

Chase: If this is your way of coming on to me, it is highly unsubtle.

Chase: Also, that means you aren't wearing pants either.

Chase: Also 2: Remember what happened the last time we were in the same room not wearing any pants?

Maddie: I actually have no recollection of that ever happening. 😇

Chase: Always happy to refresh your memory. 😈

Maddie: We're not going to sext.

Chase: Great. I'll come over in a couple hours and give you a personal demonstration. You look like you're in need of some vitamin D.

Maddie: You'll be getting some vitamin P if you as much as try.

Chase: Not sure I'm familiar with that supplement?

Maddie: A Punch in the face.

Chase: You know, I thought you'd be a lot less ardent after realizing I hadn't cheated.

Maddie: Why? Wanting to scare me off by scarring me for life intentionally is only marginally worse than getting caught with your pants down.

Maddie: And yes, I know you're not wearing any pants. It doesn't bear repeating.

He sent me a picture of the lower half of his body, sitting on his black leather couch in dark-gray slacks. I'd never seen him in anything but black suits before, and stupidly, it threw me off guard. His legs were spread, and the imprint of his huge erection traced along his inner thigh. I felt my throat bob with a swallow and sucked in a breath. A million ants were dancing on my flesh with excitement. The caption read: **Nice bikini.** I looked down, examining my breasts in my swimming suit. Was he really looking at me through the window? His windows were tinted, but I still found myself struggling not to check.

"Why does Maddie look like she's about to faint?" Layla asked. "What is she looking at on her phone?"

"Looks like a super burrito from where I'm standing," Francisco said, humming.

"Oh, I would love some Mexican food with my mojito," Layla pondered. "Check the DoorDash time for that place down the road."

I ignored my friends, typing the words I knew I was going to regret. I was too flustered—too turned on—not to take Chase's bait. Besides, it was harmless flirting. I was single. Ethan was the first to keep pointing out how casual we were.

Maddie: Is that a gun, or are you just happy to see me?

I paused, wanting to shock him. To keep this electrical current between us sizzling. So I did the unbelievable. The unthinkable. I lifted my phone and took a selfie of myself in my pineapple-patterned bikini. I didn't have a *Sports Illustrated*–worthy body. Nothing like Amber's careful strokes of muscle and surgically enhanced curves. I was tiny, with wide hips and a flat, albeit soft, belly. I sent it to him, wincing as I did. In the background, I heard Layla complaining about my inability to say no to anything. "He probably asked her to sext him, and she can't refuse because no is not in her vocabulary."

"Did she just take a picture of herself in a bikini? She doesn't even post things to Instagram that don't include flowers and sketches," Francisco mumbled, losing interest.

Maddie: You mean this bikini?

Chase: Yes, that one. Yes, I am happy to see you, and yes, I would like to pound you so fucking hard I'll leave a dent in your shape through your mattress, that new bed frame I got you, and the carpet.

Maddie: Romantic. Is that Atticus?

Chase: Anonymous.

Maddie: Don't give up your day job. Poetry is not your forte.

Chase: O ye of little faith. I can be romantic if I want to be.

Maddie: Really? Let's see. This is going to be fun.

Chase: I would like to pound you so fucking hard I'll leave a dent in your shape through your mattress, that new bed frame I got you, and the carpet. Please. <3 <3 <3

Chase: How'd I do?

Maddie: Exquisite. Pablo Neruda's got nothing on you.

Chase: Does that mean I can come over tonight?

Maddie: No. And if you ever sext me again, I will block your number.

Chase: Keep lying to yourself.

Maddie: You think I won't do it? I wasn't very hesitant to cut you off from my life the first time around.

Chase: This is not the first time around, Mad. This is real, and we both know it.

Maddie: And that doesn't worry you?

Chase: Nothing worries me.

But that wasn't true, and we both knew that.

Losing Ronan Black worried him to death. In fact, I thought it might be the very reason why Chase didn't want to love someone new.

Chase Black rejected love because he was afraid of losing it.

And me? I chased it *because* I'd lost the greatest love of all.

We were bad for each other in all the ways that mattered. I wanted everything he was afraid of, and he despised everything I stood for. A sane girl would call off the stupid azalea bet, turn around, and run away.

I leaned forward, trying unsuccessfully to peek into Chase's window. I applied most of my weight to the edge of the sun bed. I tipped the entire thing over, falling the short way to the ground, taking Francisco with me.

On our way back home on the train, I rehashed my dating situation to Layla. I told her I had two options: a relationship with an expiration date with Chase, who was sure to leave my heart in tatters, versus a safe, steady relationship with sweet, reliable Ethan.

She considered both options with a frown, then said, "On one hand, you don't want Ethan. You don't talk about him the way you do about Chase. You don't have that glint in your eye when he calls or texts. On the other, Chase is a wild card, and if you sleep with him again, you will regret it at some point. He flat-out told you he doesn't want marriage. A wedding. Kids. Those things are important to you, Maddie. I don't want you to ever give them up for a pretty face in a dark suit. But I also don't want you to wake up in twenty years and hate yourself for choosing Ethan."

She licked her lips, launching into the deep end. "The thing is, we call you Martyr Maddie for a reason. You have the tendency to forgive, even those who don't ask for forgiveness. Take that Nina girl from your work, for example. You never tell Sven about her bullying or stand up to her. You let Chase gift you a goddamn dog, Maddie, and your landlord doesn't even allow it. *And* you are allergic."

"Just barely," I muttered, knowing she wasn't wrong.

"My point is, I think losing your mom at a young age made you seek acceptance from literally everyone. That's why you're still dragging this thing with Ethan. You need to grow a backbone and just . . . say no to whatever doesn't suit you. Even if it's both men."

I munched on my lower lip, mulling her words over in my head.

"However." Layla tilted her head sideways, frowning. She wore a green beach dress that matched her electric hair perfectly. "I don't think it's necessarily bad to get Chase out of your system. One last hurrah with the devil is just the recipe to purge him out of your head. A summer fling. It could work, but only if you don't get attached. Think you can do that?"

"I don't know," I admitted. "I don't think so. But a part of me wants to. It will be the emancipation of Martyr Maddie." I chuckled. "Walking away from a broken, gorgeous man who needs me."

Something hummed beneath my skin. A carnal need to make a decision. I texted Ethan, asking him to see me Tuesday evening. When Layla and I got to our apartment building, each unlocking our own doors, I glanced behind my shoulder to see the word of the day Layla had forgotten to remove from her door from Friday.

Hiraeth: a homesickness for a home you can't return to or that never was.

The word stayed with me the entire afternoon. Soaking into my bones like the summer sun. Hitting roots in me, populating within my body. I understood it with frightening clarity.

Hiraeth.

A home that wasn't mine but that I couldn't, for the life of me, stop trying to worm my way into. A place I missed without ever visiting.

A place of my own I could call home.

Maddie: How many women have you slept with since we broke up?

Chase: Really?

Maddie: Really.

Chase: Ladies first. How many men?

Maddie: No, you.

Chase: I feel like this is highly counterproductive to what I'm trying to achieve here.

Maddie: Which is?

Chase: Your lips wrapped around my cock as I examine the top of your head for stray grays.

Maddie: I actually have a few. My mom said it runs in my family.

Chase: I can have the tweezers ready if you want.

Chase: (my romance game is strong today.)

Maddie: Thanks, but I wouldn't trust you with a stress ball.

Maddie: Also, grays are natural.

Chase: I'll take your grays. All fifty shades of them. 😉

Maddie: Now stop stalling and tell me.

Chase: Four.

Maddie: Wow.

Chase: I'm guessing it is not a good wow.

Maddie: Correct, Sherlock.

Chase: You?

Maddie: Zero.

Chase: Wow.

Maddie: I'm guessing it's a good wow.

Chase: Yeah. Although it is beyond me how you managed to withstand the tights-and-tie-combo charm.

Maddie: Ethan is exactly the kind of man I want to fall in love with.

Chase: Love doesn't work for your ass, Mad. You can't tell it who to fall for.

Maddie: You really think you're immune to falling in love?

Chase: Yes.

Maddie: Elaborate.

Chase: Yes, I really am immune to falling in love. I'm unable to. It's a nonproblem.

Maddie: Why?

Chase: I've seen the ugly side of love and now I'm all sober when it comes to the other sex.

Maddie: Tell me about Amber.

Chase: Only if you come to the engagement shoot with me on Monday.

Maddie: Do I get to shoot my fake fiancé?

Chase: Har. Har. Yes or no?

Maddie: This is blackmail.

Chase: I'd rather call it negotiation.

Maddie: I hate you.

Chase: You wish.

Maddie: What are you doing tonight?

Chase: You, hopefully.

Maddie: Try again.

Chase: Out on the prowl, since my soon-to-be temporary girlfriend is refusing to see me.

Maddie: Back to being a cheater, I see.

Chase: We're not exclusive. You kiss Ethan all the time. I bet Ethan kisses other women too.

Maddie: Forget it. Go have your fun. I hope you catch hispes.

Chase: Hispes?

Maddie: Herpes, pour homme.

Chase: Fuck, I've missed you.

Maddie: I actually stole this from Ray Donovan.

Chase: You can untwist your little (patterned?) panties. I'm currently at my parents' house, playing chess with my father. And losing. Thanks to you.

Maddie: Strawberries (re: panties). How is he feeling?

Chase: Good (re: panties). And not good (re: Dad).

Maddie: I'm really sorry. There is nothing I can say to make this better, but I'm thinking about you and your family all the time. I'm seeing Katie next week for lunch. I want you to know I'll be there for her.

Chase: The end-ness is unfathomable. Today he is here, but tomorrow, who knows?

Maddie: My mother began to write me personal letters when she first found out about her breast cancer. Little anecdotes about me as a child, about her as a mother. We bonded over flowers. I always got excited when she took me to work and there was a big order for a wedding. When she beat cancer the first time, she didn't stop writing me letters. When I asked her why, she said it didn't matter. Just because she didn't have cancer didn't mean she wouldn't die.

And she wanted to remind me she'd always love me. I think maybe telling him how you feel now is a good idea.

Chase: How did it feel? I mean, afterward.

Maddie: I felt betrayed by her. I kept thinking how could she do this to me, even though it didn't make any sense. I knew she didn't choose to be ill. I felt robbed of something. Tricked. Cursed. But then, slowly, I got back on my feet. You will too.

Chase: What if I don't?

Maddie: I'll make sure you will.

Chase: I won't let you stick around and help me.

Maddie: I won't ask.

Chase: So you'll save me, but won't fuck me?

Maddie: Precisely.

Chase: Monday. I'll pick you up at six.

Maddie: Monday.

Chase: Mad?

Maddie: Yes?

Chase: Thanks.

CHAPTER FOURTEEN

Chase

It was the same studio.

Of course it was the same fucking studio.

An industrial loft on Broadway.

I wasn't surprised. Mom had one assistant on her payroll—Berta—who was approximately eighty years old (not an exaggeration for the sake of making a point). She should've retired about three decades ago, but Berta was a widow, no kids, and Mom said the job kept her busy. Berta had a personal, ongoing feud with technology and used the Yellow Pages whenever she had to book anything outside the usual service providers the family used. Which meant that the studio—Events4U—was the same one she'd booked for every family occasion in the last century, including engagement shoots, Christmas cards, condolences, virtually every official picture taken of Booger Face, my college graduation pictures, and Katie's Himalayan cat's funeral photos (more on that never; I still hadn't forgiven her for wasting everyone's time while providing the feline with a proper burial).

I opened the door for Mad, dangerously close to crawling out of my own skin and bolting to the other side of the planet, thinking about the last time I'd been in this studio. *Who* I'd been with in this studio. It wasn't that my family hadn't visited here afterward, but I'd flat-out refused to set foot in this studio ever again on the grounds of I WASN'T A FUCKING MASOCHIST.

Until now.

Madison breezed in, her movements, like her being, swift and sunny. She leaned her entire upper body against the counter, greeting the person at the reception like she'd known her her entire life. Her pixie hair was growing a little longer than usual, sticking out playfully. It was fuck hot, and I wondered if she was going to let her hair grow and if that meant hair yanking during sex was in the cards for me.

Madison laughed at something the receptionist said, then fished her phone out of her bag and showed her something. The receptionist, I realized, was the same woman who'd taken my picture all those years ago. The memory slammed into me like a truck in a busy intersection. This was a one-person-operation business. The woman had been the one cooing at my (real) ex-fiancée and me—two nervous postgrads who'd made a fatal decision to get married before they'd known who they really were—to smile at the camera.

She won't recognize you. She owns a studio on Broadway. She sees hundreds of people every week, some of them remarkably ugly, some of them remarkably beautiful. Your face doesn't chart.

"Oh goodness." The woman, who introduced herself as Becky, pushed her glasses up her nose, blinking up at me. She was fiftysomething, athletic looking, with a gray, conservative dress, hair the same color as her dress, and enough jewelry to sink the *Titanic*. "It is you again, Mr. Black."

For fuck's sake.

"Again?" Madison smiled politely, her gaze ping-ponging from Becky to me. "Is this your second engagement shoot here?" she inquired, processing as her suspicions received validation.

I wanted to pull Becky's, Berta's, and Mom's guts out of their a-holes and make trendy scarves out of them. Rather than physically assaulting women triple my age, I took Mad's hand in mine (third time, and it was growing on me—kind of) and let the comment roll off my shoulders.

"This one's gonna stick," I clipped.

"Don't be so sure," Mad muttered.

"Oh, it will. The girl before"—Becky shook her head, rounding the counter to show us to the studio—"she was no good for him. I knew it wasn't meant to be. I have a feeling about those kinds of things. I do." She stopped in front of a white screen that had been heavily lit by projectors. A stool and camera equipment sat across from it in the darkened corner of the room. Becky flicked the camera on the tripod alive, squinting as she adjusted it. "I wasn't at all surprised seeing her back with someone else. You two, I just couldn't see it. When a couple walks in, I don't even have to talk to them. I see their body language and know if they're going to make it or not. Never fails." She tapped her manicured fingernail to her temple. I flashed her a polite, can't-fucking-wait-to-get-out-of-here smirk. I'd have dodged this entire shoot if it weren't for the fact it put a smile on Dad's face.

When Mom had told me she'd booked us an engagement shoot as a present, I'd initially turned it down, but then Dad had looked so disappointed I'd had to say yes.

"And what do you make of our relationship?" Mad asked, standing with the white background behind her. She had a gray blouse, pearled neckline, and pink, peach-patterned pencil skirt I wanted very badly to rip off her body.

"You are definitely in it for the long run. This is your happily ever after." The woman smiled behind the camera. Madison flashed me a *pshhh* look. She was amused by her. Off-base Becky wasn't. I didn't think it was all that funny.

Becky instructed us to stand close to each other, using excessive hand movements to make her point. She asked me to drape a hand over Madison's shoulder while standing behind her ("Look at that height difference, whoa!") and then asked me to put both hands on her shoulders and look into her eyes. It was cornier than popcorn, and every sarcastic bone in my body wanted to snap with rage, but I did it, knowing my parents would take great pleasure in seeing the final products and keeping in mind what Mad had told me about showing Dad how I felt.

We did as we were instructed, smiling painfully wide to the camera as Becky clicked away. Both our gazes were locked on the black eye of the camera as it flashed. Realizing we could be there for a while, Madison struck up a conversation.

"So. You're here . . . *again*?" she asked through a teeth-closed smile.

"Lean over and kiss her cheek, Mr. Black!" Becky yelled behind the camera. I did as I was told, pressing my lips to Madison's apple cheek. A jolt of something hot and unfamiliar ran between us when we made contact. Like her body swelled in my arms, becoming rounder and hotter and more alive, somehow.

"Drop it," I murmured into her skin.

"You said you'd tell me about Amber if I did this shoot with you. Spill it," she hissed, her smile still bright.

"Madison, turn around! Hug him! Look like you mean it. No, this is all wrong. It looks like you are trying to tackle him in a football game." Becky continued her commentary. Mad turned around and circled her arms around me, placing her cheek against my heart. I stared at the top of her head, and sure enough, there were two grays. They glittered against her otherwise-brown hair.

"Are you nervous?" she whispered.

"No." I scoffed.

"Your heart rate is through the roof."

"Coffee."

"When's the last time you had coffee?"

Noon, probably. Still, I was allowed to have a goddamn heartbeat, especially when I had a gorgeous woman pressed against me. "Right before I picked you up. Two shots of the good stuff."

"Liar." I could feel her grinning through my shirt. "So, Amber."

I wanted to shove her tiny frame into my pocket and zip it. She was infuriating.

"Mr. Black! Hug her back. I don't remember you so frozen your first round."

"Which you may want to stop mentioning for the sake of my current relationship," I countered loudly.

She waved me off. "I'm too old not to be blunt."

"I'm too hotheaded to have this conversation *without* a stiff drink," I growled. Madison laughed. I put my arms around her, my lips brushing her hair. She smelled of flowers and coconut and my potential demise. I needed to rethink the whole pretend-real-girlfriend idea before she caved to it.

"So. You dated Amber," she started, her warm breath tickling my chest.

"Was *engaged* to Amber," I corrected.

"Get out." She swatted my chest, looking up at me with shock.

"Madison! No battery in the studio. That's why I don't allow couples to drink before photo shoots. Things can get rowdy," Becky shrieked, unplugging the camera from the tripod and circling us with it. "Whisper sweet nothings to her, Mr. Black."

I put my lips to the shell of Madison's ear, feeling her shivering in my arms. "We were fresh out of college. Amber was different back then. Pretty, natural, *sane*. Believe it or not, she wasn't completely superficial. We took some classes together and always ended up on the same side of the argument. Although in retrospect, she'd have agreed that drowning babies as a form of contraception was a good idea if I'd promoted it. She was riding a full scholarship and wanted to marry up. That she did." I chuckled bitterly.

"Did she cheat?" The air around Madison crackled with fury and surprise and delight, and *fuck*, *fuck*, *fuck*, why was everything about her so expressive? I wanted to lean down and bite her lower lip until she moaned, but I doubted that was what my parents had in mind when they asked for formal engagement pictures.

"Not that I'm aware of." I ran my thumb across her cheek, knowing she was too engrossed in our conversation to push me away.

"What happened, then?"

"I was taking a few minutes to figure out what I wanted to do with my life. Julian was a fully formed person. He bragged about becoming the next CEO of Black & Co. Said he'd been groomed and prepped for the job. Julian and Amber got close. I drifted apart from them."

I brushed my thumb along her lower lip. She let me do that. I continued talking, but my mind was far away from the Julian-and-Amber story.

"I never corrected his assumption. Amber wanted to be at the top of the food chain. She asked me if I could promise her I'd be the CEO. That I'd give her the life of luxury she was after. I said I couldn't. I also mentioned I might want to become a teacher. Julian made her believe he was calling the shots."

"Was he? *Is* he?" Her eyes implored me.

I shook my head.

"Did you really want to become a teacher?" She sounded surprised and delighted by that. I couldn't blame her.

I shrugged. "I thought about it, for half a minute. I was a bit of an idealist back in the day. Anyway, Amber broke off the engagement. I took a few months off. Traveled the world. By the time I came back, I knew I wanted to join Black & Co. Realized becoming a teacher wasn't my calling. Amber was already engaged to Julian and heavily pregnant with Clementine. Having their son bring an out-of-wedlock baby into the world was going to kill my parents, so Julian and Amber tied the knot as soon as I landed back in the US."

I could see her doing the math in her head, arching an eyebrow. "The pregnancy. It was a close call between you and Julian."

I nodded. "That's why I said I don't know if she cheated."

"You never asked?"

"I didn't want to know the answer. Julian was my brother, and we've always had this bond. I let it go, but I stopped believing in marital love as a concept."

"Did you go to the wedding?" she asked quietly. She looked destroyed on my behalf, and I wanted to slap my own face. Because to me, it didn't really matter. It was water under the bridge. The Amber-Julian blow was nothing more than a faded scar these days.

"I was the best man." I smirked. "Showing them I gave a fuck wasn't on the menu for me."

"Mr. Black! Miss Goldbloom! Would you mind?" Becky yelled in the background, and I realized, albeit belatedly, that we'd been having the last ten seconds of conversation with our lips hovering against one another. I pulled back, feeling flushed like a middle schooler who had been caught trying to figure out the ins and outs of masturbation. Madison looked down at her feet, turning deep red.

"Sweet nothings," Becky repeated sternly, waving her camera in her hand. "Save the PDA for the honeymoon. Where *is* your honeymoon, by the way?"

"Malta," Madison said.

"Fiji," I said at the same time.

We both frowned at each other. I fought a smile. "Malta?"

"I want to take the *Game of Thrones* tour. You know, where they filmed big portions of the show. Fiji?"

"Yeah, I want to get a tan, get drunk, and bury myself inside you on the sand."

"Oh, Lordy." Becky looked like she was about to faint. "Focus! Sweet nothings. Not dirty nothings. *Sweet.*"

I moved my lips back to Mad's ear. The thing about us, Madison and me, was that our bodies seemed to be in complete sync with one another. She turned around again and pressed against me, the curve of her ass touching my erection, and I stifled a curse, breathing through my nose and trying to think about sad things to stop myself from grinding all over her.

Children living below the poverty line.

Climate change.

Starving bears.

Dad.

The last one did it. Becky returned to her place beyond the bright light aimed at the white screen, click-clicking her camera from the shadows.

"So Amber broke you," Mad whispered.

"I think I was already broken, but yeah, she was definitely the final hammer to smash any romantic bone I had in my body."

"I hate her," Mad said.

I didn't. I felt nothing toward my ex-fiancée, whom I'd spent the majority of my college years with.

I had to do something to take the Amber edge off. I didn't want to talk about her or Julian. It wasn't even the heartbreak that had made me swear off love. It was the embarrassing aftermath. The gossip mill. The humiliation.

Poor Chase got dumped.

Never was quite as hardworking and hungry as Julian.

They say Amber had to make it official with his brother because he impregnated her while she was still engaged to Chase.

Maybe Chase didn't deliver you-know-where.

Chase might've cheated first. She just did what was best for her.

I forgave Julian when he asked for forgiveness. He was the older brother I looked up to, and I was determined to let it slide and work things out between us. It was Amber I had the issue with. The fickleness of love, of what I thought love was, rubbed me the wrong way. I was infatuated with Amber in the way thirteen-year-old boys were crushing over the biggest pop star in the world. She had the looks and the lust for life, and I had the funds and ability to yank her out of her small town, thrusting her into the glamorous life she'd always dreamed of. After a brush with the four-letter word with Amber, I'd decided I wasn't a huge fan of letting someone into my life, not when the risk of watching them go was possible. All Amber had needed was the faintest hint that the horse she'd bet on wasn't going to win, that Julian was going to make it to the CEO finish line before me, and she'd dumped my ass to the curb.

Dad's illness was a bitter reminder that love was not on the menu for me.

Love = pain.

Pain = suffering.

Suffering = not today, Satan. Not today.

I pressed my lips to Madison's ear. She was staring at the camera, still smiling, but from my vantage point five hundred feet above her (she really was *that* small), I could see the horror of being stuck here for eternity in her eyes.

"I want to do very dirty things to you."

She quivered, and I smiled, my teeth tracing the shell of her ear.

"In the shower," I continued. "You could sit on my shower bench while I eat you out."

"God"—she closed her eyes on a soft moan—"that's so . . . hygienic."

We both burst out into spontaneous laughter, making Becky scowl at us. "Too much teeth. Please, let's keep it regal and classy."

I peered into Madison's face, curious to see what her next step would be.

"So now when you're about to become the CEO, is Amber trying to win you back?" Mad asked.

"I don't know."

"Do you care?"

"Not particularly."

"Does Julian know that Amber might be after you?"

Another shrug. "If he does, he doesn't mind."

"Why?"

"Because Amber was never his endgame. She was collateral in a more elaborate chess game I didn't know I was playing. What he truly wanted was affirmation that he was better than me. More of a son to Ronan than I am. He wants to become CEO. He wants to be the blackest Black in the clan."

"So why did Amber do it? Go with Julian? You're so much more . . ." Mad trailed off.

"Fuckable?" I helped her.

"I was going to say tolerable. But even that sounds generous sometimes. He just seems like a weasel, you know."

I said nothing. Becky yelled that it was a wrap, and I let go of Madison, taking a step back like she was made out of fire. But Mad was still stuck in the moment, staring at me with a vulnerable look I couldn't stand.

"It just seems unfair that you don't want to fall in love, get engaged, have kids . . . because your brother-cousin stole your fiancée. Not all women care about money and status."

"But you can never be sure." I smiled grimly. She wanted to continue this line of conversation, but I followed Becky to the reception area, choosing to put an end to it. There was nothing I wanted more than to escape the scrutiny of those green-rimmed hazel eyes. Mad trailed behind me, refusing to drop the subject.

"That's all it took? One bad experience with love?"

"Yup."

"That is so cowardly. It's like hating all carbs because you had a slice of pizza you didn't like."

"I don't like pizza either," I said breezily. Technically, it was true. I didn't like what pizza did to my hard-earned abs and wasn't planning on eating it anytime soon.

"The blasphemy!" Madison cried behind me, trying—and failing—to catch up with my footsteps. "So that's it? You sentenced yourself to a life of loneliness because of *that*?"

Had she listened to my story? Did she know many people who'd lost their brides to their siblings?

"Not loneliness," I amended. "I have hookups all the time and a great family that I love, aside from my brousin and his wife."

"But if you don't fall in love, the bad guys win," Madison insisted.

"Really?" I swiveled, pinning her with a sarcastic look. "Because they sure as fuck don't look like they're winning. They seem positively miserable, much to my delight."

There was a pause. If I hadn't known better, I'd have said Mad was on the verge of tears. But that couldn't be true. Why would she give enough fucks?

"You gonna grow out your hair?" I snapped, changing the subject all of a sudden.

"I don't know." She blinked, taken aback. "Maybe."

"I like it short."

"I'll keep that in mind."

"Really?" I asked.

"No," she deadpanned.

I stalled back in the reception to go over the pictures with Becky just to put some space between me and Madison. When my pulse no longer jackrabbited against my eyelid, I joined Madison outside on the curb. Her back was to me. She looked on edge, bouncing on the balls of her feet, hugging her midriff. I stared at her, not making myself known. She took her phone out of her purse and began texting someone. Pediatric Dude? The thought of her seeing him, flirting with him, after taking engagement pictures with me made me murderous. I stepped forward, putting a hand on her shoulder. "How about we grab a bite?" I asked.

She twisted around, sucking in a surprised breath like I'd caught her doing things she wasn't supposed to do. And for the most part, it felt that way too. Not that she owed me jack shit, but ever since this whole fake-engagement thing had started, I hadn't been seeing other people. It didn't even make any sense. I just didn't feel like making the effort with someone brand new, when Mad was right there. I channeled all my energy into getting her back into my bed.

And I'd barely even kissed her.

I needed to rectify the situation. Fast.

"I have some leftovers at home." She smiled politely. "I don't want to be wasteful."

I frowned. "That sounds a lot like rejection."

She sighed, rubbing at her eyes tiredly. "Look, Chase, you're a nice guy—"

"No, I'm not," I said, cutting her off. She faltered.

"True. But you are a real catch. Not because of your money or status but because you are funny, quick witted, smart, fun, and—yes—look like you're the product of an orgy consisting of all the Greek gods, Chris Hemsworth, and James Dean."

"Thank you for the mental image I cannot bleach from my memory. By the way, which one of them got pregnant?"

She blinked at me.

"Which god?"

"Ah . . . Chris. I think he'd rock the hell out of a baby bump."

Silence. People bypassed us on the busy street. I was officially the bastard I hated who blocked pedestrians' way.

"Anyway"—she rubbed her temple—"that's not the point. The point is, you're a catch, and spending time with you is not a good idea, because I don't want to catch feelings for you again, okay? So I'm sorry, but I don't want to be your fake-real girlfriend. Or fiancée. Or anything. Goodbye, Chase."

She turned around, walking to the subway. She bumped into a businessman. He cursed. Martyr Maddie apologized.

"Wait." I chased her, hand encircling her elbow. It dawned on me that, ironically, even though my name was Chase, I'd never done any chasing. It was always the other way around. Until now. Until Mad.

She stopped, spun on her heel, and stared at me warily. Her eyes were so full I thought they were going to overflow with emotion. I couldn't tell what it was she was full of. Intensity? Pain? Whatever it was, it made me feel like shit.

"If you care about me," she said slowly through a ragged breath, "then you will stop pursuing me. Let me live my life. Let me get over you. You confuse and infuriate and delight me. You make me feel all those emotions that I have no business feeling, and I'm desperate to move on. I *want* to want Ethan. Let one of us find their happiness. Because it is so painfully clear you don't want to ever find yours."

Now there were definitely tears in her eyes. I swallowed hard. For all my loose morals and even looser principles, I didn't consider myself a top-notch dick. I always made sure women knew where they stood with me (with the exception of Madison, apparently). I never promised anything I wasn't ready to deliver. And Maddie was obviously not on board with my offer for her. Which meant that now it really was time to let go.

I took a step back. Then another one, still holding her gaze. The world shrank around her, blurring at the edges like a faded picture.

Turn the fuck around and start walking, you tool.

Still, I stood, waiting for her to make the first move. Wondering if she'd change her mind at the last minute.

"Maybe in another life." Mad smiled sadly, her eyes shining.

"Definitely," I said gruffly.

She turned around, disappearing into the subway. I stood there for ten minutes, then spun on my heel and stomped three blocks until I found an alleyway full of trash cans and privacy. I slumped against the wall, my forehead to the red bricks, and stood there for a half hour, waiting for my heart to stop galloping.

CHAPTER FIFTEEN

Maddie

The next week crawled, minute by minute. It was exotically hot. Everything in the city looked liquefied. The concrete. The buildings. The people. Kind of like *The Persistence of Memory* by Salvador Dalí, with the melting clocks.

Tick, tock.

Tick, tock.

Had life always felt so hollow?

I made myself forget about the azaleas. About the bet with Chase. About *myself.*

I threw myself into work, sketching everywhere I could. The train to and from work. On the platform. In restaurants. On lunch breaks. Before bed. Work consumed me.

I sketched and erased and started over and laughed and cried over the DWD design, because it wasn't just a design; it was *my* design. And sure, I'd designed many wedding dresses before, but there were always rules, laid out and crystal clear.

This spring our line is going to focus on sheath dresses.

This winter is all about ball gowns.

The lace collection will be mermaid-style.

This time, there were no rules to abide by. It was just me and the chaos teeming in my mind. It was the endgame. Kate Middleton on her wedding day met Grace Kelly in her carriage met Audrey Hepburn in her signature Balmain gown.

I tried hard not to think about Chase. I took Daisy out for longer walks, watching her chase Frank. I read the word of the day on Layla's board dutifully, looking for telltale signs the nagging feeling that I was in the midst of making a terrible mistake was unfounded. I wanted to be there for Chase during this time. To be there for Katie and for Lori and for Clementine.

I even made a list of words Layla had hung up to try to sew them into a meaning.

Monday was *regret*.

Tuesday was *relief*.

Wednesday was *chocolate* (which, let's admit it, played a huge role throughout my week as I tried to forget Chase).

Thursday was *coward*.

I decided not to check the board today. I was 70 percent sure Layla was being passive aggressive after I'd told her I'd run away from Chase after the engagement shoot, leaving him standing there, confused by my behavior.

To push away the Chaseness that'd been filling my brain, I went on two dates with Ethan. I was grateful for the distraction he provided. He was endlessly patient, caring, and full of stories about his work, his patients, and his time volunteering in Africa. On Tuesday, we went to watch a war movie. The night after, he took me to meet his friends at a bar. Finally, tonight, we'd agreed we'd go to a Thai place, then come back to my place for some wine.

Wine meant sex, and sex wasn't something I was ready for with Ethan, seeing how Chase occupied every corner of my mind. A part of me wanted to take it minute by minute and just see how it played out. Maybe I *would* be in the mood. Maybe the wine would loosen me up, and we'd sleep together, and I'd realize that was all I'd really needed—a chance to be intimate with Ethan to feel connected to him.

Then why do I dread getting back to my apartment with Ethan in tow? Why does it feel like I'm on death row?

Ethan and I strolled to my building. I told him about my DWD project in detail.

"There will be a chapel train, and I'm thinking pleated sweetheart bodice that resembles a Victorian corset. Oh, Ethan, it's going to be so pretty . . . ," I gushed, noticing him stiffening beside me. I stopped right alongside him, blinking at my stairway.

It couldn't be.

But that was exactly what I'd thought the first evening Chase had been waiting for me on my doorstep, luring me into his fake-engagement plan.

"I thought . . . ," Ethan began.

I shook my head violently. Like there was something inside it I wanted to get rid of. There *was*. "You thought right. I told him to back off. Let me deal with this."

I stomped my way to my door, feeling the anger coiling hotly in the pit of my stomach, blossoming, building up, and climbing up my throat. My entire body was buzzing with wrath. How could he? How could he do this to me again? Hadn't I made myself clear? I didn't want to see him. Had gone as far as *admitting* I had feelings for him just to make him take a step back. Was there anything more humiliating than admitting your unrequited feelings toward someone? That was the basis to every poem, love song, and angsty work of art in the universe.

How selfish could he be?

"What in the world do you think you're doing here?" My voice came out high pitched, dancing on the verge of hysteria. Chase was still sitting on the stairway as I positioned myself above him. "I told you to take a step back. What is wrong with you?" I realized I was baring my teeth when Chase looked up from his phone, startled by my verbal attack. I froze.

He looked different. Disheveled and exhausted and . . . *broken.*

It was the broken part that undid me. I knew that look well. My father had worn it the entire year my mother had been dying. *Really* dying. It was still permanently inked into the place behind my rib cage. It was the hopeless look of someone whose fate had brought them to their knees.

My guard dropped. Armor clattering on the pavement at my feet.

"What happened?" I crouched down to Chase's eye level, placing my elbows on his knees. My fingers were shaking as they held his jaw and tilted his face up. "Where is he?"

"Hospital."

"Chase." I wasn't sure I was breathing. "Why aren't you with him?"

He shook his head. "I don't know."

"Do you want me to come with you?"

I saw Ethan standing in my periphery, a lone candle, long and straight and unlit. He took the scene in. It scared me. How much I didn't care what he thought, what he felt in that moment. Only Chase charted.

It was the first time I realized being Martyr Maddie was unsustainable, but perhaps being a good friend to those I cared about was something I could swing. I couldn't protect everyone's feelings.

But I would slay dragons for those who found their way into my heart.

"We need to go see him, okay?" I rubbed my thumbs over Chase's cheeks. I thought I felt him nod. I took my phone out, scheduling an Uber to take us to the hospital he indicated his dad was in. After I was done, I turned to Ethan. "I'm so sorry."

His head bowed. "I hope he gets better soon."

"Thank you," I whispered. Chase was too out of it to notice Ethan. I had to stuff him into the Uber. Wearing a ball cap, a hoodie, and a bored expression, the driver tried to make idle conversation about politics and the state of traffic.

"Your boyfriend looks trashed," he said finally. "Too many drinks?" He pinned me with a look through the rearview mirror. "I don't want no puking in my back seat."

"He's fine," I clipped.

"So are you." The driver grinned.

"I'm going to smoke your eyes like beef jerky if you as much as look at her that way again," Chase groaned. It was the first time he'd spoken since we'd gotten in the car.

"Man, talk about jealousy issues."

"We're having a day," I snapped, no longer caring about being polite, agreeable Martyr Maddie. "Mind keeping it quiet?"

"Sure. Sure."

"Stop looking at her," Chase warned again like a wounded animal. "Don't even breathe in her direction."

"You heard him," I drawled at the driver, breaking out of my sweet shell.

The driver shook his head. "Jesus."

Katie and Lori were already in Ronan's hospital room, perched on a pastel-blue sofa that had seen better days. The antiseptic smell, bright, unforgiving fluorescent light, and morbid oldness that was glued to the walls made me nauseous. I hadn't been to a hospital since Mom had died.

I hugged Lori and Katie as Chase collapsed on a seat next to his unconscious father's bed. He closed his eyes, breathing through his nose.

"He had a heart attack." Lori ran her fingers through Ronan's thick white hair, frowning down at him. "The doctors said the heart attack itself was minor, but his systems are collapsing one by one. He is stabilized but not out of the woods. Grant is on his way."

Chase didn't react. He wasn't completely there. I slunk out of the room in search of coffee and some snacks. I thought maybe Chase might wait for me to give them some space before he responded to this piece of news.

I was punching buttons on a vending machine when Katie appeared next to me, hugging her arms to her chest. She was wearing flannel pajamas and a rich coat over them. It was the first time I realized it was freezing in the hospital.

"He hasn't been sleeping," she said. "Chase."

I pretended to focus on the machine. The pretzel bag wouldn't come out. It was trapped between the glass and metallic wheel. I tried giving the machine a shake, but the thing barely even moved.

"Fuck," I muttered. I didn't curse. I *never* cursed. Katie flinched.

"I think it's been a week since he last had an actual night of sleep," she continued. "I don't know if it's just about Dad."

Was she saying what I thought she was saying? It couldn't be. I figured Katie had known Chase and I weren't really together the moment I'd told her about the cheating ex I'd caught. But why would she tell me Chase was losing sleep the entire time he and I weren't in contact? The obvious reason, *because it might be true*, just never occurred to me.

"I hate this for him. For all of you." I kicked the bottom of the machine, stifling another curse when I realized my toes had fared much worse than the machine. *Dammit.*

"Yeah," Katie mused, studying me closely. "I thought you'd know. Seeing as you guys are engaged. You're engaged, right?"

I whipped my head in her direction, realizing what it was. Confrontation. Seeing as Katie hated confrontation, I knew what was at stake here.

"Oh." I pretended to smile. "I still keep my apartment. I was home all week to work on my latest assignment."

"So that cheating story . . ."

"You should forget about that story," I bit out. I was ripped apart by the idea Katie was going to discover Chase's secret. That anyone would. "Forget it altogether, Katie. I love your brother. We're together."

It didn't feel like a lie anymore. No part of that sentence. And that scared me.

I was feeling restless. Almost violent. I placed my hands on either side of the vending machine and began to shake it with everything I had in me, letting out a scream that had been lodged inside my throat since the day I'd first seen Chase in that elevator a year ago. The walls in the hallway shook with my cry. The floor rocked beneath my feet. And yet I couldn't stop. I didn't even want to try. It was so liberating to let it all out.

The lies.

The pain.

The ache of wanting something you knew was bad for you. That was always in front of you, dangling like a forbidden fruit.

I screamed and shook the vending machine until there was no more voice in my throat. The bag of pretzels finally relented, falling down with a soft *clink*. I bent over to grab it and set it on a tray I'd placed on a seat next to the machine. It had three foam cups of lukewarm black coffee poured straight from a day-old pot and sandwiches that looked downright inedible. I began to make my way back to Ronan's room like nothing had happened. Like I hadn't screamed. Like two nurses hadn't poked their heads out of rooms, checking if everything was okay.

Katie followed me. "I won't say anything," she whispered.

"I have no idea what you are talking about." The food and coffee were dancing on the tray, my hands shook so bad.

"The thing is . . . God, I don't even know what the thing is. He seems happy when he is with you, and I think this part is real." Katie swallowed. "I think it's the only real part about him since him and Amber . . . and then after a few years, when he lost Julian too."

I finally understood what Katie was saying. Why Chase refused to become attached. He hadn't only lost his fiancée to his brother. He also lost his brother to the CEO title Ronan decided to invest him with. Everyone he loved wanted something, and when Chase didn't relent, they were quick to turn their backs on him.

Even the person he'd grown up with.

Even the person he looked up to and saw as a big brother.

"What do you make of it?" I changed the subject, jerking my chin to the door we were approaching. Ronan's room. "Did Grant say if this is . . . you know?"

The end.

Katie shook her head, folding her lower lip into her mouth. "You know doctors. They never say anything this way or the other."

I did know doctors. And she was absolutely right.

After distributing the coffees, sandwiches, and pretzels, for which Katie and Lori were grateful, I pulled a barely conscious Chase by the sleeve. "You're going to take a nap. Now."

"I'm waiting for Grant," he said icily, but he lacked that Chase Black frostbite that usually came with his tone.

"No, you're not. Once Grant arrives, I'll talk to him myself. If something important happens, I'll wake you up. Otherwise, you need to sleep."

He shook my touch from his arm, but I grabbed his elbow, tugging hard. His gaze slid up to mine. Whatever he saw in my face, he knew I wasn't going to back off. Reluctantly, he stood up. I showed him to the room next to his father's. I'd noticed it was empty when Katie and I had walked back with the snacks. I fluffed the pillows while he stood behind me awkwardly, watching. When he slid into the bed, I hesitated, then, knowing he was almost out of it, he was so drunk with exhaustion, I rolled the scratchy blanket over his body. He'd done the same to me when I'd been drunk in the Hamptons. Taken care of me without complaining about it once.

I was all but forcing myself to leave the room when Chase grabbed my wrist. The jolt his touch sent up my arm made the hair on the back of my neck stand on end. My stomach dipped. It seemed monumental. Pivotal, even. The way his eyes, silvery like a sheet of ice, met my common brown ones. His mouth moved, and I dropped my gaze to follow it, too flustered to decipher his words. It was only one word. One I'd been dreaming of hearing for many months prior to our first breakup.

"Stay."

"In the room, or . . . ?" *In your life?* I couldn't breathe. I needed to breathe, but it was hard when I pinned all my hopes momentarily on his answer.

"In the hospital. Where I can find you."

He looked so deliriously wrecked, with black-rimmed eyes, his skin hanging onto his cheekbones, like he'd lost weight overnight. I'd always wondered how you knew if you loved someone. I got my answer when he looked at me. I knew, without a shadow of a doubt, that I loved Chase in that moment.

"I'll stay." I put my hand on his.

His eyes were half-closed, his throat bobbing like he was struggling to swallow. His lips looked dry, and I wanted to press mine against them. Crazy, crazy thoughts.

"You asked if I'm over Amber," he croaked, his eyes drifting shut. The rest of him too. "I am. I don't think I ever loved her. Not really. Not like I could love you."

Thud. Thud. Thud. My heart was rioting in my chest.

"I didn't cheat, but I wanted to. I fucking wished I could, Mad. Because you were there, and you were real, and if the bullshit with Amber, whom I didn't even love, hurt like a thousand bitches, you had the potential to totally detonate my life. You were a weakness. I was so . . ."

So? I held my breath, waiting for him to continue. But he never did. His breaths grew more labored, until they curled into soft, drained snores. I put my hand on my heart to keep it from exploding.

I closed my eyes, willing myself to stop what I was doing. Romanticizing what we were. Forgetting every moment I'd loathed him. I heard Layla scoffing in my head about returning to my old Martyr Maddie patterns. Putting other people before myself.

A flash of Boyfriend Chase flickered on the screen of my closed eyelids like an old film.

Him leaning his hips into mine, his whiskey breath caressing my neck at a party. "Let's dip. Everyone's a loser, and you're the only person I can stand, which is funny."

"Why is it funny?" I whispered thickly.

"Because what I want to do to you has nothing to do with either of us standing."

I opened my eyes. Closed them again.

Chase with his back to me, watching Manhattan from his floor-to-ceiling window.

"You're a wolf," I groaned. His back was so broad, so corded with muscles I had to remind myself he was mortal like me.

"You're the moon." He grinned, tipping his head back to look at the white crystal-like ball. "You drive me fucking crazy."

I opened my eyes, feeling tears stinging my nose, clogging my throat. I closed my eyes again.

Chase and me lying on the grass, staring at the starless New York skies.

"I want to go somewhere else. Somewhere where you can see the stars at night. Somewhere pure," I said.

I could hear Chase's smile when he answered. "Weird that you mention it. I bought a telescope the other day for that exact reason. I can't see the stars, and it is driving me nuts. But I don't want to give up city life."

It was classic Chase to dislike something about his life and bend it to his own will. It was classic Maddie to dislike something about my life and give up, throw in the towel, and start over.

Another tear slid down my cheek. I couldn't help it.

Chase and me in my bed, Daisy at our feet.

"Ever feel like you're changing?" he asked.

"Always," I answered. "We're always changing. We just don't notice it because we're on the move."

"I don't want to change."

"I don't think you have much choice," I said softly. "If you don't change, you don't live."

"Maybe I don't want to live."

"You know you do."

He got out of the bed and started dressing.

My eyes fluttered open again. It was us he'd been talking about. I'd been changing him.

Chase and me on the Cyclone roller coaster. Coney Island. It wasn't a romantic getaway. I'd convinced him to come with, because I felt like having an old-school candy apple.

"You're not scared of anything, are you?" He grinned at me. Our car was the first one. It went up painfully slowly, an inch at a time.

"Almost." Our car was shaking. So was my heart. I looked down to take his hand, but he clasped his fingers together in his lap. Closed off to me in ways he didn't even know I wanted him to open up for me. "Almost anything."

I opened my eyes for the fourth time, frantic. I remembered what had happened next.

We'd both fallen.

◆ ◆ ◆

I spent the next hours trying to get as much information as I could from Grant. Dawn broke on the horizon when Grant finally said we should go home to regroup. I texted Sven I'd be working from home and went to check on Chase. He was sitting on the hospital bed, frowning at his phone. He'd been out cold for nearly seven hours.

Chase glanced up from his phone, looking delicious. His hair was messy, his eyes glinting healthily. He seemed to have gained back whatever weight he'd lost last night. The color was back in his face.

"You said you'd keep me in the loop." His voice cracked, undoubtedly to his dismay.

I strolled into the room, taking a seat on the edge of the bed next to him. "Provided there was news," I agreed. "I kept my promise."

"Is Dad conscious?"

"Getting there. He's stable, though."

"What did Grant say?"

"He said Ronan will most likely pull through."

"Fuck. Okay. No news, then."

I swiveled my head, giving him a *Really?* glare. He grabbed one of my hands and put it in his lap. Another current ran through me. Like the Cyclone when it dropped.

"I'm buying you breakfast."

"Thanks, I'm not hungry." I didn't want more one-on-one time with him. Knew I was now tipping over. Taking that Cyclone dip, after which I wouldn't be able to turn my back on him again. I couldn't fall in love with a man who promised to never give me everything I wanted from life: A husband, a wedding. Children. *Love.*

"Food is rarely about food," he said. "It's about comfort. It's about sex. It's about revenge and lust and anger. But food is never about food."

I smiled tiredly at his observation. We heard a shriek coming from Ronan's room. Both our gazes flew in unison to the direction of Katie's roar. Katie wasn't one to make a scene. Chase jumped from the bed and bolted through the door. I followed him. Katie, Amber, and Julian were standing in the hallway. Katie was panting heavily, her chest rising and falling. Her cheek was marred with red clawing marks, like she was so frustrated she'd tried to rip at her own flesh.

"You have some nerve! I can't believe you, Julian. That's a step too far, even for you."

"I just did what everyone else around here was too chicken to do." Julian sounded desperate, clutching Amber's hand a little too tightly. Amber shook his touch off the minute she saw Chase and me. Her face fell when she looked between us. I realized we were holding hands. I hadn't even been aware we were doing that.

"What's going on?" Chase let go of my hand, placing himself as a buffer between Julian and Katie. Katie leaned forward and snagged a cluster of documents Julian had been holding, waving it in Chase's face.

"Bastard brought a legally binding contract for Dad to sign, which puts him as an emergency CEO of Black & Co. He tried to slip into the room while Mom was away picking up stuff for Dad. I was outside making phone calls."

"Now, before you get your panties in a twist—" Julian was in the process of swiveling toward Chase. Bad idea. Chase sent a sucker punch straight to his face. Julian staggered back, crashing against the wall. He held his nose with both hands, gasping for breath. "Asshole!"

Chase snatched the papers from Katie's hands and ripped them to shreds. They rained at his feet, gathering around his loafers like snowflakes. Amber stared at him, wide eyed, her eyes rimmed with careful makeup and tears.

Julian dragged his back down the wall, still holding his nose. Blood trickled between his fingers, down to his shirt and the floor. "Feeling threatened, *coz*?" he hissed.

It was the first time I'd heard Julian referring to Chase as a cousin and not a brother, and I had a feeling it had been a long time coming. When I stared at Julian, such a perfect, one-dimensional Shakespearean villain in my eyes, I had to remind myself he had a life story too. That it was probably difficult to live in the shadow of your cousin, who was a decade younger, successful, gorgeous, and born into American royalty.

That Chase was seen as more talented, more capable, and more authoritative. And perhaps worst of all, that at least from the outside, Chase was unfazed by the fact Julian had stolen his fiancée.

Chase strolled toward him, smiling coldly. "Try to tamper with Black & Co.'s management one more time, Julian. I fucking dare you. And you"—he turned to Amber, who stepped back, clutching her diamond necklace with her three-inch nails—"keep him away from me if you don't want to become a widow."

With that, he took my hand and stormed down the hallway. I flailed behind him, trying to catch up with his steps.

"Where are we going?"

"My apartment."

"Your apart . . . Chase, *no*."

"Yes."

"Why?"

He stopped and turned around to me sharply. "Because," he gritted through his teeth.

"Because?" I raised an eyebrow.

"I can't sleep." He spat the words out, annoyed.

"And?"

"And I can when you are there." The rest of the words rolled out of his mouth grudgingly. "I don't know how to explain it, nor do I want to. May I be graced with your presence so I can stock up on some sleeping hours?"

I licked my lips, staring at him.

"I will not try to sleep with you." He raised a hand. "Scout's honor."

"For the last time, you weren't—"

"I was," he bit out. "For a year. Horrible time. And to this day, I misuse the knowledge of how to tie shit up."

I stifled something between a groan and a chuckle. "Okay."

He took my hand again, resuming his quest for a taxi outside, and I couldn't remember a time we'd held hands so much since our stupid agreement had started.

The devil didn't have to drag me down to hell.

I had come with him willingly.

CHAPTER SIXTEEN

CHASE

Another four hours of sleep and a shower later, I was feeling more human and less like a bag of bones and anger and untapped come.

After checking for phone calls from Grant, Katie, and Mom and getting an update in text form that Dad was still stable, I slid into one of my black suits (why other colors existed was beyond me. Black was suitable for every occasion. The only exception I made was with gray sweatpants, because those were practically considered lingerie for men) and wandered out of the master bedroom. I descended down the three marble steps to the living room. Black, sleek chandeliers dripped from the ceiling, and upholstered black leather couches and recliners filled the room. The three walls that weren't floor-to-ceiling windows were bare, raw concrete. Everything about my place was dark, indulgent, and dangerous. An apartment carefully designed in the aesthetic of a modern douchebag.

Inside the gloom and darkness sat a woman wearing an apron-like yellow A-line dress from her last night's date, with a pattern of dripping ice creams on it, her face scrunched in concentration in front of her sketch pad. Her tongue was peeking out from the side of her mouth—her MO when she was concentrating. I buttoned my shirt and watched her, not making myself known. There was something perversely predatory about watching her without being watched. My mind roamed to places it shouldn't have gone. Pleasures I hadn't taken since I'd found out Dad was ill.

Her phone began to ring. "Greek Tragedy" by the Wombats was her ringtone. It was those little quirks about Mad that made her so supremely fuckable. She wasn't exactly hipster, although I knew she dressed like one and knew her way around an indie playlist. She wasn't highbrow, but she could hold her own in a conversation with just about anyone in the world, beggar or king. She wasn't upper class. She wasn't lower class. She was Maddie class. An entirely unique, sexy species. I had to get her out of my system. I had to fuck her again.

She jumped from the distraction before swiping across the screen and tucking her AirPods into her ears. They obviously weren't charged, because Ethan's castrated voice filled my living room.

"Just checking in. Are you back home?" he asked. She looked around her. I might or might not have been standing behind a statue. *The Weeping Angel* with a cigarette tucked between her fingers, her face propped above a bar counter. An impulsive, tongue-in-cheek purchase after I'd come back from South America to find my ex-fiancée knocked up with my brousin's baby. The need to shell out a lot of money on something meaningless had been overwhelming back then. As if to say: *So fucking what? I can still drop five hundred K on a piece of shit most people won't agree to wipe their ass with.*

"Spent the night at the hospital, then came back to Chase's apartment this morning," she said apologetically. "I wanted to make sure he was feeling all right."

Another thing I didn't hate about Madison Goldbloom—she didn't pin the blame on other people. I was the one who'd twisted her arm about coming here. But she didn't mention that to Ethan.

"Oh," he said. How eloquent. Seriously, how the heck did she date this guy?

"Ronan is fine, by the way." She pinched her lips.

"Of course. I was about to ask," he said. Then paused. No, he hadn't been. He didn't care about my father. "Has anything happened between you and Chase?"

"No, of course not." She sighed.

Silence stretched across the room. These two had the sexual chemistry of a tampon and a ketchup stain together. I couldn't fathom how she didn't see it. Madison was fire, and Ethan was . . . what the fuck was he, anyway? Not water. Not earth. He was a shadow. A by-product of something else.

"Do you want to see each other tonight? We were about to—"

Hell to the goddamn no. I stepped out from behind the statue, clearing my throat. "I'm sorry, Ethan. Tonight is not going to work for us." I rolled my shirtsleeves up my veiny arms, nonchalantly making my way to Mad. I'd promised not to fuck her; I'd never said anything about not preventing anyone else from doing just that tonight. I dropped a chaste kiss to her forehead, which she wiped with a frown, her eyes blazing with horror and annoyance. I held her gaze. "See, Madison will be with me tonight."

"Chase!" she snapped. "Sorry about that, Ethan. I would love to—"

"Have a relationship in which I am both attracted to and interested in the man I am seeing," I completed for her, grinning. "I know, Mad. It'd make things so much easier."

"Nothing is more difficult than you." She tried swatting me away, but you could hear the grin in her voice. Her face was glowing. Mission accomplished.

"The word you are looking for is hard," I quipped. "And thank you."

"You are a nightmare." She chuckled.

"But the sexy kind, right? Where you wake up with puckered nipples and ruined panties?" I egged her on. She was getting flushed, her eyes wide and full.

"I'll leave you to deal with this, Maddie," Ethan said coldly, hanging up before she could salvage the conversation.

Mad stood up, waving her phone in the air. "Stop clam-jamming me!" She pretended to slap my chest.

I grabbed her hand, biting the tips of her fingers playfully. "If I'm not getting some, no one in this fake engagement is."

"We *have* no relationship!" She threw her head back, growling. "I cannot believe I tried so hard to keep you when we were together, only to find out you wouldn't leave me alone."

"Give it a few weeks," I jested.

"Stop saying that. It is disrespectful to your father. He could live for months. Even years."

"No, he can't."

"Chase."

"Mad."

She stopped, scrunching her forehead. "Why do you call me Mad? Why not Mads? Maddie? Madison? Virtually all my other nicknames."

I knew the answer. I'd known it for some time now. But sharing it with her felt like crossing a line, especially when I suspected I'd let my mouth run freely yesterday before I'd passed out on that hospital bed. I looked down, caught a glimpse of the wedding dress she was sketching, then looked back up. "You're talented," I said, changing the subject.

"And that's surprising?" She took the hint.

"No." *Yes.* "Your sketches are clean. Elegant. I wasn't expecting that."

"I can be clean and elegant. I choose to dress quirky and all over the place."

"Why?"

"Because it is my personality in textile form."

"Are you bipolar?" I deadpanned.

"Offensive." She pretended to gag. We were good together, and she knew it. I knew it, too, which was why it was exceptionally dumb of me to continue pursuing her. She looked back at the page, frowning. "I don't think people are going to like it. Sven, specifically."

"Why?"

"Too many details." She gestured toward the sketch with her hand, pointing at the sleeves, the collar, and the tulle. "Traditionally, the Dream Wedding Dress is much simpler. Cleaner lines, minimal detail, not much character. The emphasis is on the cut and the superior fit. Plus, all the dresses Croquis ever showed were pure, swan white. This one isn't."

"What is it, then?"

"Crème." She bit her lower lip. My eyes slid up from the sketch to meet her gaze. She waved the sketch off. "It's fine. Worst-case scenario, I'll cut some of the detail."

"No," I said. "You won't. It's perfect, and it's you. Keep it."

Her throat worked. My eyes dipped to her delicate neck. I wanted to kiss it.

"Okay," she whispered. "Thanks."

"Got any sleep?"

"Yeah, some."

"Wanna hop into the shower? Maybe I could drop you off at yours?"

"I'm fine."

"Good. Let's go to work. We can still recoup some of the day."

I grabbed my keys. I knew she'd follow. She never missed a chance to cease communication with me. But for the first time, I gave a shit.

I mean, of course I gave shits.

I gave a shit about Dad.

About Black & Co.

But never about a woman. Never about a date. The uneven rattle in my chest was a warning sign. My heart tested itself. *Tap, tap, tap. Is this shit working?*

I gritted my teeth and punched the elevator button, not looking behind me to see if she was there.

Three days later, Dad was conscious and good to leave the hospital. I picked him up while Mom prepared the house, whatever that meant. I drove around in circles, buying time, and he didn't seem to mind, even though *his* time was precious. It occurred to me we hadn't had a meaningful conversation about something that wasn't work since the C-word had struck. Work was a safe topic. I doubted he could remember anything from when Julian had barged into his hospital room with his contract. Dad had still been unconscious when that had happened. Grant had advised me to go easy on him and not talk about things that might spike his blood pressure. Bothering him with the Julian bullshit wasn't on my agenda.

We were circling the same side street, passing the same Pret coffee shop and the swell of the same cluster of students huddling together, and waiting on the same traffic light. There was something depressing about other people's joy while you were miserable. It was all very in your face.

"I wish we could get out of the city," Dad murmured, looking out the window. "It feels filthy in the summers without the rain or snow to clean it up. Doesn't it feel filthy to you?"

As he said that, smoke billowed from three different manholes, and some drunken frat boy hurled a beer can across the street at his friend, laughing.

"We can get out of here, if that's what you want," I said, tightening my grip on the steering wheel. I didn't want to leave the business with Julian sniffing around the management floor. I didn't want to leave Madison to fall in comfort with mediocre Ethan. What kind of name was Madison Goodman, anyway? I couldn't let her go through with it. But Dad's wishes had to take the front seat.

"Julian suggested we go to the ranch house in Lake George for the weekend. He even had it prepared for us," Dad added.

Julian would drown you in the lake if it means inheriting the business, I was tempted to reply. I smiled serenely. "He did that? Great idea."

"You can bring Madison, of course. I think she'd like it there. Lots to do. Very outdoorsy. Where is she from again?"

"Pennsylvania," I answered. "Just outside Philadelphia."

"Does she have any siblings?"

"No. Her mother struggled with . . ." I stopped.

Dad finished for me. "Breast cancer, right?"

"Yeah." I was an idiot. An idiot who needed to change the subject. "Her parents owned a flower shop. Well, her dad still owns it."

"Are they close?" Dad asked.

"Yup, real tight. She goes to see him and his girlfriend every other month. They take vacations together every year."

"You know a lot about her, don't you?" He turned to look at me, smiling. I did. I didn't remember listening to what she had to say—not intentionally, anyway—but I remembered everything she'd told me about herself. Which wasn't much, because talking was never something I'd encouraged in our relationship. But right now the burning question was whether Mad was going to humor me by joining me for another weekend outside the city. I didn't think she would.

My father's phone buzzed in his pocket, and he picked it up on speaker. "Jul," he said, his voice softening. He *definitely* didn't remember the contract. "How is Clemmy?"

"Huh? Oh yeah. She's fine." Dad must've cockblocked the real reason he was calling. I wondered if Booger Face was ever in Julian's mind. "Hey, look, Amb spoke to the maintenance company. The house in Lake George is good and ready. Should I pick you and Lori up, say, Friday morning?"

He was going to whisk my parents off for a weekend with his family? Sans Katie and me, while Dad was on the brink of dying and pretty much in hospice care? Hell no. I could smell his plan from miles away. Julian wanted to butter Dad up before he went for the CEO kill. Somewhere my sister and I couldn't stop him.

"Sounds good," Dad said. "Have you spoken to Katie?"

"No. I think she has a volunteering gig with Saint Jude's this weekend," Julian said. It sounded like he was sifting through papers in the background. Possibly more bullshit he wanted my father to sign. "You know how Katie is. Always a do-gooder."

"You should try again. Katie usually volunteers every end of the month." I butted into their conversation.

There was a pause from Julian's end. Then he recovered. "Chase. I didn't realize you were there."

"He *is* my father."

"Biologically, anyway." Julian laughed good-naturedly. "You two are very different, though."

"What's that?" I asked, taking one last turn onto that side street before making my way to my parents' apartment building. "Would I like to join you at the ranch? Of course I would. How nice of you to offer, Julian."

There was a pause and then, "Bring Maddie with you. Amber's been dying to see the engagement pictures."

"I will." *Will I?* Last I checked, Madison was going to extreme lengths to avoid me. She'd been dodging my calls *and* text messages. At this point, the only thing stopping her from slapping a restraining order against my ass was the fact we worked in the same building. Still, I couldn't not be there. She had to understand.

"Great. Looking forward to it." Julian's voice was too relaxed. Too blasé.

But I was too enraged to realize it was a trap.

Too goddamn rabid to know what I was willingly walking into.

CHAPTER SEVENTEEN

Maddie

September 25, 2008

Dear Maddie,

Today I found cigarettes in your backpack. Again. We had an argument. It was bad. You said it was a mistake. It's not a mistake if you continue doing it. You must have a reason to repeat the same action over and over again.

Whether you want to rebel or get distracted or you simply got addicted.

It's like the corpse flower that smells like rotten meat. It smells like this because it is rare and vulnerable, not by chance.

Every decision you make has a reason. Think about it.

Love,

Mom. x

◆ ◆ ◆

This time, I didn't lie to myself.

Didn't fight it or deny it. It had a name. Mom had said it best in a letter years ago, when I'd tried smoking when I was going on fifteen. It was an *addiction*.

When I saw Chase's name on my caller ID, I picked it up on the first ring. When he invited me to the ranch, ready to launch into a convincing speech, I cut off his arsenal of arguments and promises and accepted immediately. The carnal need to be there for him nearly paralyzed me. I knew, with certainty that bubbled in my veins, that it didn't make me Martyr Maddie.

It made me someone who cared deeply for Chase and didn't want to see him fail.

Layla was going to have a field day when she found out I was still playing with the devil. But knowing what I knew about Julian, about *Amber*, I felt responsible for Chase where they were concerned. Besides, our lie to his family was so big at this point it loomed over everything, my conscience included. It was a rolling snowball, growing larger each time it spun, swallowing objects and feelings and victims—Ethan, Katie, Clementine—as it descended an endless mountain of dishonesties. Even though I knew the snowball was going to hit something and pop at any minute, I couldn't stop it. Coming clean didn't seem like an option anymore. I accepted this was something Chase would have to deal with once he lost his father.

We arrived at the Lake George ranch early Friday evening.

The nineteenth-century stone building sprawled on a good portion of the ten-thousand-acre land the Blacks owned. The entire second floor was bursting with green double-doored balconies. Ivy curled up the building, the backdrop of the lake making the property one of the most magical things I'd ever witnessed with my eyes. The sun sank lazily toward the horizon, the sky surging with various shades of gold and pink.

I must've sucked in a breath when Chase helped me with my suitcases, because he glanced over his shoulder and chuckled. "This one's Dad's favorite. The Hamptons is Mom's playground."

"Which one's yours?" I asked, not fully realizing what I was insinuating.

He stopped walking, shooting me a charged frown. *"You."*

He dropped my bags. There was a moment when I thought he was going to wrap his arms around me and kiss me. I *wanted* him to do that. Badly. But he just shook his head, getting rid of whatever it was he was thinking about.

"Don't let me seduce you," he growled.

"Okay." We continued walking. "Why?"

"Because once I have you again, it will be impossible for me to let go. To let you be. To respect your decision."

He hoisted my duffel bag over my spinner suitcase, taking my hand in his free one. The charade was back in full force.

We made it to the landing. Voices seeped from the dining room. Laughing, talking, whispering. Utensils clinked. Wineglasses too. We frowned at each other.

"Julian," Chase clipped, his jaw tightening. "Must've told everyone we were running late and to start eating. Douche."

"It's time you put him in his place."

"You think I don't know that?" He glowered at me. "I let him off the hook because our parents, sister, and Clementine shouldn't suffer through what I want to put him through."

We made our way into the dining room, leaving the suitcases on the landing. The long table was fully hidden under platters and dishes. Fresh rolls, pitchers of sweating homemade iced teas, and bottles of wine were scattered on the pristine white tablecloth. The scent of smoked meat and seasoned vegetables laced the air. Saliva coated my mouth.

"Oh goodness, please tell us that story again. I cannot believe Clemmy said that!" Lori gushed.

"Start from when she walked in." Amber's tone was buttery, different. "When she saw the empty fish tank."

"All right, all right. I'll tell it again." I heard Ethan laugh.

Whoa, whoa, whoa. Back it up. *Ethan?*

I didn't have the privilege to be able to turn around and run for my life. I was already halfway inside the dining room when it registered. Chase was a step ahead of me, shielding me with his broad body, my hand still clasped in his. I felt the floor soften beneath my sandals, threatening to open its jaw and swallow me whole. My eyes connected with Ethan's from across the table. Snakes danced in the pit of my stomach, sinking their venomous teeth into my insides.

He was there, sandwiched between Clementine and Amber, holding a glass of white wine to his mouth, wearing a *Puppy Dog Pals* tie.

Looking back.

Looking *furious.*

I browsed through my memories, replaying our latest communication. Where we'd left things off. We spoke on the phone this week but made no plans to meet up. Things had reached the point of fizzling out, and I thought both of us were okay with that. Ethan said he'd been invited somewhere this weekend. I said I had plans too. We'd both been cryptic. Now I knew why.

Ethan was always on the margins of my story. A secondary character I'd gone running to whenever I'd pushed Chase away. In trying to please him, to cater to him, to *love* him, I'd given him false hope. In trying to spare his feelings, I'd done something cruel to him. Martyr Maddie, I now understood, had a dark side.

The slow, spreading grin on Ethan's face told me he wasn't caught off guard as I was. He'd known. It was a setup. My remorse morphed into fury. I straightened my spine, tilting my head up.

I didn't know when I'd stopped holding Chase's hand. When my fingers clenched into fists, my nails dug into my skin.

"Well, this is awkward. Didn't you say you two know each other?" Julian whistled low, taking a sip of his iced tea. His voice was thick with excitement. It clawed at my skin. "Dr. Goodman is Clementine's pediatrician. We thought it'd be nice to invite him over to enjoy the ranch on a rare weekend off," he pointed out when Chase threw him a what-the-hell look.

"Not awkward at all. As I mentioned before, I know Ethan and enjoy his company. We're friends." I smiled, leaning down to kiss Ronan's pale cheek. Lori and Katie stood and hugged me. I bypassed a sitting Amber and Julian, settling for a pat on each of their shoulders. I kissed Clemmy's head, then pressed a kiss to Ethan's cheek.

"What a nice surprise," he whispered as my lips brushed his closely shaved skin. His voice was paper dry.

"Ethan . . . ," I breathed. *"Why?"*

"Madison, have a seat." Chase stood across from Ethan, his death stare making Ethan flinch. I walked over to him, feeling my shoulders slump. He pushed my seat back. We began piling food onto our plates. Ethan retold the story of how Clementine had dropped take-out sashimi bits into an empty fish tank in his office on her latest visit, drawing laughs from the table.

I stiffly shoved one forkful of food after another into my mouth. I couldn't taste anything. I wasn't sure if I was more worried about Chase's family finding out we weren't together or about the conversation I would have with Ethan afterward. Chase snaked a hand between us and squeezed my hand under the table. Nuclear currents ran through my spine.

"Can I just back it up a little?" Julian rubbed at his chin, chuckling good-naturedly. "I'm trying to figure something out. Maddie said you and she are friends, Dr. Goodman. But I thought Clemmy said she saw you two hugging real long and real hard—'like couples in the movies,' I believe were her exact words—at your clinic a few weeks ago. Didn't you, Clemmy?" He turned to his daughter, then back to me. "So which is it? Are you friends, or are you something more?"

Clementine looked down, blushing.

"As I said," I gritted out, not giving Ethan a chance to answer, "I am with Chase."

"My bad, Maddie." Julian lifted his palms in surrender, taking a moment to make sure everybody was thinking about that time Clementine had told them about me kissing Ethan. "I just thought . . . well, this is silly, anyway, but I thought maybe something happened. I saw you at work the other day. You weren't wearing your engagement ring," Julian remarked as he cut his roasted chicken into tiny, meticulous pieces. "Yet here you are, with your engagement ring."

He was becoming more and more blunt, presenting his elaborate case against us. I knew I had to get out of it myself. If Chase intervened, it'd look like another bickering match between him and Julian, and like I was making excuses for him. I shrugged it off. "The ring is very expensive. I don't want to lose it or have someone cut my finger off in a dark alley for the piece of jewelry."

"Smart," Katie pointed out, popping a blueberry into her mouth. "Cutting off fingers with rings is a thing. Heard about it in a true-crime podcast."

"Are your friends happy about the engagement?" Amber pressed, a fake smile marring her lip-glossed mouth. "I should think they're planning one hell of a bachelorette party."

"My close friends are excited, yes. We're going to celebrate low key. I haven't told my colleagues yet, though. You know, life is not about flaunting expensive rings and marrying your way up the tax bracket."

Dang, dumping Martyr Maddie for a while was fun.

Amber winced. "I can see how that'd be awkward. I mean, Black & Co. and Croquis are sister companies. I wonder if people think you slept your way to the top."

"Oh, I've had this job since long before I met Chase. Marrying into money is not an Olympic sport for me." I smiled back. Chase pretended to cough to stifle a laugh. Lori polished off her glass of wine.

"Clementine, excuse yourself," Amber barked, still staring at me. Ronan snapped his fingers, and a waiter appeared, ushering Clementine to the kitchen to sample the dessert. The dining room was now a full-blown war zone. The gloves were off.

"Interesting." Julian tapped his chin.

"The things you find interesting amaze me. Is that what happens when you live a sexless, loveless life?" Chase asked dryly. Lori gasped. Ethan and Katie looked among all of us like we were crazy.

"Redirect that conversation," Ronan groaned. He looked exhausted, and suddenly, I understood why Chase hadn't been fighting back against Julian. It wasn't because he didn't want to. He knew it'd drain his father. Chase had been trying not to upset Ronan all throughout our fake engagement. He'd tried to pretend he was taking Julian's undermining behavior and petty comments in stride. But he wasn't. Julian got under Chase's skin, and today, Chase had finally snapped.

"You're right, Ronan. We should be talking about other things. Ethan, you're such a catch." Amber reached to him, rubbing his arm. Subtle as a tank. "Young, handsome, a pediatrician. I have so many single friends who would love an introduction. Are you seeing anyone?"

Ethan rubbed the back of his neck, his gaze darting to mine. "Actually . . ."

What is he doing?

The horror in my face must've been visible, because Ethan backpedaled on whatever point he was trying to make. "Not exclusively, no."

Martyr Maddie, always doing the right thing. Even if it's dating a guy just to make him feel better, Layla's voice singsonged in my head. But it wasn't just that. I was desperate to fall in love with Ethan so I wouldn't get hurt, and I'd ended up hurting him in the process.

There was silence, punctuated by good old Lori. "Ethan told me he ran the half marathon too, Katie."

Katie lifted her head from her plate, her eyes zeroing in on Ethan. "Really? Who sponsored you?"

"Doctors for Africa. What number were you?" Ethan's face opened up. So much light poured into his expression. I didn't think I'd ever seen him so . . . *present.*

"Nine two two three. Yellow shirt. You?"

"Three five two seven. Pink."

"Phew, good thing we didn't run together. We'd look like an ice cream cone next to each other." Katie wiped invisible sweat from her forehead. They held each other's gaze, a thread of something flirtatious entwining them into the same moment. Ethan was the first to look back at his plate, stabbing a piece of glazed potato with his fork.

"Maybe next time we won't get so lucky," Ethan said.

Or maybe you will, I thought. Ethan and Katie looked so easy talking to each other.

"So. Just to make sure we're all on the same page. Ethan and Maddie are just friends?" Julian filled my wineglass to the brim. Was he trying to get me drunk? Probably, based on my disastrous visit to his family's Hamptons home.

"Is that concept foreign to you?" Chase sat back, spearing his cousin with a dark glare. My hand was still in his under the table. "Or are you simply obsessed with my fiancée in general?"

"Fiancée. That's a bold statement," Amber muttered into her wineglass.

"Are we going to open the subject of bold here, at the table, Lady Macbeth?" Chase inquired dryly. Amber nearly spat her wine out. I put a hand to Chase's arm. His muscles flexed under my fingertips. He was a beast restrained.

"I can hold my own," I whispered.

"Don't I know it. I'm still hoping to get my balls back for Christmas." Chase sighed, kissing my temple. "Sorry."

It was a lie, of course, but one I appreciated, even if it was a part of an elaborate Chase act.

"I just want you boys to get along." Lori sighed, looking between Chase and Julian. "I know emotions have been running high, but nothing is worth your friendship. Blood is thicker than water."

"We don't have the same blood running through our veins," Julian spat bitterly. "Maybe that's my problem."

"Julian," Ronan scolded. "Stop that."

"Chase is obviously the favorite child," Julian persisted. He sounded like a five-year-old.

"No, you're obviously still a child," Chase bit back. "Crucifying my fiancée and trying to unveil imaginary mishaps on my behalf. It is real, and it is happening, and you can't do anything to stop it, no matter how fucking hard you try. No matter what you do. I will marry her." Chase stopped, his eyes gliding from Julian to Ethan, and finished off, *"Julian."*

But it didn't seem like his words were directed at Julian anymore. Not at all.

"Excuse me."

A chair scraped, and I turned my attention from Chase's thunderous face. Ethan galloped outside after throwing his napkin over his plate.

I followed him. I didn't know why. Maybe because Chase's behavior was uncalled for. Because he'd directed his anger at Ethan, when really, Julian was the person he was supposed to attack here.

"Ethan, wait!"

He got into the bathroom, about to slam the door in my face. I pushed my foot through the crack just as the door flew shut. I let out a yelp, feeling my skin bruising.

"Oh crap." Ethan opened the door, wincing as he looked down at my sandaled foot. "Are you all right?"

"Please." I stood on the other side of the door, foot still stuck between us to prevent him from shutting the door in my face. "Let me in."

"That's what I've been trying to do here for weeks," he said quietly. "And you hurt me."

"I know," I whispered, feeling sick to my stomach with guilt. Martyr Maddie kicked in again. True, we'd both agreed it was casual, but he'd catered to *me*. To *my* situation. In a lot of ways, we were too much alike. Nonconfrontational at all costs. "I'm so sorry," I croaked. "I never meant to hurt you."

"You're sorry?" Ethan reared his head back, the anguish in his face tearing me apart.

"Yes, of course I am," I said desperately. This was a good time to spit out the truth. That I couldn't be with him, and it had nothing to do with Chase at all. Ethan was Prince Charming, but in someone else's story. Not mine. He wasn't the one I went to sleep thinking about.

He isn't the one who keeps me awake in the first place.

"Do you regret it?" Ethan shifted from one foot to the other. I nodded. I did. I regretted hurting him.

I regretted not ending it sooner, when I'd known we had no future.

I *did not* regret kissing Chase. And that was a problem.

I opened my mouth to say something more, but Ethan beat me to it, pressing his lips against mine on the threshold to the bathroom. My arms flailed behind my body, like they were sewn artificially to my shoulders. It wasn't the first time I'd been kissed by Ethan, but this time, it felt especially wrong. I had to stop this. I started leaning back, breaking away from the kiss, my mouth ashen.

"You must have what they call an open relationship, if that's your fiancée's idea of 'good friends.'" I heard Julian's entertained voice from my right. I jerked back, spinning to find Julian and Chase.

Julian smiled smugly, his arms crossed over his chest. Chase . . . Chase didn't look at me at all. He stared at Ethan like he was about to hammer him to the ground, then stomp on his body until he set it on fire. His jaw worked. His eyes were two shades darker than their usual icy blue gray.

"What a mess." Julian shook his head, chuckling.

"Step away from her," Chase told Ethan. Julian didn't even register in his universe. I wasn't sure he'd heard him at all. Ethan did as he was told but looked between us, waiting for me to scold Chase for telling him what to do. I usually did. Chase was the only person I somehow found myself always arguing with.

Chase took a step forward. He was toe to toe with Ethan now, looming over him with his height and frame and Chaseness. My chest tightened. I realized I was scared.

"Whatever you're about to do," Ethan said, his voice steady but quiet enough that Julian couldn't hear him, "I wouldn't do it if I were you. We both know this story is far from over. The last chapter hasn't been written yet."

That was what broke me. The truth of his words. How they made Chase take a step back like he'd been hit. I'd never seen him like this. So . . . emotionally exposed.

"Right. I think we have much to discuss, *brousin*." Julian clapped Chase's back. "A quiet word in the library? It *is* our favorite place."

I watched their backs as they walked away. How Chase was shrinking while Julian swelled and filled more of the hallway.

I looked on as I realized, for the first time, that I'd killed something with kindness.

Namely, my heart.

CHAPTER EIGHTEEN

Chase

"Let's cut to the chase, shall we, *Chase*?" Julian lit a cigar, puffing away, stinking up the entire library. Punny shit. I'd be into word games, too, if my archnemesis's cover-up story got blown into the sky and I had a front-row seat.

I sat back, crossing my legs at the ankles on the desk to make sure he knew how little of a crap I gave about his whole Don Corleone act. Problem was, it was difficult to sit in the library and listen to Julian's bullshit when I had bigger fish to fry. Specifically, Ethan Goddamn Goodman, ironically the worst thing to happen to yours truly. His very existence offended me on a personal level. I officially recognized that I had an Ethan situation, which required immediate attention.

My pulse drummed everywhere. My neck. The inside of my wrist. My fucking eyelids. I wasn't a violent guy, but watching Mad kiss that tool had made me want to do things I was pretty sure were so radical there was no maximum prison time for them.

"Spare me the bullshit and just get it over with." I knotted my fingers behind my head, yawning. "And please, try not to come in the process. Your face is giving me preorgasm vibes I never cared to see on my brother's face."

That was the part I hated the most. That he was still my brother to me. Not brousin, brother. A fucked-up one, for sure, and yet.

"I very much doubt you are used to seeing people coming on a regular basis. You're too self-centered to give pleasure," Julian noted, puffing on his cigar.

"Saw it enough times on your wife's face." I rolled my tongue across my top teeth.

His smile dropped. At least now I knew it wasn't permanently stitched to his smug face. "You're an asshole."

"Well, I was taught by the best."

"I showed you how to be ruthless, not a bastard," Julian argued.

"I couldn't pick and choose which personality traits to mimic. Went for the whole package." I shrugged. It was the truth. Every single jerk move I had, I'd learned from Jul. He was the one who'd come back from college telling me about sleeping around, trying drugs, acting crassly. "Now get to the point," I urged him.

"I think we both know you're going to run this company into the ground if you take the CEO seat. I understand Ronan feels obligated to you. You're his biological son. But I paid my dues—"

"Lay off the biological-son bullshit, Jul. You're CIO. Chief information officer. You're a glorified PR girl without the tight skirt. What makes you think you can do this job better than me?"

"The fact that I have something on you." Julian frowned, as if it were obvious. "You made the entire thing with Maddie Goldbloom up. You're not engaged. You're not even dating. Your little cover-up girl is dating my daughter's pediatrician and can barely look at you. Why shouldn't I tell Ronan the truth?"

"Because you don't want to break his heart," I gritted out. "Because he fucking raised you."

"He deserves to know the truth." Julian shook his head. "I'll be doing him a public service, giving him the full picture. Why shouldn't he know who his son really is? A lying, cheating bastard. Hand over the CEO title now, publicly, and nobody gets hurt. *Checkmate.*"

I blinked at him like he was insane.

"You're giving me an ultimatum?" I wanted to be completely sure before I laughed.

"Yes."

I chuckled, standing up. I leaned down, patting his shoulder in a patronizing manner. Internally, I was a few heartbeats away from a stroke. My family finding out about Madison right now would be the worst thing that could possibly happen. Katie already knew, but she was going to keep her mouth shut to keep everyone happy, and we'd always covered each other's fuckups.

Then again, giving Julian the role was letting the bad guy win, and I'd seen enough Michael Bay movies to know Black & Co. wouldn't have a happy ending under Julian's reign. Besides, I *deserved* to become CEO. I'd worked my ass off for a decade while Julian had been busy fighting and making up with my goddamn ex-fiancée, now his wife.

I bent down, whispering into his ear, "You lured us in here knowing Ethan was going to show up. You set us up."

He sat back, lacing his fingers together. He didn't have to confirm it. His face said everything there was to say.

"You play a very dirty game, Julian. The gloves are off."

"Now, that's the reaction I was expecting after I stole your girl all those years ago."

"You don't steal leftovers. You dig for them in the trash." I smiled cordially. "But now it's on, and that side of me you just awakened, Julian? You're not going to like it."

Maddie

That night, I tossed and turned in my bed, but sleep never came.

My bedroom was right across from Ethan's. Chase was all the way at the end of the hall. I'd had the audacity to ask Katie about the sleeping arrangements when no one could hear us. She eyed me and asked, "Are you really dating Ethan?"

"It's complicated," I whispered back. She looked almost hurt, and I could see why. Katie had been adamant whatever she was seeing between Chase and me had a future. Not to mention I'd picked up on something between her and Ethan at the table.

"Complicated how?" She raised an eyebrow.

"What I'm trying to say is, Ethan is all yours," I said, meaning it. "If you're interested, that is."

"God, am I that transparent?" She put her hand to her cheek.

I'd laughed. "No, just . . . open in ways I wish I could be."

Now I needed to reinforce my claim I wasn't dating Ethan and end it once and for all. I checked the time on my phone. It was half past three. Almost morning. I knew Ethan was asleep. But I also knew that, come morning, things were going to get ten times more awkward if we didn't talk it out. After Chase and Julian had left Ethan and me, Katie and Lori had appeared from the dining room, demanding to know what had happened. I'd never gotten the chance to talk to him.

Slowly, I peeled the blanket from my body and slid my feet into my slippers. It was hot and humid, and I wore nothing but a white satin chemise.

I skated to the hallway, then rapped on Ethan's door. A gruff sound came from behind it. "Come in."

I stepped inside. The room was bathed in darkness. The outline of his body under the covers moved as he rearranged his frame, sitting up.

"Are you up?" I whispered.

"Yeah. You too, huh?"

I nodded. "Can we talk?"

"It's been long overdue, don't you think?"

I sat on the edge of his bed, twisting my fingers together in my lap. His head was pressed against the headboard. I felt his gaze on my silhouette. Thank God we were in the dark.

"Ethan, I—"

"I know." He cut me off, rubbing at his forehead. "Just . . . don't. Don't finish that sentence. I think I always knew. You were never really mine. I learned to accept that to a certain degree. I continued my steady hookup with Natalie, thinking if I kept my heart out of the race, maybe it would stay at arm's length. I thought it was a matter of time before Chase would screw it all up again and you'd come running back to my open arms. I kept waiting for you to step back from the Black fog, but he just kept sucking you in. The truth is, Maddie, it's not just that we're over. We've never really begun."

"I wanted us to be a thing," I said. Hot tears rolled down my cheeks, falling on the bare skin of my thighs. I didn't know why I was so upset. "You're perfect, Ethan."

"Please don't say that. It's what all my girlfriends said in high school." He sighed tiredly. "Perfect is boring."

I shook my head, pressing my knuckles to the sides of my eyes, drying the tears. "No, it's not. But perfect and broken do not coexist. Broken needs another broken to become whole. I have more issues than *Vogue*. I never really got over my mother's death, and . . . and . . . I have this compulsive need to please everybody. Which is why we're both here having this conversation." I motioned around us with a wave of a hand.

He laughed, sitting up fully now to be next to me. Thigh to thigh. "I've a feeling Chase is the definition of broken." Ethan sighed. "You're a good match."

I smiled sadly. "Lucky me, huh?"

"Unlucky me," Ethan countered. I swatted his arm. He was grinning in the dark. The atmosphere was shifting into something lighter. I wanted to keep it that way.

"Hey, can I ask you a question? Kind of personal, but I always wanted to know and will never get to find out." I nudged his knee with mine.

"Lay it on me."

"What's your favorite position?" I scrunched my nose. "Like . . . sexually."

"Missionary," he said. "Definitely missionary."

I smiled. *Damn you, Chase.* The arrogant jerk never got it wrong.

Ethan tucked his hands between his legs, nudging me with one of them. "Hey, do you think things would be different if he wasn't still in the picture?"

I mulled his question over for a few seconds. Honesty was the least I could give Ethan after everything we'd been through in our short, unconsummated relationship.

"No," I said finally. "You're a fully formed person, and I . . . I don't think I ever will be. I think there's a part of me still floating in the universe, searching for my mother." I stopped, frowning as I realized something. "Maybe that's why I've always been so obsessed with weddings. I've been hoping to find that something in someone else. Subconsciously. But I need to find it in myself."

"For what it's worth"—his lips found my temple, hovering over it as he spoke—"you are the best half person I've ever met, Maddie Goldbloom. Imperfections and all."

◆ ◆ ◆

By the time I left Ethan's bedroom, dawn was breaking over the horizon. The dark morphed from velvet into powder blue through the high windows. I stumbled out to the hallway, heading for the kitchen to get a glass of water. My mind was still buzzing with the realization I needed to find my missing piece in myself.

I was almost at the end of the hallway when Chase came out of his room. He wore gray sweatpants and those Kanye West–type sneakers that looked like expensive spaceships. He was bare chested and ready for an outside jog. His hair was a mess, his eyes bloodshot, though I was getting used to Exhausted Chase. It was somehow even sexier than Regular Chase.

Our gazes tangled in the unlit hallway.

His eyes dragged to Ethan's door, then back to mine. He popped an eyebrow in question. I shook my head. A barely visible gesture.

Nothing happened.

He caught it. His throat bobbed. A bubble of excitement swelled in my chest.

Beat.

Swelling.

Beat.

Swelling.

Beat.

The bubble popped when Chase pounced on me, his lips crashing down on mine with hunger that stunned me. There was nothing calculated, cold, or in control about that kiss. My back slammed against the wall with a loud thud, but I couldn't feel anything other than his tongue invading my mouth and his hands climbing up my thighs under my chemise, tracing the outline of my panties teasingly. When he found the wet patch of fabric at the center of my panties, he groaned into our kiss, squeezing his eyes shut as if experiencing something painful.

I snaked a hand between us and did what I'd wanted to do for weeks. Ran my fingers along his rock-hard abs, fingering the coarse happy trail of hair under his belly button until I found the outline of the part of him I'd always missed and never hated.

Chase grabbed my ass and hoisted me up so my legs wrapped around his waist while I was propped against the wall. He captured my jaw, extending my neck to kiss me more deeply. No. What we were doing wasn't kissing. He fucked my mouth ruthlessly, and I clenched against nothing, feeling my thighs locking in on his narrow waist with need.

"Bed," I groaned into our kiss.

"Not gonna try to talk you out of it," he groaned, his lips still not disconnecting from mine as he carried me back to his room and kicked the door shut. He was still kissing me when he toed his sneakers off. Then his lips dragged down my neck as he lowered me onto his bed, which was full of delicious Chase smell—of pine and rain and a dark forest where magical things happened. I felt so unexpectedly content that happy tears clung to my lashes.

"Chase," I moaned.

His hands ran up the sides of my thighs, hitching the thin fabric of my chemise up. His fingers danced on my skin—was he shaking?—with barely restrained urgency.

"Chase," I croaked again, desperate.

His mouth reluctantly unlatched from mine. He examined me warily. He thought I was going to stop it. To change my mind. Our hearts were slamming against one another through our chests.

"I broke up with Ethan. For good."

He blinked at me. I thought maybe he hadn't heard. Maybe all the blood had rushed down to his groin area. Based on the mammoth thing that was nestled between my legs, it wasn't exactly far fetched.

"Why?" he demanded. He sounded . . . *angry*.

Because you are worth the risk, and I'm the idiot who is about to take it. Again.

"Because of your offer."

"Be more specific?"

A temporary forever.

He was pulsating against my inner thigh. I thought I'd die if he didn't enter me.

"To be your fake girlfriend . . . until . . ." I groaned when his teeth found my nipple through my chemise, clamping on it. "Is the offer still standing?" My teeth chattered.

"It is," he murmured into my flesh.

"Then I accept."

He froze completely. I thought he'd misheard me. Why else would he stop all the deliciousness that was happening between us? Then he laced his fingers through mine, curling them against my engagement ring with one hand, and ripped the chemise from my body with the other. He did it easily, like ripping clothes was his regular gig. The punishing pain of the fabric snapping against my flesh stole my breath away. A thin pile of satin pooled beneath me on his bed. He nudged my panties aside—*the one clothing item he probably should rip,* I thought in amusement—brushing his index finger along my slit, dipping it inside me and curling it. He hit my G-spot without as much as a blink, grinning sinisterly as I sucked in a breath, my abs contracting. I'd forgotten how good he was at this.

Actually, no. I remembered very clearly how accomplished he was between the sheets, which was why I'd tried to stay away.

Chase kissed his way down my body, taking each pert nipple between his teeth and giving it an appreciative tug. The chill of his cold breath against my wet nipples made delicious shivers run down my body.

He continued his way south, kissing, dragging his teeth, nibbling. He halted at my belly button, dipping his tongue into it and giving it a swirl. I ran my fingers through the black crown of hair as he french-kissed the insides of my thighs.

Chase Black was glorious to look at from every angle, but especially when he gazed up at me with his pale eyes while sliding his tongue inside me, his half smirk still intact. His tongue began to flick inside me, and the crushing weight of an impending orgasm—and heartbreak—descended on my body like a ten-ton brick.

I grabbed one of his pillows and moaned into it, eager to keep our long-awaited reunion a secret. I felt my thighs quivering, every muscle in my body tightening, and knew I was close. My toes began to tingle and my breathing became labored as he continued tonguing me, reaching up to twist one of my nipples playfully.

"I wonder if my dad would get my insurance money if I spontaneously combust," I half whimpered, half pondered.

"Only you would say that right now." He chuckled into me as he went harder, deeper, faster, pushing two fingers into me as he devoured me. I clenched, every single muscle in my body tight and frozen. Pleasure swept over my body in hot waves.

My breath shook when I came down from the high. Chase's mouth was still pressed to my entrance. He licked his way up my stomach, then shoved his tongue into my mouth in a dirty kiss. I tasted myself and didn't feel like slipping under a rock and living there for the rest of my life. He had this thing about him, Chase. No matter how badly we bickered with each other, he always made me feel goddess-like in bed.

I pushed my hand between us and cupped the length of him, kicking his pants down carnally with my feet. I tried to lower myself to his groin to return the favor, but he pinned me back to the bed. "I'm afraid foreplay is not in the cards for us. I've been waiting for this to happen since the moment you dumped me." He reached for his nightstand, flipped his wallet open, and took out a condom before ripping the wrapper with his teeth and spitting it on the floor.

He sank inside me, sheathed and throbbing, entering me slowly, deeply, his face so concentrated and intense I couldn't close my eyes.

I arched my back, realizing how much I'd missed it. Missed *him*. Then he stopped. Chase stared at me while he was inside of me. The weight of the entire world felt like it was lodged in the few inches between our chests.

"Hey." His voice was almost a croak.

"Hey," I *did* croak.

"I'm inside you. Again." He tucked a stray flyaway behind my ear.

"All evidence points in that direction." I looked down between us where our bodies met.

He laughed, kissing my neck, then capturing my mouth as he began thrusting inside me again. He swallowed my moans with kisses, and my eyelids finally rolled shut as I gave in to the moment.

Chase grabbed the backs of my thighs, pounding into me more forcefully. I bit my lower lip to suppress a cry of pleasure. I felt my breasts bouncing as he quickened his pace. He watched as they bobbed with a hooded, dirty gaze that made me clench around him like a vise. The bedsprings whined each time he pushed into me. We moved together in complete sync.

"Mad," he groaned, looking away as if he was embarrassed about how present he was in the moment. I met him thrust for thrust, rolling my hips as he drove into me, and felt him jerking inside me uncontrollably.

"Fuck," he hissed, flattening his palm over my lower stomach and holding me still as he pounded into me like he was trying to get rid of a demon that had taken hold of his body. "No, no, no."

No?

A second climax unfurled under my belly button and spread to my legs, my chest, my fingertips when Chase flipped me onto my stomach, propping me back by my hip bones and entering me from behind. I let out a groan, adjusting to the new position.

"Fuck," he said again. "That's not working for me either."

But he was still having sex with me, and his voice sounded so strained I couldn't see him *not* enjoying it. Unless . . .

The satisfaction I felt was too much. It spread inside my chest like warm honey.

He was trying not to come. And *failing*.

"How close are you?" he hissed, the voice coming out in a short breath. The sound of us, flesh hitting flesh, and the *thwack!* of my wetness filled the room. I wondered if he was turned on by how unlikely we were in bed. How small and short I was, how big and muscular and tall *he* was.

"Close," I moaned.

He began to massage my clit as he continued thrusting into me. My entire body trembled.

"I'm coming."

"Thank fuck. Let me see." He grabbed my short hair, extending my neck and staring me right in the eye. It was such a weird, intimate thing to do. And yet I met his gaze, my eyes sleepy as the orgasm ripped through me like a current. My mouth fell, O shaped, and he let go of my hair, thrusting a few more times and collapsing on top of me.

I felt the warm, thick liquid of his come inside me through the condom. His sweaty chest was plastered on my back. My head tucked under his chin. He groaned a few more times, pumping inside me lazily. I let out a soft whimper. He was two hundred pounds of muscles and ego the size of Staten Island. Heavy.

"Am I making pita bread out of you?" he asked sleepily.

"I never could resist carbs."

He laughed. "Why is it," he said to the nape of my neck, blowing my fine baby hair with his warm breath, "that you make me feel like a sixteen-year-old boy who just found out about pussy? What is it about you, Madison Goldbloom, that drives me goddamn wild?"

"Must be the patterned dresses," I said into his pillow.

He kissed the back of my neck, laughing. "I mean, you mentioned your dad while I had my tongue *inside* you. My dick should've run away screaming. What makes you different from everyone else to me?"

The fact that he questioned it aloud was half-insulting, half-flattering.

"I'm me." I shrugged, closing my eyes. "I'm myself, and everyone else tries to be someone else around you. To fit into your neat, all-Black universe. I live in color. I guess that's a challenge for you."

Suddenly, there was nothing I wanted more than to fall asleep.

So I did.

A fallen angel, dipped in the devil's darkness, engulfed by his strong, deadly arms.

CHAPTER NINETEEN

Chase

The rest of the weekend on the ranch did not suck, unlike Madison, who reminded me her mouth was the eighth wonder of the world. It was the best time I'd had in months. Fine, *years*. The weekend consisted of good food, pleasant conversation, and mind-blowing sex. I would have low-key suspected I'd died and gone to heaven if it weren't for the fact I got an email from my accountant reminding me my quarterly tax payment was due.

If I thought I'd mythologized sex with Madison after we'd broken up to console myself for the subpar fucks I had to deal with, I was wrong. The real thing was even better than I remembered.

Longer, harder, and wetter too.

The only downside to the weekend was that Ethan Goddamn Goodman was still on the premises, horseback riding with us, sitting at our table, flirting with Katie (who looked less grossed out by the prospect of making out with my girlfriend's ex than I'd expected). For the sake of full disclosure, I didn't mind him dating my sister. He was not, I realized upon reflecting on the matter more closely, the fuckboy I'd thought he was. He seemed like the playing-it-safe, ankle-socked churchgoer my sister would be happy with. I just didn't think he was a suitable match to my Madison. I mean, Madison. Not *my* Madison. She wasn't mine. I knew that.

The night before the morning we were all heading back to the city, Ethan had to rush back to Manhattan for an emergency. He offered Katie a ride, glancing at Madison, who gave him the thumbs-up with a wide grin.

That left us free of Ethan and Katie at breakfast. Which meant I was able to do the one thing I'd been fantasizing about since I'd come up with the fake-engagement plan. During breakfast, very casually and very offhandedly, I leaned down and kissed Madison on the lips. It was nothing more than a peck. I thought people who PDA'd ought to be publicly executed in the town square. But it was enough to show everyone it was real.

The look on Amber's face—like she'd swallowed a fly—paired with Julian's appalled frown almost made me laugh.

Now that we were heading home, I was irritated with the idea of saying goodbye. My ex-slash-current-slash-temporary girlfriend was delectable, and she kept my mind off Dad's illness, which was definitely a bonus.

"Where do you want to sleep tonight?" I asked, driving at a pace that would make senior citizens look like delinquent punks. The rural view passed like flicking pictures, turning gradually into more concrete, higher buildings, and narrower pavements the closer we got to New York.

"My bed." She laughed. "Where else?"

"Mine," I said flatly.

"Daisy," she pointed out. "She probably misses me a lot."

"You could bring her to mine." *What the heck am I saying?* Seeing women's stray hairs on my pillow made me want to refurnish the whole apartment. A ball of fur on my floor would likely make me burn the entire building down.

"I think she'd freak out." Mad paused. "Actually, I think you would too. No thanks."

I waited for an invitation while Mad flicked through a wedding magazine she'd brought along with her. *For research,* I reminded myself. She knew the score. When we entered Manhattan, I finally said, "Or I could sleep at yours."

She closed the magazine, perching it over her crossed legs. "Don't you want your own space? We just spent a weekend together."

"Getting laid regularly beats personal space," I replied wryly. "Any day of the week. It's science."

"Does that mean you are giving monogamy a chance while we're temporarily together?" It was more a taunt than a question.

"Do you want me to?" I countered. I sounded like my mother and sister passive aggressively trying to convince each other to eat the last slice of the pie on Thanksgiving.

"Do *you* want to?" she answered. My brain keyboard smashed a crass reply. Was she five?

"Sure," I clipped. "I'll do *temporary* monogamy. If you do."

"If I do?" She grinned at me in my periphery. "Am I known for running around town bed-hopping?"

Good point. It was true that ever since we'd gotten into bed, it felt like I was losing a few IQ points every time I came inside her. It was like she sucked the logic out of me. The Delilah to my Samson, if he were a genius and she were . . . well, a quirky hipster. I took a sip of my coffee.

"Do you think if we ever made a sex tape, it would look weird? You're so big," Mad mused.

I nearly sprayed my coffee all over my windshield. "First of all, I would never make a sex tape—or document being affectionate toward another person in any capacity." I tucked the foam cup into the cup holder. "But let me assure you, we do not look awkward in bed."

"How do you know?"

"Because I watched us in my bedroom mirror when we were doing it." Pause. "We looked fucking epic, *thankyouverymuch*."

Mad played with her engagement ring, pouting as she processed all this. We were ten minutes from her house. She still didn't tell me whether I could crash at hers. I got irritated with her again. Maybe it was a good idea to spend some time separately.

"I think I'd like to sleep by myself tonight," she said finally. "You know, just to make sure the relationship is not too intense and we don't catch any feelings toward one another."

"Fine," I said. I didn't have the heart to correct her and point out that . . . well, I *didn't* have a heart, so catching feelings was not on the menu for me.

"Great."

I parked in front of her brownstone and helped her with the suitcases. After depositing them in her living room, we kissed on the lips, and I turned around and walked back down to my car.

Stopped at the building's entrance.

Made a U-turn and went back up, my fist already curled and ready to knock on her door. I raised my hand to knock, but the door flung open just as my knuckles were about to hit the wood. Madison stood there, panting.

I blinked, awaiting directions. Should I kiss her? Give her her space? Berate her for being so goddamn indecisive?

"Ground rules"—she raised her palm in warning—"because I know you don't have feelings, but I do, and I'm here to protect myself first."

I jerked my chin up, indicating that I was listening. I stood outside her apartment. She was standing inside. I wanted permission to get in. I'd probably agree to sell entire sections of Black & Co. for a blowie right now.

"One, no more than three sleepovers a week between both apartments. That's the ratio."

"Done," I snapped.

"Two, you take care of Daisy while I'm out of town. It's not fair for Layla to have to babysit her. You were the one who gifted her to me."

"You said you always wanted a puppy when we passed an Aussiedoodle on the street," I pointed out. I'd thought I was doing her a goddamn favor at the time.

She stared at me like I was insane. "I say a lot of things, Chase. I also said I want to get married in an Italian château."

"And?" I stared at her blankly.

"And of course I'll get married in my dad's backyard!" She threw her hands in the air like it was obvious.

"Whatever. I'll take care of Daisy when you are out of town and will not gift you anything that requires more than water or batteries to survive." I made a mental note to gift her awful things only. Heating pads and flowery planners and hand creams that smelled like desserts. The cheap shit that made Mad smile. "Anything else?" I spread my arms theatrically.

"Hmm." She tapped her lower lip. "Oh yeah. No telling anyone at our jobs about us. This thing between us has an expiration date, and I don't want to look like you've dumped me. Twice."

Mad hadn't told anyone we'd dated, then or now. I, however, didn't give a shit who saw me kissing her in the mornings when we came to work together.

"You weren't dumped by me the first time around either."

She waved me off. "They'll just assume."

She wasn't wrong. People always assumed the person with the money was the one doing the dumping.

"And one more thing." She lifted her finger in the air. I did hope it was just the one, because I was starting to think it might be a good idea to have my corporate lawyer present. Mad had a lot of rules for what was possibly going to be a two-week fling, if even that. My stomach churned at the thought of what that meant for Dad.

"Get it over with." I rolled my eyes.

"When this is done, promise me you will never seek me out or try to prolong this relationship. You said I'm obsessed with weddings and marriage, and it's not untrue. Those are things I care deeply about, even if it's not feminist or hipster or Manhattan circa 2020. Promise you will let me go once and for all. Do the decent thing and stop pursuing me when we say goodbye."

"I promise," I said, taking a step forward, erasing the space between us. We were mouth to mouth now. Chest to chest. Cock to pussy. "I promise to spare your heart. Now may I please have the rest of you?"

She wrapped her arms around my neck. "After we shower, you may."

I captured her mouth, kissing her with intent. I kicked my shoes off as I backed her into her apartment. The level of satisfaction and relief I felt at sleeping at her place should have worried me. Luckily, 90 percent of my blood flow was under my belt, so my brain didn't have much to work with.

"Kismet," she murmured into my mouth.

"Come again?" I asked. *And again and again and again.* On my face ideally.

"Layla's word of the day was *kismet* on Friday. I just looked at her door."

I made an indifferent sound to signal that I'd heard her, backed her the rest of the way into her shower, turned the stream on with our clothes still on, and peeled her dress off with my teeth.

Hands down the longest, dirtiest shower I'd ever had.

Two days later, Grant and I were jogging in Central Park. A habit we stuck to from when we were teenagers, since we both lived on the same block and were self-diagnosed with ADHD and needed to let out some energy. Sometimes we'd jog quietly; sometimes we'd talk about school and girls and work and shit (not literal shit, other than that time Grant had gotten vicious food poisoning during a ski vacation in Tahoe, which we'd discussed at length).

We usually topped the full loop, a 6.1-mile daily run, followed by a short strength training session in my building's gym before starting our workday. Since I'd spent yesterday at Mad's, only visiting my apartment to grab clean clothes and take a half-hour dump (it was decidedly ungentlemanly to occupy a lady's studio apartment bathroom just so you could scroll through every single article in the *New York Times* while you sat on the shitter, I'd been told), we'd skipped a day's worth of workouts.

"So things are getting serious, then." Grant was the vision of a runner, with his cushioned running shoes, running shorts, ball cap, Apple Watch, and special gel socks. All he needed to complete his look was a goddamn number plastered onto his back, à la Usain Bolt. I was more understated, with—you fucking guessed it, ding ding ding—*black* running shorts, a *black* tee, and *black* sneakers Katie gifted me every three months to ensure the soles of my feet weren't made exclusively out of blisters. I wasn't into half marathons like Katie and Ethan, though. I worked out because I didn't want to die young or sport a midthirties gut.

"Au contraire, Gerwig. We have a tight deadline, so I'm making the most of it. I have it all worked out."

Once Dad died, so would the relationship with Madison.

"I would love to hear this," Grant said, pretending to prop his chin over his fist, not breaking his pace. "Tell me how you worked this out."

"I'm going to spend the days with Dad. Go back to his place every day after work, play chess, have dinner, watch TV, talk, then go to Mad's in the evening and spend the night with her. That way I enjoy both worlds without getting played again."

"Getting played," Grant repeated, waiting for further explanation.

"Last time, I got sucked into a black hole of dirty fucks and clean conversation. Never again."

"It's called falling in love, you idiot. You fell in love and got butt hurt nobody sent you the memo. So you proceeded to do something mind-blowingly stupid, regretted it, got a second chance, and now, from what I'm gathering here, you are about to screw it up again."

Fell in love. Those were the words he'd used. Grant was certifiable. Of that, I was certain. The fact I trusted him with my father's health concerned me.

"I don't want a relationship," I clipped out.

"Well, you are in one."

"She knows it's not real," I said, even though it wasn't lost on me that we were about to shit all over the three-nights-a-week rule.

"It's not her I'm worried about, Chase."

We were rounding the curve, going uphill. I remembered my dad had told me the roads in Central Park were curved to prevent horse-and-carriage racing. I wondered how many other fact nuggets he hadn't had the chance to tell me yet. Grant fell behind, and I took the opportunity to flip the conversation on him.

"What about you and Layla?" I asked.

"It's over."

"Interesting," I said. It wasn't interesting, though. Grant and Layla were about as compatible as Daisy and Frank. Grant wanted a serious relationship, and Layla wanted to fuck as many people as she physically could before meeting her maker.

"Yeah." Grant sighed. "I found out she doesn't want children."

"You knew she didn't want children," I countered. It had literally been her first line of conversation when he'd met her. *Hi, I'm Layla. I don't want children, but I'm a preschool teacher. Please save me your opinion about that. Oh, hey, nice shirt.*

"Well, I thought it was flexible. You know, like people who say they won't overeat during Thanksgiving dinner because they're watching their weight but still pig out when push comes to shove."

"Children and pumpkin pies *do* have a lot in common," I drawled sarcastically, quickening my pace. Grant caught up to me. "I still don't understand why you didn't let the relationship run its course while having a steady lay."

"Because I'm not a complete idiot," he explained through gritted teeth. "I don't want to wake up two years from now with a woman who wants the exact opposite of what I do."

"How did she take it?" I asked, because it seemed like something I should do.

"Quite well, seeing as she did the dumping."

"Crap," I offered. "Sorry."

Obviously, I was an excellent friend, with great, valuable input.

"Don't you think it's ironic? Layla dumped me because I wanted to get serious. You tried to scare Maddie away because she *was* serious. Things would have worked perfectly if only Madison and I had met before you and she did. Then she could have set you up with Layla."

"You and Mad?" I bit out. "No chance. She's too weird, and you're too . . . *you*."

"Is that so?" Grant asked in amusement. He was goading me.

"Maybe I'm wrong. Maybe you could make a good couple. Doesn't matter. Bro code determines you can't touch her with a ten-foot pole because I touched her first." I paused. "And I touched her *everywhere*."

"I don't think it works like that." Grant laughed, and I felt my body stiffening. I wanted to race him up the hill just so I could roll him down it, hoping he'd break a goddamn hip. "We're not in high school anymore. You don't even like her very much. According to you, anyway."

"What the fuck are you insinuating, Grant?" I stopped running, scowling at my friend. Grant kept running in place. I'd always thought running in place was the international sign of being a pretentious dick.

Hadn't Ethan done it just the other day? Suddenly, I couldn't stand the sight of my best friend.

"Don't be so upset. Even if I ever decided to make a move on Maddie, she will never date me. Bro code may not be a thing, but sister code is real, and Maddie is a good apple. She'd never do it to Layla."

I knew he was right. I continued jogging, ignoring him chuckling beside me. It wasn't that funny. So what if I didn't want my best friend to sleep with my ex? That didn't mean I was in *love* with her.

"As for what I was insinuating," he said through a wide smile, "I believe the term I was looking for is you, my friend, are royally, crucially, and officially fucked."

CHAPTER TWENTY

MADDIE

Almost a whole Ethan-free week had passed since our amicable, grown-up breakup.

It rolled like a holiday collage. Photoshopped family dinners at the Blacks', exchanging acute opinions about the royal family's best fashionistas with Lori, whispering like a schoolgirl with Katie, and braiding Clemmy's hair as I taught her how to make ready-made cupcakes. I talked to Ronan as much as I could without monopolizing his time. I had firsthand experience when it came to dealing with a sick relative. People often preferred to avoid the sick. To converse with other family members. Those who were easier to look at, I guessed.

I learned how to ignore Amber and Julian without popping blood vessels whenever they addressed me like I was a servant. It wasn't that difficult, actually. Amber was usually drinking herself to oblivion for social-lubrication purposes and was easy to outwit. Julian was still a snake but spent much of his time either trying to sneak meetings with Ronan or locking himself with Chase in the library, where the octaves reached a few Broadway-worthy highs, even with the doors closed.

I didn't ask Chase about his meetings with Julian. It wasn't my business. I knew Julian was privy to my kiss with Ethan but guessed Chase had taken care of that. I didn't want to get involved. The more I knew, the more I got attached, and I was desperately trying to cling onto the remainder of my senses and keep my heart out of this arrangement.

My body, however, was a keen participant. Chase and I had sex like it was a competitive sport. *And we were winning.* In my bed and his, in the shower, in his bathtub, on the kitchen counter (his—I was no rookie), against his floor-to-ceiling windows, and on my washing machine (a personal fantasy of mine).

I kept waking up every morning telling myself that Chase Black was a temporary fix. Like a Band-Aid or SlimFast. Something to keep me occupied while I was waiting for the real thing to come. I refused to go to events with him, and when Chase mentioned something about a double date with Grant and a colleague of his (*Really? That fast?*), I flat-out told him there was no way I'd be seen with him in public. Those were the safety measures I was careful to take, even if the three-times-a-week sleepover rule had gone out the window.

Then a message from Ethan came. It was on the one morning I spent without Chase. At some point yesterday, I'd physically pushed him out of my apartment to ensure some me time.

Ethan sent me my azaleas back. What was left of them, anyway. The flowers were wilted, the leaves curling in gray and black at the edges, shriveling into themselves. The pot in which he kept it was coated with tar-like sand, clustered together. I held it in my arms and looked up to my windowsill, where my flowers thrived, then back to the dead azaleas again, something red and hot and angry sizzling behind my rib cage. There was a note. I plucked it out.

So sorry. Was busy keeping people alive, forgot about plant. Maybe you can save it?

Thank you for the gift, though.
—E

◆ ◆ ◆

I thought about the dead azaleas the entire portion of the first half of my day while working on my Dream Wedding Dress. I stabbed at the sketch pad with my pencil, tearing it several times.

"What happened? Did one of your kids die?" Nina taunted from her corner of the studio once Sven was out of earshot, referring to the wilted plant. "Bad mommy, Maddie."

I ducked my head down and continued working.

"Maddie." Sven appeared behind my shoulder. I jumped, gasping. "How are you?"

I opened my mouth to answer, but he cut me off with a wave of his hand. "Never mind, I'm not here for small talk. Is the sketch ready?"

"Almost." I held it to my chest protectively. I'd grown very attached to this sketch. It meant a lot to me. I'd designed it seeing myself wearing the dress.

"Let's see it." He dragged a stool from someone else's station and sat in front of me.

"Now?" I looked around, buying time.

"No better time than the present." He pried the clipboard with my sketch from between my fingers. I sucked in a breath, feeling the walls of the studio closing in on me. My lungs were scorching, I was so nervous.

"Oh," was all Sven said, after a full minute of silence. *Oh* couldn't be good. He didn't even drag out the *h*. *Ohhhhh*. Nope. Just the *Oh*. I was feeling nauseous.

Sven's brows pulled together. "There's a lot of detail here."

"Yeah," I said. "You asked me to be artistic."

"I figured you'd be sane too." He scrunched his nose, still looking at the sketch.

"You actually used the words *off the wall*," I countered, not really believing my own ears. Was I arguing with Sven? That was a definite first. I'd never challenged my boss. I suspected this was why he'd promoted me so quickly. I was his yes-woman. But not now. Not when I knew this dress was my best design to date.

Sven held the sketch out to me, his eyes finding mine. "Look, I'm not saying it's not good, but there's money to be made, and this season is all about simple strokes."

"You specifically told me there are no rules to abide by." I snatched the sketch from his hands. "And that's exactly what I did. Everyone is going to turn up to Fashion Week with variations of the same simplistic dress, and I'm going to give them something new. Something grand. Something out of this world. You gave me this assignment because you said I was ready. Well, I am, Sven. And I love this design. Love it wholeheartedly."

I thought about Chase's words of encouragement. He seemed to love it. No, more than that. He was mesmerized by it. It helped my decision to stick to this sketch. Wedding dresses weren't only about haute couture. Sometimes, they were just about seeing men—men like Chase—looking at a pretty dress and having that punch-in-the-gut feeling.

Sven stared at me long and hard. I looked right back at him. Even though it was out of character, I knew I was doing the right thing. Not only for myself but for the company.

He jerked his jaw toward my sketch. "I'll get a lot of shit about it from the bigwigs, you know."

I held his gaze. "It's also off white."

His eyes widened. "But swan white—"

I shook my head, holding my palm up. "It will sell, Sven. I promise you."

He stood up, scratching his cheek. I thought he was shocked. I definitely was, by my own stubbornness.

"When did you become so"—he searched for the right word—"fierce?"

I smiled. "Since I found out being a pushover doesn't equal being nice. Being strong is not only kind on myself—but on other people too."

◆ ◆ ◆

At half past noon, while everyone was taking their break, someone tapped my shoulder. I was still hunched over my drawing table, tongue poking out of the side of my mouth, sketching. I turned around.

Chase was standing there, lifting a white plastic bag full of containers. I could smell the pho soup and detect the paper-thin white-rice dumplings in the small plastic bowls. My mouth watered for exactly five seconds before I realized what he was doing.

I gave him a small shove, peeking to see if Nina was at her station. She wasn't.

"Are you insane?" I whisper-shouted, feeling my eyes widening. "Someone could see you here."

"And?" He narrowed his eyes at me. "I'm offering you soup, not dick. The rumor mill won't go haywire if we take lunch together."

I realized I was being ungrateful. He'd come in with the intention of feeding me. I took a calming breath, plastering a smile on my face. "Although I am very touched by your concern, I am also very adamant no one should know about us. It is temporary, and as I said—"

"Yeah, yeah." He waved his free hand like he'd heard this speech thousands of times before. "God forbid someone thinks you got dumped by the boss."

"It's not just that." I gritted my teeth. He parked a hip over my drawing board, waiting for an explanation. I looked around. The studio was empty. It was one of those summer days when staying indoors felt borderline masochistic. I glanced at my phone. We had at least thirty minutes until people began to trickle back in. Plus, he was right. We were sharing food, not orgasms. I shook my head. "Fine. Only because you're twisting my arm."

"I'll be twisting a lot more of you after we're done with the main course." He winked.

Chase quickly set the table at our kitchenette while I grabbed us two cans of Diet Coke. I told him about Ethan's azaleas, watching carefully for his reaction. I'd visited Chase's place a few times since I'd given him the azaleas but knew he'd gotten rid of them at some point. They were no longer on his living room table or anywhere else in the apartment. He'd failed the test he'd set up for himself. Not that it mattered—as we'd both agreed, this was just temporary.

"Flower murderer." Chase tsked, fishing out a shrimp from his soup with chopsticks and throwing it into his mouth. "That's a shame, considering Katie has a lady boner for him."

"She does?" I slurped a noodle between my lips. Katie and Ethan made sense, in the same way cookies and milk did. Uninspiring but legendarily fitting. A classic. Chase frowned, and I realized he mistook my contemplation for something else.

"That an issue?" He dropped his chopsticks to his soup. I nibbled on crab cake, letting him wait. I didn't like his tone.

"Nope," I said finally, popping the *p*. Chase was still frowning. I saw the moment when he decided to drop it. Change the subject. He dabbed the corners of his mouth with a napkin.

"Would you accompany me to the bathroom, Miss Goldbloom?"

"Hmm." I looked around me. The office was still empty. "You can go by yourself. I trust you're fully potty trained."

"I'm not sure where the bathroom is on this floor," he said dryly.

"That is the stupidest excuse I've ever heard." I stared at him, mildly amused by how much he wanted to lure me into his clutches.

He offered me a one-shoulder shrug. "I channel my working brain cells into managing a company that's worth billions of dollars. Priorities, baby."

"All this humblebrag," I taunted.

"You're right. Telling you I'm good is bad form. Allow me to demonstrate." Chase winked, offering me his hand over the table. I took it, watching our fingers lacing together. He tugged me forward. I stood up, glancing around and rounding the table to sit in his lap. I had a great view of the elevators and could tell when they opened. It left me a three-second window to stand up. I was safe.

"That's better." His eyes were molten silver, darkened by lust. He rubbed his thumb across my lower lip. "Much, much better."

Our lips met, hovering at first. Our eyelids dropped at the same time. We shared a breath. A pulse. The same heartbeat for a second. His mouth moved on mine. Patiently. Seductively. Almost sweetly. The thing about good kisses, I'd found, was that they were like good wine. They got you drunk before you realized it. They were spell-like.

"Is this HR-manual appropriate for Black & Co.?" I murmured into his lips. "Because it sure as hell isn't allowed here in Croquis."

"I've never read either, but if it isn't, I am liable to buy Croquis just to make it so." He kissed me again, not a trace of sarcasm in his voice. I laughed into our kiss, biting his lower lip softly.

"I should feed you more often," he said.

"You can take care of my dinner." I kissed him again. I knew we were treading dangerously close to getting caught, but for the life of me I couldn't stop.

"It's a date."

"We don't do those," I reminded him. "Remember the rules?"

He pretended to roll his eyes, grabbing my ass and grinding me against his erection. "But we still do this, so let me ask you again—where's the restroom?"

"Someone might catch us."

"They won't."

"How do you know?" I nearly purred. I reminded myself of a virginal, marginally uneducated teenybopper listening to the high school's handsome quarterback explaining to her why he could use the pullout method and not get her pregnant in the bed of his truck.

"Simple. I know everything," Chase snapped, his face masklike.

"You're not—" I started.

He cut me off. "A little faith, Mad. You only live once."

Ain't that the truth. Chase must've gathered his last sentence had gotten to me, because he smirked. "Come on. We don't have long."

I didn't know whether he meant my lunch break or at all. More than likely, he meant both.

We raced to the restroom hand in hand. Chase banged a stall door open and tugged me inside, kissing me everywhere. I murmured something about the HR manual of Croquis and my concerns about the lack of hygiene in doing what we were about to do. Then lust won over, and before I knew what was happening, I was pressed against the door, Chase between my thighs. He unbuckled and pressed himself against me, nudging my panties away under my dress.

"I love that you wear dresses." He kissed my nose. I snatched his lips before he moved away, devouring him passionately. "It makes you fuckable not only theoretically but logistically too. Thing is, I don't have a condom," he whispered into my mouth. "But I'm clean."

"I'm on the pill and clean," I said.

"Well, I'm about to dirty you up."

As he entered me, the thought that I was breaking one of my very own rules occurred to me. Having sex without a condom was most definitely real-relationship territory. Then again, *not* having sex with him right now would likely kill me.

He entered me deeply, grabbing one of my thighs and stretching it along his body.

I threw my head back, banging it against the door, then whimpered. "I'm going to die."

"Be a good sport and wait a few minutes. I'd really appreciate coming before I leave here." He pushed into me harder. I laughed. He laughed too. Was it weird that we were laughing while having sex? Probably. But it was the essence of Chase and me. Whatever we had with each other was always dipped in something crazy.

Bathroom sex proved to be less sexy than advertised on TV. For one thing, we were both sweating. The industrial AC didn't extend to the restrooms. My dress clung to my flesh like wrapping film. I looked up at Chase, surprised by the boyish vulnerability I saw on his face when he thought I wasn't looking. The orgasm built inside me. Every time he entered me, the tip of his buckle hit my clit. I was shaking all over, not exactly sure what suspended me in the air from falling flat on my butt. Physics aside, I didn't want this to end. Ever. And that frightened me.

"Come, Mad," he groaned.

"No." I kissed the curve of his jaw. "No, no, no. I want to continue. Can't you hold it a little bit longer?"

"I can," he said painfully, but he was losing himself, I could tell. His eyes were hazy, the first tremors of him coming undone, making his tight muscles dance. "But the time . . ."

Just as he said it, I came apart, letting out a loud moan, clutching his shoulders. He held me in place, but instead of pumping inside me and searching for his own release, he cupped his hand over my mouth.

I heard the door to the restroom flinging open, then slamming shut. It felt like a bucket of ice water was dumped all over my orgasm. My eyes flared, my mouth pursing behind his hand.

No, no, no, no.

He lowered me down to my feet, helping me smooth my dress over my thighs, still hard and unsatisfied. I slapped his hand away, feeling the tears stinging the backs of my eyeballs. Of course he'd said it would be okay. And of course it wasn't. I was such an idiot to trust him. But I couldn't deny my own responsibility. I was the bubbleheaded cheerleader who'd agreed to go bareback in that imaginary truck bed. Hell, I'd let the quarterback take a shit all over me.

"Mad," he said, tucking himself back in. There was something surprisingly pitiful about watching Chase still hard and wanting, trying to console me. I knew he hadn't wanted this to happen. That he'd tried to warn me when he'd heard the door. "Whoever it is doesn't know that it's you. Your legs were wrapped around me, so they couldn't see your shoes. All they heard was moaning. For all they knew, there was someone constipated in this cubicle."

"*One* of my legs was wrapped around you," I countered, while we stood in the stall, which suddenly felt so much smaller than it had been when we'd first entered it. I wanted to get out of there but dreaded leaving at the same time. "Just the one. The other was still on the floor."

"Your shoes are not that recognizable," he tried to reason. We both looked down at my shoes. I was wearing flowery heels with a yellow bow at the front. Pretty darn recognizable unless you lived on a Eurovision set.

"Maybe they didn't look down," Chase suggested.

"After hearing a couple having sex in a bathroom stall?" I laughed bitterly. "Fat chance, Chase."

"Mad." He bracketed my face, pressing his temple to mine.

I shook my head, trying to escape his touch. "Whatever. You got your way. Wasn't it your bottom line today? Getting your way?" I sounded bitter and not myself.

"Mad."

"What?" I snapped.

"Don't worry. Whatever's gonna happen, we're going to deal with it together."

My knees high-fived each other the entire way to my office. I tried to give myself an internal pep talk. Tell myself Chase was right. There was no reason to believe people knew what we'd been doing or that it had been me in the stall.

I returned to gather and dump all the food containers in the kitchenette. There a note was waiting on the fridge, typed out in a Word document so no one could recognize the handwriting:

Riddle me this: She is cute, small, and a little MAD,

but her milkshake still brings all the boys to the yard.

More specifically, I just caught her with her pants down, having sex with Black & Co.'s big boss.

The one who wears BLACK and normally dates the likes of Kate Moss.

With this kind of lip service, no wonder she just got a promotion.

So much for being Martyr Maddie, full of goodwill and devotion.

I ripped the note from the fridge and threw it into the trash can. Storming to my station, I glanced behind my shoulder. Nina was busy filing her nails, humming an Ariana Grande tune with a smile on her face. She caught me glaring at her, picked up a pint of milkshake on her desk, and took a noisy slurp.

Her milkshake brings all the boys to the yard. Aha. It didn't take a private investigator to see this as an admission of guilt. I was so embarrassed I'd gotten caught I wanted to cry. I fished my phone out.

Maddie: We're busted.

Chase: How do you know?

Maddie: There was a note on the fridge.

Chase: Shit. Do you know who caught us?

Us. He'd said *us*. That made me hopeful he saw this as a mutual problem.

Maddie: Nina Na, I think. Of course it would be my archnemesis.

Chase: Her name is Nina Na and you taunted ME for having a made-up sounding name?

Maddie: She's quarter-Korean, I think. Focus, Black.

Chase: I'll deal with it.

Maddie: That sounds cryptic and super shady. What are you going to do?

Chase: Leave it to me. I'll see you tonight.

CHAPTER TWENTY-ONE

Chase

Overall, if I had to rate yesterday, I'd give it a will-not-visit-again, I-want-my-money-back zero-star review.

Other than me not dying in a freak subway accident, everything had gone south. Mad and I got caught boning on her floor restroom (my fault), Katie nagged me about asking Mad if it was okay if she went out with Ethan (this man was hell bent on screwing his way into my close circle, or so it seemed), and—the cherry on the shit cake—Dad gathered Julian, our CFO (Gavin), and me and announced he was going to work remotely from home from next week forward. What he really meant was he couldn't even stand on both legs anymore. He still hadn't shared his medical situation with the board, and I guessed I did see Julian's point at this stage, but I would rather die than side with the asshole.

Dad had lost twenty-three pounds in less than two months and was looking a lot like death. Keeping the illness to himself was straight-up dumb at this point. And still, I couldn't exactly judge him. There was something embarrassing—almost humiliating—about dying. And he was a powerful man.

Julian had been the first to react to Dad's news. He'd hugged him, said he understood, and asked if retirement was in the cards for him. This time, Dad hadn't seemed so against it. He'd told us he'd invite us over to discuss it further.

Julian was working hard behind the scenes, spreading rumors about my performance as COO, planning to stage a vote of no confidence once I inherited the role. There was also that stupid Ethan-Madison-Chase triangle he was still banging on about, but since that could be easily evaporated—Katie was seconds from dating Ethan, and Mad and I were actually together-together—I concentrated on working my ass off and staying in my own lane. I knew I was going to deal with Julian eventually, but I hoped to drag it out until after Dad had passed away so he wouldn't be there to see it when I finally tore Julian limb from limb and threw whatever was left of him to the corporate streets, to start from the bottom at some bullshit company because no one in the city would work with him.

I got it. I did. Julian had been blindsided by my existence. Katie and I were a pleasant surprise to Lori and Ronan Black, who didn't think they were able to conceive. Let me amend—I was a miracle. Katie, a pleasant surprise. My mother had suffered from polycystic ovary syndrome, and the doctors said her chances of falling pregnant were pretty much nonexistent. Julian had spent a good chunk of his childhood believing he was the sole heir to the Black empire. My oopsie appearance when he was ten hadn't meant much to him at the time, but as he'd grown older, he'd begun to resent me more and more when he'd realized the fortune-and-power pie would need to be shared.

And he definitely did not appreciate the fact I'd proved to be better than him in every single thing we both touched.

After a disastrous day at work, I'd driven Dad back home and sat by his side, but he'd been barely conscious.

By the time I'd left my parents' house, I'd been too exhausted to go to Mad and extinguish the getting-caught fire we were currently burning in. I'd gone back to my apartment, gotten hammered, left half-apologetic messages to a thoroughly freaked-out Madison, and passed out.

This morning, I was hoping to sort out some of the clusterfuck also known as my life. I sent Madison flowers to her office. The big-ass, expensive kind. Flowers that didn't say *thank you for the casual lay* but made no room for doubt I was serious. That way, that Nina chick and Mad's other colleagues would at least know she wasn't the flavor of the week.

Throwing money at the Madison problem was the first and last good thing about my morning. As soon as I got into the office, I realized something was amiss. And when I said *amiss*, I meant my brousin's sanity.

He was standing in the middle of the office, arms spread, in a crumpled suit with a coffee stain the size of Minnesota, giving frantic directions to every secretary and assistant in sight. People around him looked ashen, scared, downright devastated. A few secretaries and interns cried. What had he done to make everyone's panties twist? Other than the obvious sin of living and breathing.

I stepped out of the elevator, considering if I should call security or punch him square in the face myself. The latter would mean a lot of legal paperwork, but damn if I wasn't tempted.

His beady black eyes ran aimlessly in their sockets, like they, too, wanted to escape the man they were in. An assistant handed him a fresh suit, and he raced to the restroom to change. I glanced at Dad's office. He wasn't in yet. I took my phone out and sent Mom a text asking if he was okay.

"Mr. Black! I'm so sorry about the news."

"Mr. Black, I just want you to know if you ever want to talk to anyone, I'm here."

"Chase—can I call you Chase?—I'll be keeping your family in my prayers . . ."

I breezed past a herd of blabbering assistants, making my way to my office. I had no fucking clue what they were talking about but was eager to find out right after I consumed my first coffee and turned from zombie to semiconscious. A hand landed on my arm. I looked up from my phone. It was Julian. He was fully dressed in a brand-new suit. That was fast. Did he possess the most useless superpower of all, of getting dressed quickly in public restrooms?

"A word," he growled.

I stalked into my office and took a seat behind my desk. He followed closely behind. I prided myself on being self-possessed when it came to Julian, but even I had my limits. Something told me I was about to meet those limits today.

"Well?" I powered up my laptop, not sparing him a glance. There was a fresh cup of coffee on my desk, and I took a sip. "Are you waiting for a royal invitation from the Windsors, or can you spit it out before lunch?" I made a show of glancing at my Rolex for emphasis. I noticed he was holding a thick stack of papers in his hand.

"I told everyone about Ronan. About the terminal cancer. How he had only a few more weeks to live," he said. My eyes darted up. His lower lip was trembling, but he kept his head high. "This has nothing to do with us. I love Ronan like a father, but he can't go around pretending it's not happening. This company feeds thousands of families. Families who deserve to know what's going on."

I couldn't argue with his logic, but I sure as hell could crucify him for telling people about it.

"You had no fucking right," I gritted out, feeling my composure slipping. I couldn't sit back and let him do that anymore. I was fed up.

"Now, that's not true. We all had the responsibility of notifying the company, but none of us wanted to do it because we feel loyal to him. Because we love him."

I was going to spit out something about how Julian never had loved my father, based on his behavior; then he slid a paper across the desk toward me.

"Ronan is not willing to change his stand on the CEO position. So you will. Refuse the inheritance."

"Are you on meth?" I adjusted my tie. "Why on earth would I do that?"

"Because—" he started. I raised my hand, cutting him off.

"Let me guess: you'll stage a vote of no confidence meeting. Rest assured, I am way ahead of you. Every single person you tried to sway against me called me up to say I needed to put you back on your meds. They're all in my pocket, and I have their full cooperation."

"No." He reddened, curling his fists in anger. "Because—"

"Madison and Ethan? That bag of bullshit?" I sat back, forcing out a metallic laugh. Talking about Ethan still felt like taking a lengthy walk in hell, fucking barefoot. "Madison and I are engaged. I spend every night at her place. My suits look like they're made of brown fur because of her dog. She hangs out with Mom and Katie more than Amber did the entire duration of her marriage with you. Hell, we were caught having sex in the restroom on her floor yesterday." I chuckled, but the admission felt sour in my mouth. It wasn't my place to spit it out. I just wanted to throw it in his face. To make sure he knew Mad and I were the real deal.

Julian banged his fist on my desk, making the keyboard fly an inch off the surface. "No! I don't mean any of this, you asshole. If you let me get a word in—"

"Just the one, please."

"Clementine is yours!" he spat out, picking up one of the papers in his hand and throwing it my way. It floated between us and landed like a feather on my desk. "She's fucking yours, okay? Not mine. That's for sure."

I sat stoically, not picking up the paper between us. Didn't take a genius to figure out it was the paternity test. Julian took a ragged breath, dragging his fingers over his balding head.

"I took the test. Finally. Amber's been teasing me about it for a while now. Every time we had a fight, she'd throw it in my face. I'm sure it doesn't come as a shock to you that things have been bad between us for a while." He gave me a narrowed-eyed glance, like it was my fault they were both D-grade douchebags who hated each other and had married for all the wrong reasons. "Three years, to be exact," he added.

"Peculiar," I said icily.

"Not really." He exhaled, his body shrinking as he did. "Ever since she found out you'd get CEO, she's been riding my ass like there was no tomorrow."

So that was what made him the way he was? Goddamn Amber?

Julian rubbed his forehead, looking around the office. "Yesterday I finally took a test. It was one taunt too many, I guess, after the weekend at the ranch. Amber was in a bad mood, and I wanted to know if she was bullshitting me or not. She wasn't. I'm not Clementine's father. Which means"—his red face morphed into a smile so nefarious I thought he was going to grow little horns on each side of his skull—"you're the baby daddy, *brousin*. Now tell me, would it not kill your parents to know you were the MIA father to their granddaughter?" He cocked his head sideways. "This is highly unorthodox. The stuff Jerry Springer drama is made of."

I grabbed the paper, skimming through it. Julian wasn't lying. He wasn't Clementine's biological father according to the test. I looked back up at him, balling the paper in my fist and throwing it into the trash can across my office with easy accuracy. I said nothing.

"Amber told me she tried to tell you numerous times," Julian accused, his lips twisting in feral disgust. I wondered if he was clinically sane. He seemed much more eager to blackmail the CEO position from me than mourn the news about his daughter not being biologically his after nine years of raising her. Only I knew Julian enough to know life had left him scarred beyond recognition from the inside. That was his way of dealing with this.

And there was something else I suspected—he'd known. He couldn't have not known. Clementine didn't look like either him or Amber. She didn't have my colors, my angles, or my expressions either.

"I suppose she failed to mention I repeatedly asked for a paternity test," I said.

"Well, you have it now." Julian waved to the trash can behind us. "Obviously, I have more copies of it."

"That's not how paternity tests work, idiot. The only thing it proves is that you're not the father. The rest of the world's male population has officially become potential candidates."

"You're grasping at straws." Julian bared his teeth. His eyes were shining. He wanted to cry. I leaned forward, no trace of malice in my voice.

"No, you're losing everything you've ever had, because you tried to steal it rather than earn it. Now get out of my office, Julian. Come back with an apology if you want a brother. I don't want to see you in any other capacity."

I knew what I needed to do, but it was going to take a minute.

Instead of getting the hell out of my office, leaving a trail of smoke and the rancid smell of desperation that clung to him, Julian sprawled on the seat in front of me.

"As for Maddie . . ." He trailed off. Hearing her name on his tongue made me want to break every glass wall in the office using his head as the hammer. "You may be together now, but I know you weren't together. Shortly before you came to the ranch, Ethan told me all about you. How you cheated on her. How she dumped you. Your little girlfriend even told him about all the women who came after her. All the hussies her boss saw going up to your penthouse. Now, let's see. What do we have here? You lied to your family about being engaged. You fathered a child with the woman your brother married, keeping this fact from them—and me—and making me raise her as my own. I can tell Lori and Ronan you probably won't be seeing a lot of Madison after he finally drops dead. That it is an arrangement. What are you paying her to cling onto your arm with starry eyes? Money? Shares? Status? Do you even see how pathetic it looks from the outside? Or maybe . . ." He got up, laughing as he shook his head, like this was nothing more than an elaborate personal joke. He was losing it. Crying. Laughing. Shaking all over. "Maybe I should just go directly to Madison and tell her about the kind of person she is dating. A man who fathered a child and didn't even—"

He never got to finish that sentence.

I pounced on him with such speed we both sailed on the floor from the momentum, crashing against the glass door. Julian hit his head. I straddled him, no longer caring that we had an audience and that I was playing into his hands. Objectively speaking, I knew I looked like a certifiable asshole. But I'd reached the end of the road. Julian had sprinted past every red line I ever had and was officially so far off the rails he couldn't even *see* the line. The idea of losing Madison after everything we'd been through—all the lies and bullshit and what-ifs and maybes—to something so stupid, so malicious, made my blood boil.

"Don't you dare say her name again." I balled the lapels of his suit, twisting them savagely.

Julian laughed, rolling his head on the carpet like a madman. "You fool. You goddamn fool. Your dick cost you your kingdom. Clementine is yours and the company is mine."

He tried to punch me in the face, but I was quicker. People gathered outside my office, watching from the glass wall, their mouths hanging open. I threw a sucker punch straight to Julian's eye. He cried out but continued trying to punch me unsuccessfully. "I *will* have your kingdom after the old man kicks the bucket!"

"Shut up," I growled.

"And in case you are wondering, why, yes, I did fuck Amber while she was still yours. Before you even put a ring on her finger. When you still lived in your dorms . . ."

I punched him again.

And again.

And a-fucking-gain.

I couldn't see past the red mist of anger and wrath.

Two burly security men stomped into my office, followed by my father, who must've arrived straight into this clusterfuck. He was holding a walking cane, hunched over it, the cane dancing between his fingers as he struggled to keep standing. His eyes said it all. He'd heard us. Every last bit.

Julian and I scrambled up from the floor, straightening our backs like two unruly punks caught shoplifting. Julian was banged up, with a black eye and open lip. It amazed me how we both were, in our core, still the same kids competing for our father's precious approval.

"Back to work," my father roared, turning around to glare at the people who stood behind him, ping-ponging their gazes from Julian and me to Ronan, whom they now knew was dying. People ran to their stations so fast you'd think their asses were on fire. Dad turned his attention back to us.

"In my entire seventy-two years of living, I've never been as disappointed as I am today. I thought I raised men. I knew you didn't always see eye to eye. I wasn't blind to the way you exchanged words and taunts from across the table during dinner for the past few years. I was terribly saddened when Amber decided to end her engagement to Chase and got with Julian so early afterward, but I held my tongue, knowing that, in essence, you were good men who were allowed to make mistakes and learn from them. Julian." He turned to my brousin. Julian stared at the floor, blinking rapidly. "From the moment we took you in, you were the apple of our eye. You're my son no less than Chase is."

Julian's head snapped up. "Then why did you give—"

"Because he is more suitable for the job," my father clipped out, smacking his cane on the carpet. "He worked harder and, frankly, made fewer mistakes. His approach is more analytical, and he is not trigger happy when in crisis. He will be CEO because, in my opinion, he possesses the set of skills that a good CEO requires. You're emotional, Julian, with the tendency for knee-jerk reactions. If you need a point of reference to why I couldn't trust you as CEO, all you need to do is look back to your behavior in the past few years, or weeks even. Taunting Chase, trying to turn the shareholders against him, trying to make me sign contracts while I was half-conscious—yes, I *do* remember that—and spilling the beans about my illness publicly before I was ready to tell people."

Julian let out a groan, covering his face with his hands. It was the first time he'd looked human in years. My father turned his head toward me, frowning.

"As for you, Chase, I really don't know what to say. Faking an engagement to Maddie. Manipulating your family in order to secure this position—"

"It wasn't about the position," I bit out. "It was about you." The admission felt bitter in my mouth. "I wanted you to think I had my shit together before we said goodbye. I wanted you to be proud."

It sounded pathetic coming out of my mouth. So much so I wanted to laugh. Dad *did* laugh. Humorlessly, though. "Evidently, you've failed. Your shit is not together. Your shit hit the fan, and now everybody stinks."

It was Julian's turn to snicker. Bastard had the audacity to enjoy it.

"Now let's talk about Clementine." Dad tapped his cane again, redirecting the conversation to the part that mattered. It felt surreal to stand here in front of my father and watch him unravel every single embarrassing thing his two sons had done in the last decade. "Both of you will need to step up."

"I will," I said without hesitation, even knowing what I knew. It didn't matter. I would always be there for Booger Face, until the end of time, in any capacity, no matter who she belonged to.

"Me too." Julian nodded, sobered. "God, I'm not a monster. And anyway, a part of me always knew, I guess. Clemmy is mine. Always will be."

Dad used the very last ounces of his energy to raise the cane, poking it in Julian's arm. "You do not treat that kid any differently. It is not her fault she was born into the wrong situation. Am I understood?" He hovered the cane between the two of us.

"Yes, sir," we said in unison.

My father shook his head, sighing. "Now if you'll excuse me, I have to go apologize to Lori for leaving her with this mess and bring her up to speed."

He turned around and walked out of my office. It was only when he entered the elevator that I noticed Madison was on the other side of the glass.

She'd heard.

About Clementine. Or at least, what she *thought* was me fathering Clementine.

About our exposed charade.

About fucking everything.

"Mad, wait."

But it was too late. She turned around and took the elevator down with Dad.

◆ ◆ ◆

Chase: You're not in your office.

Maddie: Thanks, Captain Obvious.

Chase: I'm coming to your place.

Maddie: I wouldn't do that if I were you.

Chase: I can explain.

(I couldn't, at this point, but it seemed like something people said often.)

Maddie: Which part, the one where your father uncovered us? Or maybe it's the part where you screwed my brains out in my office, then proceeded to throw it in Julian's face when he ruffled your feathers? Yes, Chase. Thin glass door. EVERYBODY heard.

Maddie: Or maybe you can explain the part where you FATHERED CLEMENTINE AND FORGOT TO MENTION IT TO EVERYONE?

Maddie: I thought I hated you then. I was wrong. This, right here, right now, is hate.

Maddie: There's nothing to talk about. This was temporary, right? You said so yourself. Mission accomplished. You screwed me. You bragged about it. Everyone knows. Now let me go.

Maddie: And one more thing. Be good to Clemmy. That's the least you can do.

It was pissing rain by the time the taxi stopped by Madison's brownstone. I tucked the papers into my blazer to prevent them from getting wet, ducking my head as I slipped out of the cab. I punched her buzzer three times, pacing back and forth. No answer. I tried calling her. She didn't pick up. I could clearly see her light was on through her window. Her plants tucked behind the glass cozily as the rain pounded on the glass from outside. I called and texted and begged for twenty minutes straight before the door opened from the inside of the building.

"Jesus, Mad. Finally. I . . ." I stopped when I saw who it was. *Layla.*

"Wow, Satan, you look like shit. Which is frankly an accomplishment, considering your genetics." She bit off the edge of a Twizzler, taking a whole lot of pleasure in watching me soaked to the bone. She was still in. I was still out. Suddenly, I wasn't sure what I was doing here in the first place. Madison had made valid points in her text messages—this was supposed to be temporary, and now we were uncovered. Done. What did I care if she knew the truth or not? Especially now, when my life was one giant fire in need of extinguishing.

"Let me in." I scowled, noticing rain dripping from my hair and the tip of my nose. How come I didn't even feel wet?

"Try again. This time nicer," she singsonged, crossing her arms over her chest. Her neon-green bomber jacket matched her hair.

"Not familiar with the term," I bit out.

"Crying shame." She moved for the door, half closing it in my face.

"Please, may I come in?" I asked loudly. *Fuck.* She reopened the door.

"What are your intentions with my friend?" She pretended to consider my request, taking another bite of the Twizzler.

Well, I would like to explain myself, fuck her six ways from Sunday, then yell at her for being so goddamn impossible, then fuck her again.

"Talk," I said, opting for the shorter, safe-for-work answer. "I just want to talk to her."

The rain was pounding on my head. Layla was taking her sweet-ass time to make a decision. The list of people I wanted to kill was growing by the nanosecond.

"She's hella upset with you, so you might get through this door, but not necessarily through *her* door." She finally opened the door all the way. "Good luck, Satan."

I raced up the stairs, taking them three at a time. When I got to Madison's door, a rush of something weird washed over me. I could almost smell Daisy and the flowers and Mad's shampoo and freshly baked goods through the crack of the door. I wanted to take a shit and a shower and a nap, then have two of her cupcakes with a side of a blowjob. I wanted her comfort, not another fucking quarrel out of the three thousand ones we had on a daily basis.

"Madison." I pounded on the door. I dripped all over the hallway, my clothes heavy with rain. I couldn't feel the lower half of my body either. My goddamn ass would probably need to be amputated after it froze off. "Open the door."

"I don't think so."

I wondered how I'd ended up here. Not just today but in general. I'd seen this side of her door so many times, always with a half-cocked plan, forever with some explaining and convincing to do, constantly un-fucking-invited.

I begged and I stole and I bargained and I manipulated her so many times it became a full-time job to be around her. And whenever we were alone, when I finally had her to myself, I kept reminding her it wasn't serious. That it was temporary. That I didn't care.

Spoiler alert: I cared. A whole lot. That was a plot twist I hadn't seen coming, and it made me stumble backward, my back pressing against Layla's door (thank fuck she'd just headed out). I let out a frustrated growl.

Shit. I was in love with Mad.

Madison "Maddie" Goldbloom, of all the women in the universe. The girl who wore patterned, horrible clothes and had a short pixie haircut that had gone out of style in the nineties and was *obsessed* with pleasing people and flowers and weddings. I loved that she was sweet and kind and thoughtful but also sassy and quick witted and made her own money.

I was painfully in love with Mad, and I hadn't even known it until it was a second too late.

"Mad." I stumbled back to her door, plastering my forehead to it and closing my eyes. Jesus. Losing my father and the woman I loved in close succession was too much. What had I ever done to karma to deserve this lubeless ass fucking?

Never mind. There was a long list of whats.

"Please."

"Chase," I heard from behind the door. Her voice was soft, pleading. "There's not much more to say. I feel humiliated. Nina has been bugging me all day at the office, and your family probably hates me, which I really don't want to deal with, and the thing with Clemmy is straight out of a Ricki Lake episode."

At least she hadn't said *Jerry Springer*. Progress, right?

"Just open up. Please. I'll explain; then I'll go."

"Not falling for that one." I heard her smile bitterly behind the door. "That's how you snuck your way back into my life in the first place."

Knowing I couldn't convince her, I turned around and slid my back across her door. Sitting. Waiting. She knew I was there. There was a pause.

"Are you sitting against my door?"

"Correct."

"Why?"

"I want you to see something. I'll wait."

And I did. I waited for an hour and a goddamn half. I heard Madison going about her evening. Cooking (pasta, basil, and olive oil—the scent was too much not to notice), feeding Daisy, and watching an episode of *You* I hadn't seen yet (God dammit). Then, and only then, she came back to the door.

"Okay. I'm ready to hear what you have to say, but make it quick."

The door was still shut. I turned around, glowering at it. Fine. We were going to do it her way.

"I'm not Booger Face's father. Here. I took a paternity test this afternoon. As soon as Julian showed me his." I slipped the paper through the door crack. I'd known I couldn't be Clemmy's father. The dates didn't add up. Not unless I'd managed to impregnate Amber from Malta, if I'd done the math correctly (and I always did the math correctly).

My eyes were fixed on the edge of the paper sitting under the door. Mad picked it up from the other side. I let out a breath, closing my eyes in relief.

"I always knew I could never be Booger Face's dad. That's why I kept asking Amber for a paternity test when she banged on about it. You think I'd turn my back on a kid of mine?" I growled. "Fuck, I love her like my own kid, and she isn't even mine. In fact, she was supposedly the very goddamn product of my fiancée and brother bumping uglies behind my back."

Silence. Ouch. Okay. In all honesty, I'd seen it coming. There was much more to my shitty behavior than supposedly not telling her I was my ex-fiancée's baby daddy.

"Who's her biological father?" Mad asked through the door.

"Some dudebro from Wisconsin. I went to confront Amber after I took the paternity test." I ran a hand through my hair. "After Amber and I broke up, she got hit with the finality of it and tried calling me, ghosting Julian, trying to make amends. By then, I was traveling and didn't pick up. She went back home to nurse her broken whatever the fuck she has in her chest. Clemmy's dad is an old high school flame. Amber said she'll talk to him. We're figuring it out so that Booger Face has the best childhood."

"What a mess." Mad sighed.

"Yeah."

"Poor Clemmy."

I sighed. "Yeah."

I loved my niece to death, but she wasn't what I'd come here to talk about.

"Anyway"—I cleared my throat—"my family doesn't hate you. Just putting it out there. Mom thinks I'm a first-rate asshole, and Dad is probably taking me out of his will. But they still like you. If anything, once I explained you didn't even ask for money or anything and just did it for Dad, you became even more heroic and perfect."

I'd call her Martyr Maddie, but the truth was lately she hadn't been that same meek, insecure girl I'd met all those months ago at all. She stood up for herself constantly and only did what she believed in.

And unfortunately, it made her stupidly irresistible.

The quiet from the other side of the door grated on my nerves. I dragged my forehead over the wood, squeezing my eyes shut.

"I don't want this to be over." The admission fell from my mouth on a whisper.

I wasn't ready to tell her everything yet. I recognized it seemed like a highly convenient time for me to realize I was in love with her. But waking up tomorrow knowing there was no Mad on the agenda seemed like a prospect worth offing myself for.

"Please." Her voice trembled. "Leave."

I pressed my fingers to her door, then walked away, respecting her boundaries for the first time since I'd met her. They said doing the right thing made you feel good.

They were wrong.

It felt shitty to do the right thing. Downright stupid. When I was back on the street, I looked up at her window, ignoring the rain pounding on my face. I saw her face pop behind the glass. She was crying.

And as I got into my Uber and the drops kept running down my face, I thought maybe so was I.

CHAPTER TWENTY-TWO

MADDIE

I'd done it.

I stood up for myself.

Martyr Maddie no more. I went against Chase Black. Flat-out refused him. I cut things off with Ethan. I even sent Katie a message, explaining how okay I was with her dating my ex-something. I was taking a proactive stance in my life.

So why was I feeling anything but empowered?

I'd always thought standing up for myself would feel celestial. Like a fully grown butterfly bursting out of a cocoon, flapping its colorful wings. In practice, I felt grossed out with myself by the way I'd turned Chase away on the day he'd hurried to the clinic to take a paternity test. I felt so empty I could feel my bones rattling inside my body as I set foot in the studio the next morning. New York Fashion Week was mere weeks away. August had bled into September, and my sketch was ready and submitted to Sven. We were supposed to start stitching the dress today. The model was supposed to be on her way to the office. Sven told me he had taken our discussion about the sketch to heart. Not only had he not made one change to my sketch, but he'd also suggested we use an everyday woman to model the dress. And by "everyday woman," he still meant a nineteen-year-old, ridiculously gorgeous model with perfect skin and silky hair. But unlike most runway models, she was a whopping size six. Super skinny and fit to the rest of the world, but on the curvy side in fashion standards.

All I had to do was see the production of the dress through, stage by stage.

"If it isn't the office mattress. Grab a ticket, gentlemen. Everyone gets a lay," Nina proclaimed as I skulked into the office. We were the only two people in. Everyone else at Croquis liked to be fashionably late. Yesterday, Nina had reached an all-time-bitch level. The type normally saved for Korean high school dramas and daytime soap operas. When I'd gone downstairs to buy a salad, condoms had spilled at my feet from my shoulder bag. She'd crammed them into it when I wasn't looking.

"Shut up, Nina," I said tiredly, collapsing into my seat and powering up my laptop.

Realizing I'd actually answered her back, Nina whipped her head around, twisting her mouth in distaste. She was wearing a Stella McCartney black day dress paired with flat Louboutins. "So *now* you have a mouth? I mean, for more than blowing important men? Figures."

Figures? What did she mean?

"Seriously." I rolled my eyes, fed up with her crass behavior. "That mean-girl cliché is super early 2000s. It's 2020. Throw shade. Finstagram me. Graduate from petty slut-shaming me. This is getting real tiring."

"You're so lucky to not have any principles," she continued, undeterred. "I bet I could get where you are if I chose to let the right people in the industry get a piece of me."

I snapped my laptop shut. "Nina," I warned, finally taking a good look at her. She was shoving pictures of her with her lobbyist boyfriend into a cardboard box. Her eyes were red. She was . . . oh God, she was *packing*.

"Spare me your victory speech, okay? I got fired yesterday, as you're well aware. Sven handed me my notice personally. Said something about Chase Black bringing his attention to the HR manual of Croquis. Apparently, Mr. Black read the entire thing yesterday while waiting at the clinic for some type of results—for what, he wouldn't say. Hopefully for chlamydia. And hopefully it turned out positive. Anyway, Chase was super happy to let Sven know I am apparently bullying you." She sniffed. But I knew she was talking about the paternity test. "Whatever, I don't even care. My first-choice internship was Prada, the second Valentino. Croquis was my *fifth* choice." She quickly wiped a tear that slid down the tip of her nose.

I stood up, making my way to her. She grabbed one of the boxes and turned her back to me. I tugged at the fabric of her sleeve. "Look at me," I said harshly. No sign of Martyr Maddie in sight. I was pissed, and I owned it.

She looked down, shaking her head.

"Nina." My voice grew sharper. "You *are* bullying me."

"It's just banter!" she cried. Bullshit.

"Why do you hate me so much?"

She looked up, giving me a *duh* look. "Why wouldn't I? Look at you. You have horrible taste in clothes, yet you feel so comfortable in your own skin. You're the uncoolest person I've ever met, no offense. Yet you're probably Sven's favorite employee. Men like Chase Black throw themselves at you and have bathroom sex with you and fire people for you. You are way ahead of the game for our age, and you didn't even go to a good college. You just . . . have it all together. I don't know. It doesn't seem natural for a twenty-six-year-old. It feels like you got a lot of shortcuts."

"Has it ever occurred to you that my life is not all unicorns, hearts, and baked goods?" I was surprised by the fact I was yelling at her, and yet here I was—literally screaming at her. "I'm super insecure about . . . well, most things, really. I live in a tiny apartment with a dog I am mostly allergic to. My love life is a disaster, my mom died when I was a teenager, and I never fully recovered from her loss. To stay on top of my game, I pretty much had no social life for the past five years and focused on working my way up. Staying an intern wasn't a luxury I could afford, as it meant I'd be homeless. Which was why I got a quick promotion from Sven, at the price of my working fifty-hour weeks. The grass is always greener through someone else's Instagram filter. No one has their shit together. Fully, anyway. We're all just pretending we know what we're doing. Those of us who do it with a smile on our face just look like we're enjoying it more."

Nina sniffed. "Well, yeah, I guess, but . . ."

"You've been a petty, jealous, out-of-control bitch to me, Nina. And I cannot and will not allow anyone to treat me like this anymore. Enough is enough. To be honest, you probably deserve to get fired. You stuffed my bag with condoms, for crying out loud. But you know what? I don't want your unemployment on my conscience, so I'm going to give you one chance. I'll talk to Sven about letting you keep this position. He will probably listen, seeing as I'm the person who got picked on. But you have to promise me you won't let the green-eyed monster get ahold of your mouth and say awful things to me ever again. Jealousy is like a fart. It stinks, we all have it, but it is best to keep it inside or release it when absolutely no one can see or hear us. Am I understood?"

She stared at me in shock, blinking the tears away from her vision.

"Nina, answer me."

"Yeah," she whispered, still mesmerized by the one-eighty I'd done. "I promise. I'm . . . I'm sorry."

"You should be."

"I am."

There was a pause.

"Why are you doing this?" She rubbed the bridge of her nose, wincing. "You don't have to. Yet you're still nice to me, even when giving me shit."

"Oh," I said breezily. "I'm not doing this for you. I'm doing this for me. Being good makes me sleep better at night. It's not that I don't suffer from the same symptoms as you—jealousy, heartache, insecurity. They're the side effects of being alive, pretty much. But I learned a simple thing recently. That gap between reality and our dreams? That's where life is tucked."

◆ ◆ ◆

In the end, I couldn't do it.

Walk away from Chase without clearing the air, no matter how badly I knew I'd hurt if I saw his face again. Plus, there was the small matter of giving him back his trillion-dollar engagement ring.

The worst part was that it wasn't even a conscious decision. I didn't go through the normal route of picking up the phone and calling or texting him to set up a time and a place. You know, like a sane person would. I just found myself going to his place after work unannounced.

I hoped—fine, *prayed*—I'd have a few minutes alone in the apartment so I could compose myself (translation: have a mental breakdown and wash my face). The odds were in my favor. I knew Chase's schedule, and it included visiting his parents after work to check on his father.

The doorman at his building, an older gentleman named Bruce, knew me by face and showed me in. Guess that was the upside of being the uncoolest person in the universe, as Nina had dubbed me. I didn't look like the type to empty a billionaire's apartment of possessions and jewelry.

"Haven't seen much of you lately. Mr. Black has been a bit of a sour face since you stopped coming." Bruce led me to the elevator. I still had the key from our first rodeo. Chase had never asked for it back, and I hadn't exactly been in the mood to initiate more conversation with him. I pushed Chase's door open just as my phone pinged with a message.

Sven: Bad news. The Dream Wedding Dress model never showed up. She was on location.

Maddie: Crap! Can we reschedule?

Sven: We don't have time. We need to start making it tomorrow if we want to get everything on time. Aren't you a size six?

Maddie: Sure. I'm also half her height.

Sven: Send me your measurements. I'll adjust it accordingly when the prima donna can finally see us for a fitting.

I gave him my measurements and hit send. For the next hour, I gave myself a tour of Chase's apartment, filing everything away in my memory, knowing it was the last time I was going to visit him. For real, this time. The azaleas, as I'd suspected, were nowhere to be seen. Not in any of the bedrooms, the bathrooms, the living room, or the kitchen. Finally, I collapsed on his couch, stared at the ceiling, and let out a sigh. I didn't remember the exact moment I fell asleep. By the time I was jarred awake, my phone indicated it was close to one in the morning. I heard Chase messing with the lock outside his apartment and sat up straight, prying away the bits of hair that stuck to the dry saliva on my cheeks.

I heard his keys drop to the floor, a groan, and then a woman huffing and picking them up for him. A *woman*.

Déjà vu of the day Chase had walked into his apartment with a stranger slammed into me. I darted up, ready for a fight. Not that there needed to be one. We weren't together anymore. Or ever. Yet I couldn't help but think of him as mine.

"Hold still," the woman murmured. He hiccuped. He was drunk. The door was pushed open. Chase came tumbling in, his black dress shirt ripped open, supported by a slender woman who clutched his shoulder to keep him upright.

"Didn't take you long to get over me," I said, my fingers balling into a fist beside my body. Every one of my muscles shook with anger. *"Again."*

He lifted his head at the exact same time the woman did. They both stared back at me.

Katie.

It was Katie.

God, I was such an idiot. Now was a good time to put the engagement ring on his table and run for my life. Still, I was rooted to his floor.

"You're here," he said tonelessly.

"You're . . . drunk," I retorted, looking at Katie with what I hoped was an apologetic expression.

She smiled, depositing Chase against the door so she could come and give me a small squeeze. "Hey. Don't worry. It's not awkward between us at all. My brother felt a little worse for wear after work and decided to go drinking with some friends. I dropped by the bar he was at before I went home and found him like this. Figured he'd need a good night's sleep before the hangover kicked in."

"Good call." I nodded.

"I'll leave you two to it."

Katie left, and then it was just Chase and me. A very drunk version of him, anyway. I felt furious with the universe for bringing Chase to me like this. Barely coherent, when there were so many things I wanted to say to him in what was going to be the last time we ever spoke.

I slid the ring off my finger. It was weird. Throughout the weeks we'd been pretend-dating, I'd been careful to remove it at work, but I'd enjoyed flaunting it practically any other time. While I was on the subway and went out with friends and took Daisy for walks. I saw other people checking out the engagement ring while I held the pole on the train or flagged a taxi or flipped a page on my Kindle while waiting for a hair appointment. I could see the wheels in their heads turning. The stories they made up for this spectacular ring. I loved this part the most.

The guessing part. My wedding obsession, I realized, was also about the meet-cute. The falling-in-love story. I'd wanted to sit each of them down and tell them about Chase. About how funny and gorgeous he was. About how fiercely he loved his family, how deeply he cared for his niece.

"So I thought I'd stop by and give this to you." I handed him the ring.

He ignored my outstretched hand, blinking as he tried to focus on my face. "Keep it."

"Chase . . ."

"Sell it. Give it away. You earned it."

I shook my head, my heart clenching painfully. "It's too much."

"I won't return it." He staggered to the living room, collapsing on the couch and turning on the TV. ESPN was his default channel. "I can't even look at it."

He looked so tired that I thought arguing with him about this was less kind than keeping the ring.

"Listen." I sat down next to him, feeling that he was drifting away from me and wanting to anchor him. "About Nina. I appreciate what you're trying to do, I really do, but please tell Sven to give her her job back. She needs it, and I don't want to get into this with Sven."

"What she needs is a lesson in manners," he slurred, frowning at the TV boyishly. "And maybe a sugar daddy to pay for all that Prada she was parading around. I looked her up on Instagram. Is this you being Martyr Maddie again? Because I won't stand for this kind of bullshit on your behalf."

"We reached an understanding." I slid the ring back onto my finger before realizing what I was doing. I ignored the warm current that ran through me as I did.

"Will it make you happy?" He swung his head toward me. The vulnerability in his expression nearly broke me. I nodded. "Fine. She can have her job back. I'll talk to Sven."

"Thank you."

"But I'll also give him some friendly advice to make you her boss. Seems fair, everything considered."

I didn't argue.

"How's your dad?" I asked, stalling. Leaving him like this, drunk and bitter and hurting, was impossible.

He gave me half a shrug. Right. Stupid question.

"I just want you to know I'll be there for you and your family, no matter what. As a friend."

"I don't want to be your friend." Chase held my eyes, sobering up for a fraction of a second. "I want to be your everything. Even that's not enough. So thanks, but no thanks."

He is drunk, my mind screamed at me as my heart lurched for him. *Plastered. Hammered. Tanked up. He doesn't mean it.*

I pulled him into an awkward couch hug, kissing his neck, inhaling his Chase smell, diluted by the alcohol he'd consumed tonight. "That's a lot to ask." I smiled sadly, pressing a kiss below his ear. I felt his words inside my body as he answered me.

"It's more than I deserve."

CHAPTER TWENTY-THREE

MADDIE

November 2, 2009

Dear Maddie,

This is goodbye. I feel it in my bones. I'm so sorry I won't be there to see you walking down the aisle. To help with your little ones should you decide to have children. I am so terribly sorry I will not be there for the breakups, and for the teenage drama, and for the small victories, and all the realizations that unfold throughout life, like thinly wrapped chocolate pieces. They all taste different, my darling Maddie. Every single lesson life teaches you is a gift, no matter the hurdles it puts in your way.

I love you, Madison. Not only because you are mine, but because you are wonderfully good, considerate, bright, and sweet. Because you are creative and your laughter reminds me of Christmas bells. Because you are all the best things about your father, and all the great things about me. You make me selfishly proud.

Before I say my final goodbye, I have another, last fun fact about flowers for you. The pretty pink pom-pom heads of the mimosa pudica look gorgeously brilliant and fuzzy, but they are actually quite sensitive. The pom-poms will fold up shyly when they are touched. They're vibrant and blossoming—but only from afar. They are, essentially, untouchable.

Don't shy away from the world. You will get hurt. You will hurt others, even if you don't mean to. Pain is inevitable through life. But joy is too. So seize the day.

Love hard.

Get lots of sleep.

Eat well.

And remember our flower rule: if it doesn't make you grow or blossom—let it go.

All my love,

Mom. x

Three days later, I took the train to Philadelphia to see my dad. I hadn't talked to him about Chase since we'd gotten back together a few weeks ago. It had seemed redundant, seeing as we weren't going to last. Dad and I had a routine. We met at Iris's Golden Blooms, where I helped him sort out his bookkeeping twice a month, and in return, I got a nice Chinese meal at a corner restaurant near our house, followed by industrial Costco ice cream in front of the TV while he filled me in on our small-town gossip. Dad had a girlfriend. A sweet lady named Maggie, whom I was super grateful for, because she kept him busy and happy and gave him all the attention I couldn't. She also understood us on another level and never once complained about the fact the flower shop he owned still held his late wife's name.

Today wasn't any different. I went through the motions: bookkeeping, Chinese food, ice cream from a tub you could hide a body in. Dad asked if I wanted to sleep over at their place. To his delight, I accepted.

New York reminded me too much of Chase. Every street corner and skyscraper was soaked with a memory of him.

The next morning I went to the cemetery. I wasn't big on graveyards. They were too much of a reminder one day I'd be a resident. But for Mom, I went once a year, on her birthday.

Which happened to be today.

I always brought baked goods, a balloon, and—drumroll, please—flowers. Lots and lots of flowers. This time, I arrived with lilacs and tulips and marigolds, laying them on her tombstone after scrubbing it clean to the point of blistered knuckles. Then I sat down next to a paper plate full of muffins I'd baked at dawn, brushing the cold stone as I filled her in on Layla's shenanigans.

"I forgot to tell you. I was also chosen to design the Dream Wedding Dress at work. After marrying half the kids on my block, I finally created my own, personal dream dress. Know the best part, Mom? Even when my boss didn't really like the design, I stood my ground and made it happen. But the thing is, I've come to understand that maybe the perfect dress I'd been obsessing about is not the thing I should be most worried about. I think I just let go of my dream man. And . . . it frightens me."

Silence stretched across the crisp morning air. Birds chirped, and everything was coated with fresh dew. I drew a deep breath, closing my eyes. "You know, Mom, I finally figured out it wasn't my fault. I know it sounds bizarre, and maybe a little juvenile at twenty-six, but there was always a small part of me that wondered if you were taken away from me because I was a horrible person. I no longer think that way. I see Katie and Chase and Lori, how they are losing the person they love most, and I get it. Life is like a game of russian roulette. You really don't know how it's going to pan out for you; you're just here for the ride. Tragedy is like winning the lottery, but in reverse. But I can't be afraid to live anymore. To let people down. To cower. No more Martyr Maddie for me. I thought if I was good and sweet to everyone,

I'd prevent another disaster. But you can't expect to win the lottery, so why should you be constantly worried about having another tragedy turn up at your doorstep? I'm done playing it safe."

I kissed the tombstone, giving Mom's name one last brush.

"By the way, you would have loved Daisy. She is a hoot. I'll bring a picture of her next time I come visit. Do you know Chase was the only man who ever entered my apartment and didn't get the pee-in-shoe treatment? Do you think it's a sign?"

I looked around me, *actually* waiting for a sign. Like in the movies. A dramatic lightning bolt slicing the sky. A flower opening unexpectedly into full bloom. Even a phone call from Chase himself would have been sufficient. Which was why the stillness of everything around me made me chuckle. Kismet didn't happen in real life.

Just as I turned around to walk away, a groundkeeper appeared from behind a tree, holding a leaf blower and sparing me a tired smile. He wore a black uniform. The tee that stretched across his chest read in white: *Black Solutions.*

"Thanks, Mom." I smiled. For me, it was enough.

Chase: Is the offer to be friends still on the table?

Maddie: You mean the one you rejected?

Chase: *While highly intoxicated and nursing a shattered ego. Yes.

Maddie: Yes. I would love to be there for you.

Chase: What are your plans for tonight?

Maddie: Watch Daisy chasing after Frank the squirrel in her quest to make love to him?

Chase: Can I join you?

Maddie: I mean, you'd have to ask them but the bar is set pretty low for Daisy if she chooses Frank for a lover.

Chase: Plus, it would be consistent with my devilish reputation to bang her roommate.

Maddie: Oh boy. I would pay good money to see your face when Daisy and Frank go at it.

Chase: You need a hobby.

Maddie: Not all of us can afford entertainment in the form of exotic ranches on lakes and mansions in the Hamptons. Us mortals have to make do with less lavish time wasters.

Chase: You mortals also have Netflix.

Maddie: I withdraw the invitation to watch Daisy and Frank recreating Gone with the Wind.

Chase: What if I come bearing food?

Maddie: Sushi?

Chase: Naturally.

Maddie: We're on. But no lip about my movie choice when you get here. I don't like your sass.

Chase: Frankly, my dear, I don't give a damn.

Chase: Thank you for taking Katie and Mom for lunch. They appreciated it.

Maddie: Technically they took me.

Chase: You paid.

Maddie: Sneakily. 😒

Chase: You're good at sneaking into places.

Maddie: Like where?

Chase: My heart.

<Chase has removed a message from the chat>

Maddie: Was shopping for sex toys with Layla. What did you delete? Where'd I sneak into?

Chase: Nothing.

Maddie: CHASE.

Chase: Platonic pizza tonight?

Maddie: Not sure I'm familiar with that topping.

Chase: It's my least favorite and includes you fully clothed. Then I'll go home to jerk off while you make use of your new sex toy purchases.

Maddie: Platonic pizza sounds good.

Chase: My turn to choose the movie.

Maddie: I want you to know that I will never forgive you for Scarface.

Chase: I was going for Love, Actually but didn't want my mascara to get ruined.

Maddie: You wouldn't cry during Schindler's List. You have no heart, remember?

Chase: Yeah, because you stole it.

<Chase removed a message from the chat>

Maddie: What did you delete? I took Daisy for a walk and things got a little intense with Frank. She almost caught him this time.

Chase: I said I do have a heart.

Chase: I keep it in a glass jar on my desk.

Chase: Okay that is a Stephen King quote. But the sentiment is clear.

Maddie: I demand a rematch.

Chase: A rematch?

Maddie: A movie of my choice which you should suffer through. I'm actually thinking of making it even more painful. How about Clemmy chooses it? Is she back from Wisconsin yet?

Chase: Last night, yeah. Let me call Amber and set it up.

Maddie: How are things between you and Amber?

Chase: I think she is starting to realize we are not going to happen.

Maddie: And Julian?

Chase: Julian and I are definitely not going to happen either.

Maddie:

Chase: He's busy with the divorce. We haven't really talked about us (idk what it is about you that inspires me to talk like a chick, but there you have it).

Maddie: I have a confession to make.

Chase: I was your best, huh? I knew it.

Maddie: I miss what we had but I'm so afraid you are going to break my heart again or dump me after this is all over.

<Maddie removed a message from the chat>

Chase: ?

Maddie: Sorry, I don't know what came over me. Forget it.

Chase:

CHAPTER TWENTY-FOUR

CHASE

"I'm seeing Clementine today." Julian stood in the doorway to my office, still sporting the remainders of a black eye, a cut lip, and the sulky expression of a middle-aged tool who'd gotten his ass handed to him in a fistfight.

I looked up from my laptop, because we were talking about Booger Face. I pressed my index along my mouth.

"First time since?" I asked, leaning back in my executive chair. It had been a shit show since the moment Julian had found out about Wisconsin Dude. The CEO bullshit had finally taken the back seat, and the reality that his marriage—his *family*—was a sham had sunk in. He looked wrecked. Like reality had finally managed to snap some sense into him. Especially as Amber hadn't wasted any time dragging Clementine to Wisconsin to hide from the social blow and had taken the opportunity to introduce the dudebro to Clementine as a "good family friend."

Julian nodded, rubbing at his jaw. "I don't know what to say to her."

"How about that you're fucking sorry?"

"Maybe without the 'fucking' part. Amber will kill me, and I think that's a hundred bucks in the potty-word piggy bank." He rubbed the back of his neck. "Wait, what am I sorry about, exactly?"

"That she's in this situation in the first place," I said. "About the circumstances. Where are you taking her?"

"I don't know. Amber just said to pick her up at five. Where should I . . . ? What does she like? Jesus Christ, I don't even know what she likes."

Julian fell into the chair in front of me with a sigh, not bothering to receive a formal invitation to come in. I stared at him like he'd just taken a shit on my desk. We were not exactly on friendly terms since he'd outed my father's illness and I'd rearranged the organs in his face. We hadn't even spoken since I'd come to rub the negative paternity test in Julian's and Amber's faces. (Literally. I'd shoved it into Julian's nose and scrubbed it up and down. It would have been the highlight of my year if it hadn't meant more bad news for Clemmy.)

"How about you take her for a burger, and Mad and I will pick her up and take her to the movies afterward?" I suggested. "It'll soften the blow."

Julian's head snapped up. "You still seeing her?"

"Platonically." I spat out the word like it was profanity. It seemed acutely unfair to get shoved into the friend zone like a pair of dirty socks after I'd given her enough orgasms to light up a refinery. I shrugged as if I didn't care. I *did* care. "Her funeral."

"Speaking of funerals." Julian took a greedy breath, avoiding eye contact as he picked up a batch of black Post-it Notes from my desk and began thumbing them nervously. "Telling everyone about Ronan . . . that was horrendous. I apologized to him. Assured him I won't be dipping my toe into the CEO scheme anytime soon. Just thought you should know."

I said nothing. Understandably, I was suspicious. He threw his head back, staring at the ceiling with a sigh.

"I just wanted something of my own."

"You had something of your own. A wife. A daughter. A good career."

"A wife who hated me despite my trying to please her in every way. A wife whom I'd promised would become a CEO's wife and, when it appeared that my promise was not going to get fulfilled, constantly threatened to leave me. I wanted the chief executive position because I thought it meant keeping Amber. She and Clemmy were the only things I had that you didn't. In trying to keep them, I neglected them, spending all my time at work. And now I'm getting a divorce." He threw his arms in the air, laughing bitterly. "Irony is a bitch."

"You can still have Clemmy. All she knows is you as her dad. As for Amber, I can sincerely say shoving your dick into a paper straw will give you more satisfaction than being with a woman who only wants you for your wallet and status. Even you can do better than that." I wasn't prepared to console my brousin after eating shit from him for three consecutive years, but kicking someone while they were down wasn't my style.

"Anyway." I arched an eyebrow when it became clear Julian wasn't going to move an inch until I kicked him out. "I have work to do. Text me where to pick Booger Face up."

He got up, looking around him like he was forgetting something. Maybe his manners. He should've knocked. He also should have apologized for the past three years. Being remorseful meant jack shit without an official admission.

"You know, Chase, you're not so bad." He stopped at my door.

I stared at him blankly. "Thanks for the lukewarm endorsement. Isn't *not so bad* synonymous with *I've met bigger shitheads*?"

He snorted out a laugh. "See? That's what I mean. I always thought you had no heart, which made villainizing you easier. You seem so detached from everything around you. You walk around with this broody dark halo around you. Almost like the devil." He frowned. A shiver ran down my spine. That was how Madison referred to me. I'd thought she was joking. I didn't think so now. "But I realized it was just you being you. And that you are capable of caring for people. You care about Lori and Ronan, Katie and Clemmy."

And Madison. I cared about Madison too.

In fact, a part of me wasn't so sure I was vastly different from my ex-girlfriend. In some ways, I, too, went out of my way to please the people I cared about. That was why I put so much on the line for Dad. But unlike Madison, my people-pleasing tendency had made my mouth write a check my ass couldn't cash. I'd promised Amber marriage. And gotten slapped in the face with her betrayal.

But I was still a sucker for those I loved.

I would always have my family's back.

Julian sent me a hopeful glance. Oh, for fuck's sake. Just when I thought we were treading carefully out of Jerry Springer territory, he went and got all *Brady Bunch* on my ass. I couldn't catch a break. I took a deep breath.

Say it.

It's going to taste like turd, but you need to say it.

He is family.

"I care about you too." I tried not to grit my teeth too much around the sentence. Julian's eyes lit up. I got it. In his mind, we'd been fucking him over, giving him the Black name without the perks, so he'd rebelled. It wasn't an excuse for his shitty behavior, but it was the incentive.

"That so?" he asked.

"Seems that way."

"Does that mean I get to keep my CIO role?"

Or maybe he just wants to cover his ass and secure his job.

"Too soon," I warned.

"Thanks, bro." He gave me a wink.

I waited until he got out of my office, then gagged.

I made a stop at Croquis to pick Mad up. Sven was by the elevator bank, rubbing an employee's pregnant belly like it was a crystal ball and gushing about babies. I gave him a nod, passing by him. A semifamiliar girl with Khaleesi-blonde hair cornered me, chasing me the length of the studio.

"Mr. Black, wait! I just wanted to thank you again for convincing Sven to give me another chance. I don't know if you saw my two emails . . . or flowers. I want you to know I don't take it lightly at all, and I'm not going to blow my second chance."

I *hmm-hmm*ed. I had no idea who she was or what she wanted from me. My eyes were laser focused on my target—Madison Goldbloom, sitting at her station in a powder-blue dress with white swans printed on it.

"Maddie and I are totally bonding. We went to lunch the other day. I don't know if she told you. We're cool with each other."

Now she was physically standing in my way, so I guessed I had to address her.

"Nadia, right?" I asked.

"Nina." She smiled brightly. "Maddie said you guys are no longer together. I'm so sorry." She put her hand to her heart. Yeah. She seemed about as sorry as Daisy after trying to impregnate poor Frank. "If you ever need anyone to talk to . . ."

I'll seek professional help from someone who doesn't want my cock in her mouth, I was tempted to finish for her, but I knew Mad would call me a jerk, and I really, *really* didn't want her to see me as the devil incarnate anymore.

"Appreciate it." I bypassed her, going straight to Madison, who was frowning at her phone. She looked up when she noticed me, grabbed her jacket, and gave me a distracted kiss on the cheek that almost made my fucking heart explode.

"Thank you. Anyway"—she smiled up at me—"I was hoping we could say hi to Ronan on our way back from the movie. I made him nondistressed banana bread."

"Nondistressed?" I ducked my head to catch her eyes. She dodged the eye contact. Everything about the platonic shit was watered down, impersonal.

"Meaning I didn't batter it. The outside looks subpar, but the inside tastes really good."

"The outside looks better than you think," I murmured, knowing it was sink-or-swim time and finally—*finally*—deciding to get my head out of the water.

It ended up being a pleasant evening, everything considered (things I considered: I had to see Julian's sour-ass face again, and Madison remained fully clothed for the entire duration).

After the movie, we took Booger Face to see Dad and stayed for tea. When it was time to go, Madison stopped me at the door and put her hand on my chest. My muscles jerked under her fingertips like she was fire.

"He doesn't look very good," she whispered, rubbing my chest in circles. "Stay with him. I'll take the train back home."

Normally, I'd try to buy more time with her. Today, I knew she had a point. I kissed her cheek. "Thanks for killing my libido and possibly my retinas with that movie. I will never look at ball gowns and tiaras the same again."

"Thanks for being a good sport about it."

She lingered. Mom and Clemmy were in the living room, doing a puzzle together. Dad was in the master bedroom. I could lean in and kiss her, and she'd let me. Her eyes were burning with that something I'd learned to recognize. A carnal hunger.

But now wasn't the time.

And definitely not the place.

I leaned back, flicking her nose with a smile. "Bye."

"Bye," she said, the word thick in her voice.

As soon as she was in the elevator, I took out my phone and messaged her, knowing the reception was crappy there.

Chase: I fucking love you, Madison Petal Goldbloom. So much it sometimes hurts to look at your face.

<Chase has removed a message from the chat>

A minute later, she replied.

Maddie: What did you send and delete? I'm going to kill you for this one day, Chase.

Chase: Dad says the banana bread was just okay. Didn't want you to get offended.

Maddie: You're a jerk.

Chase: Someone has to be.

◆ ◆ ◆

"Come in."

Dad's voice was hoarse from his lungs working at only 10 percent capacity. I pushed the double doors to his room open.

I pressed my back against the doors, hooking my thumbs into my front pockets. He lay in the shadows. Grant had explained to me that he was on a lot of painkillers but was still majorly uncomfortable. His breathing was so labored he sounded like an old car trying to spurt its last few miles before running out of gas. It had been both slow and fast coming.

"Don't just stand there, boy. Come in. I don't bite." He coughed. I took a few steps in, feeling overwhelmingly inadequate for the first time in my life. He had days, maybe. Hours, more like. And still, the world turned. We took Booger Face to the movies. We went to work. We lived. Every moment I lived away from him felt like betrayal.

He propped himself on the headboard, reaching for his nightstand and picking up a rolled cigarette. I arched an eyebrow as he grabbed the lighter next to it.

"Getting high?" I asked sarcastically.

"As much as I can with the state of my lungs. Medicinal cannabis. Does wonders for the pain." He lit up, inhaling deeply until it hit the spot. He coughed the smoke out. I sat beside him. "Maddie seems in good spirits," he remarked.

"Are we really going to talk about Maddie?" I picked up the jar of marijuana next to his nightstand, examining it.

"No, sorry. Let's talk about my favorite subject—my dying."

"Touché." I scratched my stubble. "Yeah, she is doing fine. She's worried about you, though."

"Are you romancing the poor girl?" He cocked his head sideways, taking another hit. It was surreal to sit here with him smoking pot. All he needed now was a backward ball cap on his head and a Pornhub Premium subscription, and he'd be every guy I'd known in college.

I chuckled. "She's not that unfortunate yet, but I'm working on it."

"Slowly." He tapped the ash into an ashtray.

"Let me worry about the pace. You worry about cramming as much fun as you can into the next few weeks. Look, I want to iron things out about the whole Julian crap at the office. We never really got to talk about it."

Dad waved me off. "No need. I knew, subconsciously, that this was going to happen at some point. The two of you needed to figure it out, and you did. The balance of power. Julian tried his luck with the leader of the pack and did not succeed. He is now tending to his battle wounds, and you'd be wise not to poke them while they're still fresh. As I mentioned before, I see him as a son. Clementine is my granddaughter. Nothing will ever change that. Biology could never rival familiarity.

But I will tell you this, Chase. Out of all my children, I see the most of myself in you."

When he finished talking, he took a greedy, hungry breath, like he couldn't stand the strain on his lungs of uttering a few sentences together.

"Thank you." I bowed my head.

"It is not a compliment," he deadpanned, surprising me. I looked up, frowning. He sighed, took another hit, and talked with the joint clasped between his fingers.

"I'm stubborn and pigheaded and extremely unreasonable at times. I love your mother, but I am the first to recognize I've put her through hell with my radical moods. I have no manners to speak of, and I'm sarcastic even when the time doesn't call for it—which is always. I want you to promise me something."

I hoped to hell he didn't mean to warn me against being sarcastic. I'd need to cut off half of my brain and my tongue to be on the path toward not making a dark joke out of everything.

"Hit me with it," I said guardedly.

"Give love a chance. It is rare and raw and completely life changing. A girl like Madison doesn't fall into your lap every other day. If you miss your chance with her, there's no guarantee another girl who is tailor made for you will just walk into your life. I know Amber hurt you, bad. You didn't love her, though. You wanted to get settled and get the romance thing out of the way. I saw the way she looked at you. I saw the way you looked at her."

I knew what he meant. I'd looked at postcollege Amber like a new, shiny, limited-edition car. She'd raised my stock and seemed like a good addition to my life at the time. I looked at Madison like she was a piñata full of surprises and orgasms I wanted to burst. With my dick-shaped bat. She kept me on my toes and made me second-guess what she was going to do or say. And I *had* ended up watching *Me before You*. Guess what? Louisa Clark was hot as hell.

"Open up your heart. Life is shorter than you think. And when you're in my position, bedridden, a breath away from death, you don't think about all the money you made, all the lucrative deals you signed, about the revenues and people who screwed you over and people you screwed over in business. You think about how lucky you are to be eating homemade banana bread and listening to your grandchild laughing from the other room and the love of your life being the person who made her laugh."

I closed my eyes, nodding. "I promise I . . ." I started talking, but when I opened my eyes, I saw Dad passed out. He was fast asleep, the last flame of the joint burning in his hand. I took the joint, put it out in an ashtray on his nightstand, kissed him good night, and left.

CHAPTER TWENTY-FIVE

Maddie

"Are you okay?" Sven asked as he tugged and smoothed the dress on my body.

I wasn't.

I was absolutely not okay.

The model for the Dream Wedding Dress was MIA, again, and I had to fill in for her. At this point, I was furious. It was one thing to give him my measurements. It was another completely to model the frigging thing, especially when she was at least eight inches taller than me. How unprofessional.

"I'm fine," I clipped. "You should talk to this girl's agency. She's stood us up twice in a row now. Maybe you should just get a size zero replacement."

Phew, now I really was a long cry from Martyr Maddie. The old me would never say anything remotely negative about someone. The new me, however, wanted to hold people accountable for their actions. Living with the new me, I realized, was much more convenient than sharing a body with my previous version.

"Nah, too late for that." Sven crouched forward, pinning needles around the fabric bunched at my waist. He had another row of needles in his mouth as he spoke. "Besides, even if I could get another model, I want the one that looks like a real woman. She's worth it. Trust me."

"Supermodels are real women too. In fact, women come in all shapes and sizes and colors and heights, and none of their physical characteristics make them any less of a woman." Nina raised her arm in the air as if asking for permission as they both inspected me in my work of art.

"Amen." I high-fived Nina before giving the customary bride-to-be twirl in front of the floor-to-ceiling mirror we kept in the studio mostly for Sven's daily angle check. Designers and interns and administrative assistants gathered around me to look at the dress. Crimson marred my neck and cheeks, and my skin became blotchy with embarrassment. I wasn't used to everyone's eyes on me.

"Fine. I'll amend. The model is worth it because she looks like she was born for that dress, and I don't care that she is busy. Now, Maddie, would you do me a favor and straighten your back? You look like you're about to hide inside this dress."

I did as I was told, smoothing my hand across the lush fabric of the Moonflower. I'd named the dress design after the white flower, which looked like a long dress midtwirl when it opened. But there was a catch that made me insist on the name—the moonflower only opened at night. It blossomed in the dark. Sven had said to call it something that reminded me of myself.

Nothing reminded me of myself more than blossoming in the arms of darkness.

I'd lost my mother in the midst of my awkward swing into adulthood. Only guided by my widower father, who'd been busy saving my late mother's other legacy—her flower shop.

I'd fallen in love with Chase Black when his father was dying.

And I'd fallen in love with myself, too, once I'd realized I was worthy of a man like Chase Black. Frankly, that I was worthy of anyone.

I bit my lower lip as I stared in the mirror, thinking about all the women who would hopefully walk down the aisle wearing the dress. Then about the lives they were going to have with their husbands (or wives) afterward. I thought about the children they would have. The positive pregnancy tests. The promotions. The Christmas mornings. The family vacations. Entire lives would be wrapped around the Moonflower. Thousands of women would look at this dress years from now, and it would symbolize something different to each of them. Love. Hope. Heartbreak. It filled my heart with excitement.

"Maddie." Nina stepped forward, passing me my phone, which was dancing in her palm. "You have a phone call."

I frowned at the caller ID. Katie. Did she want to cancel on our lunch plans? I pressed the phone to my ear. "Hey, K. What's up?"

"Maddie," she choked out. My heart immediately sank.

"Katie." My voice quivered. "What happened?"

It was terrible. Asking a question you knew the answer to just so it could be out in the open. So we could deal with it. Layla's word of the day today was *disaster*. I should have known.

"It's Dad." Her voice sounded soft and hoarse, like it was melting in her throat. "He died."

The next hour was a blur. I couldn't breathe. I couldn't think. I couldn't see clearly.

Maybe that was what made me burst in a blaze out of the building wearing a wedding dress that resembled a three-tier cake, before

Sven and Nina pulled me back in, kicking and screaming I had to go see the Blacks. Nina shoved me in the bathroom and peeled the dress from my body before dressing me up in my normal clothes. I shook uncontrollably, trying to call Chase and getting hit with the cold, impersonal sound of his voice mail each time. Thank God Nina had been working hard on making amends and being the best version of herself at the office. She made sure I had a taxi waiting downstairs.

The journey to the hospital passed in a blink. I couldn't decipher the faces or the words of the staff who directed me to Ronan Black's room. He wasn't there anymore when I got there. Chase was standing with his back to me, staring out the window, the empty, still-crumpled bed behind him. Lori was curled into herself on a clinically green love seat, her head tucked in Katie's shoulder. Julian was sitting on the edge of the bed, staring at his hands in his lap. Amber and Clementine were nowhere to be seen. I rushed to Katie and Lori first, not quite ready to witness Chase's pain up close.

"How'd it happen?" I asked, knowing dang well it wasn't a question they wanted to answer. On the day I'd found out about Mom, Dad hadn't wanted to talk about anything, much less the technicalities of how it had happened. And yet as friends and family had trickled in, we'd been swamped with questions. How had she died, who'd found her, and how had Dad broken the news to me?

"Mom went into the bedroom to ask him if he'd like her to have lunch by his side." Katie sniffed, holding the back of Lori's head. "He wasn't responsive. She pressed the emergency button." The Blacks had installed a medical alert on the side of Ronan's bed. "When the paramedics came in, he still had a faint pulse, so they took him here. He died within minutes."

I wrapped my arms around both of them, as if I were holding them together somehow. I breathed in their misery and kissed their heads, not sure if I had the right to do that but desperate to console them.

When their ragged breaths calmed, I stood up. Both Julian and Chase had their backs to me in different corners of the room. I went to Julian first. He was pale as an egg. He had that extra lonely shine about him, of someone who had recently lost much more than just his father. I knew he was going through a divorce and that adjusting to the new reality with Clementine wasn't a picnic for him. Cautiously, and while holding my breath, I put a hand on his shoulder, giving it a firm squeeze. His eyes dragged up to meet mine, inch after inch, so slow it was obvious he was expecting some kind of confrontation.

"I'm sorry for your loss," I said simply.

"You shouldn't feel anything but contempt toward me." He bowed his head. "But I appreciate it."

"And I know it means nothing right now, when the wound is a gash, torn open and bleeding, but I promise you, there are better days ahead. You just need to hang in there." I ignored his words.

"Why are you doing this?" His throat bobbed with a swallow. "Why do you even care? I've been nothing but awful to you."

"You were," I admitted, unable to move my hand from his shoulder. "You uncovered my lie and called me a six. You were unkind to me, but that doesn't mean I should be unkind to you. I happen to like who I am. A six, but with a ten heart."

"You heard that?" His eyebrows rose, almost comically.

I shrugged. "Beauty is subjective." It wasn't the time or place to talk about it, but I had a feeling it kept Julian busy, and that was the essence of dealing with grief. Keep going, talking, doing things.

"I wanted to rile Chase up." Julian sniffed. "I didn't mean it. And for the record—I did. Rile him up, I mean. So . . ." His gaze drifted to the window where Chase stood, still oblivious to my presence, deep in thought. "Make what you want out of it."

All it meant was that Chase and Julian loved hating each other. I couldn't allow myself to believe any differently. I dragged my eyes over to Chase. He pressed his forehead against the window, the condensation from his breath spreading over the glass like a gray cloud. The need to hug this dark, feral beast shredded me.

"Go." Julian patted my hand on his shoulder. "It's him you came for."

I approached Chase. Put my hand on his corded back. My heart coiling in my chest. Looping. Twisting. Begging. *Let me out.* I'd never been so scared to talk to someone. I didn't know if I could survive his pain.

"Chase."

He turned around, collapsing into my arms. I stumbled back from the impact but wrapped myself around him like a vise. Every inch of us was connected, pressed together. Like we were plugged in, me the charger, him sucking energy from me. His face was a wreck of emotions I'd never seen before. There was so much vulnerability there it felt like being slashed open by a sharp knife. I gathered his face and pulled him away so I could look him in the eye. Tears ran down my face so freely I was scared for my own sanity. I adored Ronan, but I didn't know him enough for his death to inspire such a reaction. All I knew was that he'd left a family who truly worshipped him. That meant he was a person worthy of my tears.

"I'm going to take you home now," I whispered.

He shook his head. "There's so much to do."

"No," Katie and Lori said in unison, standing up.

"There isn't. It's all bureaucracy now. We'll meet in a few hours and regroup," Lori insisted. "I want to take a shower. I want to get myself together. I need to tell my sisters."

The cab drive to Chase's place was quiet. We held hands in the back seat, watching New York crawl past the window. When we got to his apartment, I poured him a generous glass of whiskey and curled his fingers around it. I sat him down on the U-shaped kitchen island, then headed into his bathroom and turned the shower on. Steam covered the glass doors of the five-jet spray heads. I threw a towel on the heater, returned to the kitchen, tipped the glass with the remainder of the whiskey to his lips, and had him finish it in one gulp. Then I dragged him into the shower. "Call me if you need me."

"I'm not an invalid," he said, surly, then took a ragged breath. "Fuck. Sorry. Thanks."

I fixed him something hearty while he took a shower. I wasn't much of a cook but knew he needed actual comfort food, not some fancy takeout. You could tell his fridge had been stocked by someone else who knew he was a bachelor who didn't frequent the kitchen. I settled for beef chili with mushrooms, eggplants, and a pumpkin I found in an untouched Organic Living basket someone must've gifted him that sat lonely on the counter.

I read the recipe closely on my phone while swirling a wooden spoon inside the steaming pot of chili. The only ingredient missing from the chili was paprika. I opened Chase's pantry to see if he accidentally kept any spices. Stopped. Put my hand to my heart, letting the phone slip through my fingers and fall onto the floor.

The azaleas were there, tucked in the darkness of the pantry, which now contained nothing but three humidifiers turned on heat. The azaleas were in full bloom, bursting with colors through the darkness. White-rimmed petals, their insides bright pink, staring back at me. I took a step in and carefully tipped the plant up, seeing the secret Sharpie mark I'd made there to make sure it was the same plant.

It was.

Dark, humid, hot spaces. That's where the azaleas thrive best, I'd told him that day.

He'd remembered.

He hadn't thrown them away or let them die. He'd nurtured them.

I closed the door, stumbling back, struggling to breathe. My lungs felt ten times too small for the rest of my body. He'd done the impossible. He'd kept the flowers alive for many weeks, clearing out his entire pantry and taking care of the flowers daily.

Chase was ready for commitment. I knew that with every fiber of my heart. But I also knew that he was grieving and confused and not in the right headspace right now.

"Hey." I heard his voice behind me. I jumped, turning around.

"Oh. Hi."

"Are you making something?" He looked exhausted, rubbing a towel into his unruly hair.

"Yeah. Chili. You hungry?"

"Sure, if it's not burnt."

That was when I realized the chili was, in fact, in advanced stages of burning. By the time I reached the stove, a black crust of charred beans covered the pot.

Chase poked his head behind my shoulder, peering into the singed mess.

"Pizza?" I sighed.

He nodded, his chin touching my shoulder blade. "With pepperoni and artichoke hearts. Just like Dad liked."

Chase

Five days later, we buried Dad.

Mom had aimed for three days, but we had relatives coming from Scotland, Virginia, and California, and they all had different schedules and flights to consider. Madison had been there every step of the way, just as she'd promised. She'd gone casket shopping with Mom, had personally taken care of the flower arrangements for the funeral, and had been a great help accepting visitors into Mom's house and signing condolences deliveries.

Ronan Black's casket lowered to the gaping mouth of the earth on a gray fall day. The funeral itself had been a grand event of over a thousand people, but we'd asked that for the burial ceremony, it would be close family only. Mad had her small, warm hand tucked in mine the entire time. It was crazy I couldn't kiss her whenever I wanted to. Bury myself inside her whenever life felt too unbearable. The days after the funeral stuck together like pages in an unread book.

People brought food to our house, as if anyone had an appetite, and when shit got too real, when I couldn't muster another polite smile, Mad took over and entertained the guests for us. I doubted she had much sleep during those days. She kept working—half from home, half from the office—and was there for us until the late hours of the night.

A week after the funeral, all of us sat together and read the will as a family. Madison had insisted on not taking part in this. Called it "the clinical side of death, the one I'm not comfortable with." We all respected that, although we thought of her as an undesignated part of the family by then. Which—I was the first to admit—was another level of fucked up. We met at Mom's. The housekeeper served us cranachan parfait, Dad's favorite Scottish dessert. We consumed it while sipping the barely bearable Ogilvy potato vodka, the way he liked.

Katie was the one reading the will. She was the only sibling out of us three who didn't seem hell bent on killing someone if she didn't get what she wanted out of it, so it seemed fair.

"Mom is getting the estates, twenty-five percent of Black & Co.'s shares, and all the family jewels." Katie looked up from the paper and squeezed Mom's hand.

"Shit, I only came here for the Tiffany necklace. Well, that was fast," Julian said, pretending to stand up from his seat. Mom slapped his thigh and guided him back down. They shared a tired chuckle. I appreciated that Julian reintroduced sarcasm into our daily post-Dad routine, but I wasn't in the mood for laughs. Katie's eyes returned to the page. The paper quivered like a leaf in her hand. She cupped her mouth, her eyes glittering with unshed tears.

"I inherited all the vintage gowns Black & Co. owns that were made or used by fashion icons. Fifteen percent of the company shares. And the loft!" But I knew what was making her cry. The dresses. They meant the most to her. We had a Black & Co. museum uptown, containing famous historical dresses she loved. As a kid, she'd visited there almost monthly. I wondered if Mad had ever been. I wondered if I could take her. I wondered if she would *let* me.

"Julian, you're next." She leaned forward, squeezing his knee. If there was one positive thing about the aftermath of Dad's death, it was the fact that Julian had been given a second chance without really asking for one. It was both universally and silently agreed that he was a world-class idiot who'd acted like a douchebag of enormous proportions for the past few years, but karma had fucked him so hard—so *dry*, sans lube—that none of our family members felt particularly passionate about ruining his life further. Let me amend: I would never pass on a good opportunity to torture Julian, but I no longer wanted to ruin his life.

"Julian gets twenty percent of the shares, both properties you reside in with Amber, the Edinburgh castle, and your Dundee childhood home. There is also a personal message." She cleared her throat, peering at him worriedly. Julian lowered his head and clasped it in his palms, his back quivering. He was sobbing. The Dundee home was a nice touch. None of us had known Dad had even kept it. We'd always assumed that since Dad managed Julian's inheritance, he would sell the house. It seemed more practical. Julian also got more shares than Katie, proof that Dad had not been bullshitting. He really did consider Julian a son.

When Julian looked back up, his eyes were red and wet. "A personal message?" he echoed. "How come you and Lori didn't get them?"

"We did. Privately," Mom explained from her place on the couch. "I have a feeling whatever he has to say to you is meant to be public and heard by all members of the family."

"Okay." Julian hesitated. "Let's hear it."

"He said . . ." Katie trailed off, frowning. "Okay, this is verbatim, so don't kill the messenger: 'Dear Julian. Are you out of your goddamn mind? You have everything a man could dream of, and you're throwing it away for more work, more headache, and more responsibility? Start focusing on the important things. Money, status, and Amber were never a part of those things. I love you, son, but you are a complete pain in the ass. If you don't get your priorities straight, you are banished from heaven. I'll make sure of it. Trust me when I say you will not like the alternative. Make wise choices, and love hard. Dad.'"

The entire room burst out laughing. The first time we'd laughed since Dad had died almost two weeks ago. Katie sent me a sideways glance, lifting her manicured fingernail in warning. "I would not be so gleeful if I were you. You're next, bro."

"Lay it on me." I sprawled backward on the damask settee, jesting.

"Twenty-five percent of the shares," Katie said simply.

"That's it?" Mom raised her eyebrows. I reverberated the same question in my head but obviously wasn't enough of a brat to utter it aloud. Another 15 percent of the shares were locked up with external shareholders.

"No, you have a note too." Katie grinned, enjoying herself. I got the fewest material things. Which suited me fine, since I'd never cared for them.

Julian passed me an imaginary item from across the couch. "Your lube, sir."

I pretended to grab it. It was just like old times. When I was a kid. "A good brother would offer to apply it too," I noted.

"Seems fair, seeing as kicking your ass at chess is my favorite hobby."

We stared at each other dead in the eye for a second, then burst into laughter. Katie shook her head, used to her older brothers' antics.

"Dad's message to you is as follows: 'Dear Chase, if you're sitting here without Maddie under your arm, you've failed me and, frankly, all men as a gender. Go and rectify the situation immediately. The woman brought you back to life after years of being a shell of your former self. I'm not sure what she did, or what made you this way in the first place, but you cannot afford to let her go. Love, Dad.'"

The words sank into the room, inking themselves on the walls. Katie gave a curt nod, as if agreeing with the sentiment, then continued. "'I left something for Maddie. It's in the safe. Kindly give it to her at your earliest convenience. PS: If you fire your brother, you, too, are banished from the heaven mansion I am currently building.'"

I turned to Julian, handing him his imaginary lube back. "Looks like I'm going to be your boss for a long-ass time. I believe you'll need some lubrication for that too."

"Boys." Mom clutched her pearls, like we were back to being preteens. "Behave."

"Fine," Julian said, sulking.

"He started it," I mumbled. Julian laughed and elbowed my ribs.

Katie looked between us, then began to laugh and cry at the same time. I felt oddly compelled to agree with her mixed emotions. I was thankful Dad had left us like this. With a humorous bang, so to speak.

"And another, general message, directed at all of us." Katie wiped a tear under her eye. "'Dear family, please never forget I've always been quite resourceful when it comes to taking care of myself. Don't worry. Wherever I am, I'm okay. I miss you and I love you, and I ask kindly that you take your time in joining me. Love, Dad.'"

"False," Mom muttered. "He never could take care of himself."

Another round of chuckles.

CHAPTER TWENTY-SIX

MADDIE

I was curled into myself on the couch when the doorbell rang. I got up to answer, Daisy at my heel, barking excitedly, as she did when Chase came over. We hadn't discussed him dropping by, but the hollowness I'd felt at not being with him today, for the first time in weeks, terrified me. I flung the door open. The hallway was empty. I wondered how whoever had gotten in had done it in the first place. The front buzzer hadn't rung. I just guessed it was Layla. I surveyed the empty hall, frowning.

"Layla? Chase?" My voice bounced on the walls. Daisy whimpered, lowering her head and bumping her nose against something on my doorstep. I looked down. Was that . . . a sewing machine? It looked old school. Heavy. The expensive kind. A vintage Singer in black and gold. I crouched down, picked it up, and carried it into my apartment. There was a note plastered onto it. No sewing machine case. I plucked it off.

Maddie,

When I was a wee lad in Dundee, my mother was the neighborhood's seamstress. I witnessed firsthand how clothes transform people. Not just visually. But their mood and ability and ambition. When I moved to the States,

I decided to incorporate Black & Co., basing my entire business plan on something I'd learned from a poor widow who couldn't afford to put milk on the table. From my mother.

This is what Gillian Black taught me—if you love what you do, it will never be work for you.

To making many more dresses, and hopefully happy memories with my son.

—Ronan Black

I blinked, desperately trying to get rid of the tears so I could reread the letter again and again. Ronan had left something for me. I didn't know why it hit me so deeply. Maybe because the circumstances reminded me of my mom, and all she could afford to leave behind were letters. It took me another twenty minutes and two cups of water to calm down. I picked up my phone and texted Chase. I knew a normal person would call, but texting was our safety net. We were still treading carefully, trying not to reveal too much of our hearts. Texts could be deleted. Words spoken would be inked in our memories forever.

Maddie: Thank you for the sewing machine. How was it today?

Chase: Surprisingly not horrible. I think Julian and I are salvageable.

Maddie: I'm so happy to hear that.

Chase: *Read that.

Maddie: Still a jerk, I see.

Chase: Good thing you dumped me, huh?

Maddie: That's not exactly what happened.

I still hadn't told him I'd found the azaleas. It seemed like poor timing to talk about us when there was something so big going on in his life. Then again, I felt stuck in a limbo of feelings I couldn't untangle from one another. The worst part was that there was nothing to talk about, really. I was in love with Chase Black, and he'd friend zoned me because I'd insisted on it. Because even though he had passed the azaleas test and almost fired someone for me and taken care of me in more ways than I could count—than anyone ever had, if I was being honest—I chose to believe the stupid, cowardly thing he said to me over and over again. That he wasn't ready to fall in love.

Only he hasn't told you this in weeks.

Chase: Dinner tomorrow?

Maddie: Sure. Burnt chili sound good?

Chase: My favorite.

◆ ◆ ◆

It was the day of the runway show during Fashion Week, and my nerves were tattered and torn on the floor as I paced from side to side.

"I told you!" I growled at Sven, shaking my finger in his direction. "I told you we couldn't count on her. What kind of model doesn't show up to *Fashion Week*? What agency did she say she was from?"

The model was a no-show. I repeat: We had no one to walk the runway with the Dream Wedding Dress, which I had designed. Which I'd put my heart and soul into.

"I mean, she did get pneumonia. I know you're no longer Martyr Maddie, but a bit of sympathy would be nice." Sven winced.

I fell down into a chair, burying my head in my hands. "I can't believe this is happening. It was a dream come true."

Sven, Nina, and Layla, who'd taken a day off and tagged along for moral support, all looked at me with a mixture of horrified fascination and pity.

"You know," Layla started, "you could always model the dress yourself."

My head jerked up, and I twisted my face at her, aghast. "What?"

"It is your measurements," Nina said quietly, folding her arms over her chest with half a shrug.

"And . . . I mean, we do have the dress. All we need is a model," Sven finished, rubbing his chin.

"I can't model my own dress." I shook my head violently. "I can't."

"Technically, you can," said Layla.

"Logically, you can too," Sven pointed out.

I looked between the three of them, knowing my eyes were red rimmed. My hands shook. I hated the limelight. Hated to be the center of attention. But I also acknowledged that there was no other way. Any other model in this venue would swim in this dress. It was way too big for a regular-size model.

"God." I closed my eyes. "I'm really doing this, aren't I?"

"Seems like it." Layla took my hands, tugging me up to my feet. "It's showtime, girl."

Half an hour later, I was throwing up into a bucket backstage, wrapped in the wedding dress I'd designed all by myself. Sven had quickly hemmed up the length, and it was a surprisingly easy fix. The ball gown had long sleeves made out of crème lace, a deep V neckline, and a three-foot train. The satin nude trims, soft lines, and bare back made it uniquely memorable, or so Layla kept telling me.

It would help if I knew where Sven, my boss, was right at that second, when I needed his support the most, puking the reduced-fat turkey-bacon sandwich I'd had for breakfast into a bucket that had been the home of iced champagnes until a moment ago.

"Just please let me go to the bathroom. The nausea is only getting worse," I moaned into the bucket, heaving. Layla patted my back while Nina held the bucket up for me.

"No way," I heard Nina say, tsking in revulsion. "The dress could get dirty in the bathroom, and Sven would kill both of us. I'm not taking any chances."

"C'mon, the bathroom is occupied by models only. The only dirty thing about it is traces of cocaine, and they're already white like the dress." Layla tried to persuade Nina to budge from her stand, but the latter shook her head.

"I'm sorry, I can't let that happen. I'm actually trying to keep my job for a change."

I whipped my head up from the bucket and looked around. The backstage of the fashion show was buzzing with event coordinators, models, and stylists. All the other models seemed to be twice my height and so skinny I could make out their individual ribs when they were topless. Which was the case with nearly half of them. They walked around on high heels and skin-toned thongs, chatting among themselves.

"Where is Sven?" I whined just as one of the assistants walked briskly toward us, talking into her Madonna mic as she gave me a wink.

"Ten minutes and you're up. We're wrapping up Valentino right now."

Layla dragged a folding chair behind my butt, and I collapsed onto it, squeezing my eyes shut. I wasn't exactly a wallflower, but showing myself off was never something I'd wanted. Still, my nerves weren't solely about the show. Chase had been acting weird the past few days. And by *weird* I meant nice. He was oh so very nice. Attentive, sweet, caring . . . *not* himself. I worried he was going through a mental breakdown or something.

Which I found . . . *horrible*. I couldn't help but think something was seriously wrong, but when I'd confronted him about it, he'd played dumb. I liked it when we fought and teased and taunted each other. This new, sweet version of him disconcerted me.

"Coming through. Coming through. Make way. God, what is this, *American Horror Story*? Just kidding, Ms. Westwood. Love your stuff. And mucho respect. The Sex Pistols was my favorite band in high school. Admittedly because it made me look cooler—the music is *so* not my cuppa—but still. Have you seen my designer? Maddie? Maddie Goldbloom? Short, pixie hair, a look of pure horror on her face . . . oh, never mind. There she is." Sven giggled, waltzing past designers and assistants and models, a cup of coffee glued to his hand. He gripped me by the shoulder and yanked me up from the chair.

I wanted to throw up all over again as he righted me.

"Wow. Seriously, Maddie, the dress is not half as bad as I thought it would be. I'm going as far as calling it cute."

I eyed him skeptically—*miserably*—and nodded. "Hmm, thanks?"

"I need to talk to you." He pulled me away from the backstage area and into the hallway. A narrow white thing full of side doors leading to different rooms.

I was thinking of pointing out that I had a runway to walk in less than ten minutes, but really, no tears would be shed if I were to miss what ought to turn into an embarrassing farce.

I stumbled over my feet as Sven pulled me a little too forcefully down the hallway. Not only was I inherently clumsy, but because of my lackluster height ("*Fun size* sounds better," Layla had said, attempting to console me), I had to wear six-inch heels, which made walking impossible, let alone running.

"So congratulations—your Wedding Dress to End All Wedding Dresses has been officially purchased," Sven said airily.

"Purchased?" I panted, trying to keep up. "You mean by Black & Co.? They always pick up our collection. I thought we had a three-year deal with them."

"No, not with Black & Co. It's a private buyer."

"How could a private buyer purchase it? It's not for sale yet. And even if it was, no one has seen it. That's why we're here. To show it for the first time."

"Yes, well, the buyer is confident they'll like the dress."

"What about our commitment to Black & Co.?"

"We found a loophole in the contract. The money was too good to turn down."

"But—" I started.

"The dress is sold. This is not the issue." He cut me off, his movements a breeze. We were getting farther away from backstage and into some sort of an office floor.

"What *is* the issue?" I tried to regulate my breaths. Oh, snap. What if it had been purchased by a celebrity? What if the celebrity didn't want anyone else to see it so they could have first dibs and show it off? What if the whole runway thing was canceled and I could just go about my day and watch the show from the sidelines? I could already imagine myself seeing the dress draped on Dua Lipa on the cover of *OK!* magazine—was she dating anyone these days?—and getting giddy. Pride made my chest swell.

"The buyer has an unusual request." Sven finally stopped. We were far enough from backstage not to be seen, standing in front of a white wooden door.

I tucked flyaway locks of hair behind my ear. Sven swatted my hands away. "You did *not* sit for forty-five minutes to get your hair curled just so you could ruin it a second before the show."

So I am *doing the show? What happened to my Dua Lipa dream?*

"What's the request?" I huffed, tired of being kept in the dark.

"Well"—Sven looked around, a little queasy—"you'll have to ask the groom."

"The *groom*?"

Sven pushed the door in front of us open, and I tripped forward on my heels from the shock. A pair of big, confident hands caught me at the last minute.

Chase.

Chase was holding me.

Not only was he holding me, but he was staring into my eyes, his twinkling blue-grays full of mischief and heartbreaking warmth I had never seen in them before.

"Hi," he whispered.

"H-hi . . . ?"

I pushed myself up on both feet, aware that I probably had puke breath, and looked around me. Everybody was here. Well, everybody I knew from New York, anyway. Lori, Katie, Julian, Clementine, Sven, Ethan (*Ethan?*), Grant, Francisco, and all the colleagues I was close with. Nina and Layla slipped in just as I took count of the people in the room. Apparently, they'd been behind Sven and me the entire time.

I looked between Chase and Sven, trying to will my heart to keep from hammering its way out of my chest. Jumping to conclusions could crush me. Plus, I'd known Chase for not much more than a year. Granted, it had been one of the most intense years of my *life*.

"You have a request for me?" My mouth defied my brain as I uttered the words, internally begging him to be the groom. Or . . . not to be the groom. What if he was marrying someone else? Finally going ahead with his plan to please his family, but with some other girl? Was that why he'd been so nice and weird with me this week?

God, what if it was Ethan that was Katie's groom, and I'd just jumped the gun? My head was spinning. I needed to sit down. Chase offered me a curt nod. I needed more. I needed words.

"Please say something," I said, my mouth cotton dry. "Anything. I'm freaking the hell out."

Chase scratched his eyebrow. Such a mundane thing to do, but I'd never seen him do that before. Look unsure or contemplative.

"You've been planning your wedding since the day you were born. I know because I asked your father. I asked your father because I drove to Pennsylvania last week to meet him. I met him because I've been trying to figure you out. I think I did."

"You did?" I blinked.

"You're the type to go for public love declarations. You want the big, messy, multicolored fairy tale. I'm not sure if it can get any more public than what I'm about to do here."

Sven clapped his hands excitedly from the corner of the room, jumping up and down. "He is channeling his inner Hugh Grant. I'm *so* here for this."

Chase shot him a look, then turned back to me.

"I was just wondering if . . ." His eyes ran down my cleavage in the dress, and a smirk twisted his lips. Like he'd found his footing. I needed him to do that. Find his footing. *Talk.*

"If?" I tried to keep my voice neutral.

"If I could be the lucky bastard to destroy this masterpiece with my teeth while half-drunk and fully in love with you on your wedding night."

"Oh," I breathed.

"Oh," he repeated, his smirk widening. "I'm also wondering if I could be the man to hold your hair when you puke and not be the reason you got stupid drunk in the first place."

My breath stuttered in my chest. It reminded me I had terrible breath. As if reading my mind, Layla slid two pieces of gum into my hand, then took a step back. I shoved them between my lips. *Minty.* Chase continued.

"I'm wondering if we could get engagement photos together, somewhere that doesn't smell like the eighties, maybe, without having to worry you are about to leave there and go on a date with some bastard in a funny tie and a pair of tights—no offense, Ethan." He turned and winked at my ex-whatever-he'd-been-at-the-time.

"None taken, I guess." Ethan shrugged from beside Katie, holding her hand. I laughed through my tears. That was the best, worst marriage proposal I'd ever heard, and Chase wasn't even done yet.

"Wanna know what else I'm wondering?" He cocked a brow.

"Dying to." I laughed through my tears.

"I'm wondering if you could look at me the way you did the first time we met. Like I was a real possibility. With raw potential to be something you wanted for yourself. I want to be your every fucking thing, until we bring a replica of both of us into this world and become slaves to them, because you're into having kids and shit."

I cackled. And cried. Tears streamed down my cheeks as I drank him in, hopeful and boyish and dashing, with his imperial height, tar-black mane, and sparkling eyes that were never exactly the same color and always kept me on my toes. He took my hand. He was trembling, and for some reason, it undid me.

"In short, I'm wondering if, since you have your wedding dress stitched to your own measurements and some flowers I kept alive for you—by the way, they were a *real* bitch to keep alive—you would maybe want to marry me. Because, Madison"—his eyes twinkled with mischief and excitement and a promise to make my future brighter—"I called you Mad because I was mad about you and didn't even realize it until you walked away. After you did, I kept thinking of ways and reasons to contact you. For months, I convinced myself it was nothing more than an itch I wanted to scratch, and when Dad got sick, it gave me a bullshit excuse to hunt you down, and all bets were off. I fucking love you, Goldbloom. You soften me," he said gruffly, looking down at our entwined fingers. "But, you know, not *everywhere*."

The room burst into laughter. The adrenaline was running so wild in my bloodstream I was shaking all over. The laughter felt like honey in my throat. So that was why he'd been weird recently.

The assistant with the Madonna mic burst into the room, waving her iPad in her hand hysterically. "There you are! You're up next. Chop-chop!"

Everyone's eyes turned to her. Layla began to push the door, closing it in her face. "I will chop-chop your body if you don't go away. I am witnessing the most romantic thing in the world short of *The Bodyguard* with Whitney Houston, and you will *not* ruin it for me," she said, sulking and glancing in our direction. "And for them, too, I suppose."

"So what do you say?" Chase peered into my face urgently. He reached for his back pocket to produce a ring. I put my hand on his arm, stopping him.

"Actually . . ." I bit my lower lip, looking sideways at Layla, who widened her eyes, signaling me to say yes. "I never sold your ring. I couldn't bring myself to do it. I knew it wasn't real—our engagement, I mean—but to me, it *felt* real. A lot of the time, in fact. So I . . . just kept it."

"You kept the ring?" he asked, dumbfounded. I nodded. It was embarrassing. But maybe not as embarrassing as proposing to someone in a room full of people you knew when you weren't even officially together.

"And all those times you deleted your text messages . . ." I trailed off.

"I told you I love you," he finished. "And all the times you did it?" He cocked his head sideways.

I laughed, wiping more tears away. The hell with the fashion show. "Same."

The assistant knocked again, sticking her head in. "Croquis should have started eight minutes ago. Just letting you know. Someone's about to get fired soon."

"Yeah," Chase boomed. "And it'll be your ass, because I own Black & Co., the official sponsor of this event. Now leave!"

There he was. The man I'd fallen in love with, against all odds. And reason. And . . . no point in denying it—logic. We needed to wrap it up, I knew, even though I didn't want this moment to end.

"I don't want you to feel like you're giving in to my terms," I said softly. "We could wait if you want."

"Give in to your terms?" He frowned, looking positively aghast. "I'm not doing this to please you, Madison. I'm doing this to please *us*. You bring me joy. Showering you with gifts and love and orgasms makes me happier."

I heard Ethan groan, Layla squeak, and Sven sigh dreamily. I bit down on my lower lip to suppress a giggle.

"Then yes," I said. "Yes, I will marry you, Chase Black."

I was going to throw my arms over his shoulders, the way I'd always imagined I'd do. Like in the movies. But he picked me up honeymoon-style and kicked the door open. The assistant almost flew backward from the impact. He ran the length of the hallway while I giggled, burying my face in his chest, inhaling his singular scent. Minutes later, he burst onto the runway with me in his arms, my legs kicking playfully in my ball gown. Croquis's sign was behind us, glowing in neon lights.

Projectors pointed at us. Rows upon rows of stern-looking fashion journalists, celebrities, media personalities, and other designers eyeing us. Cameras clicked. People whistled, laughed, and clapped.

And Chase? He grinned at everyone, at everything, with that devil-may-care smile that could melt me into a puddle.

"My name is Chase Black, and I'm the CEO of Black & Co. Want to see my favorite bridal creation for this season?" he asked, putting me down gently. The dress swelled at the bottom, and I felt everyone's eyes scorching a path down my body as people took in the dress. "She's it."

EPILOGUE

Chase

Six months later

Dear Chase,

When we were in the Hamptons, and you were busy bickering with Julian, and your mother, your sister, Amber, and Clemmy were busy shopping downtown, Maddie approached me in the library. I considered it a bold move, seeing as we were complete strangers, and I was, essentially, her boss.

Madison explained her mother wrote letters to her throughout her journey fighting cancer, to immortalize her feelings toward her daughter long after she herself was gone. Naturally, I was interested. I asked Madison if she could email me copies of those letters. She said she could. I spent many nights reading Iris Goldbloom's letters to her daughter. She was, I suspect, a fine woman.

I have tried to write many letters to you, Julian, Kate, and Clementine. But in truth, expressing my feelings in words has never been my forte. I suppose I am more of a show-don't-tell type of man. Until today. I finally found something worth writing to you. Something that wouldn't feel mundane or utterly dull.

Today, I found out that your relationship with Madison was a sham. That you did it, in part, to pacify me. The fact that you went to such great lengths to ensure my peace of mind touches me.

I love you.

I am proud of you.

And your engagement to Maddie? While I suppose you thought it had everything to do with me and nothing to do with you, I knew, the day I saw your eyes light up in the Hamptons when she showed up for that late dinner, that she was the one.

Treat her well. Take care of your mother. Protect your sister. Help raise your niece.

Oh, and try not to kill your brother.

Love,

Dad

◆ ◆ ◆

I tucked Dad's letter into my breast pocket, before tightening my bow tie in front of the mirror in the small-ass bedroom with the dated yellow wallpaper. I looked sharp in a Black & Co. black suit.

"You know what stuns me the most?" Grant asked beside me, running a hand over his hair. Of course my best man wanted to look good in front of the maid of honor, a.k.a. Layla. He still hadn't gotten over being rejected. I doubted it was even in his vocabulary.

"My wicked good looks?" I asked wryly. From the corner of my eye, I saw Julian shake his head, ducking down and adjusting Clementine's floral crown. She was the flower girl, and what a flower girl she was. Mad had designed a dress especially for her, after much consultation and fuss that suggested Clementine would be the one making the vows today. "Fools," Julian muttered with a smile on his face. "Never get married, Clemmy."

"Oh, but I want to, Daddy." Her eyes widened. "With Chase."

Grant chuckled, turning back to me. "What stuns me is that Maddie still chose to marry you, even though she knows what kind of a cocky, arrogant, bas—" Grant was about to finish his sentence, but Booger Face's head flew up, and she stared at him expectantly. She had been dying for someone to screw up and roll a five-dollar bill into her potty-word jar. She was counting on new Barbie bicycles for Christmas.

"Stop it right there, good sir," Julian warned. Clementine faltered.

"Bassist," Grant finished. "Did you know your uncle can play the bass guitar, Clem?" He spun to where she was standing by the bed, flashing her a dazzling grin.

"No." She narrowed her eyes, skeptical. "He can't."

"I smell a challenge." I grinned.

"I think what you smell is the sole of my shoe in your butt for being unfashionably late." Layla poked her head into my suite. And when I said *suite*, I meant Mr. Goldbloom's master bedroom.

Yes, I was getting married in a town house in Pennsylvania.

No, I was not out of my mind. Clinically, anyway.

"Looking good, Layla." Grant saluted his green-haired ex-hookup.

She flashed him an easy smile. "Same, Grant. How's life been treating you?"

"Better than you did," I muttered into my whiskey, emptying it in one gulp. Layla took Booger Face by the hand, leading her to the bride's suite (read: Mad's childhood bedroom). Grant and Julian ushered me to the altar in the backyard. Julian was the first in line behind me, then Grant. Behind them stood all the men Madison had fake-married from her neighborhood. Layla had thought it'd be hilarious to invite them. I thought Layla's sense of humor sucked, but I was a good sport about it, because I knew Mad would get a kick out of it. Standing behind Grant were Jacob Kelly, Taylor Kirschner, Milo Lopez, Aston Giudice, Josh Payne, and Luis Hough.

Contrary to Madison's, the only ex of mine who was in attendance was Amber, who was currently sitting on one of the folded white chairs in front of the wedding arch, her sunglasses on, huffing into her glass of fizzy wine and complaining about the lack of French champagne. Mad had chosen to have a very modest event. My martyr bride was donating most of our wedding budget to a cancer-research charity. My mom and Katie sat beside Amber, who attended for the sake of playing nice with the Blacks. It didn't seem fair that Booger Face should suffer just because things hadn't worked out between Amber and Julian. Ethan clasped Katie's hand and shot me a thumbs-up. I gave him a curt nod. I still didn't approve of running tights and *Dora the Explorer* ties but didn't much care about his wardrobe anymore.

Katie had been dating Ethan seriously for four months now. Two months after Dad died, Ethan officially asked her out. Until then, he was just there for her emotionally, but I could see he was dead scared of getting friend zoned again. In fact, I was the one who'd told him to seal the deal before she gave up on his ass.

They were now preparing for their first (entire, not half) marathon together.

Mom was doing well, too, all circumstances considered. It helped that Mad and Clementine were around a lot and that Julian was attached to her by the hip postdivorce, trying to find his footing as a father after getting joint custody of Booger Face.

Amber was slowly introducing Clementine's biological father into her life. So far, so awkward, but Booger Face had us when things got too weird.

Then there was Sven, Francisco, and their newly adopted girl, Zooey, sitting in the front row. They were all wearing matching black outfits, waving Zooey's chubby hand in my direction with enthusiastic smiles. The adoption had been finalized three months earlier and couldn't have come at a better time. Mad and I were butting heads about who was to move into whose apartment. Sven pointed out he might need babysitting assistance, so Mad relented and moved in with me. They'd become closer in recent months, since Mad had stood up for herself with the Dream Wedding Dress and become his equal.

I'd paid for Zooey's entire room design and furniture for that little favor.

The pastor beside me fidgeted, pulling me out of my reverie. He let out a little gasp, and when I looked up, there she was. The woman of my dreams, wearing the dress of *her* dreams. Words seemed small for that moment. I flashed her a smile as she walked down the aisle, escorted by her father, Clementine throwing moonflowers out of a decorated basket behind her, Layla holding the hem of her train.

Mad stopped beside me, awarding me with one of her magnificent smiles.

A smile that made the world stop.

I looked down, about to tell her any of the five hundred thousand things that sprang into my mind. That she looked fucking delicious in that dress, which had been a huge success during New York Fashion Week and had already sold thirty thousand gowns, give or take, making it Croquis's second-most popular wedding dress. I wanted to tell her I loved her. Very. Fucking. Much. But before I could say any of those things, Mad turned around, opened her palm, and waited for Layla to drop her cell phone into her hand.

All the attendees in her father's backyard sucked in a scandalized gasp. She was texting. *Now.*

Mad's fingers began to move over the screen as she typed, a small smile playing on her face. I watched her, as did the rest of our guests. The pastor cleared his throat, trying—and failing—to draw her attention. My phone pinged in my pocket a second later.

I took it out. Opened the message.

<Maddie has removed a message from the chat>

Chase: Oh, no, you didn't.

Maddie: Cold feet.

Chase: You can warm them on my back when we get to Ibiza for our honeymoon. Bad circulation has always been your problem. It's a short-people thing.

Maddie: Getting farther away from getting married by the second.

Chase: Spill it. What did you delete?

Maddie: Promise you won't freak out?

I looked up at her, arching an eyebrow as if to say, *Do we even know each other?* She looked back down and typed.

Maddie: I'm pregnant.

Chase: Is it mine?

Maddie: Are you for real?!

She looked up, rose on her tiptoes, and flicked the back of my neck. I laughed, scooping her into my arms in front of our shocked pastor. And guests. *And* her harem of boys she'd "married" when she was younger.

"Then why the hell would I get freaked out?" I murmured into her lips, propriety be damned. She wrapped her arms around me. The crowd cackled.

"Your horns are showing, Mr. Black."

"That," I whispered into her mouth, catching her lower lip between my teeth and tugging, speaking low enough our audience couldn't hear, "is because for you, I'm always horny."

◆ ◆ ◆

January 1, 2002

Dear Maddie,

Can you do your mom a very weird favor? When the time comes, marry a man you can laugh with. You have no idea how important it is until you hit those sad days and the only thing to make them better is someone to put a smile on your face.

On your wedding day, make him sweat a little. Make sure he misses a heartbeat or two. See if he takes it in stride. If he does—he's a keeper (but you should already know that. Ha).

Love,

Mom. x

MADDIE

Eight months later

"I hate you so much." I grabbed the lapels of my husband's blazer, shaking him from my disadvantaged position on the hospital bed. I was past sweating and deep into dripping territory. It looked like I'd just walked out of the shower without patting myself dry with a towel. Not to mention I was about to purge a human out of my body. Yes, I was aware that women all over the world did that on a daily basis, many of them without access to Western medical assistance. But in my defense, none of these women were married to Chase Black.

"Is that a no?" Chase frowned, straightening his posture and taking a step back before I stabbed his eye out with the nearest available object.

"No, I don't want to speed up the process by having sex with you. It doesn't work that way. I'm already four centimeters dilated!"

"I have at least eight more inches I can fit into yo—"

"Do *not* complete that sentence." I jerked a finger in his direction. He raised his palms in surrender, taking another step back.

Layla rushed into my room, looking a little worse for wear. "Okay, just wanted you to know Daisy is with her dog sitter . . ." She paused, side-eyeing both Chase and me. "Sorry, I still can't believe I have to say this with a straight face. And I watered all your plants, which means they are all alive."

Daisy was doing amazing. She never peed in anyone's shoes since Chase and I had gotten back together. Apparently, all I'd needed to do in order to rid her of the nasty habit was let the right man through my door. I opened my mouth to say something, but Layla waved me off. "Yes, including the azalea in the pantry. God, to think this giant pantry could be put to good use. How's little Ronan doing?"

"Still inside my body." I pointed at my huge belly.

"Lucky bastard," Chase muttered. Layla elbowed him. I laughed. The past eight months had been a dream. Who knew that the devilishly handsome man with the mouth I wanted to punch and kiss in the same breath could be such a great husband? We'd fallen into a comfortable routine full of family and friends and laughter. We spent a lot of time with Zooey, Sven, and Francisco, as well as with Clemmy, who was obsessed with her flower girl dress and, following in my footsteps, had recently forced a classmate to marry her during a playdate. Ronan seemed like a perfect addition to an already big and loving family.

Another contraction slammed through me. It felt like someone had taken a match and lit my entire lower back. I winced, gripping the linen to the point of white knuckles. One of my nurses—Tiffany, a redheaded woman in her fifties—walked into the room, and Layla figured it was getting crowded, saluting on her way out. The nurse peeked under the blanket covering my legs.

"Yup. He is ready for his grand entrance into the world, all right. Keep breathing." She patted my knee. I'd never quite understood this expression. Did one ever stop breathing voluntarily? Specifically while giving birth?

Tiffany left the room, called the doctor, then poked her head back in. "What's it gonna be? Is Daddy staying in to watch the birth?"

Chase and I exchanged glances. We'd planned every single thing about the birth in detail—the overnight bag we'd packed together when I was only seven months pregnant, the labor classes we'd taken, the breastfeeding plan—but we'd never talked about whether he was going to stay and watch or not.

"Up to you." He cleared his throat. We held each other's eyes. For a second, I thought we'd take out our phones and do the old banter dance-off. Then my husband surprised me by taking my hand. "Please."

And I knew.

"Yes." I grinned. "He stays."

Forty-five minutes later, Ronan was out in the world, screaming up a storm. He had Chase's bright-blue-silver eyes, my brown-honey hair, and two clenched fists with curiously long fingernails. He was like a baby dragon. I laughed and cried when Tiffany put him on my bare chest. Because I knew he was a gift from Mom and Ronan.

In fact, that was the one thing I'd written to baby Ronan in the very first letter I sat down to compose to him when I found out I was pregnant. One of many I intended to write. I told him he was a great, precious gift who wasn't supposed to happen. That his daddy and I had been careful—I was on the pill and took it daily. The week the manufacturer of my birth control pills came out with a grand apology for their faulty pills, I'd realized I was a week and a half late. The idea of being pregnant hadn't even registered to me before that, so I never kept up with the dates.

I took a pregnancy test. It was positive.

Chase and I were engaged to be married. But we still hadn't spoken about the other C-word—children. I remembered the moment I'd found out. I sat on the closed toilet seat in Croquis's restroom, ironically in the very stall where Chase and I had had sex months before, staring at the two blue lines, then looking up to the ceiling and smiling at the sky.

"Touché, Ronan and Mom." I'd shaken my head. "Touché."

Now, I had a son. Someone to love. To write letters to. To see grow.

I watched Chase pick him up, all bundled up like a burrito, with his little stripy hat. My husband smiled down at him, and my heart swelled.

"How I got her to say yes to me? Why, yes, Ronan, that's a funny story. Let me tell you all about it . . ."

ACKNOWLEDGMENTS

They say writing is a lonely job, and while I agree with that statement wholeheartedly, it is definitely gratifying to see your name on a book cover and take pride in having your hard work be recognized.

This book, however, is the fruit of many wonderful women's labor, and I would like to take this opportunity to thank them properly.

First and foremost, big thanks to my agent, Kimberly Brower. I wanted to do something different this year, and you made it happen. I couldn't have asked for a better copilot to navigate my way in the publishing world.

My editors at Montlake Publishing, Lindsey Faber and Anh Schluep. Thank you so much for your amazing work, mind-blowing expertise, and excellent attention to detail. Knowing Chase and Maddie were in such capable hands made this process flawless.

Special thanks to my PA, Tijuana Turner, and beta readers, Sarah Grim Sentz, Vanessa Villegas, and Lana Kart. You ladies are my tribe.

To my best author friends, Charleigh Rose, Parker S. Huntington, Ava Harrison, and Helena Hunting. You inspire me. Thank you for holding my hand throughout this process.

To my kick-ass street team and the Sassy Sparrows Facebook group—you guys are the best! I said it before, and I'll keep saying this: you push me to become better at what I do.

To my husband and son, who are endlessly patient. Thank you for being understanding when I slip into a parallel universe and spend time with my characters.

To the bloggers and bookstagrammers who constantly BRING IT. Words cannot describe how grateful I am for the time and effort you put into your passion. You are true artists.

There are so many other people who made this book happen. Yamina Kirky, Marta Bor, Amy Halter, Ratula Roy, and more. Unfortunately, I'm notoriously bad at remembering everyone I need to thank when writing this section. Please take mercy if I haven't included you but should have.

Finally, I'd like to thank you, my readers. I thank my lucky stars for you every day. Writing is a privilege. Being able to pay the bills writing? Well, that is nothing short of a miracle.

Thank you.

All my love,

L.J. Shen

xoxo

ABOUT THE AUTHOR

L.J. Shen is a *USA Today*, *Washington Post*, and Amazon #1 bestselling author of contemporary, new adult, and romance titles. She likes to write about unapologetic alpha males and the women who bring them to their knees. Her books have been sold to twenty different countries and have appeared on some of their bestseller lists. She lives in California with her husband, son, and eccentric fashion choices, and she enjoys good wine, bad reality TV shows, and catching sunrays with her lazy cat.